Also by Ann Aguirre

The Only Purple House in Town

Fix-It Witches

Witch Please

Boss Witch

Extra Witchy

the Hocus Pocus Handbook

ANN AGUIRRE

sourcebooks
casablanca

Cover design by Stephanie Gafron/Sourcebooks
Cover art © Kateryna Vitkovska

Published by Sourcebooks Casablanca, an imprint of Sourcebooks
1935 Brookdale RD, Naperville, IL 60563-2773
(630) 961-3900
sourcebooks.com

Cataloging-in-Publication data is on file with the Library of Congress.

Printed and bound in the United States of America
MA 10 9 8 7 6 5 4 3 2 1

For Alek

1

A Spell for Skulking and Skullduggery

There will be times when you need to pass unseen, my gem. Your magic can be a mite irregular, but here's the working I use to slip away unnoticed. Strongest cast at turning times; add more will as needed. Needs must and all that.

You'll require:

- *A bit of black quartz to connect you to the soil*
- *A silver athame to etch the air*
- *Dried chamomile, burdock, and chicory, all steeped in a tea, to salute the sea*
- *Dried dogbane burned in a clay pot to honor the inner flame*

You can do these in any order, though it's strongest to work fire first, then air, earth, and water. There are no magic words, whatever the brownies may try to tell you. I find it's best to craft your own, as the old magic responds better to sincerity than rote recitation. In a pinch, you'll do as you must and let your good intentions carry the rest. I trust you'll do no harm. Even as a little one, you cared for helpless creatures. Countless times, I caught you saving creepies and crawlies, those caught in various snares. And you nearly always had a toad or a lizard somewhere on your person.

Use the sneaking spell to protect yourself and mayhap have a lark, but never to cause suffering. Not that you would, being made of joy and all. Use this knowledge well and carry all my affection with you, wherever you may go.

THEA

POOKAS JUST WANT TO HAVE fun.

They really do.

Which is why it's a shame that they've been rounded up and are confined in the royal stables for a pageant they didn't consent to participating in. House Winter loves its spectacle. I should know; I've spent most of my life fleeing from sparkling diadems and gowns made of gossamer, flower petals, and raven feathers.

Da and I were summoned from Miremorel House, our place in the wildlands, in honor of the Winter Court offering hospitality to the Summer delegation, serving as hosts for the peace talks. Among the fair folk, there's no greater rivalry than that between Summer and Winter. Though I try to stay out of such matters, sometimes I get dragged in because my presence has soothing properties, even if nobody seems to understand exactly why.

It also means that refusing this "invitation" is impossible. I'm supposed to get dressed up in a fancy gown and stand in the courtyard while the high host assembles, also in elegant attire. Then we're meant to watch the pookas prance about in their decorative regalia. Someone will sing, and then there will be an impressive display of Winter magic. Then we'll all proceed to the great hall for boring speeches and for Lord Liskaal to make promises he won't keep.

Yeah, I won't let things go according to plan. I haven't told Da about my intentions because I don't want to get him in trouble. Not that he disapproves. I learned most of what I know about fomenting trouble from him, but he's better at not getting caught. I average about 50 percent, and I don't like those odds, but I can't ignore how despondent the pookas are. Right now, they're in horse form, some dark, some pale, and all of them have glowing eyes. If they weren't locked into this shape, they'd be fleeing as cats or hares.

High fae magic can constrain and compel them, forcing them to wear elaborate harnesses and prance around with braided manes and ribbons in their tails. The visual aspect isn't the entire point, as there are layers on layers within high fae interactions. No, Winter is demonstrating their dominance in front of their primary rival, and if I were an obedient subject, I'd cooperate.

Instead, I have green and brown paint smeared on my face as I crawl through the garden toward the stables. I haven't perfected the skulking spell Da tried to teach me, so that leaves me with mundane solutions. I don't have much time, since I left this to the last minute, hoping they wouldn't be able to round up the pookas again before the pageant, as they will race from the palace grounds with supernatural speed.

I pop my head up, scanning the area. There don't seem to be any witnesses, so I open the wide doors and dart inside. Within, the pen is dim and smells muskily of misery. Anyone who could breathe in this much sadness and ignore it—well, nobody ever claimed that the high fae exude kindness and consideration. Knife-sharp beauty, yes, along with vainglorious conceit and gilded self-interest, all those things, but rarely mercy.

One thing I didn't count on, however, was the pookas being already decked out in finery. I swear softly. It will take too long to remove harnesses and unweave braids and ribbons. Maybe a transmutation spell, but my magic is wild and thready at best. When I was younger, it tormented me, but then as I got older still, I heard the whispers.

I'm not fae at all. I'm a changeling, stolen from the mortal realm.

By that point, I'd eaten far too much fae food. I can't go back, at least not to stay. I'd survive a visit, but fae magic has permeated my flesh and bones, both a poison that would kill me in the mortal realm and a cure for my mortality while I'm here. Consuming magical food, breathing the air, and drinking the water and wine conveys a certain fae-adjacent magic.

As Da taught me, I visualize the result: harnesses and ribbons shifting to puffs of silvery smoke. The magic dances just out of reach, and the number of targets complicates the process even more. I focus and strain, and—

Boom!

I stifle another curse—silver sparks instead of smoke, and they land on the provender scattered on the floor. I watch, eyes wide, as the flames spread. This is why I don't try my hand at magic more often. My heart thumps furiously, but panic solves nothing. I race to the doors, opening them so the pookas can escape.

They can't exit the compound without my help, so I run alongside the first majestic fae, the one known as Ferghus, and call, "With your leave?"

I speak the greeting because it's rude to touch an elder's mind without consent, even in urgent situations. There are always hierarchies at play, small matters that could create big problems if one misunderstands their own place in the rankings.

Hurry, comes the mind-sung response.

Now I have permission. *To the gates.*

I can hear the wild fae as many cannot. The high fae have lost these powers in exchange for more glamour and elevated magic. They can create gemstones and conjure silver and gold, travel through mirrors as well as stone and mushroom circles, make mortals wish to sell their souls for a kiss, but they don't seem particularly *happy* about any of these abilities. To me, they seem like they're starving; no excess or pleasure can ever be enough. They will never touch a pooka's mind, cavort with pixies, swim in a moonlit brook with the river nymphs, or sit on a lonely beach as a naiad serenades her lost love. I would never trade those moments; I feel at home in the glades and loughs, where the magic is thick as honey and twice as sweet.

Soon, I'll be back out there, and if I time it right, so will the pookas. This time, I'm careful as can be, and I burn just enough magic to give myself a boost and borrow the bounce to scramble onto Ferghus's back. He doesn't break stride, leading the charge through the garden toward the gates.

Fire crackles behind us, an acrid smell nearly unknown in the heart of the Winter stronghold. Everything here is white and silver, apart from the gardens. Those are carefully curated with deep green and icy blue, flashing past in a blur of cool and wintry hues.

We nearly trample several wild fae servants in our ride to freedom, but shouts echo in our wake, and the sentries will be expecting us.

I hunch low, aligning my body against Ferghus's back, and hope nobody gets a good look at my face. The mud and verdant paste will help obscure my features, but there's a short list of folk who would dare such an uproar. With magical aid, it probably won't take them long to hunt me down, despite the precaution of concealing my identity. The reckless ride jolts my spine as we vault the hedge that separates the courtyard from the ward, a common area where guests are made to wait so they understand the importance of those who dwell deeper within the palace.

The gates are closing in response to the smoke or the horns or perhaps even the baying of the coin-shìth, who will be tasked with tracking us. I'm lucky they're howling and not barking; that would be a death sentence for the pookas and me alike. I calculate our speed and find it will be close, too close, if I don't stack the odds in our favor.

When I reach for the magic again, it burns, a slipping-slithering badness that creates a dark and fraying thread around the periphery of my vision. The black bleeds red when I insist on pulling taut, holding the gates steady, steady, steady—

Stop.

Stop.

I hold and I hold and I hold until pain is a color, glowing all over my body, brightness and burrowing, a worm made of needles trying to eat my skin. My ears whoosh and pop. We're through, and the pookas put on speed, a glorious and thundering escape. Behind us, the gates crash closed too late, and the silver metal rings out a peculiarly dissonant tone.

Ahead, the wildlands unfold before us. No easy paths, just light game trails and flora that smells like home. Ferghus trots to a stop as soon as it's safe, and I slide off his back.

We honor you, he sings. *Thea-friend, we are a whisper away. We guard you, always.*

We are kin, I sing back. *Always, Ferghus-friend.*

The herd shifts. Scatters. They're ravens and cats and goats and hares now, all racing in different directions. It will be impossible for House Winter to provide the scheduled entertainment, and they will lose face before House Summer. Concern for my dad often keeps me relatively compliant, but I have no loyalty to Winter. I've seen how they treat the wild fae.

I'm on my own, no regrets. Ferghus has been a good friend, and the other pookas deserved my aid as well. Returning to the palace would be a terrible idea, especially since I don't like the place at the best of times. Mudge, my da, has a suite in the stable complex, and I'm always welcome in the loft I occupied as a child, but I prefer his sylvan cottage, Miremorel House, a cozy little nest within a hollowed-out mushroom. Da told me that they're tiny in the mortal realm, but plants and fungi grow to towering sizes here, feeding on the magic.

I have spent my best times at Miremorel. But it might not be wise to show up where they'd expect me to hide, as there will be hell to pay for today's work.

It might behoove me to go a-roving in the wild, drink with brownies, and barter with hobgoblins, some of my favorite people in the entire world. I've read stories that travel across the fairy rings, tatty books left by human visitors, and the writers always get it wrong. Brownies may complete house chores, but they're not peaceful like the fables say. If I gave a brownie a dish of cream in exchange for housework, I'd be slapped so hard, my ears would ring. And I've never been swindled by a hobgoblin. Not once.

I pause, breathing in the sweetness of the air. Inside the palace, it smells…tame, purified by layers of protective magic. Out here, there's earth and moss and peat and the complexity of so many flowers that there's a war of enticing scents. Darkly luscious inkberry mingles with the bell ambrosia, marrying the appeal of velvety darkness with a silvery sheen, an aromatic echo of the swirls of scintillating light in the sky. This is where I feel most free, entirely at home. I can *breathe* out here.

In a luxuriously self-indulgent motion, I stretch, feeling my shoulders ease. More tension trickles away when I pull my shoes off and sink my toes into the loamy earth. The wilds love me back, as brambles never tear at my skin and leaves caress me when I pass by. A dangling strand of ivy shivers in delight when I whisper, "Good day to you, green-friend."

I set my course in the opposite direction of Miremorel House. Da doesn't need my troubles to come knocking at his door, even if he's not in residence. The guards might wreck up the place if they're aggravated enough.

Hmm. I could visit Macha. She lives a day's walk from the palace, past the point where the glade becomes fen. Though I know the way in my sleep, she can be cantankerous. I once spent some time as a lizard because I showed up without notice, and I have no desire to repeat the experience. Not Macha, then.

Who else would take me in?

As I walk, I contemplate where I might find refuge. Ordinarily, one's parents should be their first port in a storm, but Rain and Fen have never been that for me. Nominally, I am their daughter, but not by blood. Their indifference has haunted me my entire life. No one has ever addressed the fact that my presence is a crime that's received no redress—that the culprits among the Winter Court who stole me from my mortal kin to punish Rain and Fen for their forbidden love have yet to be uncovered. I feel so conflicted because I shouldn't even *be* here, yet I love the wildlands with my entire soul.

And that brings me back to the changeling status, a tarnish to my name that I can't shake, no matter how virtuously I behave.

And I decided long ago that I much prefer to be bad.

2

> ***Silent Resistance***
>
> *The artist carved this piece as a frieze in a granite wall. It depicts a figure trying to hold back a wave with their hands, but it is obvious to the observer that the person will soon be swept away. It is the intention that matters and that moment of resistance. The outcome may be foretold, but the subject will hold for as long as they can. Even if the struggle is futile, they still devote themself to it. And the struggle matters.*

KERBOROS

"FIND THE CULPRIT," LORD LISKAAL orders.

Word is already spreading how some reckless soul has freed the pookas, thus sabotaging the peace talks between Houses Summer and Winter.

I have been pulled from my meal to do my hateful cousin's bidding yet again, and I clench my jaw against the outrage that threatens to overwhelm me. If I spoke even a whisper of my white-hot hatred, Lord Liskaal would separate my head from my neck. And while I can heal most injuries, I am no Dullahan. I keep my eyes down because this false subservience allows me to survive.

Lady Valnevi is present as well; unlike most consort-and-liege relationships, they wed with mutual adoration in their hearts, not for mutual benefit. They are thin and pale, more like ghouls who feast on pain and terror than the beautiful hosts immortalized in human poems. Clad in silver and white, they represent the worst and most capricious cruelties Winter has to offer.

I curse my blood and fate silently as I incline my head. I waste no words on this pallid pair, now busy eating each other with their eyes. The palace staff speak of their perversions with secondhand glee, and their chambers are said to receive a regular rotation of all manner of visitors. I do not give a damn what they do privately, but I'd prefer never to see either of their smug, wretched faces again.

"Why are you still here?" Lady Valnevi demands in a shrill tone.

"Merely waiting to be dismissed," I reply.

"Get out," Liskaal snaps.

I stride from the great hall without looking back. I'm still so cursed hungry that it makes me crosser than usual. And I have quite a reputation. Just as well. I loathe most beings and would enjoy spending the rest of my life in silence and solitude.

A pox on both Lord Liskaal and Lady Valnevi.

On my sire too, while I'm cursing people. If he hadn't tried to wrest the gilded crown from Liskaal, I might not be in this situation. I was barely whelped when the rebellion failed, and to this day, I cannot be certain why Liskaal spared me when he executed the rest of my kin. On my bleakest days, I suspect that it was so the humiliation of my line would never end and he could punish me in perpetuity for my father's sins.

"Hubris and avarice," he once whispered to me, and at the time, I didn't understand.

Now that I do, I find a grim sort of satisfaction in completing the tasks set to me as efficiently as possible, so that I may resume what little peace I'm permitted. They call me his hound, the beast that exists only to heel to his hand.

It would have been kinder to kill me. But Liskaal is not known for compassion.

And I serve because I am waiting. This isn't my destiny. Not forever. I have never been able to pinpoint an alternative, and it is safer not to anger the Lord and Lady of Winter. So I hunt. And watch. And wait.

But I have been sowing seeds and tending my garden for an eternity now. Eventually, my darkly beautiful belladonna shall bloom.

And my cousin will be stunned, not because I will complete my father's work. Entirely the opposite. But for now, I keep up appearances and offer silent apologies to those I'm forced to hunt. Retracing the culprit's path will not serve as well as visiting the stables. That is where I shall commence. They would have lingered, opening each stall, so it will be easiest to find traces of them to follow.

But I don't quicken my pace, now that I have left Liskaal's sight. Instead, I take a quiet pleasure in returning to my quarters. If I'm questioned, I'll justify the pause to collect tools of the trade. I have obscured my methods sufficiently that no one can determine how my magic functions, whether I use rituals or elemental aids.

My room is humble, intentionally so. Though the same blood runs in our veins, Lord Liskaal houses me with the wild fae. He thinks I should mind this obvious insult. The truth is, being hidden from the upper echelons allows me considerably more freedom and solitude. I would enjoy even more of both.

I have no artwork on the walls, no treasures that can be taken. As a child inside an enemy stronghold, I swiftly learned that anything I valued could be stripped from me. And so, I learned to treasure nothing but my own sovereignty. There are only carvings on the walls, and no one would know that I made them, fanciful shapes created in silence, over the long years of my exile.

As I enter, I touch the beard of a water dragon that I shaped when I was young. It's a quiet little ritual that comforts me. Friends are a luxury I cannot afford, loved ones even less. I have been alone for so long that silence feels more natural than conversation. I eat what remains of my meal, left on my table, toasted brown bread with mushroom-walnut paste covered in creamy white cheese. It's not as delicious as it was before the interruption, but I savor it nonetheless.

To add to my subtle defiance, I also tidy my dwelling before collecting my weapon, the only blade I am allowed to carry, its haft etched with Liskaal's personal crest. It is the closest thing to a brand on my skin, a possibility they did discuss and eventually discarded.

Outside, the light informs me that I have dallied long enough. Any longer and I risk provoking displeasure. My disrespect must be measured in microns, not meters. As I step into the passage that leads behind the serving annex, a brownie greets me with too many teeth. I respond with a single word: "Erdene."

"You're off hunting, then?" she asks.

"It is my mandate."

A pause as she checks to be sure we're alone. "Such a waste, that one in the big white room." She makes a sound betwixt lips and teeth. "It should be you," she adds.

It's not the first time she has expressed such sentiment, often in less oblique terms. Erdene isn't the most cautious of wild fae, and I distance myself from her, not due to antipathy but because I must be so careful. Even this exchange is enough to prompt a wave of executions. I ensure that my expression does not change when I incline my head, slipping past her as a silent shadow. There is no response more accurate than what she's already articulated.

If things were different, if my father had chosen his course with better strategy and greater foresight, it *would* be me.

And then I despise myself for the thought. Because in any future where I lead the Winter Court, it means my brother still perished. I would gladly swap my luck for his, as the world would've been better off if Geraint had survived in my place. He was a force for good, a bold and bright soul whose loss dimmed the glow of the fae collective. Geraint was endlessly patient with my questions and my curiosity, and I—

I miss him.

Fighting a tide of melancholy, I head for the stables, where the fire has been contained with misty magic. The smoldering bits are still warm, and I acknowledge the warning with a nod at the brownie who offered it. Nobody tries to stop me from entering the premises, however. They must be aware I serve at Liskaal's whim.

Once I ensure that there are no watchful eyes to observe my process, I kneel and touch the ground, sending forth fluttering tendrils. They coalesce into spiderlings, dark blots of energy that skitter to and fro, sensing familiar patterns and building a web in my head. I close my eyes, mentally reviewing what transpired here.

Thea.

Of course it was Thea, but I needed confirmation to track her. The spiders try to lead me toward the gates, but I already know that was how she escaped. Instead, I climb the ladder to the loft and surround myself with her belongings. I sit amid her pillows and blankets and childhood playthings. The whole space is permeated with her essence; I drink it in until I can *feel* her.

With some targets, attuning to their signature is torture. But with Thea, it's a pleasure. She feels like wild places, like laughter and lightning, like warm breezes and swift-running rivers. When I reach for her, I feel clean. *Ah. There.*

If I could, I would let her go, but disobedience would mean revealing one of my closely kept secrets, and so I open a portal.

3

A Spell for Gilding and Glamour

You're not interested in fancies and fripperies, but I can teach you how to make yourself into the brightest of diamonds. At some point, you may want to look your best to captivate someone special. I remember your first crush, my gem. You were devastated when that dryad said you were too young and she'd never leave her tree to be with you anyway.

Now, I do think your natural charms are enough, but should you wish a little boost, I'll gift that knowledge. Here's the working I used in my courting days. Strongest cast in the dark.

You'll require:

- *A bowl crafted with rose quartz*
- *Soap made with fresh rose petals, dried lavender, and lemon verbena*
- *A flax towel hand spun by someone who loves you, warmed by a flame you kindled*
- *A silver mirror to confirm your allure*

For this working, you fill the bowl with pure, warm water. Lather the soap in your hands and wash your face gently. It's part of the ritual, though the simple care may leave you glowing even without a glamour. You're a beautiful soul, and it won't take much magic for others to see you as I do.

Rinse the suds using the quartz bowl. Pat your face dry with the linen towel. Take up the mirror and do three recitations. Choose the features you love about yourself. In my courting days, I said to myself, "Mudge, you've fine bright eyes. And look at that magnificent hair! And that friendly smile. Why, anybody would be lucky to get your attention."

Finally, know this: Anyone worthy of you won't need a glamour to see your worth. They'll know already, but there's no harm in wanting to stand out. Use this working well, and know that my fondness for you knows no bounds, my darling daughter.

THEA

I'VE MADE IT TO THE outskirts of the swamp when the air thins around me and energy crackles fiercely enough to lift my hair in the static charge.

This is such bullshit.

A moment later, a portal opens and Kerboros, House Winter's enforcer, emerges. His name is similar to a legendary dog Da told me about. Humans believe it has three heads and guards the gates of the Underworld. And to be honest, Kerboros has some qualities in common with a ferocious, bite-drunk cur. It feels like cheating, how quickly he ran me to ground. But then, the court and those who serve them have powers beyond my reckoning, most of which are used to keep the wild fae beneath their collective thumbs.

"Your presence is required," he says.

Then he nudges me toward the portal. Kaleidoscopic energy swirls around me, bursts of color and pops of sound that leave me reeling; off-balance, I tumble into the courtyard with such force that I land on my hands and knees, scraping the skin. Blood smears the ground when I brace myself. I know better than to rise. My stomach churns. Traveling this way is a good test of abdominal fortitude, as I'm a shudder away from tossing my guts on the paving stones. I'm not sorry because the pookas were miserable, and my pride ranks below their sorrow, so I'll apologize before anyone asks me to.

It's not the first time. I've learned it's helpful to pretend penitence eagerly.

As I raise my head, I realize the entire coterie is present. Lord Liskaal and Lady Valnevi, encircled by courtiers and social climbers, regard me icily. Small wonder, as I'm more of a tree climber, and today, I'm also smeared in green and brown goop. I can't wait to get this over with. I hope these two supercilious assholes exile me to the wildlands today. Rain and Fen possess enough power to protect me from execution, but banishment from court? Yes, please. And my so-called parents wouldn't object to that decision.

For me, it would be a dream come true. *Please send me to the wildlands with orders never to return.* I'm so excited about the prospect that I could scream.

"You have despoiled what should have been a joyous and momentous occasion," Lady Valnevi proclaims after a protracted silence. Before I can say a word, she continues, addressing the court instead of me: "I should censure this scapegrace appropriately, but other matters weigh heavier for the nonce. We cannot allow inconvenience to destroy the accord we have so painstakingly brokered."

I have no idea what she's talking about, but I have a bad feeling.

"An accurate summation, and most generous, my love." Lord Liskaal lifts her elegant hand and seals a kiss against her silvered glove.

Lady Valnevi gestures. "Take her. Have her washed. Everything shall proceed at midnight, as originally planned."

Panic catches fire in my veins, and I lurch to my feet. Liskaal gestures, and his people march me toward the annex, where guests and less important visitors are housed within the royal compound. The crowd parts reluctantly, yielding only enough space for me to get knocked by shoulders and elbows.

The Lord of Winter makes one final command: "Make her presentable."

Kerboros watches in silence, though his eyes flash. And then he's gone in a swirl of gray cloak; he's all bronze and midnight, and I wish I'd managed to kick his shins. In the Winter Court, most have raven-dark hair or a blue so pale, it gleams white. There are variations in skin tone, with those of inky tresses having light skin and the blue-haired fae usually deep as midnight. Kerboros is the rare exception, warm skin and raven hair and eyes gray as cloud cover. The ladies and maids run the gamut in complexion, but I don't recognize any of them.

"This way," a court lady murmurs.

"Oh, you're bleeding. Let me heal that first." A brownie, bless her, appears from behind the rest.

She's small and wrinkled as a nut, though that's no indication of her age. Deep-green hair curls all over her head, fine as moss, and she beams as a soothing warmth permeates my skinned palms and knees. I know her. This is Da's friend Erdene, someone I've known as not quite an auntie but who's been kind when our paths cross.

"That feels better. You're gifted." My smile conveys appreciation, but I know better than to thank her.

Mortals who stumble into our world thank us for *everything*. Those words create obligations, offering proof of indebtedness, and once you're locked into a bargain, it can be difficult to extricate yourself. I have no desire to work in the kitchen in Erdene's stead while she lolls on a cushion.

Erdene bares her sharp teeth in a delighted smile. "Mudge has raised you well."

Mudge is my real dad, in my heart's core, but there are no documents binding us, nothing that proves we're family, other than our love for each other. But the quickest way to make me smile is to praise him. "I think so too."

Erdene turns to the others. "The rest of you, go. I'll make Thea ready."

At her touch, drowsiness suffuses me, and my muscles go lax. My knees wobble as she guides me toward the bathhouse, the only aspect I like about the Winter Court. The luxury is so excessive that it could steal your soul, all gleaming polished white stones and the cascade of steaming water from bright platinum pipes. There are huge tubs with scalloped edges, one steaming hot, one comfortably warm, one icy cold, and so many magical unguents and potions devised to make one more gorgeous and glamorous.

Belatedly, I inquire, "Ready for what?"

"We'll discuss that later," she hedges.

Probably I should dig for more information, but Erdene herds me to the cascading water, and she has such big eyes. They're clear as topaz, fringed in a delicate web of green lashes, a shade deeper than her hair. Though she comes only to my shoulder, she is, as many brownies are, deceptively strong. Her grip tightens, though not enough to hurt me.

"A bath? Now?" I ask.

"You could use some looking after, my dear. How did you ever get so grubby?"

"I smeared myself with mud and moss on purpose."

"Silly child." But it's a fond scolding.

Brownies can be nurturing, the flip side to their unruly streak. I sigh and strip down, immersing myself in the silky, crystalline water. I've heard the Summer Court has myriad natural beauties, but in the Winter Court? Water is life, whether it's free-falling in a sleeting rain, fluttering in snowflakes, or frozen solid.

She opens a pot, releasing the glorious fragrance of distilled dreaming dragonberry, a fantastical peppery sweetness that heats the skin. There are crystals ground into the mixture, and she uses a hagstone to exfoliate until my skin feels brand-new. Rejuvenated, I scrub away the grime and exhaustion so that my whole body tingles.

Afterward, I get a full beauty treatment, with Erdene massaging me with scented oil, anointing my feet as I sip some lovely floral tea. The spices are bright and piquant, all yellow and gold on my tongue, so this must be a Summer import. Winter teas tend to taste blue or green, sometimes with faint notes of purple. I've never sampled black tea, though the humans supposedly have it. I wonder how rich and delicious it must be, like drinking the night itself. But while I daydream about the mortal realm sometimes, I don't want to go there. Da says they have nearly destroyed all their wild places, which means there's nowhere I'd feel at home.

After the massage, Erdene smooths a bright blue mask upon my face and covers the rest of me with steaming towels. An ice bath will follow; in the Winter Court, they believe it adds a glow in addition to all the magical benefits. Normally, I would be fidgeting by now, but Erdene is humming the most soothing song, all soporific bliss. I recline and wait until the hot cloths cool. The cold plunge is shocking, but I do feel invigorated.

The brownie eyes me critically. "With your coloring, I think you'd shine in silver. What do you think, my darling?"

She holds up two gowns, neither of which I'd prefer to put on. I was prepared for punishment, and while primping wouldn't bother some folks, for me, it's torture. I want to object, especially to the pinchy shoes that I suspect Erdene will soon insist on, but I'm so sleepy that I can't be bothered to complain. I stare muzzily at the dresses.

The first is ivory, and it has so many layers. The thing is diaphanous, and if I wore it, I would feel like a cream cake adorned with curtains that belong in a maiden's bower. The silver dress is sleeker, with long sleeves and a fitted bodice, holding a delicate shimmer when the light glides over it. Sometimes it's matte and sometimes it's a river.

"Definitely the silver," I decide. "But what—"

"You must be hungry. How long has it been since you've had a bite?"

I struggle to hold on to the edges of my initial question. Or objection. What was I about to say, anyway? I can barely remember what Erdene asked now. Hm. I skipped breakfast, I think, and I walked for so long in the woods. All the way to the edge of the swamp. "I'm not sure."

My head feels fuzzy, and I can't remember what I intended to do before we got here. I'm getting ready for something important, am I not? That's true as it can be.

"Let me send for some biscuits. And fruit, perhaps?"

"That sounds good."

Erdene passes me some undergarments, and I sleepily start getting dressed as she moves off to whisper to someone standing outside the bath. I ruminate on how Winter's hound hunted me down without hesitation, how grim he looked when he herded me through the portal.

I've never seen the man smile, but when he looks at me, in particular, it's like he chills even further, a glacier for a soul.

On her return, I ask, "Why does Kerboros hate me so much?"

"Don't take it personally, my dearling. That one hates everybody." She adjusts the strap on my underdress. "There's a bit of unseemly gossip about him. Are you interested?"

"Yes, please." I shimmy into the dress, eager for inside information. Brownies have all the best chatter, as the high fae tend to treat them like inanimate objects.

"His family's related to Lord Liskaal, don't you know, on the patrilineal line. And there was some ugliness, I've lost track of when. But rumor has it that our Kerboros feels that he's the rightful Lord of Winter while being forced to serve."

I stare, wide-eyed. "But that's incredible. I'm surprised Lord Liskaal hasn't had him executed or banished for his bad attitude."

"Betimes, it's best to keep your enemies close, and as Lord Liskaal compels Kerboros to hunt, the lord proves that Kerboros is his hound, and the owner never asks the dog if it's happy to be chasing prey."

"He's angry because he's powerless, then." I instantly find it difficult to dislike Kerboros as much as I did before.

The assistant returns with a plate that Erdene accepts with a gentle smile. She turns to me again. "Indeed. Have a seat, eat your treats while I do your hair."

Dreamily, I nibble at the sliced dew pear and honey wafers, so light and thin, they melt on my tongue in a pop of sweetness. Erdene has a little basket full of trinkets that jingle merrily when she hooks the handle across her arm, and then her hands are so very busy. I love when people play with my hair, and I've experienced that so seldom. It requires no effort to let her tug and weave gently, murmuring as if I'm her doll.

At some point, I lose track of time, drowsing like a little sprite in the sun. She gives me a soft tap on the shoulder. "Finished. You look like a princess."

Oh no.

No.

She's not humming anymore, and my mind is clear as a bell. "You stupored me!"

"Just a little, my dearling. Didn't you enjoy it?"

"That's not the point!" I yank at the tight dress and touch my hair. Ribbons and gems, all cunningly interwoven into a complicated arrangement that would take me forever to unravel.

It's as if I've traded places with the pookas.

"Tell me what's happening at midnight." My tone is cold as wrought iron, and I could happily freeze all the water in those pretty platinum pipes right now, if only my unpredictable magic would cooperate.

Erdene tilts her head and shows me her teeth, all softness gone. "Gladly. You're getting married, my sweet."

4

> ### *Isolation*
>
> *The artist carved this piece from fallen wood. The carving uses one continuous piece with the planed side of the log serving as the base. It depicts a fox hidden in an impassible thicket. Polish and oil highlights the deep patterns of the grain, mimicking dappled fur. Tangles of thorns encircle the fox to keep it safe. Or to keep it from escaping. The fox is clearly on guard, tail raised. Foxes are social creatures. But this one is alone, aware that it must be wary at all times. These brambles offer no solace for a kit ensnared in isolation.*

KERBOROS

AFTER LEAVING THE GREAT HALL, I'm free to pursue my own ends, though I remain watchful as I wend my way deeper into the corridors used by the wild fae.

There are always those who seek to elevate their status at someone's expense, so I give no sign of my intentions until I return to my quarters, where I can spy to my heart's content. I don't do this because I enjoy it. But information is currency, and I sell secrets. Over the years, they've kept me safe.

I settle on the floor, as my powers serve best when I'm grounded by earth or stone, and I summon the tendrils, shaping spiderlings nobody else can see. My mother taught me this secret magic in the dungeons while awaiting execution; it was how we received news of the outside world when the guards would tell us nothing. Though she resembled the high fae, she came from older lines, where the magic runs deep and sometimes dark. I have heard rumors that my mother may have been related to Macha, the swamp witch, but she never spoke of that connection, and it could be unkindness that followed after her passing.

There will be consequences for Thea, and I wish to learn what they will be.

This time, I set different parameters and search for ripples aligned with her essence. The spiders find her at once, but I don't linger over her getting her hair styled. There must be more ominous overtures in play.

Soon, the spiderlings draw my inner vision to the spectacle of a hobgoblin named Mudge being dragged from the kitchen, where he was about to polish off a pear and cheese tart. The palace is warded against wild fae magic, weakening it to the point that many cannot perform powerful spells at all. Mudge says a few words. My spies cannot provide audio, but I usually don't require it. I can discern a great deal from these echoes, traces left from recent events. He's absolutely cursing them, but in the end, he goes quietly.

They likely threatened Thea. Love is a tether and a weak point.

I uncoil from the floor and roll my shoulders. It seems I will visit the dungeons next. This isn't the first time, but I wish it could be the last. If I ruled the Winter Court, I would do away with that desperate place entirely.

The cells smell of misery.

To me, misery is unwashed bodies and salt and copper, tears and blood. There's waste as well, an animal musk born purely from terror. I wish these awful odors weren't so familiar, but it reminds me strongly—

Stone. Stone. Stone. Interlaced, before my gaze. I will not remember. I will *not.* The stones in the wall are gray, seamed in dark brown. I count them until calm overtakes me. I have visited the dungeons many times, usually in secret. I greet Melas, the boggart in charge, with a slow inclination of my head.

He's a good-humored soul, and I don't begrudge him the role he plays. Others, as I know all too well, revel in the power they hold over the most vulnerable.

Today, I have caught Mel in the midst of a meal, something gray and viscous. The broth bubbles, and something squirms, rippling beneath the limpid surface. This dish smells oddly of the sea. I do believe Mel has a taste for tentacles. I have been amassing such useful observations for ages; much use have I for these trifles.

"Have you come on his lordship's orders?" he asks, tilting his head with a quizzical air.

Mel seems surprised that I've come empty-handed. Normally, I bring bread or slivers of soap for those imprisoned for irritating Lord Liskaal or, occasionally, for no reason at all.

I shake my head silently. "Is Mudge here?"

According to my intel, he should be.

"It's not been long, but yes. He's in the fourth cell."

"I'll speak with him." It isn't a request.

Mel isn't inclined to argue. He chucks the control stone, allowing me to pass the checkpoint. There is a glowing crystal behind me, and I tap the stone against it. The discordant sound echoes within me, and it feels like a sideways wrenching when I arrive on the other side, a dungeon so deep that it's elsewhere entirely, not even part of the Winter realm in the most technical sense.

I don't want to remember, but it's impossible to forget the first time I saw this place. After my father's failed rebellion, we were *all* brought here—the family members who survived. My brother, Geraint, died for our father's ambition, and I sometimes wonder if he was the lucky one. He died believing he could bring about a brighter future for the wild fae if he fought hard enough.

I watched Winter's warriors cut him down, his blood so red on the whitest snow. And my father? My father *knelt.* He surrendered after Geraint had given everything to his cause. I was too young to fight, but I had daggers, and though I was still a child, I followed my brother against my mother's wishes. I remain unable to shake the horror that lives in my skull, even to this day.

In my mind's eye, I see them now, crowded into one cell. My mother knelt on the floor, weeping silently, while my father fixed a spiteful stare on the opposite wall. He wanted to rule but not to suffer or sacrifice. And I, stone-faced, was determined not to display my despair or terror. Determined to give my enemies nothing. I lost track of the days, waiting for execution.

No, it is not easy for me to visit these cells. And yet, this errand won't wait.

The first cell contains two sleeping sluagh. For obvious reasons, I leave them be. I count my steps as I pass the second cell, ignoring the hag's piteous cry, knowing that if I step close, she will use vicious nails to rend my flesh. In the third cell, a redcap sings eerily in the dark, and the stench of copper clings to my throat.

Soon, I find myself standing before Mudge, who clambers to his feet with a facile grace. He always looks so serene, regardless of his situation. It is an aspect of his character that I admire, even as I find his demeanor frustrating. The hobgoblin aims a smile in my direction and stops on the other side of the bars. The redcap pauses, no longer inflicting his uncanny song on an unwilling audience. While he appears to pay us no attention, I know better. He's listening. In fact, the *walls* are listening.

"And how can I be of service?"

"I came to warn you," I say then.

"About what?"

"I know you have your own intelligence network. There's no point in denying it, but I'm wondering how much you know. About why you're here." Best to keep my words vague.

"That would be telling." Mudge gets a canny look in his eye as if weighing how much he should reveal.

Clever of him, as he has no notion whether I can be trusted. Those in the Winter Court tend to serve their own interests. But I have joined no factions, forged no alliances. I exist outside the seasons spent jockeying for position.

In my way, I am both untouchable and inviolable.

"I'm trying to help you. Believe that…or not. It's all the same to me."

"I'm listening," Mudge says.

"I'm sure you've gathered that they rounded you up to use you against Thea."

"I did suspect that," he admits.

"But do you know what they're planning for her?" There's a limit to how much I should stick my neck out, even for Thea.

She's…good. In the way that few are among our kind. I witnessed her joy at setting the pookas free. And it's not the first such valiant stunt she's performed. No, she's infamous in the Winter Court for toeing right up to the line, weighing her worth against how much she can annoy Liskaal with her small rebellions. My cousin uses her as he uses everyone, and I don't wish to see her bright light dimmed.

"Not the particulars as such."

"I can only advise you to encourage her to cooperate. There will be dire consequences otherwise." That's all I can say with so many prisoners listening to my words.

"Will they ask something of her that she cannot bear?"

How am I supposed to answer that? I lift a shoulder. "If you want her safe, ensure she understands that this choice isn't a choice at all."

I turn then, leaving Mudge to consider what he'll do to keep his daughter from harm. I hurry through the dim corridor, not breathing deeply until I touch the control stone to the crystal and appear on the other side behind Mel, who slurps up the last of his meal.

"Finished?"

"Yes."

I depart without another word and retrace my route. On emerging from the recessed staircase, I hear footsteps, a larger group making their way toward the prison annex. Just in time, I slip around the corner of the building, hiding out of sheer instinct. I narrowly avoid encountering Thea and her guards. For as long as I have known of her—and she's grown up dashing in and out of the Winter Court—I have never seen Thea thus. The sight of her leaves me reeling, and I stumble against the cool stone, damp moss cool against my fingertips.

In such finery, others might find her beautiful. To me, she is the essence of sorrow.

They have polished and plaited the wildness out of her. Her face has become haunting, heartbreaking because she is pale and glittering, *la belle dame sans merci* from that old human verse. The handmaidens have plastered over her vitality, confining her, enforcing her smallness in a gown that makes her resemble everyone else in the Winter Court. Until this moment, I didn't realize how much I cherished her fierceness. Now that it's gone, I feel the lack in a bone-deep ache, searing loss married to a weeping wound.

She passes so very close to me that I smell the sweetness of crushed flower petals and the woody herbs that must have been in her bath; I breathe the honey in the cream they massaged into her skin. If I reached out from my hidden vantage, I could graze the sleek fabric of her dress.

The wan light of a distant lamp finds her face; Thea is not smiling. Living at court will destroy her, one way or another. The spiderlings have shown me glimpses of documents and of secret meetings. I have a grim feeling down in my bones.

Now she's gone, marching down into darkness.

Erdene flashes a cunning look in my direction, as if she knows I'm lurking in the shadows. But then, I am *always* lurking in the shadows.

I wonder if Thea knows how long I've taken joy in her tiny rebellions.

I wonder if she knows how long I've loved her.

5

A Spell for Luck and Light

Sometimes we turn our magic to blessings for others, those we hold most dear. There will likely come a time when you wish to shield someone and keep them safe. To attract all manner of bright and beautiful things. In truth, I cast this spell for Rain and Fen when their daughter was born. Soon after, they discovered your true nature, and then you came to me, precious gem. Goodness cast in a wide net comes back to us sevenfold, you see.

I'll write out the working I use to send fortune and fair winds to those I adore. Strongest cast at the height of light.

You'll need:

- *A piece of sharp green jade*
- *One white beeswax candle*
- *A large bay leaf*
- *A golden censer*

Take up the jade like a pen, the leaf like paper, and etch your wish for protection or luck or blessings, whatever wonderful boon you wish to bestow on your loved one. Craft it carefully and be specific. Leave no room for misunderstandings. Once I wrote that someone I cared for should never stop laughing. You can imagine how that was twisted, most unpleasant indeed. Even with the best of intentions, there will always be a spark of mischief in our magic, a yearning toward trickster trades and leading folks astray.

Once the message is complete and incorruptible, light the candle with the magic spark I mentioned. Burn the bay leaf in the censer while visualizing the joyous outcome of your spell. Mind, the more distracted you are, the more this can go wrong, so don't risk this working when your mind's restless. Blessings will keep, but curses run you ragged trying to catch them. Finally, lift the censer and gift the wishes to the wind to unleash the full effect. If the result is good, you'll hear a sound like tinkling bells, and if something's gone wrong, a discordant tone along with a deepening chill.

Courtiers have made you feel unwelcome, as if you cause trouble by being different. I wish I knew more about your heritage, but whatever people say, you're no demon out there devouring souls. Things go wrong for me all the time. Don't blame yourself if you don't master a spell on the first try. Your best is good enough.

THEA

I HAVE NO WORDS.

In my time on the fringes of the Winter Court, I have been passed over, punished, penalized, and pushed around, but I've never been disregarded to this extent. I struggle to get the question out. "Does Da know?"

"He's currently locked in a cell. His cursing was memorable to say the least. He's lucky Lord Liskaal didn't take his head."

The initial burst of warmth freezes into a kernel of fear, and it burns in my heart with winter frost. Erdene doesn't need to tell me that my dad will remain a hostage until I comply; I've dwelled at the edge of the ice for the entire span of my existence. Slowly, I get to my feet, regarding the brownie with a faint feeling of betrayal, although she couldn't have stopped this.

She could have warned me.

But she wore a mask of kindness instead, lulled me, who's never known a mother's softness or care, and made me waste precious time. Though I don't know the hour, I collect that I won't be allowed to try to free Da. The person Erdene spoke to earlier is most likely a guard, if Lord Liskaal operates true to type. There is probably more than one posted outside the bath. I'm not known for my obedience.

"I see," I say softly. "If you expect me to be meek, even for a moment, I must be allowed to confirm that he's unharmed. In person."

I expect Erdene to push back, but two sharp raps sound on the door, and she turns from me to answer it. The gown binds me, and my hair feels like an unbearable weight, exacerbated by the flounces and furbelows in my updo.

She speaks with them briefly, and a moment later, Erdene beckons. "They're ready for you in the great hall, but you'll take a detour on the way, my chick. Try not to fret. Things will work out as they're meant to." As the guards encircle me, she *winks*.

Does that mean—do the lesser fae have a plan?

Generally, I'm not the sort to wait around for a rescue, as proven by my pooka-liberation mission earlier. But I don't know what I can achieve when six armed fae march me with great determination toward my supposed wedding night. Based on what Lady Valnevi said, I'm being used as a peace offering, though as always with the high fae, it can be a double-edged blade. The Winter Court provides fresh blood to Summer while removing a thorn from their own side.

If I had a choice, I'd rather go to the Autumn Court, where they don't seem to care about such machinations at all. That said, Lady Mirralee holds her cards close to her chest, so perhaps she has an agenda she doesn't reveal to outsiders. Lord Sorren of House Summer *loathes* Lord Liskaal and would be delighted to gnaw at Winter's borders, though he's a tad too indolent to declare outright war without great provocation. Instead, he pecks at Winter, keeping tensions at a simmer. In fact, even the Springtide Court would be preferable, and allegedly, it's governed by an eccentric, ancient fae who acts endlessly amused by everything. According to widespread gossip, Pelleril declines the use of a title and tells everyone to call them *Pell.*

For a moment, I contemplate tearing off this dress and sneaking away from this mess. But considering Da, locked up to keep me in line, love surges through me, deep and powerful and nigh overwhelming. He's always been there for me. I don't have to think much; it's not even a sacrifice, as long as he's safe. For Da, I'll marry a boggart or a Dullahan or even a fachan, no questions asked. If I had the focus and the supplies, I'd cast a luck spell for him here and now, but I have to trust that he's unharmed.

I haven't been paying attention, but we're approaching the administrative side of the palace complex. The serving quarters are behind, even farther from the center, and past there, the door to the antechamber leading to the prison. Inside the holding area, a bored boggart picks his teeth with a stone knife. His gray skin is marbled with darker veins, and his eyes are small and red. He has large fur-tufted ears, a scaly, hairless tail, and a round, comfortable belly.

"I wasn't told to expect visitors!" He frowns at the lot of us.

A guard replies, "She'll speak with Mudge, so bring him out. We're not sending her into the cells in such a pretty dress."

I smile a bit. That's an entirely fae response, a certain reverence for beauty that I appreciate, although I don't always agree on the definitions. The boggart grumbles as he passes into the deep with the control stone, and when he returns, Da follows behind him, whistling a song that I could identify in my sleep. The mournful melody speaks to me, as it always does. Da says "Tha Mi Sgìth" is about a fairy who fell for a mortal girl at first sight, but he never says more, just gets a soft and sorrowing look, faraway for a moment.

I scan him from head to toe. Olive-brown skin, hazel, if you will, though I seldom encounter that word applied to anything but nuts and eyes, a tousled mop of silver hair, sharp canines that protrude a bit, and a full underjaw. He has pert ears and a weathered face, and he's not quite as tall as I am now, shorter by a hand or so. Da has the gentlest eyes of anyone I've ever known, sweet and calm like a forest pond, and twice as green.

"You came, my jewel?" He's always called me that. I think Erdene's changeable endearments started with him. "There was no need. I'm well enough as you can see."

Indeed, he doesn't appear to be injured, just a bit rumpled. "I had to be sure."

"They've promised to let me go. After. But I'll stay here if you need time to…fix matters. In your own way." Though his words are vague, he's giving me permission to run.

Leave him to Lord Liskaal's uncertain mercies.

Ah, no. I could never.

Before the guards stop me, I take two steps and hug him fiercely, my true dad. He smells of lichens—woody, and sharp, and slightly sweet—cedar, and a bit of brackish water, but not in a bad way. "No. It's all good. Wish you could be there, though. Maybe for my next wedding?" I manage a lopsided grin as he laughs quietly.

"How many are you planning, then?"

I shrug and step back. "Who knows? I live by my gut most days."

"Your gut's golden. It'll never steer you wrong."

I angle my hands, shielding them from the guards, and check to see if the boggart is paying attention. He's slouched in his chair, perusing an illustrated book. He might understand what I'm saying, if he looked over, as the wild fae have learned to speak silently when we're blocked from mind singing. But the jailor's loyalties likely lie with the high fae, so I'd rather he didn't catch us. This entire area is shielded, so I can't touch Mudge's mind with mine. Swiftly, I sign, *I love you. Be careful.*

Because his hands are bound and the guards are watching, Mudge only nods, his thickly lashed eyes watchful.

I turn to the guards. "Our deal has been honored. We can go."

My attendants pick up the pace, making up for lost time, and we jog to the great hall, so I'm breathless when we reach the massive doors. They bang open with a grandiose *clack*, and like everything else in the Winter Palace, they are white etched with silver, and rivers of light glance off the glaring skull-white of the floors and walls, making it difficult to focus. Finally, my gaze settles on the crowd arranged in a semicircle before the thrones currently occupied by Lord Liskaal and Lady Valnevi.

It's a little unnerving how much they resemble each other, but that's by choice since the high fae can shift forms as I might change clothing. I can only surmise that their ideas of beauty are thin, as narrow as what fits through the eye of a needle. The oversize chairs should diminish them, but somehow they don't; they appear to be carved out of actual ice, though I don't think that's the case, and within the semitranslucent crystal, there are flickers of faces with screaming mouths.

So. Unsettling.

Gradually, the whispers quiet, and there is no music to soften the tension. On happier occasions, where the wedding isn't so much of a criminal sentence, there would be musicians and acrobats and scintillating displays of fae magic, like birds shaped from pure light and wintry crystalline flowers that bloom from smooth stone columns.

"We are gathered here today to put aside old wounds and grudges and usher in a new era of peace," Lord Liskaal intones.

The guards step to the side, and I proceed with measured steps toward the center of the hall. My would-be spouse should be arriving soon.

I search the crowd for any familiar faces, and I recognize Lady Almira. She is dressed in a gown that resembles the one I refused, all diaphanous layers so fine, they could've been woven with spider silk. When she moves, her skin shimmers, hints of ocean pearl mirrored in the tiny shells she wears instead of gems, a nod to her family's undine connections. I don't recognize the lord beside her, but he is cloaked in white feathers, his suit a misty gray, the shoulders bedecked with crystalline thorns.

Shadows shift across their faces, and in the ebb and flow, their features are first austerely beautiful and then monstrously terrible with hints at feral natures covered by a deep, impermeable glamour. It's impossible to know a high fae's true appearance unless you've grown intimate with them. And I have no such relationships among the nobility.

Not even with those who have been recorded as my parents.

I'm not surprised Rain and Fen aren't here. From what I know, they've been visiting their daughter in the mortal realm, bringing gifts and showering love. She's their real child. I'm the changeling.

And while there are ways my birth family could contact me, so far they haven't. I don't know if I want them to. They didn't even notice that I had been taken. Maybe I shouldn't blame them, as the fae glamour the infant left behind to resemble the one taken, and as the magic fades, any lack of resemblance is attributed to a child's natural changes.

Which leaves me in a strange state of in-between, belonging nowhere and sought only by the wild fae.

"Where is the delegation from the Summer Court?" Lady Valnevi asks.

A courier rushes into the room and flies like an arrow directly to her side, whispering with no small amount of agitation. When you don't fit in, you acquire the ability to read the room and determine the prudent course. I don't always act on that information, but I always possess it. Based on body language, there's been a complication. That could be good for me, but not if it harms Da in any fashion.

Lady Valnevi clenches her jaw and speaks through her teeth. "Then *find* them. Who allowed them to wander our halls unescorted?"

"Yes, my lady. At once."

"There will be a short delay," Lord Liskaal says smoothly.

This may be what Erdene mentioned before, and I'll pay tithe and tribute to the palace staff for the rest of my life if this is a distraction and they're freeing Da. That's the best I can hope for in this silly dress.

"In the meantime"—Lady Valnevi rises as she speaks, prowling toward me like a white serpent—"I would have you seal the marital agreement."

"Seal?" I ask.

In answer, she produces a blade of pure ice—out of nowhere, or her body—and slices the tip of my finger. Before I can agree or protest, my bloody fingerprint joins another on an ornate vellum scroll that I haven't been allowed to read. I lean closer, trying to skim some words, but Lady Valnevi draws back, as if she might be contaminated by my proximity.

"It is done," she says.

Then the hall quakes with a subterranean shiver, and all the lights go out. Beneath my feet, I feel the continued vibrations, as though an immense beast lumbers in our direction. The palace brownies hastily kindle illumination, but foxfire? It's whimsical and unreliable, ghosting around the hall. *Something* is making the lights very nervous. I get only the barest glimpse before I'm hit from behind, not so much blackjacked as trampled.

I pitch forward, and a court lady kicks my temple with her dainty, sparkly shoes, and that's the last thing I see for a while.

6

Naked Blade

This piece is carved into the inside of a door, the outline of a sword with an emblem etched into the blade. The details of the emblem are vague, incomplete, so it's impossible to discern what it's meant to represent. And the blade itself is flawed, with lines indicating where it will, one day, break from that implicit fault. There is no hand present in the design to wield the blade, nor is there a sheath to shelter it. The blade is the focus, the beginning and the end.

KERBOROS

IN DISTANT HALLS, I HEAR the shouts, a great clamor spreading like a wave.

But I never volunteer my time to the Lord and Lady of Winter.

No matter the situation, while they do compel my service time and again, I never proffer it freely. Had I the power, I'd sabotage everything related to Thea's forced nuptials. As far as I'm concerned, whatever has gone wrong can continue on its way. I remain in my quarters, ignoring the ruckus, carving the first shallow shapes of a new bas-relief.

And I smile.

It is not my problem until I'm summoned to deal with it. I continue slicing delicate strips from the wall that curl downward like the peels of a desiccated fruit.

Whatever has occurred, they will demand that I remediate the crisis. At this point, I doubt that my distant cousin would know how to act without first steering my hand wrapped around the hilt. He thinks that if I do violence in his name, the court will loathe him less.

For I'm the perpetrator; I hold the weapon. But he is shortsighted and imperceptive. Everyone else sees, as well as I do, that I'm not the wielder; I'm the dagger.

For now, however, I'm permitted to choose the angle of my cuts, create a design of my own making. The artistry is soothing. I'm repeating patterns I find everywhere—in the scales of sea creatures and the shells they leave behind.

It is a rare peace that cannot last.

The sounds intensify, until eventually, they culminate with the sound of small fists thumping on my closed door. I take my time in responding, knowing that each tick of the clock will feel intolerable to my accursed cousin, the Lord of Winter.

Lord only of his own sight line.

There are quiet rebellions all around him, and he lacks the wit to discern them because he is always scanning for overt resistance, not seeing the subtle markers of disrespect. The whole court despises my cousin and his consort, and I doubt the courtiers would weep if Summer conquered the realm and imposed new leadership, a puppet more amenable to their terms.

Not that I'm willing to serve as such.

Once I complete my arrangements and escape from Liskaal's influence, I will never permit anyone else to make me dance.

Before opening the door, I clean my artistic tools and put them away with precision that must feel maddening to the person who has demanded entrance three times with urgent rapping. Only then do I respond to the summons.

"Yes?" I regard the brownie with a calm mien, unmoved by the chaos spinning in the shadows behind us.

"Lord Liskaal needs you, sir."

I say nothing.

But with every moment, the urge to smile plucks at me. I must not, of course.

I must behave as if I know nothing about what's transpired and have no insight as to how the Summer delegation came to vanish within our walls. If that's what has occurred. I will put my faith in nothing before confirming it for myself.

The brownie takes the direct path instead of sticking to the corridors allotted for the use of the wild fae. This choice reveals much about the urgency of our mission. The great hall is empty as we pass through, and it smells of trampled flowers. Something large and angry rampaged here, terrorizing the court. Blood here. And here, drying now. Those who serve will be up all night, scrubbing away stains from the gleaming white.

I guessed at the chaos from the distant noises, but I'm not a guard.

I suppose if I was ordered to fight, to defend the Winter Court, I would comply. But that is a waste of my magic, and for Liskaal's many faults, he's not a complete dolt. He tends not to squander valuable resources, and there are other bodies better suited to protecting empty rooms and halls.

"What transpired?" I ask.

It would seem strange for me to evince no curiosity, so I ask even when I may be able to surmise. Through my spiderlings, I specialize in secrets. And there are always those who pay for such. As I work through intermediaries and dead drops, nothing could be traced back to me, and someone who wanted to pass unnoticed might find my knowledge useful.

The brownie is young, nervous. Her gaze darts into all the dark corners before she speaks in a tiny voice that reminds me of ringing bells. "I'm sure I don't know, sir. It's better for you to get your information from the source."

"You didn't see anything?" I press.

People tend not to like me. I encourage it. She's no exception, trembling from the question like I might blame everything on her and offer her to the Lord and Lady of Winter. As if I'd do that to my worst enemy, let alone a kitchen brownie whose name I can't recall.

"I truly don't know," she squeaks. "But I've heard a lot of confusing nonsense."

"It would be helpful if you shared that information." Even when I try to sound reassuring, I come across as gruff.

At least, I suspect that's true from her audible gulp. Then she squares her shoulders and lifts her chin, making eye contact. "You didn't get this from me, yeah?"

"Understood. To be frank, I don't even know your name, so I wouldn't be able to provide that intelligence to anyone who inquired."

That seems to soothe her, and her tension eases. "Right. Well, someone I know who was in the serving hall said it was a fachan! But how in the world did the beast get past all the guards and wind up running wild?"

"An excellent question. I appreciate the information."

As we pass through the palace, I notice that the damage appears to be largely cosmetic. Someone wanted the compound on high alert, but not to mount an offensive. A fachan qualifies as an excellent diversion, and it allowed the Summer delegation to slip away in the confusion.

"Did they catch the creature?" I inquire.

She shakes her head. "It disappeared, along with those bigwig guests. People can't just vanish, can they?"

"Not usually," I agree.

It is possible. With the right preparation. And if someone like me isn't tasked with finding the lost. Thoughtful, I let the silence stand, analyzing the information I've acquired. An illusory fachan, perhaps, with agents judiciously placed to create physical evidence of its passage? That would have provided cover for the real escape. Even if Liskaal has come to the same conclusion, he won't view the situation as I do. He'll see this as a subtle statement that Summer has no intention of withdrawing their claim on Winter's border.

The brownie leads me to the lord and lady's private chambers. "Here we are. Good luck to you."

That is a curious thing to say. I knock twice and wait, turning to watch her scurry away before their attendant opens the door. He is high fae, beautiful in the manner many are, with perfect features, pointed ears, pale skin, and ink-dark hair. His eyes are like silver pools, reflecting nothing. And he is clad head to toe in their colors, his fitted uniform white and silver, showing every line of his body.

He makes a sweeping gesture to invite me in. "You're expected. The

Lord and Lady of Winter are wrapping up in the throne room. They will speak with you presently."

I keep my face still, suppressing instinctive scorn. Such absolute self-aggrandizement—they rushed me to arrive when they're not even here to receive me. It feels like the ultimate in posturing. They never stop posing, those two, so enamored with their own importance that they can't see the moving forest for the trees.

There's a human story, written by some famous bard, about how a noble house will fall when the forest comes for them. I've forgotten the particulars, but yes, these two will never realize what's happening—that I've cut all the cords—until it's too late. All I need to do is play my role for a little longer.

Even if compliance burns like fire.

7

A Spell for Succor and Sustenance

Even cooking can be magical. It should be, in fact. Kitchen spells needn't be complicated. The simplest of spells can bring the greatest joy. This one can be tailored by changing out the spicing herbs and the type of ingredients. Without further ado, I'll share the working I use to cheer you up when you've had a rough go.

You'll require:

- *One silver spoon*
- *A copper cauldron*
- *A sizable piece of bloodstone*
- *Generous amounts of cinnamon, allspice, and ginger*

You'll need other ingredients for best results. You could drink it as a tonic, using only water, but it wouldn't be filling, and magic can't create nutrition from nothing. We can create only the illusion of fullness, and that can have wicked consequences. Feckless mortals have starved on glamoured fae food, never realizing they were eating air. When I cook for you, my gem, this spell adds the warmth and satisfaction you experience, whether it's a bit of cracked barley or a handful of rolled oats. It'll be even better if you have a little fruit or some nuts. Having both makes for an exceptional outcome.

Use the bloodstone as your cooking surface, and funnel energy until it's good and hot. Set the cauldron on top, then add your ingredients: grain, water, nuts, fruit. Allow it to heat while focusing your will, funneling your love and good wishes into the pot along with the spices. You can speak the spell if you wish, though I usually don't. If I do, it'll be, "Let this food bless and nourish my darling girl. Let it serve as fuel for all the wondrous things she'll do, and let her feel my love in every bite." I'd be honored if one day you used this spell for me, but it'll serve well wherever you roam.

THEA

IT IS SO FLIPPING DARK.

When I rouse, I cannot be certain how long I've been out, and I feel weak, but anger sizzles in the air around me, tingling on my skin. Without meaning to, I lift my head and feast, silently drinking in the blazing wrath that Lord Liskaal disperses as he paces. This ability is probably why I—and others—survive here in the Winter Court. I take a situation from explosive to volatile and from volatile to salvageable, simply by existing.

The Lord of Winter glares at the courtiers and guardsmen assembled before him. "An unmitigated debacle, and for once, Thea had nothing to do with it!"

I stumble while pushing to an upright position. It's unsurprising that nobody rendered aid while I was unconscious. Erdene cannot freely traverse the great hall, and Da is locked up, so my head is still bruised and I have scrapes and cuts on my hands and knees. I might be able to heal myself once I feed a little more. *Easy enough.* Fortunately, everyone in this room is angry—and not with me. Over time, I've learned that righteous wrath tastes different than violent fury. I do strive to control myself at all times, though the effort is sometimes painful. I can't remember when I didn't feel hungry.

My movement, however, draws Lady Valnevi's attention. "You're awake. Since you did sign the agreement, the marriage and the treaty are binding. But if you cannot implement some plan for cohabitation, the Summer Court may manufacture cause for dissolution."

I blink. "If I don't move in with some random person, the realm could go to war?"

"Summer wants part of our territory," Lord Liskaal snaps, as if I ought to know that.

One of the courtiers speaks, rambling about redrawn boundaries from some conflict that I'm too young to recall. I certainly haven't studied fae history, as Da provided lessons of an entirely different variety. He's not a generalist, but rather specialized in mischievous magic and wilding ways.

I shouldn't articulate how much I don't care about any of this while he's still locked up. I need to be tactful. "I cooperated. If you want me to help further, keep our agreement." I pause delicately, because Lady Valnevi has no choice. Unlike me, she can't renege on a deal. "Where's my dad?"

A familiar hobgoblin slips through the crowd, stealthy as a shadow, and until he speaks, I'm pretty sure I'm the only one who notices him. Spells for skulking and skullduggery indeed. "I'm here, my gem. The commotion was fierce. Are you hurt?" Warm, rough hands take mine, and he tries to turn them palm up to assess the damage.

Not wanting to worry him, I quickly turn that scan into a hug. "Not really."

Lady Valnevi makes an ominous sound at the back of her throat. "I did not give you leave to speak," she says to Da, though her gaze lances through me.

I wonder who let him out. Possibly the boggart, though Da is endlessly resourceful. "Apologies. I thought I should let Thea know that I'm safe and sound."

As far as I'm concerned, this marriage can be dissolved. If they want me to live as a hostage in the Summer Court, they can offer me a better reason than pretending they want to avoid a war. In truth, they wish to feign reluctance so they can claim they exhausted all avenues for diplomacy before being forced to military action.

Perception is everything. They need to shellac some righteousness atop their overweening ambition. I don't know for sure that Summer even wants more of Winter's lands. Given what I know of their character, Lord Liskaal and Lady Valnevi might be the aggressors, trying to steal from Summer.

Regardless, those two are nothing if not deceptive. So if I cooperate and leave Winter, taking my calming properties with me, tension will subside in the Summer lands while Winter gains the space to foment resentment. And when Summer no longer wishes to do battle, Winter will attack.

I'm a cursed gift, after all.

The document I signed is crumpled on the floor, and I stoop to pick it up. Earlier, I didn't examine it closely, but the signature is scrawled to the point of being illegible. If I squint, I can make out the letters. Devan J. Fenelon. Nobody I know, then, or at least no one I recall meeting when various Summer delegations visited.

Lord Liskaal shares a speaking look with his lady. Her silvery lashes flutter. But before she can speak, a harried guard sprints into the room, wheezing out a few desperate words: "We have completed the search as you ordered."

"Well?" Lady Valnevi screeches.

"They're gone. The entire delegation is gone."

"Gone *where*?" Lord Liskaal demands.

"Unknown. There were signs of a struggle in the quarters where they were assigned. I've been assured that the front gates never opened."

"Portal magic. Kerboros should be waiting for us to debrief." Lady Valnevi tries to seem unaffected, but her lips twitch, revealing her distress.

If the Summer envoy comes to harm during a diplomatic mission, the Winter Court will bear all the blame, and they're not ready for battle yet. They thought they had more time to gather support and get alliances in place, but it seems some crafty schemer is trying to accelerate the timetable. I make eye contact with Da, who tilts his head ever so subtly toward the archway that leads out of this grand and gleaming hall.

I move so slowly that it hurts my joints and sinews, and with each incremental motion, I expect someone to turn on me and shout, *She's running away!* But they've momentarily forgotten about me in light of current events. Eventually, I make it to the corridor with my da right behind me, and I let out a sigh that's more like a groan of relief.

"That was…" He makes a gesture as if he's dusting away something unpleasant. "Shall we go home?"

"Please," I mumble, as the aches and pains and exhaustion set in.

He's quiet as we tiptoe through the palace complex, adroitly avoiding guards and messengers racing about in reaction to the vanishing of the

Summer delegation. It doesn't take long for us to reach our sanctuary. His room is above the barn, and mine is a loft within that space, ample when I was small, a bit cramped now, though I'll call it cozy.

It is decorated with shiny things I've given to him over the years. There's a padded bench for sitting and sleeping, a low table set upon a rug woven by brownies out of pooka hair, and a few shelves fastened to the walls. In the loft above, there's a sleeping mat from river reeds and dried flowers, along with a plethora of pillows. I can't wait to crawl up there and collapse.

"Have you eaten, my jewel?"

"Erdene gave me a snack."

"Nothing substantial, I'll wager."

He's right about that. The dew pear is long gone, and I only nibbled the honey wafers. But unlike our cottage in the wildlands, we don't have the means to cook.

But I should have known that wouldn't stop him. He gets busy with some ground grain and dried fruit; then he pours some water from a flask and sets the copper bowl on the table. With a focused frown, he wriggles his fingers, and the bowl heats slowly, slowly, until the ingredients thicken into groat porridge. He even put this spell in a book, and I already know how lovely this will taste. Even better, it will warm me from the inside out, comforting me now as much as it did when I was small.

"I adore you for this." I take my spoon from the little box on the table and dig in.

"Have you heard from Tara lately?" he asks unexpectedly.

I haven't seen my childhood friend in such a long time. Her father never approved of me, and he was angry at her mother for allowing the connection. I shake my head, mouth too full to answer. The repast is simple and creamy yet chewy with bursts of sweetness. And it's spiced with love and kindness, the rarest flavors of all. Quickly, I empty the bowl and lick my spoon clean. Da pets my head as he takes the dish away.

"She's working in Summer, probably busy at the inn," I guess.

He sighs, showing a wistful expression. "That's what comes of growing up, I suppose. We have so much to talk about, but..." A pause as he studies my face. "You look done in."

"I am," I admit.

"Ferghus is in the wind with his herd, is he?"

I nod. "It was worth it."

"As long as you feel that way, I do as well," he says.

"I'm sorry they dragged you to the dungeon because of me." It comes out in a rush.

"If you have energy for apologizing, you have spirit enough to discuss how we're getting you out of that dratted marriage contract."

If I run, he'll pay the price. I know that, and he does too. There's no world where I allow anyone to hurt him. So I manage a smile and stretch my mouth into a yawn that swiftly becomes real. "What's that? I can hardly keep my eyes open."

"You can't kid a kidder," he points out. "But I'll let it be. Ready for bed?"

"More than. You get some rest too." I hug him for a long time and then edge up the ladder, gingerly using my scraped hands to pull myself onto the platform. Earlier, when Da asked if I was hurt, I said, "Not really." He hasn't noticed that I'm a bit beaten up, and I don't want him to.

It takes a few painful contortions to strip off that wretched silver dress. I fling it away with a muttered curse. As I tumble onto the pillows, I tip my head backward. On the ceiling, there is a whole world, still sparkling with pixie magic. Da called in a favor from a friend named Shereth, who painted the forest scene to cheer me up when I grew old enough to ask awkward questions about why Rain and Fen paid no attention to me, though I was supposedly their daughter. Twenty years on, the rivers still sparkle and the pookas still run through the flowering trees. I can even smell the floral and honeyed perfume of the wildlands, thanks to her deep woodcraft.

A few of my childhood things are still in a chest at the back of the loft, but I haven't looked in there for ages. There's nothing of value, apart from my own sentimental attachment. The sound of Da moving about below and eventually settling himself to sleep soothes me as well. Before I know it, I'm gone.

Without realizing how I got here, I'm standing in the garden outside Miremorel House. The sun is a blessing, and the air is bright and pure, the song of the brook nearby calling to me in the distance. Here, I know the shapes of all the rocks, the colors of the mossy stones, and I could sketch the trees from memory.

I love it here. But where's Da?

"I'm waiting for you," someone says in a sunny tone. "Find me."

I spin in a circle. "What? Why?"

The more obvious question is *who*, but I'm too savvy to fall into that trap. Asking a fae directly for their name is quite a dire offense, a misstep I wouldn't make even if I have spent more time in the wildlands than at court. Though I don't see anyone, there are certainly multiple places to hide. I pace across to the broad-branched tree that shades our cottage. There's a tangle of foliage, leaves practically woven into a verdant screen.

"They'll make you if you don't volunteer. I rather think that you're not the sort who enjoys being forced to comply. Have I read you wrong?"

"Not at all," I admit grudgingly.

Some might find it bewildering or vexing to converse with a

disembodied intelligence, but there's a water sprite near Miremorel House who doesn't much enjoy leaving her brook, so I'm used to it. Truth be told, I've had some lovely chats with Nerys. She's got a wicked sense of humor, and she always knows the best gossip. Even here, people are always whispering to trinkets and tossing them in fountains, never wondering where that water goes.

"Then heed my warning. They'll blame you if they can. Punish you if you let them." The voice is light and melodic, delicate as butterfly wings and flower petals, but there's also an inherent power that pleases my ear to the point that I find myself languorously smiling, when the words are, in fact, most alarming.

"'They'? Do you mean the Lord and Lady of Winter?" That's the only deduction that makes sense, considering the day's events.

Which means this isn't a dream. It's a Sending.

8

> ### *Glorious Chaos*
>
> *This piece is carved into the wall directly across from the door, hidden from sight unless one knows where to look. Unlike most of the reliefs, this one combines color and texture. It is both a relief and a fresco, a figure of a woman astride a pooka, glorious hair streaming behind her as she rides. Other figures give chase, but she is untouchable, untamable as the wind and cannot be bound. Only the woman possesses the gift of color. Everything else is presented in natural hues, varying shades of brown. She is the focus of the piece and the center of everything.*
>
> *She is freedom. She is glorious chaos.*

KERBOROS

I CAN COUNT THE NUMBER of times I have visited Liskaal in his chambers on one hand.

It must be serious this time.

The fact that he doesn't wish to have this conversation in the great hall, to pour salt in the obedience-shaped wound and humble me before the court? This is practically unprecedented, and it signifies a crisis so profound that I relish the moment in a heated flush of delight.

Is your empire crumbling, Cousin?

I articulate none of these thoughts, striding past the attendant to the antechamber where I wait for the Lord and Lady of Winter. They leave me tarrying long past what is reasonable or polite, but eventually, Liskaal appears, his usually pristine person bearing visible signs of distress.

"Find them," he barks.

"More information will be required." I can't track someone from thin air with no details, although I have been cautious enough to conceal the range and scope of my powers.

If Liskaal understood what I do, he might recruit someone to replace me. And that I will not permit until my plans are complete.

"The entire Summer delegation has vanished, including the scion pledged to wed Thea de Winter as part of our peace accords."

"Will Summer consider this an act of war?"

Liskaal paces, ravaging his pallid hair with a careless hand. "They might. But I did not summon you for idle talk. You'll take the abandoned bride and hunt down her spouse. Before word spreads beyond containment."

Amusement sparkles through me.

Dear, credulous Cousin, the brownies are already whispering tales as fast as they can share them. Soon, everyone will know that things have gone drastically wrong.

"We'll leave at first light," I say. "Do I have leave to visit the suite where the Summer delegation was housed?"

"To get their scent?" Liskaal offers the icy quip, his mouth curled in a mocking smile. "Of course. Do it now before the traces fade."

I merely nod.

I enjoy how much it irritates him when I fail to respond to his jabs. But every hurt forms scar tissue over time, so I no longer feel those needles. Some days I feel nothing at all.

Except when I catch a glimpse of Thea.

I wheel just in case my expression quickens even a fraction, yielding Liskaal a hint of my true inward state.

To me, Thea de Winter is freedom. I love her—or maybe the idea of her—the way I admire a pooka running unfettered or a bird arcing across the sky. She has never once been bowed, and she *never* obeys. She is the most intractable, glorious chaos, and I treasure her rampages, even from a great distance. I don't know her, so, of course, I don't *love* her.

But what she represents? Resistance. Defiance. And kindness.

Such kindness for all the wild fae.

And devotion to Mudge, who would walk through fire for her. Among the wild fae, it would be tough to find someone who wouldn't. Thea brands everyone she touches with her quintessential fire, leaving them forever changed.

Liskaal has no notion what a boon he's offering and would probably rescind the order if he realized. I don't linger lest that happens, instead aiming myself toward the quarters formerly occupied by the Summer contingent. While I do sell certain secrets, I don't know how Summer vanished within these walls.

The palace compound is finally quiet, and I encounter no one on the way. The rooms are unlocked and wildly untidy, as if some revel occurred here shortly before. There is wine spilled on the floor, pooling crimson here and golden there, and there are feathery strands tangled on the light fixtures. Not spiderwebs but something similar, gossamer-like, carrying an unusual scent.

I close my eyes, feathering my senses outward. There should be a burst of magic if they left through some portal, unless it's a magic unknown to me. I have never traveled to the mortal realm, and I'm unfamiliar with how witches might work a transport spell.

Could we be facing interference from beyond our realm?

Impartially, I analyze the facts, reviewing what I have observed in the past twenty-four hours. Nothing unusual. No traces of outside influence. There would have been whispers in wild fae circles if even a hint of outside presence had been known. No, it doesn't make sense. This didn't happen because witches made a pact with Summer…

I close the door and bring forth my spiderlings, reviewing what happened in this room. But the spiders show me what the evidence suggests: The Summer delegation drank a lot of wine, frolicked, and sprayed some fluid that made everything shiny and sticky, and then they rolled around in it. Not quite an orgy, but along those lines.

And then they left the room through this door. When I try to send my spiderlings after them, deeper into the palace, the little hunters stop.

I'm missing something.

This is a suite, connected rooms made to house a large party. But the Summer scion would have been assigned to the largest space. I'll go over that territory again.

Frowning, I move into the primary bedroom with its ice-white furnishings. The doors to the wardrobe stand open, nothing inside. I close them thoughtfully, feeling the tug of…something. I close my eyes and scan in here. Not a tingle. Not a spark.

I'm already intrigued by the Summer scion because for the first time in what has sometimes seemed like an endless existence, I am…stymied.

How did they vanish?

No magic can explain this. There should be traces for me to follow, even if I'm unfamiliar with the one who compelled the parting of the ways. There are always trickles, runnels of energies soaked into nearby objects.

But this room is dead to me, silent as a cell before a prisoner cries out.

I cannot report my failure. My dreadful cousin might cut off my head if I admit that I don't know where the quarry has gone to ground. Hunting is what I do.

As I turn to depart, a thought strikes. The fluid that they sprayed, did it dry into those feathery strands? I breathe in the scent again. Moonmallow. It blocks magical energy for a time, and used in conjunction with a glamour…

Could it be that simple? Oftentimes the simplest explanation is true. I examine the premises one last time, and when my supposition proves plausible, I laugh.

For the first time since I accepted that I'm alone in the universe, I laugh and laugh and laugh, practically beside myself with glee.

If my theory is correct, the Summer delegation used my information about the secret passages concealed within the palace. They created the signs of a bacchanal here in alliance with some wild fae, and the whole group used moonmallow. Most likely, the wild fae, disguised as the Summer delegation, went into the palace so they would be seen, then *not* seen, once they dropped the glamour and resumed their own identities. A powerful illusionist must have created the fachan diversion, and allies flipped tables as corroborating evidence. Meanwhile, the actual Summer host crept out through secret tunnels, their own magic concealed.

Two things are absolutely clear in this moment: Lord Liskaal is in no fashion prepared to face the Summer Court, and I cannot wait to see how it all unfolds.

9

A Spell for Mischief and Mishaps

I'm sure you're surprised to see a spell along these lines. But sometimes, people need to be reminded that everyone's the same. We all have hopes and dreams, and they need to drop their fancy cake or spill their wine at some formal occasion. Even better if it ruins an expensive outfit. This spell won't call a plague to their houses or burn anything down, but... Tripping at the wrong time. Dropping something important. Knocking things over at the worst moment. Oh yes.

I call this working the Great Equalizer. Nobody looks important with a sticky pudding down the front of their vest, do they? Only use this if you're aggrieved and fed up with someone's nonsense. Unlike most, I'd caution you not to put too much of yourself into it, lest someone trace the mischief back to you. It's best to go gently and wait. The mischief will find its time, and if you're lucky, you'll be around to see it. If you're even luckier, you'll only hear about it and escape all blame.

This one is best cast in the dark. You'll require:

- *A sharp piece of black tourmaline, uncleansed*
- *Rue, hyssop, and wormwood*
- *A malachite mortar and pestle*
- *One large hawthorn leaf*

Grind up the herbs with the mortar and pestle until they turn into a paste. Use the black tourmaline to write a single word on the hawthorn leaf, something simple, like: Fall. Trip. Spill. Picture the spell's recipient clearly in your mind, then use your magic to incinerate the leaf until not even embers or ashes are left. There should be only smoke on the wind, winging its way toward your target. Cleanse all your tools thoroughly afterward, both the tourmaline and the mortar and pestle. You might also wish to do a cleaning ritual for yourself as well because you don't want spells of this sort traced back to you, my gem.

Once those matters are tended, wait. It may not happen immediately, but wild spirits have a good sense of comic timing. In my younger days, I had more fun than I should admit with this one, and you take after me in that respect. When you were just a tyke, you toddled to the palace kitchens and took a single bite from every pastry you could reach.

It was sheer chaos, and I laughed myself sick.

THEA

"HOW DO YOU KNOW SO much?" I demand.

Soft, silken laughter surrounds me as I spin in all directions.

I wake in the loft, heart thundering, though I'm not sure if it's fear or excitement.

The morning is quiet, and since the windows are narrow, more designed for ventilation than viewing, they don't let in much light. Already, the dream is fading, drawing me back from the brink of some vital realization.

I need to…what?

The voice seemed insistent that something must happen, but I've lost the thread. Before I can pull the skeins of my unraveling thoughts together, two ferocious thumps sound at the door.

"Already?" Da mutters. "T'isn't even fully done dawning."

"Open the door, hob." That scowling tone belongs to Kerboros; it can be no other.

I bristle at the implicit insult in that manner of address and launch myself down the stairs. There are few souls in the Winter Court who irritate me as much as Lord Liskaal's hound. Despite the fresh understanding I received yesterday, he still treats people terribly. Since he's suffered, he ought to know not to vent his spleen on those who had nothing to do with it.

But Da opens the door with his customary good nature. "What do you need, then?"

"Thea's presence is required in the great hall. Immediately."

My dad immediately protests, "She hasn't eaten or washed. Give us a bit."

"Five minutes."

It's more of a concession than I expected, but I'm glad for these moments. Last night, I meant to ask, but my head was so spun, I forgot. I'm aware we have curious ears, so I ask Da silently, *The lord and lady seemed surprised to see you last night. How did you get out?*

He levels a long look on me, and then he mind-sings, *Erdene. She's more than she seems. She's an important friend, my gem. Don't ever cross her.*

"You're wasting time," Kerboros says.

"I'm going." The last thing I want is for Da to end up in the cells again. I find comfortable clothes tucked at the back of the loft and shimmy into them as fast as possible. If only I could retrieve the wispy fragments of the dream. It feels important.

With a silent look of reassurance, I hug my dad, lingering to enjoy his familiar comforting smell and the warmth of his hand patting my back. I mind-sing, *I'll come out on top. Who raised me?*

That's my girl, he sings back.

As I follow Kerboros out, an imp of mischief takes me. I'm famished after yesterday's shenanigans, and I feel like messing with him. I stare at his wide back, armored in dark leather, and flex my fingers until a shimmer of power responds. Nothing a fae would notice, because it's innate and mine. There's a blood-bright ember of rage burning inside him, and I have a little taste. Hot as fire, deep as death.

Mmm. Kerboros is heady.

His steps slow. And he turns to me, a frown wavering between his fearsome brows. "I might have been discourteous when I relayed Lord Liskaal's instructions."

"You could apologize to Da," I suggest. "If you regret it."

"I will do so."

I draw a little more as we walk, feasting until the top of my head tingles. Kerboros is a veritable river of wrath, and it's fascinating to watch his body language shift. Soon, his shoulders ease, and his movements become...languid, for want of a better word.

If I didn't know better, I'd say that he's almost smiling.

"I had forgotten what this feels like," he says in a wondering tone.

"What?"

"Peace."

He lowers his head, just once, as if basking in the sensation. Then his gaze hardens. "Don't do this again. Without my edge, I am a pet, nothing more."

I didn't think of it that way. "I apologize. Normally, I only skim a little and not very often. Around here, there's no shortage of arguments, conflict, and chaos."

"You keep blood from being spilled," he says matter-of-factly. "It is well-known. That is why Lord Liskaal has forgiven you for so many absurd stunts. He knows that enemies who think to strike at him here will have their venom sipped away without realizing why. And then the toothless serpents may nip, but without impact."

This is the longest conversation I've ever had with Kerboros.

"I thought I was a nuisance."

"Sometimes. But irreplaceable as well."

No one's said that to me before. At least, outside of Da, who thinks I'm all the lights of heaven, a treasure, and a gem, all lovely, shining things.

Before long, we reach the great hall, and I pat my dark curls. That's as good as it gets.

This morning, Lord Liskaal and Lady Valnevi are alone, no courtiers to get in the way. Kerboros remains by the archway, leaving me to approach on my own.

"Thea," Lord Liskaal says.

I bow. "How can I serve?"

They swap looks, and then Lady Valnevi says, "Your marriage should have sealed the peace between two courts, and now your partner has run away, possibly at the sight of *you*. What do you think we should do in such a situation?"

I manage not to flinch. I've heard worse. "I'll find them." The words burst out before I fully realize my intent to speak.

It's like I've been prompted by the voice in the dream. Now I remember them exhorting me to volunteer before…

I don't know. I can't recall.

But I feel like the consequences will be dire if I don't step up.

"On your own?" Lady Valnevi doesn't seem impressed with my offer. "When our best trackers cannot follow their trail?"

I glance at Kerboros, who remains impassive. Does that mean he failed to find the traces of their passage?

He gives nothing back, just a figure staring straight ahead. In the brighter light of the great hall, the configurations etched into the dark leather of his armor gleam faintly with silver, and I'm a bit fascinated by the pattern. Is it a leaf or a flower or a tracery of—

"Thea." Lord Liskaal's stern rebuke for not paying attention is shaped like my name.

"I use other means," I say. "I'll find…" Oh no. I've forgotten my spouse's name. "The Summer fugitives. I'll assemble a team."

Lord Liskaal seems to make a snap decision. "You may recruit no more than four people, Kerboros will accompany you and make regular reports." The Winter King pauses. "This is your last chance to prove your worth to the court. If the alliance fails and we go to war, we will have no need for one who pacifies our enemies."

Right. Because you'll be killing them. And Winter enjoys its little cruelties, but they aren't so depraved that they'd chop up foes who have lost the will to resist.

But maybe failure isn't such a bad thing? I can permanently live in the wild. And—

"Before you decide that this mission is not critical to your happiness, understand that we mean there will be no shelter for you anywhere in our demesne. Not in the wildlands, not in the four courts," Lady Valnevi says.

My breath catches. "The mortal realm is a death sentence."

"Then you grasp the stakes," Lord Liskaal says smoothly.

I bow again, seething silently.

Then I back out of the room and save my outrage until I round the corner. Arching my back, I tilt my head to the ceiling and open my mouth in a scream that I can't voice. Kerboros looms behind me, a royal shadow cursed to serve as well.

"We should source provisions," he says.

Experimentally, I sign, *I hate them so much.*

But he only stares at me, hands still as stones in a pond at his sides. I guess he doesn't understand the quiet tongue of the wild fae. That will make it easier to communicate with others in front of him.

"Like what?"

I've never taken gear into the wilds, and I never have trouble finding food or friends or a place to rest my head.

The scowl returns. "Are you being intentionally obtuse?"

"No. But bring whatever you want. I just don't like carrying things."

Kerboros snarls a little. "Do not ask *me* for supplies later. And don't attempt to seek shelter with me either."

I laugh, though there's precious little humor in the sound. "I would never. Did they give you a deadline?"

"We have ten days."

The severity of the situation starts to sink in, and I fight a wave of panic. I don't *find* things. I wander in the wildlands, seeking beauty and wonder. "That's not long. We should get moving, I guess."

"I will meet you at the gate." Kerboros doesn't turn away immediately, however. He watches me go for some reason.

With a wave of acknowledgment, I rush to the stable to share the news with Da. My words spill in a confused rush. "I'm building a team or leading one or both. Ten days. I might be banished."

"I'll go with you," Da says, as soon as I finish speaking.

Quickly I shake my head. "I need to know you're safe. If you're at Miremorel House, it'll motivate me, knowing you're waiting for me at home."

He takes one of my hands in two of his. "I know you're trying to spare me hardship, no traipsing around the wilds like we did when you were little. But I'm the one who's meant to be protecting you, don't you see?"

But he did, protected me for so many years, and now *I* want to keep him safe. Plus, I'm concerned about how perilous this might prove. And he's my dad, the one person I can't risk, even if his skills could help. If something goes wrong and then he's gone, there'll be nobody in the world who loves me.

I don't say that.

"You caught me." I flash a cheerful smile.

Hesitating still, he squeezes my hand gently, and I feel the ridges and scars of hard work. He carved toys for me and built furniture with these hands. He carried me when I was tired and set me on his back when I bloodied my knees. Da doesn't like letting me endanger myself, but there's one thing I can say to get his approval.

"I want to do this on my own," I say softly. "I need to. It's part of growing up."

His face droops. "Ah. So it is, indeed."

"But even so. I'll want some of your yummy porridge when the adventure's done." Best to comfort your loved ones by saying true things.

He laughs with apparent delight. "And so you shall have it, my jewel. You have your special bracelet?"

"Always." I show him the pouch on a string around my neck that holds that keepsake and various bits and bobs for spellcasting.

"Thanks for indulging me. I'll slip out of the palace confines before the lord and lady get wondering where I've gone. Find me at Miremorel when it's done."

"A wise precaution." I give an approving nod. "But before you go, do you have any suggestions about who might locate a group so sly that even Kerboros can't track them?"

"I'd call the pookas first," Mudge says, after a moment's thought. "They owe you. And once you have a ride, you might chat with Macha."

I think for a moment before, "And if Macha doesn't feel helpful, maybe Nerys will? She knows everything that goes on."

"The perfect start," he agrees.

We hug, and I hold on a little too long, my eyes misty when we part. I feel it in my bones. The next time I see this kind soul, everything will be different, but I can't put a finger on the flavor of the change.

The world?

Or me?

Either way, I give Da time to get free, and then I make my way to the gate, where Kerboros is pacing. A pity I'm already well-fed, because he looks angry again.

"I have been waiting for—"

"Why? I never said when I'd be here." I cut off the complaint in a cheerful tone. "Let's get out of here while we can. Before something else goes wrong."

"For once, I agree with you."

It's too bad that I hate the way Kerboros portals so much; the abruptness of his shifts nauseates me. Otherwise, I'd ask him to take us to the pookas. But though time is limited, I'd rather travel the slow way.

Besides, I suspect I know exactly where they are. Once we pass the gates, I set a brisk pace along a footpath worn by the wild fae who have been banned from the mushroom circles and portal stones.

Usually for causing chaos.

Moss dots the trail, the flat stones placed ages ago now half covered by greenery. The air is humid, scented with loam, and the trees cast a verdant shadow, their branches woven into archways with leaves that whisper as we pass. Giant mushrooms like the one Da turned into Miremorel House rise here and there, caps polished with wind and rain. Their undersides glow with phosphorescence that lights the deadwood and damp leaves below.

Roots break the surface, making progress treacherous beyond the track, and ferns cluster around the trunk of an ancient solitary tree. I recognize this one, feeling a hot blush creep across my cheeks. I hope the dryad doesn't see us passing by. But she wasn't cruel, and neither is her forest; they both reward curiosity with rare gifts.

"Where are we going?" Kerboros asks, after we've been walking for a while.

"Do I need to confide my plans? You're here to spy on me after all."

Hs jaw clenches. "Not by choice," he snaps. "Had I an alternative—"

"But you don't." I can be annoying too.

Before he can respond, a gruagach stomps into view, armed with an uprooted tree.

10

> ### *In Plain Sight*
>
> *This piece, unlike most in the collection, is abstract. It's a frieze that encircles the entire room, a narrow band atop all the walls. Over many long years, it has been carved in geometric patterns that do not repeat. Lines meet at unusual angles within the bordering framework, and sometimes there are three or four lines running parallel or intersecting at odd intervals. People have speculated that there may a be a message hidden in code, but that some cipher may be required to discern the secret written in plain sight.*
>
> *No one has ever decrypted its hidden meaning.*

KERBOROS

THE GRUAGACH IS AS TALL as a house, wide as a hill.

His marbled gray skin resembles patchy stone, and he's covered in tufts of dark hair that grows all over his body in luxurious patches. He has broad features, heavy brows, and a mane of hair that gleams in the light, even caught up in a topknot as it is. The fur on his shoulders grows into his beard and sideburns, making it difficult to see his mouth.

I step forward, intercepting the gruagach before he can attack.

Though I'm no expert, I'm familiar with many of their customs. Often, they enjoy testing their wits against travelers, though a loss might prompt a display of temper. I can't obviously throw a contest, however, as that would be insulting. To avoid violence and navigate this encounter, I need to be judicious.

"I challenge you," I say swiftly.

"To what?" the gruagach asks.

"A battle of the brightest—for right of passage."

The gruagach glances at Thea for some reason and then sets down the arboreal weapon. We're safe for now.

"Go on, then," he says.

A riddle. If the stakes weren't so high, I might savor this exchange more. After thinking for a moment, I offer, "I speak without a mouth, and I have no body, but I come alive with the wind. What am I?"

"Starting with a simple one, I see. An echo! My turn..." He pauses, tapping his large foot as he considers, and the resulting vibration sends tremors that rock the earth beneath my feet. "I'll try to match your level. I can't be seen, can't be felt, can't be heard, and can't be smelled. I live behind stars, under hills. And empty holes, I fill. I creep softly and follow after. I devour land and kill laughter. What am I?"

He's good, I realize.

I'm not familiar with this one, and it's rare that I need to contemplate such things, but the answer comes to me ere long. "Darkness."

"I had *the dark* in mind, but I'll accept your answer as correct," the gruagach returns. "This is fun. I can't wait to hear your next one."

"Do I get to play?" Thea asks.

The gruagach responds before I do. "Certainly! Take a turn. We'll both guess."

"How far can you walk into the woods?"

I quirk a brow at her. That's an unfair type of puzzle; it doesn't have a set answer and is dependent on the size of forest. It seems the gruagach agrees with me as we make eye contact, and then he says, rather gently, "That's not a proper riddle, is it? We need more information to provide a definitive answer."

Then I nod, showing that I agree with the giant fae's assessment.

"Wrong!" Thea says with a smile that makes me want to smile back. "The answer is, of course, *halfway.* Regardless how big the grove is, once you pass the halfway point, you're not walking in anymore. You're walking out."

I stare at her, silently stunned. It feels like she's just won the game, not with complex wit but with unassailable logic, and I don't know why I'm surprised. Over the years, I've witnessed her brilliance. She navigates the court with the precise amount of respect required to keep her out of the dungeons, and she's well aware how useful the Lord and Lady of Winter find her skills in keeping tensions manageable. Over the years, she has tested the bounds of their patience and tolerance, knowing where the lines are drawn.

I respect her so much for that.

The gruagach laughs, a deep and booming chuckle. "That's rich! Never thought of that, but you're entirely right."

"One more round each?" I suggest.

"Grand," the gruagach agrees. "I'll have another turn. Too much of me can weary the heart, especially among those who fear my art. I'm precious to some, terrible to few, and occasionally wished for like a dream coming true. I'm fragile as glass and easy to fill. At riddle's end, I'm lingering still. What am I?"

"Is it silence?" Thea asks, just before I say, "Silence?"

"You're right! Both of you." Rather than being upset, the gruagach seems so pleased that he bounces, creating more vibrations nearby.

Trees lining the path sway in response to his enthusiasm. With an inner jolt, I realize I'm nervous about my next offering. I'm well aware that Thea doesn't like me, but I want her to regard my intellect highly. That makes very little sense and matters hardly at all in the larger scheme. Yet I cannot shake the inclination.

"I am a silent witness, keeper of years, and I am inevitable, despite all your fears. Inescapable, I cling to the world, dancing in sunbeams and lighting on banners unfurled. I gather everywhere as memories decay, yet with a touch, I vanish, as my presence dismays. What am I?" I cannot resist glancing at Thea to see what she makes of this one.

"I can think of a couple of things that make sense," she says in a pensive tone.

"Is it a cobweb?" the gruagach asks.

"That's a good guess. Not the answer I had in mind."

"Then maybe…dust?" Thea tries.

Of course she got it.

I incline my head. "That's it. Well done."

"I think that's the first time you've ever complimented me. Need to make a note or something. Let's see. I'm doing a silly one, so don't expect anything deep. What words are a one-letter difference between a delicious dish and abject begging?"

"I hate these types of riddles," the gruagach says with a gusty sigh.

They're not my favorites either. So many words, and it will take forever to run through all the possibilities. It feels like she's cheating, but I can't say that I mind. "I yield. Tell me the answer?"

"Peas and pleas," she says promptly. "The *L* makes all the difference."

"I don't know if I'd call peas delicious," the gruagach complains.

"You haven't tried Da's pea porridge! It's *so* good. He's promised me some for when we're done with this adventure."

Adventure? Is that what we're having?

Finally, Thea wins. I can't resist any longer.

I smile.

11

A Spell for Swapping and Sunshine

There will come a time when you're journeying, my gem. I'll do what I can to ease your path. This charm can sweeten the weather, and I'll share my secret to staving off the rain, at least until you get where you're going. Now, we shouldn't meddle overmuch in such business. If there was no rain, the trees and flowers couldn't grow and the brooks would dry up. Not only that, but the rain makes us treasure those sunny days.

That said, sometimes we do need to coax an hour or two more. My only caveat is, if you enjoy the sun now, there will be rain later. The universe tries to stay in balance. You're not changing the totals, my jewel. Rather, you're borrowing future sunshine. That means it'll rain when it was supposed to be sunny at some point. But since timing matters, mayhap that rain won't inconvenience you, if you've gotten where you were going. It might trouble others, so do consider that before you give the weather a tweak.

This working is best performed in the light. You'll need:

- *A significant amount of sunstone, honey calcite, and tigereye*

- *Broom, saffron, and alder*
- *A golden censer*

Arrange the stones in a protective circle, alternating types. Take care not to place two pieces of the same type next to each other. This spell is deceptively simple, and so much falls upon your clarity of mind and the focus of your will. From within the protective circle, add the herbs to the golden censer. Use your magic to incinerate them to smoke, and then focus your will. Concentrate on the smoke carrying your wishes far and wide, until it becomes...more. A manifestation of your will. This is not quite a summoning, but near enough that the protective circle is a wise precaution. You can use different stones for different charms, but these are attuned to the sun.

Keep your mind fixed on fair winds and bright skies. Once you're certain that the smoke shadow is bound to your directive and will go forth to stave off rain and whisper sweetly to the wind on your behalf, only then carefully unseal the circle. You can do this by moving a stone or stepping outside the boundary. The smoke should wing away and keep the clouds at bay for the time you've specified.

This charm is stronger when cast on someone else's behalf. The last time I used this spell, it was your name day, and you were so disappointed that we wouldn't be picnicking to celebrate that I moved the clouds for you. Do you remember how it stormed that night? All things in due time.

THEA

WHILE THE RIDDLING WAS FUN, we do have a schedule to keep.

This will probably embarrass Kerboros, who seems to think he's saved the day by defusing the tension. His smile is...unexpected, sunshine breaking through a bank of darkest clouds. He's so proud of himself that I shouldn't burst his bubble.

But this gruagach, Timuir, is a family friend, and while he looks moderately terrifying, if people would stop screaming when they see him, they'd discover that he's quite a nice person.

"It's been lovely riddling, Uncle Tim! How have you been?"

Kerboros shoots me an unreadable look, but within the span of a few heartbeats, he relaxes his battle readiness and keeps his own counsel. Though I don't expect him to comment, I'm minorly disappointed that he's so self-contained. I do feed on excess anger, but he keeps his fury so well leashed that usually I would need to touch him to gain any sustenance. And I've promised not to do that again without his consent.

"You know," Uncle Tim says with an eloquent head tilt. He probably doesn't want to say more in front of Winter's hound.

I nod, understanding the words unspoken.

"Where are you going with that?" I gesture to the tree trunk at our feet. It does resemble a club, and anyone might reasonably expect a gruagach to use it for smashing.

"Building a dam for Macha. She can be so picky about the type of wood."

"Oh, we're on the way to see her as well. Do you want some company?"

"Normally, I'd say yes, but..." Uncle Tim shoots an apologetic look at me.

Yeah, Kerboros is making me unpopular in the wildlands.

"Don't let me keep you, then. Take care of yourself, and mind your bad knee!"

I get a wave of acknowledgment as Uncle Tim strides off, his footfalls shaking the immediate area. We haven't found the pookas yet, so even if he *had* been willing to travel with us, we couldn't have kept up. A gruagach takes five steps for every one of mine.

Once my honorary uncle leaves my line of sight, I turn toward my companion, but before I can speak, he does.

"Do you know everyone in the wildlands?" Kerboros asks in a mild tone.

Mild for *him*.

"Mostly." I'm not being facetious.

I wonder if he'll inquire about my plans again. I'd rather not have to make up something to satisfy him, though I doubt he's asking from his own curiosity. The Lord and Lady of Winter will be demanding updates.

Instead, he gestures, indicating we should get moving now that the path is clear.

The weather is perfect, no mischief sending storms in our direction. If I know Da, he's got the wood folk casting charms for fair winds and bright skies to ease our path. I aim a burst of brightness in Mudge's direction as I head for the pookas' favorite grazing spot.

Kerboros is quiet, bordering on morose. He doesn't look at me, but he isn't admiring the scenery either. It makes me sad, how little savor he seems to find in life. I've heard only a snippet of his story from Erdene, but I can't fathom how alone he must feel. The irritation I used to experience in his company is slowly easing into empathy. After all, I know what's it like to feel alone at court, and Kerboros can't even take refuge with the wild fae.

I push onward, past the tangle of thorny brambles and feathery foliage. The wildlands offer so many shades of green: moss and myrtle, pine and phthalo, so deep it's nearly black. Ahead, the trees thin, yielding to a grassy meadow, and the green deepens to gold. Wildflowers grow amid the waving fronds, while honeybees drift from bloom to bloom, tasting the nectar. The breeze is warm and tinged with the scent of mint and clover.

As expected, I find a few pookas grazing on the sweetest grass anywhere in the wildlands. Including Ferghus, who owes me a favor. I don't enjoy keeping score on kindness, but we need a ride to Macha's hut. I bow even deeper to the pooka king than I did to the Lord of Winter. Hopefully, Kerboros won't share *that* in his report.

"I could use your assistance," I say.

It would be gauche to speak of debts. I have their attention now, and Ferghus touches his thoughts to mine. I greeted him verbally so as not to presume on our connection, but his silent response assures me that I'm still in his good graces.

What would you have of me?

A ride to Macha's domain, or as near as you feel comfortable.

The swamp witch can be…sensitive. To say the least. And many wild fae prefer to avoid her territory entirely.

Easily done. Do you need us to rid you of your burden? It would be easy.

I collect he means to get Kerboros lost, not to bury him in a bog, but with pookas it's tough to say. They're intense beings with passion to spare. They run for joy, and they hold grudges against those who curtail their fun.

Pookas also have…interesting ideas as to what could be considered entertainment.

He can stay, I send back.

As an extension of our regard for you, so long as he does not provoke us.

I turn to Kerboros, who has watched our silent communication with a faint frown. I speak quickly. "They'll take us to Macha's place. Please don't give them any trouble, just ride quietly."

"You make me sound like an agent of chaos," he snaps.

We both know that's me, I say to Ferghus.

The pooka lets out an amused sound and lowers his body for me to mount. It's more of a struggle for Kerboros since his pooka won't help, but he manages to swing astride, and then we're off, racing through the wildlands at breakneck speed.

I mind-sing to Ferghus, more curious than anything else: *Do you know anything of the Summerlings who went missing from the Winter Palace?*

The wilds are silent, Ferghus sings back.

Hm. That's unusual.

The Winter lands should be eager to speak of Summer crossings. I don't know what to make of the fact that Kerboros can't find the portal that took them, and none of my usual allies have news either. If Macha can't point us in the right direction, I'll be out of ideas.

For now, I enjoy the ride and the option not to talk with Kerboros. His pooka isn't making it easy for him to stay on its back, but the Winter hound clings with stubborn determination that I can't help but find admirable.

The forest flies by in a blur, and I breathe in the freshness of the green air. Pooka speed is tremendous, however, so we don't ride long before the terrain shifts, yielding to the springy ground that heralds the start of the bog. From there it will grow wetter still, until the plants grow dark and twisted, guided by Macha's hand. Not because she's a bad person but because she wants the region to look unprepossessing. It discourages visitors. The swamp stretches as far as the eye can see. Technically, Macha exists at the edge of Winter's borders, but her domain touches all *four* territories, making her swamp the center of everything.

Stagnant pools fill with the scent of decay—wet earth, rotting vegetation, and a coppery tang it's best not to contemplate. Gnarled trees jut from the ground, draped in curtains of moss and parasitic vines. Ferghus trots to a stop when it grows difficult for the pookas to maneuver, and I slide off.

"You run like the wind." I admire his skills verbally instead of thanking him.

You noticed. He preens a bit.

Nearby, Kerboros has swung down without a word. His pooka touches my mind briefly. *It was bearable. He didn't speak.*

"Call on me if you can use my help," I say. Then I add, "Be well."

And free, Ferghus adds.

"Always," I agree.

A life lived in chains isn't worth living. Everything I've done has been structured to keep me out of the hierarchy, not beholden to anyone, though the Lord and Lady of Winter are trying to change that. To affix me to a post through this wretched marriage.

"How far to the witch's house from here?" Kerboros asks.

I shrug. "I walk until I find her hut or it finds me."

"That is…a peculiar response."

But it's accurate. Macha's hut is…not ambulatory but *mobile* is probably the best word. The house has a few spots that it fancies, and Macha rotates through those locations, depending on her mood and the weather. The swamp witch is mercurial, so why wouldn't her abode be the same?

We walk deeper. The air smells faintly of sulfur, a mixture of the standing water and the types of plants that thrive in this environment. Every step squelches. The silence is broken by the occasional croak of a hidden frog or the distant mournful cry of a bird. I'm used to the eerie atmosphere, but Kerboros curls his lip.

"Not to your taste?" I tease.

"I doubt I need to answer that."

"Is anything?" I ask, not really expecting a serious reply.

But Kerboros appears to be considering his response as he steps over a bubbling patch of mud. Best he didn't put weight on it. He'd be swallowed to the chest in a blink.

"Yes. A cool, moonlit night outside the palace walls before the water freezes, when the air is so bright that breathing feels like the ringing of a bell."

I had no idea Kerboros had even the merest streak of poetry in him. But thanks to his evocative words, I can picture the scene beautifully, even feel the crisp clarity of the air in my throat.

"That does sound lovely," I admit. "Have you enjoyed many such moments?"

"Less than I would prefer."

"Your employers don't seem like they would offer you much space to breathe."

"Employers?" He lets out a bitter laugh that echoes sharply enough to slice the drooping branches from the dark and daunting trees. "You can call them what they are out here. I'm their eyes and ears after all. There are no others who would report back."

"Captors, then?"

"Closer to the mark," he mutters.

"Do you have no promise of ever regaining your freedom?"

Perhaps he could sign a pledge promising never to plot against—but no. I curtail my own thought because that's pure foolishness. Lord and Lady Winter don't trust the good intentions of others, even when documents have been signed. If they did, they wouldn't have sent me on this ridiculous quest, given that the marriage is legal on paper.

The quiet lingers to the point that it seems Kerboros won't reply.

Then he says, "Only threads of possibility so thin that they're fantasies more than paths."

"Dreams are important. They give us the strength to carry what we must."

"For as long as we must?" he asks.

It is quite a different question, posed by one of the fae. I'm naturalized, and even I don't know how long I'll live, provided I'm not poisoned or murdered by my enemies. More accurately, Lord and Lady Winter's enemies. I have friends, but the people who care about me and who I adore in return aren't welcome at court. I imagine Nerys living in one of their fountains and stifle a smile. And Tara hates pomp and ceremony as much as I do.

"I'm probably not the best person to ask about that. I'm very young." I feel a bit self-conscious about it, actually.

I'm not even half a century, only a bit past a quarter. I haven't seen mortal realms rise and fall in a flicker of my scrying pool. It can be difficult getting people to take you seriously if you're less than a hundred. In the clay realm, I probably wouldn't live that long.

Here? Nobody is sure because I'm a rare sort of changeling, not human, not moon touched, but other. Even here.

"Old enough for them to make use of you," he returns with the faintest trace of salt.

"That is true."

The stillness alerts me first.

As we've moved deeper into the swamp, I didn't notice initially, but now I realize there are no other noises. The frogs and birds have either fled or stopped communicating. No chirps or chitters or grunts, no scrambling about in the mud. There should be things hopping and skittering, but as one approaches Macha's domain, the wild creatures become leery. As they should be. Because there are traps scattered all around, snares for the unwary, magic trip wires, and cunningly disguised objects of power that will do all manner of things to a curious fae.

And I can't afford to spend a week as a lizard. Not now.

Swiftly I put up a hand, signaling Kerboros to stop. "We're close," I whisper. "We must petition her properly and hope she's in the mood to help."

"If she isn't?" His hand flexes toward his weapon, and I shake my head swiftly.

"You mustn't. While we're technically in Winter right now, this is Macha's realm. By the time anyone heard what befell us, it would be too late. Let us be humble and respectful and see how it goes."

His jaw clenches, and he speaks through his teeth. "You ask a great deal, do you understand that?"

"I do. But Macha is a great sorceress and must be greeted accordingly. And don't—" A sharp *snap!* followed by the *whoosh* of powerful magic interrupts my warning.

Oh crap. Too late.

12

Open Book

This piece is carved into the edges and top of a bedside table. It's a deceptively simple design with the edges of the table carved to look like pages of a book. At the bottom, it's slightly wider, creating the sense of a cover while the lines for the pages are softer. The seam down the center creates the illusion that the tabletop is an open book and the wood has been polished until the wood grain could be mistaken for some mysteriously blurred text. Various creatures have been etched as well, adding to the impression that this is a picture book instead of a piece of furniture. But the mood of the creatures captured thus is dark and ominous. Their postures are tense; they are caged in the confines of these pages when they yearn to be anywhere else.

KERBOROS

I HAVE NEVER BEEN THIS angry.

Incandescent with rage—that's the phrase. And I *do* feel so hot that I might be glowing strong enough to be used as a light source. Clenching my teeth, I pace, seven strides forward, three across, seven back to where I started. Trapped.

In a bottle. On the deck of a tiny ship.

I can't blame this on Thea either, because she was about to warn me not to touch anything, I think. But I saw what looked like an altar on the ground, a fascinating array of objects, including this ship in a bottle. I sensed no ominous magic, nothing that would have warned me that I could become part of the display.

And now I'm an exhibition. I've already tried to open a portal, but I have no access to any of my abilities. Whatever pulled me in also neutralized my natural talents. The same sick helplessness that I experienced in the dungeons so long ago spills through me in a dreadful wave. I have not been this powerless since I came of age in my cousin's court.

With great effort, I stifle the panic and gaze past the cloudy glass of my ridiculous prison. Thea is unfathomably huge, looking around the area, presumably for me.

"In here!" I call.

My voice bounces off the walls, and I can't tell if she hears me. I don't have a good grasp of what her magic can achieve, but she moves around, until—oh. She's kneeling. I *think* she sees me. Feeling so foolish that it nauseates me, I wave both my arms, trying to attract her attention.

She says something, but the sound is muffled, so it's like the burbling of a brook. Or perhaps that's the actual water nearby; I can't be certain. Pausing, she seems to be waiting for my response, so I shake my head and cross my forearms to signal that I don't understand. I don't want to reveal my knowledge of the wild fae's secret sign, but the situation is too urgent for me to prioritize hidden advantages over personal freedom.

I do hope I'm not too small for her to follow my gestures.

The bottle is dampening all sound, I sign. *I can't hear you.*

She signs back, *Again? At your size, it's a little hard to follow.*

I repeat the gestures, slower this time. Thea seems able to understand me, but it might not be enough to secure my freedom. Panic and terror battle in my mind, and I must control myself. I must stay focused on my current predicament. I can't get lost in the dark. I can control this. I can. I can.

I can't.

The dark behind my closed eyes is full of fluttery things, and the sound of sweeping wings carries me into the past—that dark dungeon where my family waits. And when I arrive, I'm forced to concede that part of me has never left that place.

The cell is minuscule, and it smells of copper and misery. When they came for my father, I didn't get to say farewell. He maintained his facade, insouciant until the bitter end, pretending that we would be delivered by his allies, pretending that all would be well, and so he denied me a final moment of closure, a word of advice, or a single reassurance. Instead he said, "I'll see you soon," as if his rebellion had not entirely failed.

He never acknowledged Geraint's sacrifice.

I lose track of how long I wait in silence with my mother. She sits on the cold stone floor, weeping. I kneel beside her, and she reaches for me, holding on with desperate intensity. Her arms are like iron bars, and they do burn like cold iron, a desperate and terrible grip; she squeezes until I can't breathe, as if she might drain the life from me in her grief because she knows something dreadful.

They don't bring us food or water, and the thirst is terrible. One prisoner is screaming. Someone else is crying. Other than my mother.

When she finally lets go of me, she's left bruises on my shoulders. "Ori. When I am gone, you will be alone. You will not be able to trust anyone. And your life may become difficult. But promise me—"

The cell door clangs open, revealing two figures in hooded cloaks. They stride in, knocking me to the floor as they jerk her upright.

"Mathair!" The high fae word for mother *escapes me, and I feel ashamed by it.*

While my father yearned only for power, my brother dreamed of a world undivided by such rigid castes, where one didn't need to speak high fae to rise in social status. It feels as if I've let him down, just as I'm failing her. I push to my feet shakily and rush at them, but I'm too small. Too young. Too weak to stop them from taking her. They knock me down, and the door clangs shut, leaving me alone in the darkness.

Always. Alone in the darkness.

Tremors set in, and I squeeze my eyes shut, pulling my arms around my knees. I won't look at the walls or touch the hash marks my mother carved. It doesn't matter what happens to me. There's no one left to care if I live or die.

Warmth. There's warmth now. That's different. In this nightmare, it is always cold, and I wake with tears on my face. But there's a deviation in the pattern.

Someone is speaking to me. And I think—

When I open my eyes, still shuddering, Thea is on the ground beside me, arms about my shoulders. She's hugging me, gentle but firm, and she rubs slow circles on my back. Nausea roils within me, and I don't know if I can contain it. The only thing that would make this day more humiliating is if I cast up my morning meal.

Her voice is quiet. And kind. "It's okay. It *will* be okay."

She doesn't know. She can't tell that I've just relived the worst aspect of my continued existence. While it's not ideal, I can live with this level of vulnerability.

"I fear confined spaces." Even to my own ears, my voice sounds rough.

I let out an unsteady breath, and suddenly, my arms wind around her too. It's not a rational decision, more of an instinctual need. I am *starved* for touch, and I fight the urge to bury my face in the soft skin between her neck and shoulder.

"Me too," she admits. "That's part of why I hate it at court so much."

"Because you feel trapped?"

"Yeah. I like it much better in the wild." She's still rubbing my back, patient and kind.

I can't contain the words. "My entire family died for my father's ambition. Liskaal's soldiers cut down my brother, Geraint. I wasn't supposed to be there, but...I saw everything. Those who had promised to support my father did not appear on the battlefield. Liskaal might even have ordered them to raise Father's hopes so my cousin had an excuse to purge us."

"I'm so sorry," she whispers.

"Geraint was"—I pause—"not like me. People loved him. *I* loved him."

Tears sting my eyes, and I loathe that I've been rendered so pitiable with such impunity. There's nothing I can do to make the swamp witch regret this; most likely, it's incidental to whatever purpose she had in mind when she set this snare.

"I have five parents," she says then.

"What?" It's not a secret that she's a changeling, but I didn't expect her to speak so candidly. The shock steadies my emotions, and I stare at Thea, waiting for her to continue.

"My mortal, biological parents. I'm not even sure if they noticed that I'd been swapped. Then there are Rain and Fen, who don't want me either. They've been looking for their real daughter for as long as I can remember."

"Why are you telling me this?"

She smiles slightly, though there's a bitterness in the twist of her lips. "So you won't feel exposed. A secret for a secret."

"I appreciate what you did. Intervening. I was trapped in a memory. The dungeon. My mother, before her execution." I swallow hard. "She called me *Ori*."

Thea repeats, "Ori. It's cute, I like it."

Cute. No one has ever applied that word to me.

While I appreciated her fierceness before, the way she brooks no tethers to her freedom, her sweetness speaks to my soul. I'm as afraid now as I was trapped in the cell. Because I'm starting to care for Thea as a person, not an avatar of freedom, so much that I ache when she pulls back at last.

And that gives me something to lose.

13

A Spell for Softness and Sleep

Sometimes, my gem, the world gets the better of us. It becomes difficult to focus, let alone rest. But to carry on, we need to get a good night's sleep so we can rise and shine and find that things look brighter on the morrow. No matter what challenges you face, you'll need to bolster your spirits by putting your heart at ease. I'm prone to worrying, as are most beings with sensible heads on their shoulders. But there's no need to borrow trouble when it comes to the door uninvited, all on its own.

To set aside your cares, you'll need to cultivate the proper frame of mind. Or perhaps it's not you who's got the troubled spirit. You could use this charm to help someone who's important to you. At any rate, it's effective for soothing hearts and minds and making those exposed to the soothing energies more inclined to rest at their ease. It doesn't cloud the mind or aught like that; it simply makes daily concerns feel a little less pressing for a time. A gentle working, this one is, perfect to let people take a deep and healing breath, cast off their cares, and get a good night's sleep.

This one is best cast right before you rest your head, whenever that may be, and go soft with your spell work. You'll need:

- *Topaz and malachite*
- *Dried marshmallow, meadowsweet, and motherwort*
- *A copper censer*

The steps to this working are simple. Place the topaz and malachite at the bottom of the censer. Use your magic to heat the whole container. That will be the most difficult part of this charm for you, my dear daughter. But I believe in you. Not just for this working, but for your entire life. I know you'll do great things. But more importantly, I also know you'll do kind things. Now then, you have a hot censer and some dried herbs. Place those on top of the hot stones. They'll create a soft little puff of smoke, and the gentle aroma will allow you to rest easy. As the censer cools, the scent will lessen, but you should be well asleep before then.

If the smoke troubles you, place the censer some distance away. It should still be in the same room where you're sleeping, though. This spell serves a dual purpose. It eases your nerves and keeps nightmares at bay. Or it's supposed to. Whenever I use this working, I enjoy the most delightfully dreamless sleep. I wish for you that blessing as well, my jewel. Sometimes the blessing of silence is all we need to set us to rights, and we don't realize how much clamor there is, even in our own heads, until it ceases, just for a night. Sweet dreams, and know that I'm lighting a candle so you never lack a glimmer to guide you home.

THEA

"ARE YOU FEELING BETTER?" I ask.

I try not to show how shocked I am. Before I touched the bottle, Kerboros had curled into a ball and stopped responding. Knowing that we're on a deadline—and failure has fatal consequences—I never would have chosen to join him inside if I hadn't been so scared for him. The exterior world is muffled, and I don't think he's noticed that he isn't out yet.

That I've come *in* instead.

The attention to detail is impressive, frankly. I couldn't admire some of the intricacy of the model until I shifted in scale. Now I marvel at the perfectly veined leaves on the trees dotting the distant hill, while in the foreground, a small ship dominates my view. There is a pier with crates stacked on it and a coil of rope, but we are the only beings in the tableaux.

"I'll be fine," he says softly.

On some level, I can't believe that we're hugging. But I'm too conscious of his heat and his scent for this to be an illusion. I wouldn't put it past Macha to mess with our minds, but each of my senses confirms that this is real. I can't say how long he stays curved around me like a vine, but I register the moment he realizes that the environment is the same.

He lets go of me and eases to his feet, gazing at me with a complicated expression. By which I mean, there is a pleat between his brows but his eyes are soft and his mouth seems almost to be curled up on the sides. Nobody has ever looked at me this way before—with this entanglement of gentleness and exasperation.

"Why did you do this?" Kerboros asks.

"We couldn't communicate." I pause, unsure how to describe his behavior.

"Because I panicked."

That's accurate. I swallow my own anxiety, trying to ignore the ticking clock in my head. Morally, this was the right choice, but it may not have been a good decision. I'm so scared of being sent to the mortal realm to die. Will it be painful? I don't know what they eat or how to act. I won't understand the local customs, and I don't have anywhere to stay. I wheeze, forcing the fear away with brute mental force.

I let out a shaky breath. "Let's hurry. I spent a week as a lizard in Macha's domain, and we don't have much time."

"A week?"

"Seven sleeps. It's tough to track time as a lizard. I mean, I wasn't stuck *inside* a trap, but my physical form limited my travel options. It's worrying when you're small enough to be eaten by a bird."

"I should think so. My magic doesn't work in here," he adds.

Half closing my eyes, I reach for the wild eddies of fae magic that are capricious with me at the best of times. But the air is still and quiet. Is this what it's like to be human? Will I feel like this over there, once I'm exiled? The idea of never seeing Da again, or any of my friends, Tara and Nerys, oh—

I realize he's waiting for me to respond.

"I can't use mine either. Do you mind if I test my innate abilities?"

Before, I promised I wouldn't feed from him again without consent—and I shouldn't have done it in the first place, even though Lord Liskaal has given me tacit permission to drain anger as needed to keep the populace compliant. I…hate the fact that I need to, but sometimes hunger slips the leash, and I sample. It's instinct for me, and every day, I battle my nature. I long to be someone who contributes, not someone who leeches from others.

But self-control leaves me unsatisfied, always hungry, always on the verge of doing something dreadful. The silence makes me feel guilty for asking, so I add, "Never mind."

"Go ahead. I'm furious with myself for delaying us, so there's plenty to spare."

Us. What a curious word, one I never expected to hear from Winter's hound.

I shouldn't call him that. Something has shifted between us, and it feels wrong to dismiss him now that I've caught a glimpse of his secret heart. Silently, I extend a hand. If he takes it, that will persuade me his assent is more than empty words.

Kerboros gazes into my eyes for a beat, and then he puts his fingers on my palm, just the barest whisper of touch. A frisson pops on my nerves, but before I can analyze what I'm feeling, appetite takes over. His energy is dark and lush, filling me in a rush of dusky-purple wrath. I can feel the heat rising in my face, a sensual flush, and he makes a sound deep in his throat.

I break contact, heart rate up, breath coming in soft gasps. "Wow. Was it good for you too?" My voice sounds embarrassingly husky.

He startles me with a laugh. "It was. I have no outlet for those emotions. If Liskaal suspected how I *truly* feel, he would judge me too great a risk, regardless of how useful he finds my service."

I clear my throat. "Accurate. You weren't kidding about the anger."

"At least you won't starve while we're stuck. There's something unexpectedly fulfilling about nourishing you."

My chest feels tight. I never thought I'd meet someone who finds me less than odd. Some fae find my presence disturbing and would gladly return me to the mortal realm. There's a bit of a flutter within the constriction, and I struggle to keep from revealing just how touched I am by his words.

"Good to know," I manage to say. "We should check our surroundings. Macha never makes a trap impossible to escape."

"There's a way out?"

"If we're clever enough to find it. She's not a bad person, just...testy. She uses these snares to deter visitors."

"One would have to be quite determined to persist," he agrees.

"I'll just..." I make a vague gesture toward the dock and hurry off, the heat lingering in my cheeks.

That was beyond awkward. Let's not focus on that part.

If Macha left objects to be examined, maybe there's a clue. I peer into the crates and examine the rope. They look like normal items to me, and nothing happens when I put the rope in the crate. I try the other one just in case. Nothing. There's no result when I hop into the crates either. I try stacking them, to no avail.

Wishful thinking. I didn't really imagine it would be that simple.

Maybe I'll explore the hills away from the ship. If I find a ring of tiny mushrooms, that would absolutely be the portal out. But the distance is deceptive, and it takes what feels like a long time to walk the length of the hills. I don't find anything but random plants and flowers, and the light seems to be fading outside.

Kerboros is on the dock waiting when I get back. "Anything?"

I shake my head. "What about you?"

"Unfortunately, no."

I could cry. The ticking clock is even louder in my head, but I'm so tired. It feels like forever since I said goodbye to Da. "I need to rest. I'll catch a few winks, and then we'll get back to it. We have to get out of here as soon as possible."

Ugh. I regret my cockiness in assuring Kerboros I'd never need gear, as I can always find a friendly face, someone who's willing to shelter me. I guess I'll curl up with a coil of rope. While that could be fun under the right circumstances, I don't have the energy to get creative. Nor do we have the time, even if I had the verve.

"I'm missing something, but I'm no longer at my sharpest," he admits with a trace of reluctance. He sweeps off his cloak and spreads it out. Then he produces a blanket from his pack. "We can share," he adds.

I don't question his generosity. Before he can rescind the quiet offer, I settle on the edge of the makeshift bedroll, bemused to find that the fabric retains his heat. The feeling is curiously intimate but not unwelcome. Not anymore.

"I'm surprised you're open to this," I whisper.

"Why?"

"Because I was so sure the wildlands would provide, and you said you wouldn't help."

"That was before. I don't know that coming in after me was wise, but your kindness means a lot to me." There can be no mistaking his sincerity.

It feels like the antisocial layers are sloughing away, revealing a Kerboros known only to me. "I appreciate it, as our predicament has me eating my own words."

"And nothing else," he notes.

Despite the dire situation, I laugh, settling in further. "I deserve that. I should've asked Uncle Tim for a snack. He has pockets full of treats that could sustain us for a week."

There is *something* I can do to help us rest, however. I sit up and delve into the bag hidden beneath my shirt and quickly perform a spell that should preserve our peace, at least according to my dad. The smoke is soft, just as he promised, a faintest trickle that reminds me of expensive incense I've smelled burning in the Winter market.

"What's that?" Kerboros asks.

I'm not sure if he means the spellbook or the ritual. Quickly, I explain, "Gifts from Da. To help me cope with my magical…differences."

"That was kind of him. I see where you get it."

"He's the best." I try (and fail) to ignore the fear tapping at the back of my brain. While I am exhausted, I don't know if the anxiety will let me sleep.

"You've got a remarkably bright soul," Kerboros says.

With the consequences for failure looping in my brain, it takes forever to drift off, and I awake with a yell at finding a stranger's face right next to mine.

14

Hidden Fire

This is the tiniest piece in the collection, measuring smaller than the artist's hand. It is a stylized flame, concealed on the wall behind the bed. Five arcs rise from the center, giving the impression of heat in the shape and movement of the carving. Details become finer and more minuscule toward the heart of the fire, indicating color shifts. This carving has been painstakingly finished despite the fact that it's hidden from view to the casual observer, and a deeper stain has been applied to the piece, a shock of color in contrast to the lighter tone of the rest of the wall. This piece represents the vibrant inner life that cannot be shared but could be discovered by a devotee of the artist's work.

KERBOROS

A SHOUT STARTLES ME, AND I roll to my feet, laying hands on my blade before my eyes are fully open.

Thea sits nose to nose with… *Who is that?* I would have sworn that we were alone in this accursed trap—oh, perhaps this fae just stumbled in and was startled to find us sleeping. It's the most logical explanation, though it doesn't mean I can relax my guard.

"Get away from her!" I order. "It is the height of discourtesy for an unknown person to violate her boundaries in such a way."

The fae rises in a smooth motion. "Friends call me *Zeph*, though I can't say *you* look particularly amiable."

Thea waves a hand, rubbing at her eyes with the other one. "Stand down. If…" She casts an inquiring look at the newcomer, though I've no idea what she's asking.

"They," Zeph supplies.

Oh, I see. Zeph does present an androgynous aspect, and it's polite to establish preferences before settling into a longer conversation. Thea is better at these details because she's had more experience talking to people. I snarl at them when necessary and glare in silence when possible. My attitude usually results in people leaving me alone.

"If they intended to harm us, they could've done it while we slept."

Reluctantly, I lower my weapon. She might know this person. I refuse to embarrass myself again like I did with the gruagach. Uncle Tim, indeed.

"True enough. But where's the fun in that?" The words are light; the tone offers more complexity.

Since I often imply more than I'm permitted to express, I could infer any number of meanings. Perhaps Zeph means it's not fun to hurt people if they're not awake to react. That would never occur to Thea; I'm certain she thinks they mean there's no pleasure to be gained from harming others at all.

I skim them from head to toe, trying to take their measure. They are elegant, no question, but in a casual, disheveled fashion, not with the studied grace of one who lives and dies on court opinion. Possibly, that untidiness springs from being lost in the wildlands and stumbling into one of Macha's traps.

They are small and lean, neat rather than well muscled, with an angular face and large amber eyes. Their skin tone is on the lighter end of gold with a shimmer of metallic. Pointed ears, like many high fae, but a shock of greenish-gray hair. I can't say that I have ever seen anyone who looks quite like this Zeph.

Nor can I place their accent. Autumn has a particular twang, and Spring offers a charming lilt. Winter imbues a certain crispness to the consonants. And Summer? Summer is all languid drawl. Zeph...is a mystery. Much like Thea.

I analyze their raiment, fine enough to pass in any of the courts, but not so luxurious that they seem to be high ranking. They wear loose trousers held up by glittering suspenders with crystal buckles adorning the shoulder straps. Their shirt is sleeveless, revealing intricate thorny patterns twining around their arms in varying shades of green: here, jade, there, sage, and a forest of vines around their wrists. The patterns flicker a little, dim, and brighten—magic, then—but perhaps muffled by this ensnarement.

"Concluded your inspection?" Zeph asks cheerfully. "Did I pass muster?"

"Don't mind Kerboros. He thinks everyone is dangerous," Thea says.

"He's probably righter than you realize," Zeph replies.

Thea laughs like they're joking, but I don't get the sense that they are. "How did you end up in here?" she asks.

Without waiting for the reply, she bounces to her feet, stretching with fluid moves that strike me as beautiful. When she bends and arches, her body is a poem, an ode written in lightning and air. I wish to capture her grace, carve it in wood or stone to see if her lines hold the same magnetism in stillness as they do in motion.

"I came in for a nap, of course. It's such a peaceful spot. Nobody ever bothers me." Zeph pauses, cocking their head as if struck by a thought. "You did come on purpose, didn't you? Never tell me you're stuck."

The humiliation stings. I repress the urge to check for some large and unusual insect that might be causing this sensation, except we're the ones captured in a terrarium. I fix my expression as best I can and let Thea do the talking. She seems to enjoy it.

She brightens. "Does that mean you know how to get out?"

"It's simple once you learn the trick. You'll kick yourself when you realize how easy it is." I'm not imagining the edge of mockery in their tone or the significant flick of a look.

Zeph is desperately amused at my expense. Such tremendous entertainment to see Winter's hound indefinitely detained by a vexatious swamp witch.

Thea glances between us, brow raised. Then she does something stunning. "We did the best we could, and we hadn't given up. We were resting before round two."

We. She's taking my side.

I'm not used to being part of a *we*, however small the context. It gives me a quiet pop of pleasure, right in the center of my chest. If it wouldn't make my affinity so obvious, I'd step closer to Thea to reinforce the impression of our unity. In fact, it takes all my self-control to stay where I am.

"You said yourself it is a peaceful place to nap," I add.

"True. I was asleep when you got here, or I'd have given you a hint."

"Were you?" I'm not smiling.

For once, neither is Thea. It seems as if she may think it's strange that this fae could sleep through us calling back and forth, providing updates on all the areas we searched. But before I can question them, she appears to make a choice, and her expression melts into her customary sunny charm.

"You must've been exhausted," she says, either choosing to believe them or pretending to. Since she's navigated the Winter Court successfully, it could be either.

"You've no idea." Suddenly, Zeph pivots and steps off the dock, dropping into the blue surface below. And disappears.

The water. The water is the portal out.

Without hesitation, I follow.

15

A Spell for Portals and Passage

Ever since you were a tiny thing, you've loved little more than going. It didn't matter where. You were always enchanted by the prospect of the next journey, the next surprise, the next wonder to be uncovered. I loved taking those jaunts with you as you grew, teaching you about our world and the wild folk who dwell hither and yon. And as you've become independent, I also love keeping the porridge warm and a soft bed waiting for you after a good, long wander.

Now then, you already know about mushroom circles, but you won't always be near one, will you? So you must have a mode of travel accessible for emergencies. This spell requires complete focus, so don't attempt it if you're suffering stress or simply having a dreadful day. To portal where you're meant to be and not end up somewhere entirely wrong, keep your wits about you. Opening a portal is a little different than a passage charm. The latter allows you to pop into another room, perhaps past a locked door. Not that I'd speculate regarding your intentions about such an endeavor.

The former takes a fair bit out of you, especially if multiple beings pass through with you. I've never been able to bring anyone with me when I create a passage.

You'll require:

- *A hagstone made from a stalactite (agate will substitute in a pinch)*
- *Dandelions, basil, and juniper berry*
- *A bronze kettle and a tin cup*
- *Clear water blessed by a nixie*

Heat the water in the kettle, using your magic, then steep the fresh herbs until you have a savory tea. Pour it through the hagstone into the tin cup. Down the drink in one go while you focus on opening the path. You'll feel energies gathered, though you may need to take some nourishment from anyone who might be nearby, as this is a large working. The portal should look like swirls of energy in the same hues as your aura. You've got a lovely silvery-white corona, my gem, so your portals, when you succeed at this spell, will reflect that shade. Pass through quick as you can, as it burns energy to hold such a fold in the world. Let the portal go when you're safe, and reward the nixie who provided the water. Speaking of which, Nerys sends her love.

To grant passage, the steps are similar, but be familiar with the space you're trying to enter. If you can't picture it in your mind's eye or see it with your actual eyes, you can't safely transit to that space. Otherwise, the wild fae would be robbing vaults every day. Alas, we're limited to places we know by heart, but it's a lovely spell if you find yourself locked out of a warm house in a pouring rain.

Writing these notes has me missing you something fierce. You're ever and always the joy of my life and the jewel in my imaginary crown.

THEA

WHEN THE OTHERS VANISH, I jump in too.

It's got to be the exit, right? I surface in brackish swamp water, not too far from where the ship-in-a-bottle trap lay in wait for Kerboros. There's no need to warn him not to touch anything. He's got that lesson etched on his bones now.

I can't believe I shared the lizard story. It took a week before Da found me. I was much younger then, and he was fearful to the bone.

But he didn't punish me. Instead he told me calming stories while he painstakingly unraveled the spell, sharing lore he's gathered of "my people," though I can't verify the authenticity or accuracy. From time to time, Da has also shown me relics from the mortal realm, including various religious texts. I find an academic interest in such things. They are fables to me, nothing of worship, but there was a story about a primordial garden and a tempter snake, as I recall. The front of Macha's demesne—where we are now—that's how I imagine that eternal garden from the human stories.

The trees are bent but not stunted. They grow together in a wall to protect her, branches intertwined. Beneath the water that surrounds the small peninsula, juts of dark root tangle with white flowers growing upward toward the light. Above, green moss drapes the branches like bridal veils and pixies flutter in gossipy clusters on iridescent wings.

Shereth, the one who painted the mural on the loft ceiling, isn't here, and the others don't greet us. Swamp pixies tend to be cliquish. Nearby, a small yellow lizard lounges on a log. I wonder if it's anyone I know. They're not trying to get my attention, however, so they could be enjoying the break.

"Where are we going?" Zeph asks cheerfully, falling in step beside me.

I glance at them. "We were visiting Macha before we got sidetracked."

The air is perfumed with pollen, and deep breaths make me feel as though I'm hovering on the verge of a great sneeze. In the distance, something splashes into the water, swimming about us in slow circles.

"Should I be concerned?" Kerboros asks.

About the thing in the water? I shrug. Presuming Macha wishes us harm, she hardly needs a beast to do her bidding.

"This should be fun," Zeph declares. "Do you mind if I spectate?"

"Not at all. You did get us out of the bottle. Wise sorceress, if you're willing to speak, prithee let me know," I call, directing the last statement in a louder voice.

I've had the most success with that greeting where Macha is concerned.

Kerboros gives me a look as the silence builds, and then I hear the rattle of reeds that could be mistaken for bones. That's the sound of Macha gliding through wind chimes that line the perimeter of her home.

"It's been some time since I saw you," the swamp witch says in a silken tone.

Beside me, Kerboros starts faintly, likely in surprise. People are never prepared for her beauty, I think. In legends, swamp hags are wizened old crones with matted gray hair and gnarled, clutching hands. But Macha is ageless like a forest, with dark green hair that flows down her back in a river of silk. She wears a simple gown with many hidden pockets, and her features are exquisite, pointed and foxy, full of clever, knowing amusement. Her eyes are endless shadows, black like onyx, and she gazes at me briefly before her attention shifts to Kerboros.

"I've been conscripted," I say wryly.

"The Winter Lord does enjoy evaluating the extent of his reach," Macha says. "Whom have you brought me?"

I'm surprised by the gently protective instinct that makes me want to shield Kerboros from the sharpness of Macha's interest. "This is Kerboros." I gesture at the sharply scintillating fae on my left. "And Zeph."

"Oh my. I'm entirely spoiled for choice today, I see." The faint trill on the word *entirely* indicates the intensity of Macha's intrigue. "I had no notion that Winter's hound was so..." Clicking her tongue, she circles him with predatory fascination instead of finishing the thought.

Kerboros withstands her scrutiny without moving. "Your interest is noted."

Good. Neutral is the best way to handle Macha. She doesn't respect those who beg for her favor, but she's also easily offended. There are those who have approached her and remain trapped in the form she chose for them when they irritated her, mainly wild fae without an innate ability to shift.

"I'm suffering greatly from all this lack of attention," Zeph says then.

Macha turns her regard in their direction, angling her head. "Hmm."

"Is that a good *hmm*?" they ask.

"There's a puzzle to solve," I cut in. "I hope you can figure it out." It never hurts to appeal to her wits. Or her vanity.

"I'm willing to listen, though I make no guarantees."

Succinctly, I explain how the Summer delegation has gone missing and none are able to track them using any type of magic known to Winter. "You're the most powerful person in any realm," I say. "So I thought..."

"That I could track for Lord Winter?"

Oh no.

I shake my head quickly. "Not at all. But maybe you could give us a hint? You'd know if unusual magic was used anywhere near your domain."

I'm taking a risk. If Kerboros tells Lord Liskaal that I've implied Macha is the real power in the Winter realm, it won't end well for me.

I'm about to start gnawing my nails when Macha speaks. "I may be willing to have a look, but…I require incentive. Tribute, if you will."

This is the best possible result, but I don't know what I can provide that she doesn't already have. But I still say, "I'm willing to negotiate."

"You can't pay the price," she says silkily while staring at Kerboros.

He tenses. Yet he can't ignore our mission objective either. "What do you require?"

I hope it's not blood.

"Nothing you cannot spare, Winter hound, though I should name you *spider*. A memory. You know the one I want, seeing as you relived it recently in my snare."

Despite the fact that I'm used to Macha, her tone sends a shiver through me. I don't know if this is a good idea. The loss of memory is like death to a fae because they're eternal, and they carry time with them. Kerboros must be old beyond my imagining, and if he yields this to her, it will be the same as surrendering a little bit of his life.

I wonder if I could persuade her to accept a lock of hair instead. Kerboros has gorgeous hair. Long and dark, shiny, and threaded liberally with silver. It looks like it would be extremely soft, basically the only part about him that does. His skin is warm copper in this light, with the faintest patina of green from the canopy above. I wonder how I look to him—odd, when I rarely consider my appearance at all. In fact, I have been known to paint myself entirely in mud from head to toe.

I had good reasons at the time.

Giving him time to consider is the right move, I don't speak because this is his decision, between him and Macha. I won't interfere. If he thinks this is a bad idea, I won't press. We can figure something else out.

A powerful feeling simmers inside me; I don't want anyone to hurt him ever again. He's started to feel like someone I should risk myself to protect. On the surface, it's ridiculous. He's a renowned warrior, deadly with a blade, and famous for having an even sharper tongue. His words cut deep, and he wears solitude like an icy crown. But inside him remains a boy terrified and alone in a dreary cell.

I might be the only one who knows that about him.

If Kerboros looks to me for help, I'll see if I can turn Macha from this notion. I do have a flair for words and an affinity for bending people to my will, usually by sapping some of their anger. But Macha is a force more than a person; I cannot feed on her emotions. Mostly, she feels... watchful, to my attenuated senses. Is that even an emotion? It's certainly not a feeling that offers me any sustenance.

"I'm already under a compulsion," Kerboros says in a graveled tone. "A secondary constraint would—"

"No. You must take my word for it, but that is not my intent. You will gain no tether to me, should you make this bargain."

Again, I repress the urge to intercede. My hand twitches with the urge to touch Kerboros, to pull him away from Macha and her tricksy ways. Bargaining with the swamp witch, he'll never win. She keeps her beauty by stealing from others—life, time, memories, magic—and her loveliness is legendary.

Please don't hurt him. He's been hurt enough.

"Then I am willing to trade for your expertise," Kerboros answers.

Macha's delight is unnerving as she glides toward him and frames his head in her hands. Her long nails curl downward, pricking into the top of his skull, and shadows flicker, darting inside his head like tentacles made of smoke and spite. Though Macha isn't evil per se, she does take some joy in tormenting others.

He flinches, and then the smoke tentacles withdraw, glowing with orange at their tips.

The swamp witch inhales her prize and then faces me. "That could have seemed cruel. But if you knew what I know, you might call it a kindness."

I can't piss her off. "Maybe so. Should I accompany you?"

Even when I lived here as a lizard, I never saw the inside of Macha's home. I don't expect that ever to change. She's revered and feared, but no one *knows* her. Not intimately. I've heard stories, of course, tragedies—a mortal artist who broke her heart long ago. But I've never gotten confirmation, and I think she prefers to maintain that air of mystique.

Yet it's better to be sure.

She sears me with a stare. "Wait. I will attempt to discern what you wish to know."

16

Sacrifice

This piece is carved from fallen wood. It depicts a woman on her knees, sobbing into her hands with abject despair. Each detail is carefully rendered, including her torn clothing and tumbled hair in disarray. Only her face is hidden, though her posture reveals the depths of her grief. Her back is bowed. Her shoulders are rounded, heavy with whatever brought her low. She holds herself like a woman who has been sacrificed for someone else's good, and perhaps she wasn't consulted as to whether she wanted to pay that price. The statuette imbues a deep uneasiness, as if the artist witnessed something unspeakable, so terrible that it had to be purged from the soul through the slow, inexorable scrapes of a blade.

KERBOROS

THE INTERLOPER HAS VANISHED.

Did Zeph lose interest and wander off? It seems suspicious that they didn't say farewell. When I turn to Thea to inquire about her thoughts, I find her studying me closely. Is she concerned about the aftermath of whatever the swamp witch did?

"Are you all right?" she whispers.

"Why wouldn't I be?"

"Because you lost a memory. An important one, most likely."

I hesitate. "I'm aware that…there used to be pain. Now it feels like…"

"Like what?"

"If you'll forgive the analogy, it feels as if a wound has been lanced. And the poison is gone, leaving a space instead of a festering core."

The sensation troubles me somewhat. It feels as if I've lost something significant, but when I reach for it, there's nothing. Only smoke where there once was fire. I shake my head, impatient with myself. I have spent enough time on retrospection during my solitary pursuits. In another life, perhaps I would be an artist. That work has granted both solace and joy through dire tribulations.

"Then I do hope it wasn't bad. What she did to you."

"As do I. But failure isn't an option, and I had to sacrifice something, or the consequences for both of us would be unbearable."

Her eyes widen slightly. Then her lips curve. It seems that I've pleased her, judging by the sparkle in her eyes. But I remain unsure what I said that summoned such a delighted expression and how I might replicate it.

"She took a memory about your mother, I think," Thea says. "Based on what we talked about before. You told me that she called you *Ori*."

"*I* shared that with you?"

I don't remember telling Thea; the thread must have unraveled when Macha stole my memory of my mother. I know I had one, but I can no longer recall what she looked or smelled like or how her voice sounded. The name Ori is familiar, and it makes me ache in some inchoate way, yet I can't summon specific recollections. Thea knowing this about me feels...important. Intimate, even. She's a living link to a memory I've lost forever.

"Yes. I'm so sorry."

"About what?"

"The memory. Your compulsion. Is there no way for you to emancipate yourself from Winter's service?" she asks.

I could tell her that I lied to Macha—that I freed myself from the need to follow Liskaal's orders some time ago. But I need an opening for my plans to succeed. I can pretend and be patient for a little longer. I would like to trust her, but the risk is too great, and I've been alone too long.

I respond to her question, ignoring her sympathy. "My cousin would need to believe that I pose no threat to his rule."

A frown creases her thick, arched brows. "Impossible. How do you prove you'll never do something?"

"Precisely. You might be the only person who's ever grasped my situation." Freedom will never be given to me; I must take it.

"That might be because you discourage conversation," Thea points out.

I'm under no illusions. She wouldn't spend time with me if we hadn't been assigned to hunt fugitives together. Yet I cannot say that I regret this particular task.

"It has been longer than I can recall since I spent this much time with anyone."

She smiles slightly. "Are you complaining?"

"I am not."

Has her expression warmed? In the light, she is lovely, all amber hued, with eyes like gemstones and hair that tumbles wildly down her back. This is how she's meant to be seen, framed by the wild greenery of Macha's yard. We stand a few paces apart, just…gazing at each other, and I know I should say something.

Thea steps closer.

As if I'm pulled toward her, I do as well, wondering what will happen when I reach her. A touch? Perhaps she'll ask to feed from me again. I've grown used to the feeling and would even welcome channeling some of that rage toward a brighter purpose. There is a faint tension now, and she reveals it by biting her lip. I've seen that sign in others, people participating in a courting dance.

My heart kicks in my chest at the mere idea. But she can't mean it that way. It's impossible.

I'm Winter's hound.

Before I can react, Macha sweeps into the front garden with a triumphant gesture. And pauses. "Oh. Have you forgotten that you're recently married?" she asks Thea.

I swallow an instinctive curse.

She has been granted to another, promised without her volition, and now my wrath is back, rising in an inevitable tide. Not that it matters. Power grants authority to anger, and I have never sought the former. I learned from my father's mistakes. While I do scheme, I do so quietly, furtively, and with altogether different ends.

Thea clears her throat. "We weren't doing anything."

"Mm," Macha says with an articulate lift of her brow.

I want to protest, but it seems better to redirect. "Never mind her personal life. Your aspect tells me you've learned something vital."

"You cannot find them because they did not use magic. They passed from the palace using concealed tunnels and have made their way through natural means."

That confirms my theory. When I opened the secret panel in the wardrobe, I suspected what had transpired, but it's good to have my supposition validated. That means the Summer delegation has numerous allies, conspirators concealed within the Winter court. If my cousin truly compelled my service or my loyalty, as he did in the old days, I would be forced to reveal precisely what I know. But all bindings lose power over time, and those who feast on cruelty grow complacent, secure in their displays of force.

"You have eyes everywhere," Thea says.

"Indeed I do. Every lizard, every serpent, every toad whispers to me."

Thea seems to believe that flattery is the way to go. "You're incredible. Second to none in secrets and skullduggery."

"Most impressive," I add, because she might be correct. While I have heard of Macha, I have never met her ere now. And I recall the rumor about my mother. I wonder if she'll address it. "Will you permit a personal inquiry?" I add.

Does the swamp witch smile slightly? "Personal? Hmm. I'll allow it from you. But don't make a habit of this."

"People said that my mother…" How do I ask this? Simplicity is best, I think. "Were you related to her?"

To my surprise, she steps closer, carrying the scent of night-blooming flowers. When she circles around me, I feel faintly concerned but not threatened. "I did idly wonder if they shared those stories still."

Thea is watching this exchange, wide-eyed. "Wait, you didn't answer him."

"In a sense," Macha says to me, ignoring Thea entirely. "Your mother *was* descended from one of my daughters."

Thea opens her mouth to respond. I hold up a hand to forestall her, because she's practically vibrating with curiosity, and judging from the look in Macha's black eyes, if we press too hard on the subject of her daughters, we will not leave this swamp. "I appreciate the information," I say in as formal and respectful a tone as I can muster.

"I'm not your grandmother. There's little blood that binds us," Macha says. "But you *do* carry some of my secrets, dear spider."

"What does that mean?" Thea wants to know.

"You may find your quarry where it is always spring," Macha declares. "Or I might be lying. How much do you trust me?"

Now she's amusing herself with us, as there's no suitable response to that question. Instead, I bow.

The swamp witch takes this as a cue to terminate our conversation. "I will tell you no more. That would remove all the challenge, and I shall enjoy monitoring your progress."

I suspect we must take the swamp witch at her word. She does not appear to be accustomed to denying herself entertainment.

"Hopefully, she's pointed us in the right direction," Thea whispers.

A thunderclap sounds, and Macha morphs into a conspiracy of ravens, flying off in different directions. I blink. "Not one for long farewells?"

Thea shakes her head with a sigh. "Not really. Not for as long as I've known her. I admire her flair for the dramatic, however."

Thea pauses, and I can tell she's biting back a question. If I had to speculate, I'd imagine she's wondering about my relation to the swamp witch. Normally, I would already be moving, but as our time together is limited, I treasure it all the more, trying to extend these small moments and engrave them in my memory just as I would a frieze on the wall.

"Something you want to ask?" I suggest.

She seems to think for a little longer, then says, "No. Ready to go?"

If she doesn't have a question, I do. After seeing how my preferred mode of transport impacted Thea the first time, I won't inflict it on her again without permission. "Are you willing to travel through my portal magic?"

"It can be…rough. But it's fast." She straightens her spine. "Try to be gentle."

A molten spark sears me, and I can no longer doubt that she's developed some personal interest in me. How utterly unexpected. "No one has ever requested that of me."

She flashes a saucy grin. "You know, I rather *do* enjoy being the first."

"And so you shall be." She has no idea what she's doing to me, what she's inviting. There's a faint edge to my voice, the timbre of a growl.

Now she sounds a trifle breathless, a warm flush in her cheeks. "Well, then. Let's get to Springtide."

I extend my hand, waiting until Thea accepts it, and then I pull us through a hole in the world.

17

A Spell for Alacrity and Adventuring

If you're perusing this page, you must be embarking on a grand undertaking. This charm won't start any fires or save any fair scions, but it sets the right tone. I call spells like these "mood boosters," albeit some can be quite powerful. For instance, my granny Tash loved to fool about with one we privately called Horrid Laughter. It's one thing to giggle at a jape, quite another to be unable to stop braying like a beast.

That said, this is a good one to cast before you set out. It puts everyone in a festive mood, eager to see the sights and battle difficult odds. It can also lift the spirits at the journey's lowest ebb. There may be a few who object to having their emotions tweaked, so be cautious. Avoid conflict when you can. I'm not telling you to hide your light, mind. Just know when the fight is necessary.

This working will respond best in the light. You'll need:

- *Jasper, iolite, carnelian in your pocket, warmed up with your hand*
- *Angelica blossoms for everyone in the group*
- *A tin mug*

- *One swallow each of wilding wine*

'Tis best if you frame this as refreshment and not as a spell or a charm per se. Angelica blossoms are a delightful snack, and who would turn down a taste of a lovely jasmine honey wine? Any flavor will do, however. I'm rather partial to dew pear acacia. Whatever you have should suffice, as long as you maintain lightness of heart. With the stones warmed from your grip, first offer the angelica blossoms with a cheerful spirit. Once all companions partake, pour the wine and proffer a sip to each. If the charm is taking hold, they won't resist despite using a communal cup.

Your gentleness can seduce them from "they" to "we" in a trice. I find it's best to give a little toast. You can be clever or witty or funny as a drunken boggart or even try to sway their hearts. I use this, now and again: "Here's to stealing, fighting, and drinking. When you go thieving, take only your true love's heart. And when you do battle, let it be for the defenseless. And when you drink, please raise a glass with me." It's a rare soul who can resist, and once they've enjoyed your food and savored your wine, they'll feel a bond, my gem.

Never underestimate the power of moving someone's heart. People will go to war on orders and flee when the tide turns, but they'll defend their homes to their last breaths. But you already know that. The beavers taught you this lesson in the wildlands. I'll never forget finding you covered in mud from top to tail, guarding your stockpile of sharpened sticks. You were ready to fight a small sprite army to protect that beaver dam.

THEA

WHEN I TAKE KERBOROS'S HAND, my fingers tingle, all flaring heat, like being struck by lightning—or a pixie's wrath.

That sensation yields to the awful portal lurch that churns up my guts. But the colors of his aura, echoed in this swirling vortex, are so freaking pretty. Kerboros brings stardust and wonder, sea-glass blue and sparkling iolanthe shot through with frost and silver. I thought he was colorless at first, but no. Instead, he's *all* the colors, compressed so tightly it looks like shadow.

Once the shimmering fades and my eyes adjust, I notice that we haven't landed in the Court of Springtide. *Dammit. Nothing ever goes as planned.*

And ordinarily, it'd be an adventure, figuring out where the heck we are. Somewhere else could be the most fun I ever had. But I think about Da, waiting patiently at home for me. Even if he's not currently in the cells, I understand that he's a hostage until I find my spouse and convince Lord Liskaal that I can make that relationship work.

Fear slithers up my leg and grazes my throat with its fangs. I don't let it bite. I force away my emotions and box them up, as I've been doing with my hunger for my entire life. I try to silence the ticking clock in my head. *Please don't hurt my dad. He's all I have.*

Strictly, that's not entirely true. There are people who care about me, dear friends who will miss me if I'm banished to die a slow, excruciating death, experiencing the horrid withdrawal that comes from the sudden cessation of magic. But Da? Losing me would destroy him. He's the best parent in the world, and I can't let anyone hurt him, no matter what. Internal resolve slowly forces fear of failure to submit.

Kerboros paces, intensely perturbed and glaring at the golden meadow as if it has personally offended him. I take stock of our surroundings. Tall grass—a delicate golden green, tipped with lacy white flowers here and there—sings as the wind passes through the field. There are pops of color: purples and pinks brightened by a cheeky occasional orange. The air smells sweet too, gentle in my lungs. Other than the flowers, I don't recognize any landmarks. No sloping hills or rock formations. Not even a mushroom ring.

That makes me feel…uneasy. It's a little unusual not to find trees of any kind in the wildlands. We guard our sacred groves and honor the dryads who dwell there. Here, it's best to presume everything is alive and listening—and behave accordingly. Da didn't teach me anything in particular about flower fae, so I'm at a loss.

Not somewhere I want to be.

"Hello there. What took you so long?" The familiar voice seems to come from nowhere; then Zeph pops into view amid a profusion of blooms.

"Were you waiting for us?" I tilt my head, baffled by so many things, but currently, I'm wondering how Zeph got ahead of us.

They couldn't have known where we were going, right? This was a misfire of Kerboros's magic, not where we're supposed to be at all. Some wild fae are tricksters, so they might be joking. While most fae can't lie directly, they can jest and tinker with meanings and misdirect all day long.

"What makes you say that?" they ask.

"Never mind." Getting a straight answer will require more energy than I possess.

I consider deploying a useful spell that Da crafted for wayfaring, but I decide to save it. Because, usually, when I think things can't get worse, they do. Hope for the best; plan for the worst. That credo has never steered me wrong.

"Do you know where we are?" Kerboros asks in a grudging tone.

I shake my head. It must gall him, knowing that we're here because his magic misfired. From all my observations of him, he seems tightly wound, focused on efficiency and obedience. Lately, though, I've seen glimmers of something else. An ungovernable streak he's been repressing with all his might, and it calls to me. The feelings I had before rebound even stronger. In Macha's grove, I wanted to protect him. In the aftermath of his terror, I comforted him.

And now… *Oh no.*

There's no time or space for me to feel this way. I'm not sure when empathy shifted into intimacy, but now the feelings are deeper still. I like the way he looks and the way he smells, and he's so very warm. My cheeks are suddenly white-hot as I imagine—

"Thea?" Zeph prompts.

"What?"

"You're so red. Are you quite all right?"

I wave a hand, trying to cover my embarrassment. I'll die if Kerboros realizes how I feel. I grope my way back to the original topic and turn the question back to Zeph. "What about you? Have you been here before?"

They aim an impressive smile at me. "Many times."

"Tell us what you know," Kerboros demands.

"But you don't seem to be here on purpose," Zeph muses in a faintly mocking tone. "You do seem to make a habit of blundering about, don't you?" They gaze across the flower meadow and laugh softly.

The sound raises goose bumps on my arms because it's so devoid of humor. It's like Zeph hates Kerboros. And I guess I understand why. People who don't know that he's been forced to do his cousin's dirty work might think he's horrible. In fact, I used to number among them, but now I know the truth, and I have Kerboros's back. Maybe he's not my person, exactly, but I…care about him. A lot has happened in a short time, and I can't pretend things are the same as when we first started traveling together. I fold my arms, making it clear I don't trust Zeph.

"The better question is how you ended up here ahead of us," I point out.

The slender fae turns cool eyes on me. "Are you accusing me of something?"

This whole encounter feels off. Why did Zeph disappear before Macha provided our lead, and if they *are* tracking us, could they have been sent by Lord Liskaal to keep tabs on us? None of those answers are apparent, and I can't decide how dangerous Zeph is; therefore, it's better if I don't provoke them. They also said they know where we are, which means we need their knowledge.

So I fasten on a smile. "Of course not. No need to argue. If you meant us any harm, you wouldn't have shown us how to escape Macha's trap."

"A reasonable deduction," Kerboros allows.

I hear a soft chime, and then a shower of sparks cascades around us. Emerging from the blaze of light is a small humanoid form with delicate wings cast in shades of blue, the smallest fae: a pixie. I take a step back.

Unlike me, Zeph reacts with delight. "Rosalina! There you are. I wondered if you could find me. Ready for an adventure?"

"Hmm," says Rosalina, gazing first at Kerboros and then at me.

Zeph lets out a bubbling laugh. "Don't be like that. This is important."

"Is it?" Rosalina asks. "Well, it had better be. I had plans, you know. I don't exist to be at your beck and call."

Oh dear. A grumpy pixie, one who feels put out with Zeph for making demands. And why are they doing that exactly? I don't remember inviting them to join our expedition. While I did receive permission to recruit a small team, I had other allies in mind. But now I don't have a way to communicate with people I've known all my life.

Time to make the best of this. I wonder if good manners and a can-do attitude will appease a crabby pixie. "Hi there. I'm Thea." I indicate my companion with a nod. "That's Kerboros. We met Zeph at Macha's place. Not sure why they're helping us, to be honest."

The pixie snorts. "Because they're nosy, meddlesome, and easily bored."

Zeph laughs. "I can't dispute that even if I want to. Rosalina knows me too well."

"As long as you admit it," Rosalina says. "Anyway, these are the Golden Fields. Home to various beasts and boggins."

"Boggins aren't dangerous," I say immediately.

They're the smaller cousins to boggarts, who always get a bad rap in mortal stories. So do hobgoblins, and it irks me to no end.

"Definitely not," Rosalina agrees. "At least not intentionally. They're just large compared to me. And when one is small, there are increased risks." She eyes me with a skeptical expression. "Please do mind your step."

"We're not lummoxes," Kerboros says.

Suddenly, I'm so sleepy, I can't keep my eyes open. That doesn't make sense. We slept in Macha's bottle, so I should be hungry, not tired. But I don't know if we should pause for a meal in the middle of these flowers because the scent is making my head tingle. I blink, fighting the urge to curl up right where I am.

Rosalina pinches me. "Get moving. It's not safe here."

"The flowers have a soporific effect?" Kerboros guesses.

Zeph grins. "If only that was the worst of it."

As they speak, a bloodred flower growing on a meaty-looking green stalk nearby unfurls long unusual petals, revealing a deep disturbing maw.

"Let me guess," I say. "The flowers will eat us."

18

Defenseless

This piece is carved into the wardrobe doors, done in two panels. On the left, a figure extends their arms crossed before them as if to block harm. Since they're without a weapon or shield, however, there are deep cuts on their forearms from where blades have struck. On the right, swords and knives are etched, attacking from all angles, rendered in faithful sizes, so the wielders cannot be seen. While the victim might appear to be defenseless, they could also be viewed as stoic, taking wounds in service to some ideal. Their features are barely present, lending an eerie and faceless aspect. The subject could be anyone or no one at all.

KERBOROS

"ONLY IF WE STAND STILL long enough," Zeph replies.

I would like to say that it will be easy to get rid of Zeph, but I suspect that we've acquired a shadow; I can either use them or get accustomed to being annoyed. I have existed in the latter state for a long time, and this could be intentional surveillance. I don't believe in coincidence.

They may have been dispatched by Liskaal or his evil queen, Valnevi. That seems like the most probable explanation. The Lord of Winter does not enjoy leaving me to my own devices, as my awful cousin seems to think that I will foment a rebellion given the least opportunity. Just like my father. Liskaal has no clue what I'm really up to, or he would be far more worried. My schemes have nothing to do with ruling the realm and everything to do with—well, sometimes it's better not to think too hard on your own intentions. You never know what abilities others might be hiding.

"Let's go," I snap.

I will not meet my end digested by flora. All around, the flowers are stirring. They don't seem to be ambulatory, but they *are* hungry, snapping as we pass. As I get moving, I draw my weapon and ensure that Thea is with me.

She's right at my back, and Zeph must be behind her, as their quick-silver presence registers at the rear of our group. Rosalina flutters ahead as a scout, calling out directions. She guides me right and left as more plants awaken.

It occurs to me that I'm putting an unusual amount of faith in a stranger and spare the energy to hope this pixie isn't trying to murder us. Flowers lunge as I race past. I try to turn to check on Thea, but I pay for breaking focus when I veer too close and one of them sinks needle-sharp teeth into my arm. I swiftly slash myself free, and the snapping flower mouth lands behind me, still twitching. Thea vaults it while Zeph skirts around, and I wheel, sealing my hand over the wound.

I keep moving, blood steadily seeping through my fingers. That enflames the flowers, who let out hungry hissing sounds. Since Rosalina didn't slow when I was bitten, I can barely see her. I can't hear her calling out directions either. The end of the meadow isn't far, but I can only guess at the best route, and sometimes I'm wrong. I slash a path with my dagger, my forearms bitten as I go. At first, it's an endless battle.

Rosalina finally notices that we're in trouble and circles back. "All you had to do was keep up. What's the matter with you?"

I'm too busy slicing to spare her a sharp look. More and more flower heads hit the ground. I'm starting to enjoy this. As we go, the smell of their own fluids makes the feral blooms wary, and we eventually pass from the carnivorous flower field. Since I was leading the charge, I'm the only one who's been harmed. What are a few more scars atop the ones I already possess? I quickly scan Thea from head to toe, confirming that she's unharmed.

And she catches me. Her gaze settles on mine, and she cants her head, asking a silent question. I don't know what I'd say, if we didn't have two onlookers. The truth would doubtless shock her greatly—that I care more about her continued safety than my own.

Then she makes a bold move, signing, *I'm all right. Were you worried?*

I dip my chin ever so slightly. It's a barely there nod, the faintest acknowledgment of what I feel for her, and my heart skips at the prospect of growing closer to her through this admission. When I begin to fear what my face may reveal to her, I turn to study the landscape. The flat plain has given way to uplands, gently rolling hills covered in light-purple flowers. These don't look aggressive at least.

Rosalina is circling the area, studying the terrain and the flora. "Lavender boscage. And cobalt summercomb."

It's beautiful in the distance, but I am not a botanist. I cannot imagine why that's significant. "And?"

My injuries sting.

"Doesn't that mean we're closer to the Summer lands than Springtide?" she asks.

Oh. Now I comprehend her line of thought. Faery is a series of joined territories with thin boundaries leading to other spaces or zones entirely; it can be confusing. But she can identify the region based on the summercomb. As I understand it, the realm has driven more than one mortal cartographer mad.

Thea scrutinizes the area as well. "Is that right, Rosalina? We're near Summer?"

"Call me *Rosa*," the pixie says.

"I didn't have a chance to say so before, but it's nice to meet you." Thea is skilled at making people warm to her, and the pixie is no exception.

"It was hectic, sure enough. Maybe we'll get along," Rosa says.

"That's a nasty bite." Zeph looks like they might poke the injury, so I step back.

"Oh no." Thea rushes over. "How bad is it?"

"I need only a respite, and I can heal myself." Now that I'm no longer running for my life, I can clean the wounds and—

Thea takes my wounded arm, and I let her. Experiencing her touch is worth suffering a little. She has a strip of damp linen cloth, and she carefully blots away the blood, seeming anxious as she checks for foreign matter. She meets my gaze with a tender aspect while pressing gently. "I thought some of those plant teeth might be lodged in here. Do you feel anything?"

I can't answer the way I want to, and my heart is racing. "It's fine. I can do it."

She offers me some water.

I accept the flask and sip from it, gathering the strength to address all the little cuts. "Your kindness is a gift."

Nodding, she whispers, "I feel so silly for refusing to pack my own supplies. I was so proud of my connections and so sure the wildlands would provide."

"I'm sure if we weren't traveling so far afield, they would have," I say, trying to be gentle with her. It's such a rare impulse, wobbly-legged and newborn in its presence.

"You two are sweet," Zeph says with an enigmatic expression.

I straighten as irritation prickles over me. It feels like Zeph is needling us, and that's...odd. At least, partly so. I'm used to creating conflict, but people normally like Thea. Zeph strikes me as a free spirit, so why does Thea rub them the wrong way? Still considering the question, I focus and pull enough magic to close the punctures, though the expenditure leaves me exhausted and hungry to the point of feeling unsteady on my feet.

"I can feast on nectar," Rosalina says then, as if she can read my physical state. "But what do you three plan to do?"

I don't mind sharing with Thea, but it annoys me faintly to provide for Zeph. I make the offer anyway. "I'll divide what I have. It's simple fare. Just fruit and honey wafers for now and dried vegetables for later. I'll make soup. We need a break after that run."

My knees are too weak to carry me far, so I'll prepare food for everyone. I set up the warming-stone cooking circle and then heat it with magic. The pot rests directly on the stone, and I add the dried vegetables to it, along with herbs and spices, plus a handful of barley grain for added heartiness. Thea helps, adding a few things to the pot. She also shares water from a tin cup she produced from somewhere.

"That frankly smells delicious," Zeph says.

Without deciding to do so, I check on Thea. She's curled up near

Rosalina, looking like she might nod off at any moment. I offer a first course of honey wafers and fruit, and then when the soup is done, we take turns eating out of the pot. I have my own cup and bowl, but it seems better to share. Such things build communal bonds—or so I'm told. I've never attempted to make anyone like me.

Still, it's companionable passing the pot around. We each take a few bites, before circling it onward, and then it returns. We continue this way until all the warm soup is gone. And the stories are true. I feel… connected. Perhaps for the first time in my life, I'm part of a collective.

My mind drifts to Macha, who stole the memory of my mother and whose line I distantly carry on. I wonder if I get my tendency toward solitude from her. Yet, if she once had daughters, she wasn't always alone. She is older than our recordkeeping, and the secrets she must have to share might encompass volumes enough to fill a library. Somehow, she knows about my spiderlings, but I have no fear that she'll share that information with Liskaal. Instinctively, I understand that if the Lord of Winter forced her to choose a side, he would not be pleased with her decision. And he wouldn't live long if he interfered with her territory either.

Interrupting my reverie, Thea rubs her belly with what sounds like a happy groan. "That was exactly what I needed."

After making soup, there's not enough water left for everyone. I do have a bottle I can fill, if we find a stream. Rosalina scouted before, but I probably shouldn't be the one to ask. I don't know how to approach people, and pixies can be…difficult. They often resent being seen as messengers and servants, and I understand that sensitivity better than most.

Zeph might be able to cajole her since they know her better. Presumably. Otherwise, she wouldn't have responded to their request for aid. And for that matter, what did they even tell her? I eye them both, then dismiss the notion of asking for clarification.

“We have time to forage,” I say. “Before we set off again.”

“Are we on a schedule?” Rosalina asks.

“We are,” Thea replies. “I think we have nine days?”

“What day do you think it is?” Zeph cuts in.

I provide my best guess.

They open a small timekeeping device, a fae invention perfectly attuned to the oscillations in temporal energy. Then the date and time displays on the crystal. “I don’t like to bear bad tidings, but we napped longer than any of us realized.”

Stunned, I just stare for a moment.

Impossible. “We only have *one* week left?”

19

A Spell for Courage and Comfort

There may come a time when you feel disheartened, as if you cannot face what comes next. This working will help to center you, remind you of why you came so far in the first place. It's meant only for you, and there could be consequences if you attempt to sway others with this one. I would caution against it. Forcing emotions on other souls could be construed as coercion, and there is a line we ought not to cross, even if we can.

I hope this charm leaves you feeling as you do when you first come home and you get a big hug. There's always a warm bowl of porridge waiting, and I tried to distill that solace and safety into a rite that would reassure you in that same way. I've tested it myself, and it passes muster. You might be surprised by how simple it is, but sometimes the simple things are the best. Simple joy. Simple life.

At my lowest point, you reminded me of this when you were a wee tot, barely toddling. I put you down amid a garden of flowers, and you didn't uproot a single one. You sat in wonder watching a pixie sampling the nectar.

(Yes, that's how you first met Shereth, and she told me you were a special child that day.) Most children want to take, but you only drank the wonder in, starry-eyed and full of joy.

This one is best cast quickly at the height of light. You'll need:

- *Silver and garnet jewelry*
- *Candied ginger*

First, put on the jewelry. It might seem like such a simple thing, but objects have power. Objects that matter to us, charged with emotional weight, possess even greater potency. This is why I gave you the earrings I made. Think of them as a talisman charged with my love, or you can look on them as armor. While you've never been enamored of such things, the court ladies use their pots of paint as a sort of armor, concealing their true faces and presenting what they wish the world to see. It's another sort of glamour, my darling gem.

As for the candied ginger, it's tasty, good for you, and it bolsters the heart and mind. You'll feel it warming you from within, emboldening you and readying you for whatever the world brings. Nibble it slowly, or gulp it in one bite. That's up to you. Your choices matter.

THEA

WHILE THE OTHERS ARE BUSY, I perform the spell for luck and light; I need all the help I can get.

As soon as I finish, inspiration strikes. Tara. We're near Summer, and she'll *unquestionably* be useful. Plus, I haven't seen her in ages. She's a young hobgoblin who boarded with Da and me for several seasons while learning about our customs. When Tara went home to Summer, I missed her terribly, but we've kept in touch, and we visit as often as can be arranged in the wildlands, even when the climate is politically sensitive.

Lately, that's all the time, as Lord Liskaal is convinced something is brewing—that someone is scheming against him. For all I know, that's true. But I don't give a damn who rules in the four courts. I just want to live my life. Yet they insist on making it my problem.

At least I have a direction now.

"Let's head toward the Summer Court. No more portals." I glance at Kerboros, hoping he doesn't take this personally. "We don't know why your magic is compromised. We can't risk using it until we figure out the malfunction."

"A reasonable precaution," he says.

Thank goodness.

"Everyone feel ready to continue?" I ask.

In answer, Zeph falls in step with me as Kerboros sets out following Rosa. She seems to be willing to scout, but he might not trust her reports. He's known for coldness and suspicion even among the skeptics in the Winter Court, which makes the soft moments we've shared even more special and rare. I remember the way he clung to me, battling terror, and the way I held him back, as if my arms alone could keep him safe.

Suddenly, I realize that Zeph is addressing me. "Have you spent much time in the Summer Court?" they ask.

I shake my head. "My travel is strictly monitored by the Lord and Lady of Winter."

The rulers don't trust me, and they keep me tied to court through my bond with Da and their need of my ability to keep hostilities in check through passive exploitation of my abilities. That's why I haven't even been allowed to spend all the time I'd wish in the wildlands. I have…a quota to meet, I suppose.

"Why?"

Zeph is displaying an unusual amount of interest in me. "Why are you so curious?"

Kerboros likely thinks I trust everyone too quickly, but it's more that I'm wary yet I don't display it. It's safer that way. Better to be judged as happy-go-lucky and not a threat than someone who needs careful observation.

"You're famous. Stories have circulated outside of Winter about your pranks—and how preciously you're held by Lord Liskaal."

"That makes it sound like he adores me," I say, shocked.

"Is that not the case?"

"Oh, good light. If that's the current rumor, I'll be lucky if Lady Valnevi doesn't skin me alive. *No.* Emphatically no. He doesn't see me as a love interest."

"Ah, so you're available. What about me, then?" Zeph wheels in front me, walking backward while maintaining intense eye contact.

They hold the fervent look as they slow their pace, letting me get closer. Closer. Then they take my hand, and—we both dissolve into giggles at the same moment. They literally can't sustain the seductive expression, and I'm tempted to ruffle their hair.

"No. I don't think we have any spark at all."

"Alas, I feel the same. I don't think I can seduce you."

"Did you want to?" I ask, mildly curious.

They make a vague gesture, spinning to face forward and quickening their step. "It occurred to me that it might be convenient."

"You're so strange." If I sound mildly offended, it's because I am.

"Ignore me. That's the advice Rosa gives everyone, and it's usually the best course."

I laugh, reluctantly amused by their self-deprecation. "She hasn't had the chance with us. Between your sudden arrival and the carnivorous flowers—"

"Yes, it has been chaotic, hasn't it? And there I was, ready for a nap in the spot where I thought I was least likely to be disturbed."

"I'd apologize for interrupting, but I suspect I'll need your help. Which I appreciate, by the way, even if I don't entirely understand why you're here."

This is a test. I wonder if they'll address my implicit curiosity or sidestep the issue. I can learn a great deal by what they don't say. Earlier, I attempted this query, and Rosa stepped in; Zeph let her answer stand without offering any information of their own.

"You were trapped," they say unexpectedly. "I knew how to help you, so I did. And once I've started something, I like to finish it."

"A quirk of completionism?" I suggest.

"That and pure nosiness, as Rosa said before. It's entertaining to participate in other people's conundrums."

They have a point. Da raised me to be helpful, which sometimes crosses the line into interference. I don't do it for amusement, though. I help because it's what my dad would do in the same situation. I'll probably never be as instinctively kind, as my own nature constantly whispers to take and take and take a little more: *Just a taste—they'll never miss it.* I exist in a state of perpetual hunger, afraid of doing harm and becoming a parasite.

"This way, don't dawdle." Rosa seems to know how to find the Summer Court, and if she doesn't, I'm too disheartened to take charge at the moment.

It stung to find out that we spent three days in Macha's bottle trap. This isn't like the relaxing lizard vacation; I wasn't trapped back then, just transformed. And I was too young to put myself in Da's shoes, so I had no clue he'd be so frantic. At the moment, I'm scared to the point of feeling queasy, battling terror of being banished to the mortal realm and the slow, awful death that awaits. My biological family is there too, but—

"Are you all right?" Kerboros asks.

Lost in thought, I didn't notice when he dropped back and Zeph sped up to speak to Rosa. "Do I not look that way?"

He studies me critically. "You seem tired. And…" He hesitates. "Unwell?"

"I'm worried. I hope Tara can help us, but I'm not sure about our next move. I hoped Macha would have more specific info, and that idea ended up wasting so much time."

We never managed to find Nerys either. Maybe I should have gone to her instead. Unlike Macha, she's always happy to have visitors.

"My fault," he says softly.

"No, I didn't mean…" I pause. "It doesn't matter."

"What does, then?"

I find myself telling him the truth. First because I don't have anything left to lose, but also because I've come to trust him in the past few days. "I was thinking about my mortal family. In the human lands."

"Do you want to meet them?"

I lift a shoulder, unable to give an answer. "I'd be lying if I said I have no curiosity whatsoever, but I'm afraid it would hurt Da. As if my curiosity would be the same as saying that he isn't enough."

"I do not believe he would see it that way," Kerboros says at once.

I glance at him in surprise. "Why do you say that?"

"You two share an extraordinary bond. The depth of your love is apparent even to someone like me."

"Like you, how?" I want him to clarify, but he doesn't.

Instead, he fixes his gaze on the rolling green hills ahead. The wind lifts his dark-and-silver hair so it streams behind him like a banner. I like the warmth of his skin and the honesty of his eyes, and even the scars he hides beneath the black garb. When he's not scowling, he's—

Beautiful. I'm not afraid to shape the word silently, but it is a step too far to imagine anything between us ending happily. At best, it would be a few stolen moments of pleasure, and I would feel guilty the whole time. I'm promised to someone else. Part of me thinks that pledge holds no weight since I made it under duress, but my obedience is what stands between my dad and dreadful things.

This once, I'll behave and resist temptation. I force myself to focus on his words.

"I regret my clumsiness in Macha's demesne. I suspect you're thinking about the mortal realm because you're worried that you'll be exiled there."

That is unexpectedly perceptive. I clear my throat, unwilling to admit he's right. I have questions about his connection to the swamp witch as well, but this doesn't feel like the proper time for a long discussion. "Before the worst comes to pass, we have a week to find Devan."

"Do you think—"

Before he can complete the question, Rosa calls, "The Summer Palace should be visible over the next rise."

20

The Sun of Summer

The artistry of this piece is rough, compared to the others in the collection. It may be reasonably surmised that this is one of the artist's first works. It is carved into the inside of a wardrobe door, a carefully kept secret. The sun is stylized, large and asymmetrical, with rays arcing out at odd angles, forming intersecting triangles. The knife work is ragged and tentative, lighter scrapes followed by deeper gouges, as if the artist didn't feel sure about the project. There are geometric patterns hidden in the background, like lines on a scrap of parchment. This feels like a love letter, but one that the artist couldn't create in words. The sun remains the central figure, and it is vaguely anthropomorphic in an aspirational way. Some of the rays have been gilded with both wax and paint, but the project remains incomplete, lending it a rustic aspect.

KERBOROS

IN THE DISTANCE, A STATELY castle gleams like pure gold against the verdant hills.

The lines are gentler than the Winter Palace complex, more gentle curves and seductive spires, minarets touched with glittering gems. I have never seen the Summer lands with my own eyes. I breathe deeply, noting the sweetness of the air. There is a balmy quality that differentiates this realm from the Winter lands, distinct from the variance in flora. White and purple flowers dot the emerald carpet here and there, and trees and bushes grow along the game trail. There isn't enough foot traffic for there to be a path, as most of our people travel by portal magic or mushroom rings.

Yet Rosa doesn't hesitate; she arrows toward the castle, and I wonder how she knows we're approaching the right side. There will be gates set aside for each type of guest. Nobles of rank or visiting dignitaries should use the front, but I suspect we qualify for postern doors. None of us possesses proof of status or even a token that proves we're conducting Lord Liskaal's business.

We certainly don't have the authority to be here.

"We shouldn't use our real names," I murmur.

"Why not?" Zeph asks.

A sharpening of Thea's aspect tells me she understands. "Because we're recruiting someone to help us locate the Summer delegation."

"Who went missing in the Winter lands," I finish.

"Oh. Oh dear. Yes, that would be rather awkward and might lead to unfortunate misunderstandings," Zeph says.

"I can only be a pixie," Rosa warns. "Size-changing magic is too taxing to maintain for long, but I can be a *different* pixie."

With that, she expels a glittering cloud of magic, and when the sparkles fade, she is a new person. I should do the same, a glamour that will prevent anyone from identifying me. I have never dared dispatch the image that is eternally focused on Winter's hound, a recognizable enforcer throughout the realm. I concentrate on shifting my features, blurring them, softness here, a gild for my hair.

There.

Zeph has already conjured another look, this one even more fanciful—pink hair, amber eyes, and haunting features; they'll draw attention wherever we go, but any description provided will certainly be wrong. I wonder if we should all risk disguises or if some should wait outside the palace compound in the settlement beyond. Wild fae often live near to the court in their own villages, close enough to work or answer a summons. In Winter, the two have combined, thanks to my cousin's inability to cede control on any trifling matter.

It takes Thea a little longer, and she uses a ritual that is unfamiliar to me. When she's finished, she looks...the same? Perhaps a little more alluring. But then she ties up her hair and makes a few changes with cosmetics as well.

"It will have to do," she says with a faint sigh.

"I doubt Liskaal has people looking for us specifically," Zeph says. "Since he tasked you with this mission, and you're supposed to be reporting back."

"There will be spies." I know this with absolute certainty—because many of his people also report to me. "However, you're correct in one sense. He will be tracking my movements...and Thea's to the best of his ability. I cannot say whether he would predict our attempt to obfuscate our movements."

"And he couldn't have anticipated us recruiting Zeph and Rosa," Thea adds. "We didn't know them before."

Rosa makes a disgusted noise, radiating ire in Zeph's direction. "I hate court business. I hope you appreciate my forbearance."

"Couldn't manage without you," they say in a cheerful tone.

Thea appears pensive, staring toward the small gate. "Splitting up seems like a good idea. Larger groups are more memorable, and we do have an unusual composition."

She is correct. Two high fae, one pixie, and…Thea. Who is unique in these lands. I would add *irreplaceable* if anyone asked.

"If they don't already know Zeph and Rosa are with us, perhaps we shouldn't be seen entering the Summer Court with them." It feels like the wisest course.

I am not suggesting this simply because I prefer having Thea to myself. It is the logical path, offering maximum protection to everyone in our group.

"Suits me," Zeph says. "Rosa, are you with me?"

"Against my better judgment," she grumbles.

Thea stops them as they move toward the postern gate. "Wait. How will we find each other again?"

"No worries, love. I could find you in the dark." Zeph flashes what I presume is meant to be a charming grin, and I clench my jaw.

Their knavish discourtesy deserves a rebuke, and I wish I could deliver it. My hand twitches toward my weapon, and I take a breath. They probably didn't mean for it sound so…suggestive. It may be a reference to Thea's aura, nothing more, but anger still simmers at the bottom of my soul, tinting everything crimson.

I stare at them, narrow-eyed, as Thea laughs. "I suppose that's true.

Which is a sign that it might be tough for me to go unnoticed, but I'll try my best."

"Mm, fascinating." Rosa flutters off with Zeph, following like a young fae chasing a butterfly.

"Let's give them a head start," Thea suggests.

I have no objections. Silently, I open my pack and offer a flask that still has a little water left. Tepid, at this point, but she looks pale. I fight a smile when she accepts it immediately and wonder how it would feel to be close enough to someone, truly close, that they would accept me without question, always believe me, always take my side. I suspect I'll never get nearer to that than this—these precious moments with Thea.

"Tell me about Taragon." It's an abrupt conversational gambit, and inwardly, I wince at how bad I am at this. It sounds like an order, not how I meant it at all, but I don't know *how* to show interest. I can't force myself to say more—to explain my curiosity or to clarify the peremptory statement.

In my childhood, Liskaal killed anyone who showed partiality for my company, and I drove people away rather than see them destroyed for displaying even a whisper of kindness. I'm playing a dangerous game with all the irons I have in the fire, but if all factors align, I will, one day, succeed in securing my release from the Winter Court.

Thea laughs. "Yes, boss. Right away, boss."

I press my lips together briefly, feeling so absurd, it stings. "Please?"

"Better! Don't worry, you'll figure out this talking-to-people thing. I can be your training partner."

Partner. A stunning pang—it feels like I've been punched in the chest. Even if she's joking, I hate how much I relish that word.

It requires all my aplomb to speak in a repressive tone. "If you insist."

"I'll stop teasing you. Taragon… Let's see. We met when she was fostering in the Winter Court. Her family owns a tavern in the market, on the mercantile side of the palatial plaza. She stayed with me and Da for a few years, and we got close. At one point, we were like sisters. We tried to stay in touch, but correspondence can be irregular between the courts, and arranging visits in the wildlands is a challenge too. For different reasons."

I nod. Communication between the courts can occur through scrying surfaces, like crystals, pools, or mirrors, or messages that arrive in the form of written letters, carried sporadically by whoever happens to be traveling. Both options carry a risk of tampering or interception, so it's often better to visit personally whenever possible. But Thea lacks an innate facility with portals, and the mushroom circles can be slow since mushrooms sometimes choose not to cooperate. In addition, Liskaal controls her almost as tightly as he does me, albeit for dissimilar reasons.

"So you haven't seen her in a while?"

"Unfortunately not. But she'll be an asset to the team. If you think Da is likable, you'll be amazed at how sweet Tara is. She could make a pixie purr."

"High praise indeed."

"I think it's probably been long enough," Thea says then.

I glance at the gates. No sign of Zeph or Rosa, so I agree. "Let's find your friend. It should be a memorable reunion."

Eyes wide, she lowers her head with a soft groan. "I really, really wish you wouldn't say stuff like that."

21

A Spell for Friends and Fraternization

Sometimes, my gem, through no fault of our own, we lose track of our friends. Time or distance has their way with us, and we fall out of touch. I'm guilty of this myself, and I have a few old companions I'd love to see once more, but our paths haven't crossed in longer than I care to recall. At such times, we can take matters into our own hands, make it more likely that old friends will be drawn in our direction, and we can enjoy a sweet reunion, catch up on recent exploits, and swear never to let the connection lapse again.

With this particular charm, you must truly want it, however. An idle fancy or simple curiosity won't carry your wishes on the wind. This spell will be carried only to a true heart's match, someone near and dear who would greatly move you to behold them again. Your will makes all the difference, spiced by the warm regards of long-held fondness. I have no doubt that if you went wandering, I could use this working to bring you back to me, as I have never known anyone I miss more than you, darling girl.

This charm is best done in full daylight with no hidden intentions. You'll need:

- *A round piece of yellow moonstone*
- *Peppermint, yarrow, and one pink rose petal*
- *The spark of your friendship*
- *Your cupped palm*

This spell is simpler than most. Your bond and your intentions will do most of the work. In your cupped palm, place the moonstone, the peppermint, yarrow, and rose petal. For you, my jewel, this may be the difficult part, but focus as much as you can. The spark of your friendship should burn bright enough to consume the herbal components, but not heat the moonstone enough to burn you. You should have a warm stone and ashes in your hand, if the spell succeeds. Blow the ashes to the wind as you think of the friend you wish to see again. Then tuck the warmed moonstone against your heart. You should have a neck pouch among your bits and bobs that will allow you to carry it so. If you loosed enough of your affection, you should receive a sign that your friend is thinking of you before the moonstone cools.

Do you remember when you first met Tara? She was brand-new to Winter, and one of the court ladies was bullying you, demanding that you fetch and carry for her ride. Tara arrived with all her boxes, and that sly minx cast some mischief when she saw what was happening. That court lady tumbled headfirst into a horse plop, and my, how she screamed. You two were fast friends after that.

THEA

"WHY NOT?" KERBOROS ASKS.

To some degree, I understand his confusion. He's likely not the superstitious type; he doesn't believe anything particularly bad comes from challenging the universe. But I *am* that sort of person, always wary of grim omens and ill-starred signs. Maybe it comes from watching people's faces, ever alert to a shifting mood that could threaten my existence. I can't remember when I realized that I don't belong here—I'm an interloper uprooted through the vagaries of fate—but it's been a factor for as long as I recall.

I wave a hand, not wanting to get into it. "Never mind. It would take too long to explain."

Making a concerted effort to shift my mood, I decide to be enchanted instead of anxious. I've never visited the Summer Court before. I gaze around in wonder. The marketplace smells of warm sugar and hints of fruit, probably from the stall a few steps away that has slices of peach drizzled with honey. They also sell various dried fruits, neatly labeled in decorative handwriting, in glittering jars, each a different hue. Though I was born in the mortal world—and promptly stolen from it—I don't know how things look there. Somehow, I doubt common objects are as pretty as they are here.

Kerboros doesn't seem as delighted as I am; his face is inscrutable. The plaza is noisy, merchants calling out to passersby, speaking silly rhymes to attract attention to their wares. Most of the custom appears to be from provisioners who work at the palace. Now and then, I spot folks who must be visiting from the wildlands, but I try not to draw attention to myself. It will ruin everything if I'm recognized.

Da once told me there's a famous mortal poem about a goblin

market. I got curious, and he traded one of his precious treasures to get me a little book of verses. I read it and found it prettily written but a bit long and entirely silly. As if goblins have nothing better to do, and most I've known aren't interested in fruit at *all*, let alone using it to trick twitterpated maidens.

No, this particular market is full of all types of fair folk. There's a stall selling pear and honey wines, another selling whimsical spun sugar shapes, creatures and flowers, that melt on your tongue in a burst of sweetness. I spot another vending hair ribbons that glitter in the light and another stall draped with silk spun from cobwebs. There are charmed objects too—a mirror that lets you glimpse your true love and a chalice that turns water to wine—and I'd *love* to spend hours browsing, but we don't have the time.

My stomach lurches, reminding me that I'm not allowed to be here. Lord Liskaal would view this visit as treason, so I can't get caught in the Summer lands. Neither can Kerboros. I don't know if Liskaal's spies managed to keep pace with us, and the uncertainty makes my stomach hurt. Why in the realms did Kerboros's magic deposit us here? It's like the universe wants us to fail.

When the anxiety pangs fade, I discover that I'm hungry. Again. But I can't tell if it's for food or life force.

"We should stop dallying and get to work," Kerboros says.

"Right." I sigh. I wish we could look around; it's my first time at the Summer market, but there's so much to lose. I made a kind choice before instead of a prudent one, opting to comfort him when he got trapped in the bottle. So it's sensible to forgo amusement now. Everything has a price.

He gives me a searching look, and then his features relax into a half smile. "But there's no reason we can't combine investigation with exploration."

Kindness from Kerboros? I feel like I've won a major victory without raising a sword, and I yield to my urge to celebrate, doing a happy little dance that makes him chuckle. I imagine reaching for his hand, lacing our fingers together, and enjoying the warmth of the day, with no other worries. Just the two of us.

My heart aches over how much I want these stolen moments with him. I can't believe he's the one who suggested we combine business with pleasure. If I let myself, I could get lost in him—in those deep eyes, a shade of gray that can gleam like silver or look dark as a storm cloud, depending on his mood. His whole face captivates me, its sharp lines softened by his current expression.

I clear my throat. "I'd like that."

"You're staring," he murmurs.

I shouldn't flirt. But then, I do lots of things I'm not supposed to. "Do you blame me? I have the most intriguing man in the Winter court all to myself."

Kerboros pretends to look around. "You do? Where?"

Laughing, I nudge him lightly. "Don't pretend. Not with me."

He sobers, studying me with a steady regard. "I won't."

Suddenly, I recall how he held out a hand, waiting for me to decide whether I trusted him. Now I do the same. Kerboros doesn't hesitate. His fingers twine with mine, and the warmth gives me a delicious tingle. *I want those hands everywhere.* Now there's no hiding my smile as we walk deeper into the market, a trifle aimless, bound together in this moment because we've chosen to be.

We'll ask about Tara as we shop; I'm excited to see her because it's been a long time, but as soon as she joins the group, it will change the dynamic. Right now, I don't know Zeph and Rosa well, and I'd be lying if I said I'm not deeply attracted to Kerboros. There's something between us, a spark that could build into a blazing fire in a better time and place.

But Tara knew me when I was little, and she has some embarrassing stories to tell. Spirits save me, if she shares any of those tales… Well. I don't want Kerboros to think badly of me.

No time for fretting. Better to accept this moment for what it is, precious and stolen.

I try to decide who might be the best source of information, but the market is so pretty that it's tough to concentrate. Even the vendor stalls have an artistic bent; they're not just hammered together from fallen wood. Colors limn the sides with silken streamers affixed to the tops, and artful patterns are etched into the lower frames.

This is a bustling, wondrous place. Observing the denizens of Summer as they pass, I notice they seem happier too, calling out to one another without timidity or hesitation. There's a boldness in their stride as well. Even the pixies are smiling, which, if you know anything about pixies, is a big deal. Despite her occasional brusqueness, Rosa is one of the *nicer* ones I've met. Da's friend Shereth is an outlier, sweet as spun sugar.

Kerboros quickens his step, tugging on my hand, and I match his pace. He's heading toward a stand that I never would have predicted. They're selling sticky buns shaped like nautilus shells. Da always called them *sea cakes*, and I haven't had them in such a long time. Kerboros buys two and turns to offer me one.

"I noticed that you have a sweet tooth," he says gruffly.

He…noticed? I swallow the urge to ask, *Since when?*

"That's so kind." I take the cake right away. Even though we *did* have lunch, we didn't have dessert, so I eat the treat in two bites. So delicious, light and fluffy like a cloud, delicate sweetness with a hint of fruit and flowers—and it dissolves on my tongue in a burst of honeyed goodness. "This is wonderful," I add, fighting the urge to hug him.

I wonder what he would do if I did. The idea makes me chuckle, and he gives me a narrow-eyed look, as if he might be the butt of a joke. I suspect he's used to that.

I don't think he'll ask, but…he does, taking a careful bite of the cake. "Will you share what you find so amusing?"

"It's more that I'm happy," I reply, which isn't a lie. It's not the entire truth, and I decide to share the rest. "I'm happy, and I want to hug you. But I thought you'd be appalled—"

"You may," he cuts in.

"What?"

"Hug me."

I stare at him, stunned, but I don't hesitate for more than a moment. I rush at him and wrap my arms about his middle, as he's rather tall, and I mean for it to be a joyous, playful moment, but from the instant his arms come around me in turn, there's a rush of heat, a conflagration of sparks, all over my nerve endings. He has no right to smell this delicious after days on the road, like woodsmoke and dried herbs. His hand moves idly on my back, dragging up and down, and I squeeze my eyes shut in response to the stunning tingles that follow each sweeping caress.

I feel a little dizzy when he lets go of me. "Wow," I mumble.

"I should buy you cakes more often." Kerboros is smiling slightly, a feline expression of contentment visible right around his eyes.

I never would have guessed him capable of such a look. "No objections on my end."

"That was an enjoyable break," he observes. "But we should focus."

"You have a point."

As I spin in a slow circle, I try to recall everything Tara told me. Her family runs a tavern nearby, but I can't remember the name. When we were kids, we didn't talk about *work*. Instead, we caused as much chaos as we could—pretty much what I'm known for.

I decide to start the research at a nearby booth where they sell handmade silken shawls, gorgeous artisanal work with fringe and lace. The hobgoblin sings out a poetic patter about his work: "All the colors of the rainbow! Coquelicot, carmine, cobalt, celadon, citrine! Come and see, purchase and preen!"

"I've got this," I say to Kerboros.

He releases my hand with apparent reluctance. "I await your success."

My hand is warm from his touch, and it takes genuine effort to walk away. "I was wondering if I could ask a question," I say to the shawl seller.

"Of course!" he replies. "What do you like? I made everything you see on display with these two hands." He wiggles his short fingers for emphasis.

"Your work is beautiful, but the question is unrelated."

He sighs, losing some of his enthusiasm. "Fine. I'm listening."

"Do you know a hobgoblin named Tara? Her full name is Taragon."

The merchant frowns, heavy brows pulling together. "Do you think all hobgoblins know each other or something?"

Yikes. I don't think I can come back from this.

"Sorry," I mumble.

Then I skedaddle, deciding I need a new vector of approach as I return to Kerboros. He smirks as I close the distance between us.

"That seemed to go well," he observes.

"Not my best effort," I admit. "I was abrupt. Do you have a better idea?"

"I suspect we shouldn't ask any *other* hobgoblins," he tells me.

"I deserve that." I laugh because I don't mind him teasing me about my lack of finesse. At least, I *think* he's teasing.

We move deeper into the market, and this time, Kerboros chooses our contact. He approaches a boggart selling carved stones. Kerboros takes a moment to examine all the wares, and I'm close enough to catch the conversation.

Kerboros says, "Your work is exceptionally skilled."

"I'm delighted to hear it!" The artisan seems thrilled with the compliment.

They discuss patterns, methods, acid washing, and a bunch of stuff that I don't follow about working with stone. It's clear Kerboros knows a lot about stone carving, and I'm fascinated by this revelation about him. As I'm about to tune out, Kerboros makes a purchase from the stall.

He tucks the stone in his pack, and then he says, "By the way, do you happen to know a hobgoblin named Tara?"

"Do you mean Taragon?"

"Yes, that's her name."

"I've seen her around the market, buying supplies now and then."

I step closer, unable to resist chiming in. "I think she works at a tavern, but I can't remember the name."

"There's loads of taverns around," the boggart says, not unkindly. "You know who you should talk to?"

I shake my head.

"The herbalist, just around the corner. Tempest knows everyone. And come to think of it, I believe I've seen them together before. At any rate, if anyone can point you in the right direction, it'll be them."

"Understood," Kerboros says.

We step away from the stall as the vendor greets a potential customer. It feels like we're on the verge of a breakthrough. Once we find Tara, our group will be complete. Tara can talk *anyone* into anything. That's another reason why I want to find her, not simply because we're close, both emotionally (in the past) and geographically (right now). I hope she can help me talk my spouse into giving this relationship a try.

Or maybe… This idea taps at the edges of my brain, as if looking for a weakness. Maybe she can think of a way out of this mess. Two heads are better than one, and she's clever as well as kind. Either way, with the deadline galloping at us like a wild pooka, it's do-or-die time.

I don't want to be with Devan J. Fenelon; my heart has other inclinations entirely. I steal a look at Kerboros and wish I was still holding his hand. That peek catches him in the midst of returning a fallen rag doll to a young brownie, who scampers off with a delighted giggle, dragging the doll in the dust behind her. *This* is the enforcer others call Winter's hound. To me, he's someone else. Someone who's kind to children, who buys me cake and lets me hug him. My cheeks heat, and I poke at them.

"Have you been stung?" Kerboros is very close, his face near to mine.

My breath hitches. "No."

As I debate whether to confide how adorable he's acting, a hobgoblin shouts, "Out of the way, coming through, hot bread for sale, hot bread! Get your hot bread!"

He's pushing a trolley laden with loaves, and Kerboros reacts so quickly, it makes my head spin. In one motion, I'm in his arms, twirling with him out of the main flow of traffic. My pulse was stuttering before, and now it's racing. I gaze up at him, staring at his lips.

And the look on his face—nobody has ever hungered for me like that. He dips his head. I lift my chin.

We're jostled by a passerby, and my forehead smacks into his shoulder. At least they didn't ruin a kiss.

My voice is husky when I say, "Let's go find Tempest."

22

Wild at Heart

One might be forgiven for missing this piece entirely, as it's carved into the bed, a little secret the artist keeps close to his chest. This maiden has been carved into each leg, the only artwork replicated within the space. But this woman is shown four times, each a different pose, a different scene. The common factor is the woman's expression, unfettered and joyous. The first depicts her in a wild wood, surrounded by adoring wild creatures. Another shows her astride a pooka. The third finds her trailing a hand in a wildly rushing river. And the final scene provides a glimpse of her perched high in the boughs of a tree, holding a round and perfect apple. The beholder might wonder whether she is the embodiment of freedom or temptation. Possibly, the artist perceives her as both.

KERBOROS

THAT MOMENT WITH THEA LEAVES me giddy.

We almost kissed. It wasn't just me; she felt it too. I don't know what I've done to deserve this, but I could shout from the joy of it. Somehow I contain myself and consult a random brownie for directions. She tells me to head for the outer edge of the market, toward the archway that leads into the palace. Thea follows, close enough that I feel her warmth at my back.

The stall is large compared to the others, twice as wide, with a table displaying tinctures and salves in front and shelves behind arranged with potions. Purple silk banners drift in the breeze, matching the cloth that covers the tabletop.

Thea seems interested in their wares, and I wish I could indulge her further. Left to my own devices, I'd give her the world. Through my incompetence, we've wasted so much time. Guilt chews at me.

Tempest greets us with a smile. They have long white hair caught back in a braid and twinkling lavender eyes. As with many fae, their face is smooth, no lines to determine their age. Not high fae, I think, but I don't recognize their features. Something about the angle of their cheekbones and the width of their shoulders whispers of a different lineage, not one I've encountered before either.

I glance at Thea to see if she wants to do the talking. She is known for being social, popular among the wild fae. She shakes her head silently, and I suspect it's because the misstep with the shawl vendor has rumbled her confidence. Based on my observations, she can't be accustomed to failure.

I step closer to the stall, willing to try for her. "We're told that you might know Taragon." The statement sounds abrupt, even to my own ears.

Tempest cocks their head. "Told by whom?"

"I didn't catch his name—the stone carver on the other side of the market."

"Ah yes, you're referring to Fenstig. I understand that you need information, but I also have a business to run. So let's talk about potions before, shall we?"

"I'm in the market for a potion," Thea says immediately. "What do you have?"

She's bright-eyed and eager, peering at the jewel-hued bottles. I can see that the conversation won't progress unless I let her peruse Tempest's wares. Not that I've got the right to *let* her do anything. Thea can do whatever she wants; she's proven that time and again.

Thea bounces a bit as Tempest points to a particular set of potions. "I have one for buoyancy, one to turn you green—"

"Why would I want to be green?" Thea asks.

"You might be surprised by how many people are interested in that one," Tempest replies. "But be warned, it's not easy being green."

Before she can get drawn into a lengthy discussion, I indicate a potion at random. "We'll take that one." Tempest wraps it up, and I pay for the purchase and then tuck it away in my pack.

"Don't you even want to know what it does?" they ask.

I shake my head. "Not really. The situation is urgent, and I need an answer."

"Right, yes, the referral. What was the question again?"

I do wonder if Tempest is fully in command of their faculties; they seem so easily distracted. But rudeness means starting over at a new stall, and I cannot use my cousin's name to enforce compliance, something I have become too adroit with over long years.

As I restrain my impatience with the scatterbrained potion seller, Thea chimes in with congenial charm. "We're looking for my friend

Taragon. I always called her *Tara*. Her family owns a tavern in the area, but—"

"Tara. Oh." For a second, a shadow clouds their sharp features, but then they force a smile. "You're in luck. I know her well. Her father too, what a good soul. A good, kind soul." They repeat the words with a strange note, not quite sorrow, but...bitterness, perhaps?

I might be wrong. The details I notice about others tend not to be emotional in nature. When I glance at Thea, I see a flicker, and she tilts her head, raising a brow, which I take to mean she noticed something odd about Tempest's tone too. But we're not here to investigate the potion maker's failed relationships.

"Could you provide some directions?" I prompt.

"Certainly." Tempest turns and gestures toward the other side of the market. "Keep walking that way, straight along, then turn left when you see the statue of the rearing pooka. Go past it and duck between two tilted buildings. A green ivy bower connects the two, quite a picturesque archway. Pass through that courtyard—and don't worry if someone yells at you. That's Ragh, and he's kind of a curmudgeon."

"How come?" Thea asks.

"There's a sad story, a lost love or a heartbreak of some sort. I've forgotten the particulars. He used to be the jolliest of sorts, but now he just shouts at passersby." Tempest makes a tsk-ing sound.

"I suspect our journey doesn't end in a courtyard," I say, hoping I don't sound as annoyed as I feel. It's my fault we're behind schedule in the first place, and everything feels like it takes twice as long when I have to be polite.

"Indeed not. Keep walking until you come to the other side. That's the back end of Toad in the Hole. That's the place for you to start. If Tara isn't in, they'll know where she is."

Finally.

"You've been an amazing help." Thea smiles at Tempest, leaving me mildly dazzled by the bright beauty of her expression.

When she bounces off, I do my best to keep up.

She follows the directions and indeed a sharp voice does scold us roundly when we cut through the courtyard. But Thea ignores Tempest's instruction to disregard the chastisement. "Do you object to us using the shortcut because we're tracking dirt? I can sweep if you like."

A round creased face appears in the upper window, and then the brownie pops out onto the sloping roof, creeping toward us with a suspicious stare. He is small, even for a brownie, clad entirely in gray from head to toe. His eyes are narrowed, focused on Thea with a puzzlement bordering on outrage.

"Are you calling my courtyard dirty?" he demands.

"Not at all. I was just hoping to make you feel better about our passage."

"That's absurd," Ragh says. "Nobody cares about my opinion. Haven't for ages."

"Well, they should."

"Why?" he asks.

"Because everyone matters," Thea replies.

The conviction in her voice pierces me like an arrow. I suddenly don't care that we have little time to waste. She's correct. I don't know Ragh, but now this moment is critical to me as well. We should do what we can to make him feel less hostile.

"If you wanted me to feel better, you wouldn't offer to do chores. You'd provide a tangible token of apology."

Since I recently bought something that might suffice, I produce the glimmering rose quartz, so pretty and delicate, carved into an actual rose. Fenstig has a talent that outshines my own, and I planned to study this piece at my leisure. Then, if I felt brave enough, eventually, I might have given it to Thea as a gift. But it can serve a higher purpose now, comforting a brownie who feels overlooked by the entire world.

"Would you like this?" I ask. "As a tribute of respect."

Ragh scampers to the edge of the roof and peers down at the artist's work in my hand. To my surprise, he presses a hand to his lips, eyes going wide and soft. "It looks like the last flower I had from Govannon. Before he went away to Autumn."

"Then this was meant for you," Thea says softly.

A sudden pang startles me; this isn't like me, not at all. I surprise myself by asking for more information. "Who is Govannon? And what happened to him?"

"The love of my life. And I wish I knew. The uncertainty eats at me. He went to the Autumn lands to work, and he was supposed to send word when he had a place for us. But it's been so long, and naught but silence."

"Have you tried searching for him? By magic or otherwise?" Thea seems interested too, as we now have something in common with Ragh.

"I did. Nothing came of it. I can only conclude he doesn't want to be found," the brownie says in a sorrowful tone. "I wish he'd told me that he wanted *us* to end. I loved him enough to let him go for his sake. And for his happiness."

"Take this as a memento of happier times," I say then. I lift my arm, and with a burst of magic, I lend enough animus to the stone rose so that it pops from my palm to Ragh's in a smooth motion.

The brownie holds fast to the gift, clutching it to his chest. "You don't know what this means to me. I feel...tranquil? I'd nearly forgotten the word, let alone the sensation. Go in peace and with my blessings."

If Thea nibbled at his anger, there might be tangible reasons for his improved mood. But it's better that he ascribes it to the conversation and the gift. We cannot be discovered here. If we're caught, they will execute me. But I care less about my own fate than what becomes of Thea.

She waves, unaware of my bleak thoughts, and continues toward the tavern with the brightness of her being burnished to an incredible sheen. When I view her aura, she's shining silver from head to toe, so good that it hurts me to gaze upon her. I shift my attention to the back of the tavern.

Toad in the Hole is gray stone, braced with pale wood, whitewashed first, pastel hues painted on top. Such gradient colors lend an enchanting effect, more like fish scales, or perhaps it's meant to suggest an amphibian resemblance. There are window boxes with flowers tumbling from them, trailing vines creeping to the eaves. From within, I hear the sound of voices rising and falling in conversation.

The back door stands open, and she enters without hesitation. It never seems to occur to her to wonder whether she *should* do something. On my own, I would verify if this is a kitchen entrance, meant for staff. I follow, feeling as though I've adopted the role of guardian, destined to fail at keeping Thea out of trouble. We emerge in a kitchen with a huge scarred table, a variety of knives, and ingredients scattered about. It smells of hops from the brewing beer and yeast, likely from the freshly baked bread cooling on the counter nearby. If I'm not mistaken, I also detect mushroom stew, and I would love to try both.

Perhaps not right now.

Two surprised brownies turn to face us, one wearing a stained apron. The other holds a tray of drinks.

"You're not supposed to be in here!" the apron-wearing one scolds.

Thea grins. "Then we'll go out there."

She breezes by before the encounter can escalate. Past the rosy heat of the kitchen, the inside of Toad in the Hole is dark and cool. In the common room, tables and chairs, stools and stumps are arranged haphazardly all around the space, furniture suitable to accommodate guests in all shapes and forms.

The bar is an enormous tree, carved to suit the shape of the space. An artisan used magic to preserve the surface, enhancing it to a glorious sheen that highlights the pattern of the grain. Based on the char marring the sides, I suspect it suffered a mishap in a sudden storm. We try not to kill trees, but sometimes they expire, and we make use of the remains. Some find fae woodwork grisly; others won't even work in stone for similar reasons, though true stone spirits are few and far between. And those that do remain are ancient, rarely stirring from their deep and ageless dreams.

A young hobgoblin with dark-green skin, light-brown hair, and radiant yellow eyes breaks into the widest smile imaginable when she spots Thea. "Is it really you?"

Thea yelps as they slam together in a vigorous embrace, but she holds on, beaming. "It is! I finally found you."

"Didn't even know you were searching," the hobgoblin I presume is Taragon says. "Let me look at you." She pauses. "I'd love to say you're better than ever, but really, you could use a good washing up. Whatever have you been doing?"

"It's a long story," Thea tells her.

Taragon smiles, showing all her teeth. "An interesting one, I hope."

"Definitely that." She turns to me with a gesture. "This is Kerboros. He…" She hesitates, seeming unsure what to say.

I take solace in the fact that she's not introducing me as Winter's hound. "I am tasked with helping Thea," I say simply.

"Taragon Toadpearl." The hobgoblin greets me politely, adding, "It's a pleasure."

"I'm hoping to interest you in the quest as well. It's juicy," Thea adds.

"You have my attention. I gather you foresee needing my silver tongue?"

"That's part of it," Thea allows. "I do imagine we'll need your talents before the journey is through. Are you in or are you in?"

Taragon laughs. "Have you forgotten that I was raised in a public house? Even from you, I would never accept the first offer. But let me get you both a drink while we talk. Negotiation is thirsty work."

"Negotiation or reminiscence?" Thea asks with a smile.

A rather cunning look crosses Taragon's face. "Can't it be both?"

"It can! Of course it can." Thea's shoulders lower, tension releasing at Tara's answer.

It seems that she might not have been certain that Taragon would be delighted about their reunion. Since they were childhood friends, she might feel awkward about showing up suddenly and asking for a favor. I've become rather experienced at gauging her moods, and right now, I believe she's smiling with relief.

Thea adds, "Then I *could* use a drink. Do you have any cider?"

"Coming right up." Taragon turns to me. "And what would you like?"

People rarely ask me this. "Honey wine, white blossom if you have it."

"We certainly do," Taragon replies. "Settle yourselves over there. I'll join you in a jiffy." She indicates a table at the back of the tavern.

23

A Spell for Concessions and Compromises

Betimes you'll need people willing to hear what you have to say, mayhap with a favorable bent. Now, I would never use this handy charm to swindle someone, but the details, my gem—the details! You can gain a great deal of ground with a word, a nod, a smile or a wink, or a promise to find common ground.

Don't make the same mistake I did. Once, I tried. And once, I failed. I used this one to try and make someone stay. It didn't work. Of course it didn't. Because that wasn't a compromise that could be made. I just didn't know it at the time. But if you choose wiser than I did, you'll find it most helpful indeed. I've kept it simple so you can do it swiftly—without attracting undue attention.

This one is best cast in the shadows, done quick and quiet. You'll need:

- *A pinch of cinnamon for your drink*
- *A spark of magic to charge your charm*
- *The breath of your whispered wish*
- *A heartfelt toast shared between all involved parties*

For this working, the dash of cinnamon can be added to anything you're drinking, though it will seem most natural in beverages enhanced by such a spice. The spark can be a pretext of warming your drink, and then you propose the toast. Best to keep it simple. Soft with the magic, delicate as air. The warm feelings will come, as you drink and converse and find a compromise that tilts toward you. Be prepared to face aggression if someone feels you've influenced the outcome unfairly or tampered with their free will. This is the toast I use:

"May your troubles be less
And your blessings be more.
And nothing but happiness
Come through your door."

It's the toast I use at most gatherings, so people don't bat an eyelash when they hear it. I'll never forget the time we had guests at Miremorel. Food and wine for us to make merry, and you were supposed to be sound asleep by then. As I raised my glass, you scrambled onto the table and took the words right out of my mouth. You're always full of surprises, my gem.

THEA

BRIEFLY, I THINK ABOUT SPICING my drink with cinnamon, but Tara has paged through the grimoire Da wrote for me.

She might realize what I'm doing, and if she agrees to help, it should be her decision, not even slightly influenced by my erratic magic. As we settle at the table she indicated, I contemplate Ragh. He was so hurt and angry that my hunger slipped its usual leash and I fed from him without meaning to, without needing to touch him. The hot prickle of shame digs into the nape of my neck like tiny claws.

Normally, I control myself better.

But I'm always starving, a bottomless pit that can't be filled. I'm wrongly made, awful and misshapen, and I should have asked permission. It might not go well for me if anyone realized. The fae are prickly, and I never forget for an instant that I wasn't born here. That they could banish me on a whim for any reason or none at all. It feels like the threat's always existed, silent and unspoken, but now it's been read out in a guaranteed promise of doom. I must be careful at all times. Not too needy. Not too hungry. Not demanding more than anyone can give when what I really want is an emotional feast, for someone to throw wide their heart and invite me eagerly to devour *everything*.

Kerboros chooses to sit beside me, and in my peripheral vision, I see him studying me with an intensity that makes it difficult for me to turn my head. Instead I watch Tara deftly filling our mugs at the bar. He clears his throat, and I still don't look. *Intentionally* not looking. Somehow I've become awkward and tongue-tied around him.

After what nearly happened in the market, I'd rather straddle his lap and nibble his neck. I want to find out if his stern mouth turns to silken heat under mine. I want—

Oh, stop torturing yourself. There's Tara.

She bounds toward us with a graceful stride that doesn't even rattle the glasses. The other fae speak unkindly of hobgoblin allure, but Tara is lovely, just as Da is the definition of dapper. Today, she wears a splendid skirt that bells about her generous hips, bright as a sunbeam in yellow, and the white blouse she's tucked into it shows the pretty curve of her shoulders. Even her apron is cute, deep green striped with pale gray.

"Here we are. I'm so happy to see you! How long has it been?" she asks.

I shake my head as I divvy up the drinks. "I don't remember. It feels like forever."

"So," she says, plonking onto the opposite bench, "tell me everything."

Kerboros stays quiet, so I do the talking, giving her an abridged version of our current situation. Her eyes widen as the story unfolds. I finish with "And that's where we are."

She shakes her head. "Those pookas would have been fine. Aggravated but fine. I love you, but you're *so* impulsive."

That wasn't what I wanted to hear.

But before I can speak, Kerboros does. "In Thea's defense, the Winter Court would have proceeded to barter her to the Summer Court even without that complication."

I turn to him, pleased and stunned in equal measure. "You don't think I instigated this entire situation? Really?"

"Of course not," he practically snarls. "They're using you. As they use everyone."

Tara waves a hand, taking a sip of her drink. "Details. I'm used to dealing with the consequences of Thea's actions."

"Wait, are you—"

"*Our* actions, ordinarily," Tara clarifies. "I was always in it up to my neck, and I never learned to back down when we dared each other either."

"As I recall, it was your idea to hide all the royal sheets in the stable loft," I remind her, exercising all my inner fortitude to restrain a chuckle.

Kerboros stares. "That was the two of you?"

"No sheets were harmed, and the brownies magicked them clean," Tara says swiftly.

I take a sip of the cider. It's cool and refreshing, just the right tang from fermentation, and I roll my shoulders. Now that we've found Tara, things should improve. People find her ebullience irresistible, and while some think I have a way with people, Tara outclasses me.

"I hope you will consider the request. Thea needs you." Kerboros maintains a severe mien, even as he advocates for me.

When he first tracked me down with the pookas, I could never have imagined *this*. Whatever's blooming between us. This yearning is far more potent than the cider I'm sipping, sweet and lush and exquisitely forbidden.

"Before I agree, I need to know something." Tara turns to me with a somber look, eyes locking onto mine. "And I'll know if you're bamboozling me."

"Go ahead." Suddenly, I'm nervous without knowing why.

"Do you want this marriage? I mean truly."

How can the answer be yes?

I've never met Devan J. Fenelon, who apparently loathes me so much that running away seemed like the best option. It stings, remembering how Lady Valnevi said so in the great hall. While Lord Winter obsesses about conspiracies—some deep and intricate Summer plot to incite a war between factions—I fear I know the truth. The stories have preceded me, and rather than insult Lord Liskaal, Devan has elected to flee. Given the option between life forever in flight and me, my prospective spouse chose to become a fugitive. My pride would be battered to bits if I let it sink in.

I glance around to make sure nobody is paying us any particular attention. Then I shake my head. "What I want is to escape. You weren't wrong when you said you're an expert at getting me out of trouble. Lord Liskaal wants to embed me in the Summer Court, and I can't find a way out of this. Kerboros was correct when he said I need you."

Tears fill my eyes, but before the first can fall, Tara moves around the table to wrap a warm arm around my shoulders. "You can't cry. I haven't even started the negotiations. If you start bawling, I'll feel too guilty to demand the right to name your firstborn."

"Is that what you want?" Kerboros asks, seeming shocked.

I emit a shaky laugh, wiping my eyes, and make a counteroffer: "Second born, and the child has the right to review the name *and* approve it when they come of age. I haven't forgotten that you named our stable cat Yardlad."

Tara laughs. "It was so funny when tongues got twisted and they'd call him *Lardyad.*"

"I had an uncle named Lardyad. Venerable soul," Kerboros says in a stricken tone. "Show some respect."

I blink. "Really?"

His face doesn't change. Still, that impenetrable stare. Then: "No." And his mouth, ever so slightly, curls up on the ends.

A joke? A smile? What in the world is happening here?

Tara chuckles. She doesn't seem to realize how momentous this is. "Though it goes against my better judgment, I'll accept your terms."

I burst into tears then. Kerboros leaps to his feet as Tara enfolds me in her arms. She thumps my back gently, and my head droops to her shoulder. Her familiar scent comforts me as few things could; maybe only a hug from Da would feel more like home.

"What did you do to Thea?" a sharp voice asks.

Blearily, I peer over her shoulder and find a strange pixie hovering nearby. One beat, then two, and I realize this is Rosa, though she's changed her appearance again, different still from when we parted. Zeph is with her, still wearing the disguise they chose earlier.

"Friends of yours?" Tara asks.

I point. "Zeph. Rosa. I mentioned them before."

"Then the first round is on me. You'll have to pay for room and board tonight, and I won't be able to join you. My father won't be delighted that I'm haring off on adventures again just as he thought me committed to settling down."

"Oh no." I sit back, frowning. "Do you want me to come with you? Explain things."

"No offense, but it will be better if you're not involved in this conversation."

Chagrined, I hunch my shoulders, aware that Tara's rather staid father considers me a bad influence. "I understand."

"I'll cover our meals and lodgings," Kerboros offers.

Rosa scoffs in a loud pixie undertone. "You mean Lord Winter will."

"That's generous," Zeph cuts in. "Shall we take our food and drinks with us and enjoy a break before traveling on tomorrow?"

I stand, enticed by the prospect of a hot bath, a delicious meal, and clean, soft sheets—in precisely that order. "That sounds heavenly."

24

The Blue and the Burn

This piece started as part of a shipwreck, rescued on one of the artist's journeys. The wood is gray and weathered, exposed to elements and salted for good measure by a restless sea. It seems to have arrived from the mortal realm, doubtless driven through one of the swirling sea portals that siphon materials from human enclaves. Two forms have been carved, and the lines have been painstakingly burned dark, offering a charred yet strangely beautiful effect. The figures are vague and small, though it is uncertain whether they are meant to be young or instead depict sprites or pixies instead of larger beings. They touch only at the hands, arms arcing away from each other, and it lends an air of melancholy to an otherwise simple scene. Blue pigment has been washed over the wood, though not the pyrographic designs. Those lines remain black and stark, two small figures holding hands. For now. For as long as they're allowed to.

KERBOROS

ON THE OTHER SIDE OF the kitchen, the Toad in the Hole boasts a bathhouse.

The space is simple and clean, nothing unnecessary. Stones have been smoothed together so seamlessly that it feels like a cave, skilled magic in the making of this place. For once unconcerned with such craft, I sink into the warm pool with a raw sound I would never make if I wasn't alone. A charm would have sufficed to remove dirt and tidy my person, but it doesn't offer solace for sore bodies. Hunting can be exhausting work.

Traveling with Thea? Well, that is pure temptation, and holding back has my body in a tight coil. I untie my hair and dunk my head in the water, holding my breath to force away more prurient thoughts. These days, it's so difficult to restrain myself and not reveal how heated my regard has become.

Earlier today, I wanted to kiss her so fiercely that my toes curled in my boots. I still want to. Just…want. Endless oceans of it.

I remind myself that she's spoken for. *Promised to someone without her permission*, a quiet voice reminds me. She told her friend she wants out of that relationship. Not that she wants to build a life with Fenelon. But even if she longs for me as much as I crave her touch, my cousin would never permit me such joy.

I burst from the water to find Thea slipping into it. It has been longer than I care to recall since I shared a communal bath. I have enough social grace not to gawk in response to her arrival, but every fiber of my being vibrates now that she's here. Her hand flies to her mouth, and her eyes widen. She must not have seen me beneath the bubbling water.

"I was here first," I say, hoping she's not about to object to my presence.

"I'm surprised, not complaining," she shoots back.

She settles on the opposite side of the stone bath, which is large enough to hold two or three additional patrons. More if they're sprites or pixies, less if they're gruagachs. Her skin is gently flushed from the heat, her brown hair damp and wispy around her pink cheeks, which are a little hollower than before we set out, and she has new mauve crescents beneath her eyes. Weariness or something more? Isn't she receiving satisfactory nourishment?

"Are you hungry?" I truly must get better at finding segues to inquire about such matters. I always sound brusque, demanding information as if it's my due.

I am not my cousin.

"More than you can ever imagine," she whispers.

I *loathe* the thought of Thea suffering, would crawl out of my skin to prevent it at this point. "Then take what you need from me. You have my explicit permission."

She hesitates only a second, and I suspect the fact she moves at once is more a testament to her state of starvation than any desire to be closer to me. "Have you washed your hair yet?" she asks unexpectedly.

"Not yet. I haven't been here long."

"It's so pretty. To be candid, I was admiring it when you hauled me back to Winter after I released the pookas."

"My hair?" I never receive compliments, and I'm not sure how to proceed. But…it's not a bad feeling, knowing that she appreciates one of my physical traits.

"Gorgeous," she affirms. "And if you're willing, I'd like to propose an exchange…your energy for my service. I don't accept handouts."

"By all means," I breathe.

There are cleansing products arrayed in pots and jars behind us. She chooses something that smells like distilled sunshine, not a scent I would have chosen for myself, and lathers my hair in long, soothing motions. Her fingers are gentle on my scalp, creating a cascade of tingles that spark long-dormant nerve endings to life. My whole body reacts to her touch, coming to readiness with an alacrity that's both impressive and awkward.

Under the water, I pinch my inner thigh just to be sure this is happening. I'm naked in the bath with Thea. She's behind me, and the water blurs my body, so hopefully she won't notice. I focus on the scalp massage so intently that it takes me a moment to identify that warm lassitude stealing over me. My muscles relax, ones I hadn't even realized were taut. An eternity of tension releases when she fills a jug and rinses my hair in tender, careful motions. The edge of frustration softens. So does my anger and my perception of being trapped. With my senses so blunted, Thea could do something dreadful to me, but she's not that sort of person. And if she cared about me deeply, personally, I might learn to tolerate the trap my life has become.

On this journey, I'm closer to attaining freedom than I've ever been before. At some point, I wonder if I'll have to choose between my painstaking plans and ensuring Thea's safety. She wants a home, a place to belong. And *I* want to be free. Even if she cared for me, I'm not sure those needs can be mutually met.

Gently, she wrings the water from my hair once she finishes. "How does that feel?"

"Incredible."

"You're not dizzy or light-headed?"

If I said yes, it would be for different reasons. I want her with a physical ache, and I can't find the words. I don't dare look directly at her. Not now.

"Kerboros?"

Oh no. She said my name.

"I'm well." Even to my own ears, I sound hoarse, my voice thick with the yearning I fight to swallow. The longer I spend with her, the more difficult it becomes.

"Your face is red." She sounds…amused?

I risk a look at her then, and her eyes are lambent, glowing in the half-light. "We're in the bath. It's warm. Very warm."

"Pity. I thought maybe it's because we're so close and we're both naked."

The sound I made before tries to emerge, and I disguise it as a cough. I have no expertise in carnal matters, no finesse. For ages, my reputation and my bad attitude have driven people away, kept them safe. But now there's Thea, her face too close to mine.

"It's cruel to tease," I murmur.

I'm unraveling, just like my hair, now swirling around us in the water. I feel the echo of her hands on my scalp, brushing the tender skin on the nape of my neck in an exquisite torment, here and then gone, and I feel like I might spontaneously combust or boil the water around us.

"Who's teasing? I want to kiss you." There. She's said it plainly. "I wanted to earlier."

And I can't take any more. I can't, I can't.

I can't.

With a groan, I cup her face in one hand and set my lips to hers, hungry and clumsy and needing her like I've allowed myself to need no one ever. She responds instantly, wrapping her arms about me. Her mouth is silk and heat, her tongue endlessly curious. We tangle and hold and kiss, pressing again and again, lips and bodies, until I lose my mind, my breath.

She makes a gorgeous sound right into my mouth, and I give it back, unable to pull away or protect myself. I don't care if she loses control, if she drinks me dry. For her, I would happily shrivel to flower petals and be carried off on the wind. I shape the curves of her back, her shoulder, her hip with my other hand, and then I tug gently on her hair.

Her head falls back, exposing her throat, and I press worshipful kisses against the warm, wet skin. She squirms and moans, her breath coming in great gulps. Her whole body is quivering now, and just as she's about to crawl on top of me, I hear voices.

I wrench away, feeling the loss of her touch like the thrust of a diamond-sharp blade. When the bathhouse door opens, we're on opposite sides. I fumble for a sponge, willing my body to settle down. I put soap on it and scrub my arm, unable to speak as Zeph and Rosa join us for their own ablutions.

"How's the water?" Zeph asks.

"Hot," Thea replies.

If the situation wasn't so ridiculous and inappropriate and utterly unlike me, I would laugh. "But not unbearably so."

She smiles at me, a secret look, and if it's possible, I get even harder. "Really? I'm about to melt over here."

Rosa tests the water, seeming not to sense the undercurrents. "I'm with Kerboros. That's tepid at best. Ah well, it'll have to do."

Our travel companions disrobe, rinse off, and slip into the bath. Soon, their presence neutralizes my physical alacrity. Zeph stretches and starts scrubbing; as they do so, they say, "Apparently, they have two rooms free. How do we want to divide them?"

"I'm not sharing with her," Rosa says immediately, pointing at Thea. "Gender sorting is asinine—we're basically strangers."

Zeph nods. "That's fair. And you're always welcome with me."

Rosa eyes us both as if she fears we'll attempt to take up space in Zeph's quarters by force.

Though I don't display my jubilation, there are fireworks going off within me. "Acceptable."

"You don't mind sharing with me?" Thea is teasing me. The mischief in her voice nearly makes me pull her into my arms again. "Are you sure?"

With heroic effort, I disregard that provocation and respond levelly: "Thea and I are used to each other now."

She laughs. "You can say that again."

Two can play at this game.

"In fact, sometimes I find her company agreeable."

Zeph angles their head, a speculative look on their unfamiliar features. "Is that so?"

"Mm. She's like a mermaid in the water."

Thea chokes, sitting up, now seeming mildly alarmed by what else I might say. Perhaps she's onto something here, goading people for amusement. This *is* entertaining. "Er, I wouldn't go that far."

I probably wouldn't have said anything too scandalous, but Rosa steals the opportunity. "We found your friend," she says to Thea. "And now we're ready to move on to finding… Wait, who are we looking for again?"

The smile fades from Thea's eyes, leaving them despondent. "My spouse."

With what we've just done, that reminder stabs me like a knife in the chest.

25

A Spell for Insight and Innovation

Sometimes, we feel trapped. This is a deceptively powerful charm to sharpen mental acuity and help you access ideas that might not have occurred to you otherwise. Not a glorious working or a dramatic one, but there's power in micromagic too. One never knows how the ebbs of power will flow back toward us. I tend to use this one right before I sleep. My dreaming mind often crafts the most miraculous solutions, and I wake knowing precisely what to do when I was floundering the night before.

One thing I wish I'd known before I reached this age, my gem: It's fine to admit you don't know, even if you're consulted by someone whose opinion matters. There's no shame in not knowing. And there's value to be had in seeking a solution together. Shared weight is easier to carry, and nobody is exhausted when they're helping from their hearts. I was blessed with the gift of you, but nobody provided a how-to guide or an answer key, so I'm doing my best to provide the tools you need to thrive.

This one is best cast right before rest, and go gentle with your spell work. You'll need:

- *A small round piece of green tourmaline (substitute green turquoise in a pinch)*
- *Pinches of cinnamon, ginkgo, and mugwort*
- *A sprig of foxglove*
- *Silver chalice*
- *Clean rainwater*

This working is a little different; there are multiple steps, so I'll begin with the simplest. Place the foxglove and the tourmaline (or turquoise) under your pillow. Steep the cinnamon, ginkgo, and mugwort in the chalice. You can warm it with magic, but be patient and take your time. You can't rush creativity, or the results can be...erratic. You might end up with an obsession to set off on a wild-goose chase instead of the outline of a brilliant notion. Now, I'm no stranger to going off half-cocked, but in magical matters, it's best to be entirely cocked to avoid unwanted consequences.

Once the components have steeped and the water changes hue, dip your fingers into the liquid and flick them across your pillow, three times in total. The top of the pillow will be misty but not wet. Flip it over so the anointed fabric touches the foxglove and the tourmaline or turquoise. Now prepare for bed as usual, and brace for interesting dreams.

*But you're no stranger to those! Once, you woke in the middle of the night and crept out into the wildlands, desperate to speak to Nerys because you dreamed something bad had happened to her. When I caught up to you, nothing would do but for us to go to her stream and check on her. And while we were there, we saved her from being caught in the backlash of a hex gone awry. Her stream dried to a trickle, and if we hadn't been there to aid her in breaking that hex, something bad *would* have happened to her.*

You'll never go wrong following your heart, no matter where it leads.

THEA

I'M A TERRIBLE PERSON.

Not because I regret what happened between me and Kerboros. But because I don't.

After reminding Rosa of our quest, I should feel riddled with guilt. The others talk around me, but I can't focus on the conversation.

Before, if you'd asked me, I wouldn't have said I was this unreliable. While technically I may not owe loyalty to a contract I signed under duress, I *still* feel conflicted about my lack of remorse. I've lived my entire life trying to prove that I'm not a parasite, and yet despite my intention to protect Da at all costs, I've stumbled. Maybe even fallen?

No, I refuse to use that word. I can't fall in love.

My heart thunders in my chest, burning through the energy I've siphoned. This mistake—I wonder if should I call it that, considering how much I enjoyed myself? Regardless, those stolen moments threaten everything I hold dear. If news of my dalliance with Kerboros gets back to the Lord of Winter, it will go badly for my dad. Fear lashes at me, but some greedy part of me also wishes Kerboros and I could pick up where we left off. Though I've romped with people before, I never felt like this.

I don't know what to do about it.

"I'm clean enough," Rosa says, breaking into my convoluted thoughts.

"Me too," Zeph adds.

I notice Kerboros angling an intent look in my direction, but I don't meet his gaze. And I think he's taking that badly because when I steal a glance in his direction, his face is cast in its customary lines, all sternness and imperturbable angles. Yet, somehow, I also perceive his hurt, buried so deep, I'm not supposed to sense it.

"I shall retire too," Kerboros declares abruptly.

"I'll be up in a moment," I reply.

First I need to speak with Tara. If I can find her. Earlier, she said she needed to convince her family, meaning her father, about accompanying me on this journey. But I don't think her parents dislike me enough to drive me out if I knock on their door.

To convey the illusion of relaxation, I linger in the water until everyone leaves, and then I dry off in a hurry, dress, and head to the family quarters on the other side of the public house. They have self-contained rooms; at least that's what Tara told me when we were younger. I've never visited, but I suspect I can find it, based on her stories. I follow my memories as best I can, and once I arrive at the suite I hope is theirs, I rap lightly, hoping Tara answers and not her father. Fortune favors me, as she appears and steps outside, putting a finger to her mouth.

"Mum just dragged the old man to bed," she whispers.

"Do you have a moment to talk?" I ask.

"Of course," she says. "But we shouldn't stay up too late."

I fully agree with that, but the turmoil in my heart makes it difficult for me to settle. Tara leads me back into the tavern, now closed for the night. She pours us both drinks, cider for me, proving that she pays attention to the details. Before she can ask, I spill everything. By the time I finish, my voice is trembling and tears stand in my eyes.

She takes my hand. "Thea. Breathe. Now listen to me...you have no relationship with this Devan. I've heard rumors, and I've comforted more than one heartbroken soul. Devan's a relentless flirt and seducer! Don't give it a second thought. You're essentially a captive, and you had no choice. You only agreed to this mess because they threatened to banish you. And because they might hurt your dad."

"But that's why I think I'm horrible," I protest, hoping she'll understand.

My dad is my whole world. I can't believe I fooled around with Kerboros in the bath and risked Da's safety like this. If anyone was spying—

"From what I know of your father," Tara says, calmly cutting off my dire thoughts, "he'd be sad that you feel guilty. Mudge wants you to be happy, whatever that entails."

"Where he wants me to be happy, I need him to be safe."

"In an ideal world," she says in a sorrowful tone.

I don't know if Tara's implying that it's impossible for both to coexist—my happiness and Da's safety—but she's never been one to sugarcoat things. And I can deal only with the reality I live in. I sigh over a sip of cider, realizing this can't be fixed with a confession, though it helps to hear she doesn't think I'm awful.

"Thanks for listening."

"Are you really not planning to tell me more about the steamy bath action?" she asks, waggling a roguish brow.

I let the silence build as I finish my drink. "It was the best kiss of my life." Then I amend, "Several of them, actually. How about you? Are *you* seeing anyone?"

A shadow flickers in her usually cheerful demeanor. "I was. But Tempest broke it off rather suddenly. These days, I don't know what's going on with them at all."

My eyes widen. "Tempest? They told us how to find you but didn't mention..." I trail off, unsure how to phrase the rest.

"That we used to be together?" Tara guesses.

"Yeah. I'm sorry it didn't work out."

She tries to smile, but I can see she's still sad about it. I round the table and offer a hug, which she accepts, squeezing me until my ribs ache. I rub Tara's back gently, holding on until she lets go. Da taught me that, along with everything else. You don't tap. You don't fidget. You let the person you're hugging decide when you're done.

"Do you want to talk about it?"

She sighs. "Maybe at some point. Tonight? Not really."

"I did get the impression that they had some complicated feelings about your dad." When her head snaps up, I realize that maybe I shouldn't have said that.

"What made you—"

"Just an impression," I interject. "It's nothing they said. I'm probably wrong."

Best not to mention that Kerboros caught the weirdness too.

Tara frowns. "How odd. I didn't even realize they knew each other."

"I should get some sleep," I say, hoping I haven't made things worse.

She rallies then and manages a teasing tone. "Are you sure? I do believe you're sharing with Kerboros. Maybe you'll finish what you started."

I hate that she feels like she needs to hide the fact that she's hurting, but sometimes pretending we're okay is what lets us carry on. The kindest thing I can do is play along. "Now I regret confiding in you," I joke.

"No, you don't."

I smile; she knows me too well, and there's a particular comfort to being known. "Good night. See you in the morning."

By the time I tiptoe into our room, Kerboros is wrapped in a blanket on the floor. I regret that I won't get to snuggle in bed with him, but I imagine he thinks the way I reacted earlier means that I regret everything. He's likely misinterpreted my actions, and maybe we'll never share a moment like that again, one where he lets down his guard and allows himself to *want.*

I don't know how I feel about that, but I need to rest while I can. The bed is calling me, so I crawl under the covers and drift off, listening to the comforting cadence of his breath nearby. Then I rouse to a thunderous bang on the door; it doesn't feel like I've been asleep for long, and I hear Tara calling my name.

"Get up, get up! We need to get a move on, slugabed. We have to go shopping."

Groggy, I comply and get ready as fast as I can. Kerboros is already out of the room, so we won't have a chance to discuss what happened yesterday. Maybe that's for the best, or possibly I'm a coward for thinking so.

It doesn't take long for us to meet in the courtyard. As a group, we head toward the market back the way we came.

Instead of scolding us from the rooftops, Ragh offers a friendly wave. "Good to see you, friends."

Tara turns with an astonished look. "What sorcery is this? I need an explanation."

"Thea worked her usual magic," Kerboros says, a hint of a smile in his tone if not reflected on his face.

And I experience a delicious frisson at his approval. Hopefully, that means he's not upset with me. All the bustling and fretting has me hungry again. Yesterday I got too distracted with the kissing to fully take advantage of Kerboros's generous offer. I fed a bit but not enough. *Never* enough. I'm so afraid of hurting someone.

It would be much easier if I knew anything. Like how much energy I can draw without inflicting permanent harm. When you grow up surrounded by people who are different than you, who don't share your needs or traits, it's difficult to articulate how confusing and isolating it can be. No matter what I do, I may never find my place here. I may always exist on the fringes, tolerated but not welcomed, except by a select few.

I trail behind the group. Since it's early, the market's crowd is thin, just a few fae here and there. Tara rushes around with Rosa, consulting the pixie about her list, while Zeph is unusually withdrawn, on par with Kerboros. Zeph's behavior troubles me; they're not being candid about their motives, and I wish I knew if they're dangerous.

We probably can't trust them, but I don't have any concrete reasons for my worries. Maybe I'm just hungry. Because I'm distracted, staring at their back, I stumble into someone who already seems wobbly on their feet. In reflex, I grab their arm to steady them, but the moment my flesh makes contact, their energy breaks over me in a sensual wave, exuberant and sparkling; I've never known anything like it. The high crackles through me, electricity in my veins as euphoric bliss illuminates my nerve endings.

More.

More.

More.

Hunger consumes me, blocking every rational thought. A creature of mindless need, I take and take and take—until my victim collapses. My lips peel away from my teeth, and I lunge, unhinged with vicious voracity.

Only the screaming breaks my focus.

26

Flight

This piece is difficult to find, as the artist concealed it on purpose. The room has no windows, but it does have shelves. And the artist has carved this into the wood behind some innocuous tomes, a silent rebellion that might attract scrutiny, should some powerful or malicious person happen to identify it.

It is, of course, the artist's family crest, which has been stricken from all official rolls. It is illegal to recreate these lines, especially the winged pooka in the center. Though pookas can shape-shift, they rarely choose to take form as a winged horse, since it's much easier—and requires much less magic—to fly as a raven. But that's the point of the design, as it represents commitment to the improbable, the embodiment of seemingly unattainable dreams.

The artist last saw this standard held aloft by his elder brother, before abject failure, before the doomed rebellion met its end on a flower-filled field that provided only a feast for crows. Before dungeons and loss and execution. Before. The heraldry has been recreated from memory, so it may be inaccurate or shifted somewhat from the original depiction. But the idea survives, even in hiding.

Unrealistic dreams can come true. And bound people can be freed.

KERBOROS

"DEMON!" THE CURSE RINGS OUT in thunderous tones.

I whirl as the body drops, and Taragon screams, falling to her knees. The supplies she was carrying scatter all over the ground nearby. She pulls Tempest into her lap, stroking the pale hair away from their face. Around us, the sparse crowd is multiplying, people shuffling out of cottages and alleyways to add shocked murmurs that rival Taragon's weeping. Tears stream down her face as she tries to rouse Tempest.

"What's wrong? Are you sick? Is that why—"

"The demon drained their life," someone shouts.

Thea sways, her face as pale as milk beneath the usual honeyed hue of her skin. I catch her by the elbow to keep her from hitting the ground. My nerves prickle at the rising hostility all around us. The cries for help are drawing people out of their homes and businesses nearby, and instinct tells me that we don't have long. Spectacle always provokes interest, sometimes vicarious glee at another's misfortune, and occasionally concern, but whatever the reason, it means too much scrutiny for us to linger.

"Fetch the guards," someone shouts.

"Leave them alone!" It's a familiar voice, and I seek to match it among the encircling faces and pointing fingers.

Ragh, the brownie Thea befriended, is attempting to intervene on her behalf but pitted against the fury of the onlookers, with Taragon crying and his small stature, it's unclear how much weight his support will carry. I will not risk Thea's safety.

"Send a runner to the palace," a pixie shrieks in the shrillest of tones. "The strange one killed Tempest. Just look at them!"

"Guards!"

Someone else takes up the cry. "Guards!"

We're surrounded. And I make a swift decision, hauling Taragon to her feet. She seems too stunned to resist. My last transportation spell went awry, but we *cannot* be discovered in the Summer lands, particularly under these conditions. If we're apprehended in Summer, especially after their delegation disappeared, we'll be executed as spies or assassins. My familial history guarantees it. And even if Summer remands us to Winter's custody, we can't justify our presence here. Liskaal will have our heads as traitors; death stalks us at every turn.

I can't let them hurt Thea. I'd rather die.

Fear makes me feral, wild as a lightning strike. I wrench on the magic with all my might, focused on crafting a portal to carry us away. In the course of my sanctioned hunts, I've traveled a fair bit, and I focus on a mushroom circle in the wildlands, not far from Springtide, where Macha told us to search. It's not too late; I can make this right.

The energy crackles as the golden vortex appears, a massive undertaking, as I need to hold it steady long enough for our group to pass. I nudge Thea forward first, and she clutches Taragon, who seems stunned to the point of disorientation. When Thea moves, the crowd parts, all of them unwilling to suffer Tempest's fate by touching her, even in an attempt to hold her back. Her face crumples, eyes huge and fevered in her pallid face. Twin roses burn in her cheeks, a riotous color gained from harm inflicted on another. Her pain is a tangible force; it hurts me to breathe, just gazing at her.

They vanish through the swirling eddies of golden energy. Zeph, Rosa, and I rush simultaneously, and as soon as my feet hit solid ground, I close the portal. Exhausted, I topple to my knees. I wasn't ready to pull that much power, and my head feels like it's on fire, throbbing to the point that I hear a high-pitched whistle within my skull.

I remain on my knees, uncertain whether I have the strength to stand. Since I'm trying to keep my brain from exploding, I don't immediately realize that our situation has deteriorated. It takes Rosa's exclamation for me to take stock of our surroundings.

Oh. Oh no.

"Macha's tits! Where in the wilds are we?" she demands.

I've never been here before. But I've heard the stories, horrific tales meant to frighten the very young, and I recognize this place from those eerie fables.

"The In-Between," Zeph says, before I can.

"The In-Between?" Thea repeats. Her tone makes it a question.

Rosa sighs, a supercilious expression on her tiny face. "Honestly, didn't that hobgoblin teach you anything? Your ignorance is embarrassing."

"Do *not* talk about my dad," Thea snaps.

For the first time, I see dangerous energy swirling around her. I don't even need to shift to another spectrum of vision; the tendrils are crimson with violence and rage, the need to hurt Rosa to stop those words from emerging.

Who is Tempest, exactly?

And why—also how—did their energy change Thea like this? To say I'm worried is a massive understatement. But to be fair, I feel like scolding Rosa as well. Thea didn't mean to hurt Tempest; it was an accident, and I'm certain the others understand that as well. Or perhaps they don't.

Perhaps they've never harmed anyone unintentionally or otherwise, never been faced with two choices, one bad, the other worse.

I address my words to Thea. "The In-Between is a liminal space between the wildlands and the territories granted to the courts. Here, there is no ruling entity to provide visual cohesion, so it's a place where lost things wash up."

Taragon wipes her eyes, dashing away the last of the tears. Her expression is grim and conflicted as she regards her friend's anguish. But she takes a moment to collect herself and chooses not to accuse Thea. Not to spit sharp words, even though her behavior in the market square indicated she once had a close bond with Tempest. Then she spins in a slow circle, taking in the environs.

The area is shrouded in fog, brackish water on the boggy ground. It pools around our ankles, and I feel occasional nudges, even through my boots, that hint at creatures swimming in it. Gray and withered roots rise above the rocky ground like tentacles that have been left in the sun yet are concurrently rotting from within. I cannot make out any features of the landscape in the distance. It all looks the same, bleak and featureless.

"We've established where. The more pertinent point is, how do we leave?" Rosa says.

Zeph appears pensive. They're so quiet, reacting so little to current events, that it sets off mild alarm bells. "An excellent question," they respond.

I'm more concerned about the fact that my previously flawless magic has gone wrong. Again. Twice in a row?

That is completely improbable. More likely? Sabotage. While I can't completely rule out external interference—because who knows what magic was ricocheting around the crowd—I don't know if it was a result of enemies of Winter who recognized us, someone trying to prevent our escape, if it could have been a coincidence or…

No. None of those answers feel right.

I don't like this possibility, but someone *within* the group could be working against us. Taragon wasn't present for the first misfire, and she was sobbing too hard to have done anything. But I don't know about Zeph or Rosa. We accepted them on faith, but perhaps it's time to scrutinize their motives.

I won't confront them yet. I don't have any proof.

Belatedly, I realize that I'm still on my knees. Thea comes to my side and offers me a hand. Her gaze is weighted, silently daring me to reject her. But here's what I don't say as I meet her gaze: *Drain me dry. I'm not afraid. It's worth it to experience the joy of your touch.*

I accept her help, savoring our fleeting contact. I'm unsteady, but the headache is receding. My mouth tastes sour, an acrid touch in my throat that makes me suspect I barely avoided depositing my breakfast on the marshy soil.

"What do we know?" I ask.

"Only that it's difficult to leave," Zeph answers.

"Any of you been here before?" Tara sounds rough, her voice thick and raspy with intense grief.

Rosa scoffs, whirring in tight, angry little circles, her wings fluttering too fast to be seen clearly in an impressive display of aerial agitation. "Definitely not. Pixies are smarter than this. *This!* This is what I get for helping big folk."

"I'll make it up to you," Zeph promises.

They pat their shoulder, offering a perch, but Rosa refuses with a snarl and a headshake. She seems truly enraged, blaming Zeph enough to avoid getting close to them. Their flicker of surprise suggests the enigmatic fae wasn't expecting her to be *this* furious while *I* wonder why they're so serene.

"You always say that, and I'm still waiting," she grumbles.

Their relationship intrigues me; it is not romantic, but they seem to be close. Are they friends? More like family? And how far would Rosa go for Zeph if it came down to it?

As I wonder, water jets upward in an explosive burst, and something rises from the murky water, all open mouth, flailing tentacles, and snapping teeth.

27

A Token for Fighting and Ferocity

This isn't the usual working, my gem. One never knows what might happen, and one day, you might find yourself facing a fight, through no fault of your own. I'm well aware that you don't go seeking trouble, but sometimes it finds us. You take after me in that way. In my youth, I could never pass up a chance to stick my nose in, and I rarely refrained from interfering if I thought my meddling could change someone's life for the better. You get your curiosity from me, dear daughter. Never let anyone tell you different.

And so I've crafted something for your protection, using my magic and the best of the protective stones. It's one use only, and you'll know what to do as soon as you put the bracelet on. Keep it with you so I can protect you even from afar. I'd never suggest you take up training for battle, as it's neither where your heart nor your inclinations lie. But all the same, it would make me feel better if you kept this with you. I expended a fair amount of time and energy upon it, and it should serve you well in the right circumstances.

You'll need:

- *Amber and obsidian moonstone and white agate, strung into a bracelet on fine silver thread*

There are no complex instructions, no ritual to complete. When you're in grave danger and all hope seems lost, put the bracelet on. Let my love do the rest.

THEA

IS IT...A GIANT WORM?

No. Not exactly. It's not like any worm I've seen. For one thing, it has. . .appendages—not quite limbs, not quite tentacles. For another, it's vertical more than horizontal; this is a hideous creature with limbs all over its body and a giant, gaping maw at the top. The creature is mottled gray, striations of color running with mucus or slime, and the limbs strike out violently, lashing the water.

It doesn't seem to be able to see us. But it senses us some other way.

This seems to be a beast of endless grasping hunger, and I experience a moment of horrified recognition. Is this because of me? If I was distilled to my essence, is this how I'd look? *No, that can't be true. This can't be because of me, right?* I didn't summon this monster.

As I wrestle with the fear that I'm calling these somehow, another creature pops up, smaller than the first, then another. And another. They might be a horrible family.

"What *are* those?" Tara breathes.

"The more pressing question is, how hostile are they?" Zeph adds.

Rosa snorts. "I'm pretty sure they want to eat us."

I have no answers, but I touch the pouch I wear around my neck. Da has always insisted it's an emergency measure. If ever there's a time to put on the bracelet, it's now.

I'm not a fighter. I prefer to slink in and out of situations, and when confrontation can't be avoided, I'm better at keeping my eyes down and pretending to be contrite.

But I don't think these creatures can hear us, so they wouldn't be interested in an apology. Maybe they sense us through the vibrations of our movements? I shift to test that theory, and a boneless jelly tube slams into the soil, knocking me to the boggy ground. As I roll backward in the foul-smelling water, I yank to break the strings on the little bag.

And put the bracelet on.

My arm glows with faint amber light, and the gemstones crumble to dust, leaving me with the thin silver band and a shimmery golden blade that's like an extension of my hand. I don't need to practice with it; I can swing it as easily as moving my arm. It leaves a shimmering trail when I slice the air experimentally. Courage that could only come from my dad suffuses me.

You can do this, my gem. You can do anything.

For a moment, I hear his voice—or an echo of it—and then I hear Tara say, "Thea, what're you trying to prove? Get away from there! Kerboros, do something."

I'm not proving anything. I'm protecting people I care about. This isn't natural to me, and I'm not happy about it, but I won't cower. Not when this is my fault. Maybe in more ways than one.

Can't worry about that right now.

Kerboros doesn't respond to her. Instead, he draws his sword with a metallic *shing* while Zeph summons twin glowing spheres, white as moonlight, but they look searing hot, like the white that burns beyond the blue in the fiercest of fires. I gesture at Tara to get back, and Rosa needs no such warning. The pixie darts off, well above and out of reach.

Tara mutters, "Oh, suddenly you're a sword fighter, are you? With a fancy light sword and everything. Don't think we won't talk about what happened in the market."

Despite the situation, I almost smile. Trust Tara not to let me off the hook even for an instant. I know she's upset, but with this beastie whipping its legs around wildly, I can't pause for a chat. I dive and roll again, hacking the limb that nearly flattened me.

"Get to higher ground," Zeph shouts.

I don't ask; I leap.

As soon as I light upon a small outcropping, Zeph launches the spheres, not at the creature but into the marsh. The energy dissipates, making the water roil and boil around the beast. That maw opens to emit the most horrifying sound—too shrill, too loud, too much agony entirely—and it goes wild, slashing in all directions.

"You're cooking it?" Rosa asks.

Zeph shakes their head, working up more energy for a second try. "Not fast enough."

"Don't expect *me* to eat it," the pixie says.

I'm a bit trapped, but I should be able to edge around the perimeter and reach the back appendages, reducing its mobility. Kerboros whispers a word that I don't catch and glides across the surface of the water, barely touching it. His magic is so damn impressive; this is why there's a prevailing theory that a particular religious icon was a wandering fae.

I'd have to focus on my spellbook to attempt the same feat, and even then my chance of success is relatively low. Da tried so hard to teach me—to enable me to use fairy magic like I belong here, but it's not my forte even at the best of times.

The humongous monster charges at me, flailing against its own death. I dodge the slash of a limb and roll forward into disgustingly warm water. I fend off the limbs with an expertise granted from my father's magic, but that boost is waning. I can't hold out much longer. Even as I frame the weary thought, Kerboros spins into motion, his sword a silver blur. He is blindingly fast, killing the smaller creatures so quickly that I can barely follow the movements.

But the final kill? Doesn't go as I would've expected. My light sword shimmers once and fades, so instead of blocking the attack, the tentacle knocks me arse over teakettle. I bounce hard and land at Tara's feet. Rosa flutters overhead, a tiny bow in her hands, and she fires rapidly into the creature's yawning maw.

She laughs, vicious glee in her midair twirl. "Doesn't matter that the arrows are small. The poison will do it in."

Zeph has managed to summon more energy, and Kerboros is poised to stab the monster in the throat, but it shudders violently, insides churning through the mottled hide, and then…it just keels over. That's my lesson from this fight: Never underestimate a pixie.

Once the bodies stop writhing, they dissipate into mist. I frown, glancing at the rest of the group. That thing knocked me down. And now it's just…gone? I check for bruises and scrapes, and yes, I'll have some mementos of that fight. While things can be weird in the wildlands, they're usually not weird in *this* way.

"What just happened?" I ask.

"I'm not sure," Zeph says in a thoughtful tone.

"Illusions?" Tara suggests.

Rosa shakes her head. "Poison doesn't kill illusions, sweet cakes."

Kerboros steps out of the water and closes the distance between us. He's single-minded in checking me over, searching for signs of serious injury. There's nothing subtle about his concern anymore, and I like this feeling far too much to protest. I let him hold my shoulders and study me to his heart's content.

"You're unscathed?" he asks in a deep voice.

"More or less."

"Sorry to cut into your moment," Tara says, "but I need to talk to Thea. Now."

Right. The reckoning is at hand. We've just fought a monster, and it was far too much like looking in the mirror, after what I did to Tempest. Intention doesn't mitigate injury. Tara wanted to help me, and now I've hurt someone she cares for.

I don't know what to tell her, except the truth—I fear I'm changing into the monster that I have spent my life trying not to become.

28

All the Wrong Angles

This piece features triangular patterns, cast in unfamiliar angles, but it rests in the corner of the room, unfinished. Perhaps the artist couldn't see how to complete the work. As it is, partially done, a crystalline delicacy has been imposed on an irregular slab of misty limestone. The matte surface of the stone is dusty, veiling some of the deeper etchings. The carvings are neither certain, nor precise, and it seems likely that this piece was an early effort, before the artist acquired any level of expertise. But one who has studied the artist's works as a whole could envision two possibilities. One is an arcane tablet with mystical runes only partly imbued, an incantation to unlock untold power. The other? A relic from the mortal realm—an unfinished gravestone.

KERBOROS

AS TARAGON PULLS THEA ASIDE, I stop myself from following.

They have much to discuss, and I have something on my mind as well. The adrenaline is still fading from the fight. I will not focus on the way my pulse echoed in my ears when the creature attacked Thea.

We're trapped in the In-Between; it's not the time for personal matters. In my earliest days, I heard a few stories about the place while playing with others in the Winter Court. They whispered of the swamp witch who sent bad changelings there, where they languished forever, unloved and unwanted, never to be seen again.

Now that I've met Macha, I wonder how many of those tales she spread personally to keep folks from pestering her with inane requests. Apart from Liskaal, I thought I had no family left. Macha would likely be horrified if I used that word to describe our connection, but I do find kinship with her. I'd spread gossip as well to protect my own solitude.

My parents had no time for such rumors, too involved in sowing the seeds for my father's rebellion. In fairness, the obsession began and ended with my father. My mother…I can't recall anything about her specifically. In the abstract, I'm aware that she taught me about the world and how to ignore those who said we were lackeys, or toadies, or hangers-on, clinging to the frayed remnants of past glory, unable to let that hint of distinction go when it passed to a different line.

My head feels strange. While I know we failed, I can't remember how anymore. It's all blurred edges and a wistful ache. But my anger at my father remains, a kernel of fury embedded deep in my soul, burning like a coal. The worst part of those allegations is that they were at least partly true. My father *was* fixated on besting Liskaal. But only *he* wanted that. Not me and my mother. And certainly not my older brother, whose name

I rarely mention, the first casualty of my father's hubris. Geraint wanted something else entirely—to free the realm from Liskaal's tyranny and make the world better for the wild fae. That idealism did not protect him.

I shake my head at the pain crimping my chest. If it isn't time to worry about Thea, it's not time to dwell on the past either.

"The rest of you," I say, "remain together. I'll do some scouting and return."

Rosa bristles immediately. "Who put you in charge?"

I don't care to argue with a pixie. They're known to be contentious, capable of feuding for ages over the most trivial matters. Skirting her question, I say, "Feel free to leave, then. If we separate completely, however, it may be difficult for us to reunite later."

"Then what makes you special?" the pixie demands in a suspicious tone. "Why are *you* going if it's not safe and you might not make it back?"

Zeph reminds her, "He's Winter's hound. His only work is hunting for his cousin."

The usual sting pierces me at the accuracy of the allegation. I'm good at what I do, much as I loathe the undertakings I'm charged with. Before anyone can object, I stride away from the group. Because I have a suspicion that has been growing for a while, and I need sufficient time alone to confirm it. Ten paces out, the mist envelops me. It feels clammy on my skin, like unseen leeches prowling for a place to feed. I disregard the distraction and keep moving until I'm sure I'm out of earshot.

It occurs to me then.

This is the opportunity I've been waiting for. I'm no longer bound by Liskaal's magic, and I planned to set the scene, craft a compelling narrative that proves I met my demise. Only then will I be free of his disgusting influence. And I can live quietly, anonymously in the wildlands, far from any court. There are spaces less dangerous than the territory Macha has claimed. I even narrowed it down to a hospitable area between Summer and Autumn, where no one would ever find me. No one searches for the unloved dead, and even if they did, nobody could locate a hunter who doesn't wish to be found.

Opening a portal to anywhere would be much easier for one person. I can walk away from all this. Thea's problems aren't mine, are they? She isn't mine to cherish or protect. I barely know Taragon, Rosa, or Zeph. Is there any reason for me to stay? To risk myself when I've spent my whole life avoiding the altruism that ruined my brother?

To my surprise, I feel…conflicted. My head tells me to go. But my heart…

Well. It won't hurt anything to find out whether my suspicions are correct first.

I can decide once I know. I close my eyes and focus on the magic whirling all around me. The energy is intense, rivers of power to be pulled. For the greedy or the unwary, the consequences could be swift and painful. Anyone who craves control could easily be driven mad, and in overreaching, they might immolate themselves or be absorbed in these uncertain eddies.

I am more cautious; I take only what is needed. As an added precaution, I build a mental barrier in case of a mana surge, and then—

"Help! Help me! Is anyone out there?!" The hoarse voice seems to come from all around me. "I thought I heard someone. Am I losing my mind? It's been so long…"

I can barely discern the hoarse croak of the last few words. There are no other ambient noises, no insects or wind rustling through the reeds. For that matter, there are no reeds. It might be a trick—or a trap, something meant to lure me closer. But if the creature we fought earlier could communicate verbally, it chose not to do so.

It's a risk to waste time out here. I have no way of knowing what properties the mist contains, whether it's acidic or poison or drains magical energy. I could end up as a hopeless soul calling out for aid if I tarry in the inexplicable, soupy fog. Winter's hound would cast only one spell and return to the group, but Thea has reminded me that I used to be more—and could be again.

I realize I can't leave someone screaming for help. I'll finish the other spell once I determine whether this is a trick or a genuine plea.

I won't abandon my companions either. I'm like my brother after all, much as I didn't want to be, much as I tried to cut out my own heart and keep existing as an automaton. And so I shift and center my mind. I don't have an imperative from Liskaal to sharpen the urgency, but the sound of the target's voice is fresh in my mind. I don't dare try to summon my spiderlings. The In-Between might transform them into hideous monsters and force me to fight them. I lock onto the voice, slowly opening my senses to let a faint trickle of power provide the pull. Even so, my barrier wobbles against the sheer volume of magic; it's raw here, heady. I could get drunk on this and decide I'm a god.

There. That way.

I follow the pull, keeping my eyes down. Wispy, glowing balls dart around me, each trying their best to lead me off track, but I know better than to follow a wisp. They're not sentient, per se, and as I understand it, they're more echoes, remnants of fae folk that came before and perished but haven't accepted their fate yet. In the mortal realm, I believe they're known as ghosts.

It feels like I've been walking for a while through this blank and terrible place. The pull is no stronger, and I'm starting to doubt myself. The call hasn't come again. My magic has failed twice before; perhaps I'm wrong in suspecting sabotage, and there's something awry with me instead? Angry with that possibility, I step incautiously and nearly fall, my footfalls creating a noisy slosh on the slimy stones.

"I did hear that! I did. Who's there? Is someone here? Anyone?" So very close this time, that agonized voice.

I rush forward, determined to locate whoever this is, and reach a clearing not unlike the one where I left the rest of the group—with one key difference. A skeletal tree rises from the promontory like a gaunt gray hand, branches bare. The withered trunk is scarred as if blasted by lightning, though the pallid, shrouded sky cannot possibly produce rain. Not here. Most of the branches have broken, riddled with damp rot; only two remain, outstretched to the sides like arms flailing in protest of decay.

And perched on the left limb is a gnome in a bad state. He's small of stature and of frame, his once-dapper brown pin-striped suit is torn and dirty, and his luxurious beard hasn't been trimmed in ages. Thick brows overshadow his eyes, but he leaps to his feet unsteadily upon my arrival.

"You. You're actually here! You are, aren't you? Here, I mean." He peers at me with a heartbreaking blend of skepticism and hope.

"Yes. I'm here. I heard you calling out." Though I don't normally wonder about such things, I ask, "What are you doing up there?"

"Avoiding monsters," he says, as if that should be obvious.

Considering the creature we just fought, that is a more sensible answer than I expected. "Come down if you wish. I'll guide you back to the rest of the group."

Ragged laughter bursts from him. "You were with others and *abandoned* them?" The guffaw swiftly chokes off with a strangled cry. "You absolute dolt. We'll never find them. Never. You didn't save me, you doomed *yourself*."

I ignore that in favor of completing my original task. First I craft the intention and then the question. This is an adjunct of my finding magic, and there's immediately a tug, answering my inquiry. A faint orange glow burns through the mist; that's how powerful the positive reply is. If this had failed, if I'd erred in my suspicions, I would have focused on Thea.

If she was on the other side of the universe, I could still find her with my eyes closed.

"This way," I say to the near-hysterical gnome. "And keep up if you don't want to be left behind."

Not that I would do that to him after all he's presumably been through. Judging by how he pauses before scrambling down from his perch, he's nowhere near certain of my good intentions. "Bah. Anything is better than that blasted tree. Let's go."

Time feels…changeable here. I don't have any better word for it. Now that I'm familiar with the sensation, it reminds me of being trapped in Macha's bottle. On an academic level, it seems plausible that she draws strength from this place, bolstering her swamp with swirls of wild magic from the In-Between.

That also means we need to hurry. The days might be melting away as we walk, and there's nothing I can do about it. But I don't fear the consequences of failure. Liskaal will go through me before harming a hair on Thea's head, and I don't care who I have to kill. For her, I will fight to my last breath, the last drop of blood. I wonder if Geraint felt no regrets at the end, if he felt it was a good death because he'd given everything to the cause.

The stakes are high. I might perish when we leave this place, but the time I've spent with Thea? I think it might be the only time I've truly lived.

The gnome is silent, creeping in my wake with a stealthy lightness that says he doesn't want to fight monsters. We walk until the mist begins to clear and the glow brightens, revealing Zeph in the distance, covered in a shimmering aura. My magic whispers, *Them. Guilty. Guilty. Guilty. They interfered with your spells.*

Spy? Saboteur? All I know is that they cannot be trusted.

For now, none of them can see us. Beside me, the gnome remains quiet and still, unable to see what I do—the certainty of betrayal. It's a spell known only to me, part of the tracking magic that makes me such an effective hound, much as I loathe the role.

Now the question remains: With all of us trapped, what can I—or perhaps more saliently—what *should* I do about this treachery?

29

A Spell for Regret and Remorse

My gem, this may come as a shock to you, but I'm not perfect. I muck things up now and again, and while I'm always sorry, sometimes it doesn't change the outcome. When people are hurt, the results matter more than my intentions. Yet guilt can consume you when you allow it to. Since I'd rather you avoid that torment, I'm offering a spell that may grant your heart peace in times like this. It's important to acknowledge your part in what went wrong, but if there was no malice in your mind at the time, you can admit that you caused harm without carrying that shame with you until the end of days.

This may not be possible, but gather those involved in the event. First, apologize sincerely. They'll know if you mean it, and while forgiveness isn't owed, you can take comfort in the fact that you did the right thing. You don't control how other people react, only your behavior. So we start by offering contrition. If they feel so moved, once you've spoken your piece, then invite them to participate in this ritual with you.

This spell can be cast at any time; that's the magic and the beauty of it. You'll need:

- *All willing involved parties*
- *Hyssop, cinnamon, comfrey*
- *Clean water*
- *A vessel to make tea*

The tools here are less important than your intentions. This brew might be strong tasting, and you might need to sweeten it, if possible. If it isn't, you don't need to drink the entire cup. Simply sipping the drink you made together and talking honestly will comfort everyone. I hope your hearts feel lighter once you do.

The pain should ease by the third sip, and if you feel like ending the ritual with a hug, that will feel even better. I remember the first time you fought with Tara. Do you recall what it was about? I confess that I don't, as I came on the scene late with the two of you sobbing like your hearts would break. We had this tea that day, along with honey wafers and cheese toast. You were laughing together again by bedtime.

THEA

"I'M SO SORRY," I SAY immediately, as soon as Tara pulls me from the group.

I notice the tear streaks on her face, and I take a step, meaning to hug her, but she holds up a hand. "Not now. What *happened* back there?"

"I don't know," I whisper, misery lacing my tone. "I touched Tempest to keep them from falling, and something came over me." I can't explain that hunger, even now. "There was an unusual quality to their energy."

It's not a justification, certainly not.

Tara sighs, shoulders rounding. "They *are* mysterious. I don't even know where they're originally from."

I blink at that. "Not Summer, then?"

"No. They're maddeningly reticent about their past. And I thought they'd open up in time, if I was patient. Instead, they ended things between us."

"Without explaining anything?"

She nods. "It's dreadful, not knowing if they've recovered."

From the harm I did.

I flinch and produce my spellbook from a small shoulder bag. "Would you consider doing this spell with me? We've done it a few times over the years."

Though I seldom let anyone look at this book Da wrote especially for me, I hand Tara the tome and show her what it says. Her aspect softens. "I remember why we were fighting. You wanted to steal all the dough from the palace kitchen and put it in the wishing fountain to see what would happen."

I cringe at the reminder. It's coming back to me. "And you said that it might be funny, but it was a waste of food and hard work and we might get the cooks in trouble."

"You said I was mean," Tara reminds me.

"Then you called me a knobhead."

She laughs, which I'll take under the circumstances. "We insulted each other until we both got so mad that we burst into tears."

"That's when Da came in and we had tea. I have the ingredients right here." I pat the pouch around my neck.

"You've already apologized for what happened with Tempest. And I have cups," Tara says. "Very well. Let's do it."

We work quietly together until the tea is brewed. I didn't recollect this part from when we were little, but Da was right. The brew smells strange, and the taste is medicinal. But it's warm, and I listen as Tara begins to speak.

"Tempest...they're important to me. We met in the market. I stopped to see if they had anything that could improve the quality of wine starting to turn. Amend the vinegary taste. My dad likes to cut corners," she adds self-consciously. "At first, we were friendly acquaintances, and then they distilled a decoction especially for me. For our wine issue."

"Oooh," I tease. "A custom concoction."

Tara playfully makes a fist. "Shut it, or I won't tell you anything else."

But she doesn't get the chance to say more. "I can't believe you two ridiculous baggages are having a tea party," Rosa snaps.

Her wings flutter faster than the eye can see as she zips back and forth, trying to rise over the fog. She finally swears, a series of vicious and venal curses that practically blister my ears. Mentally, I make notes: *Gag-sacking seed jerker* is a good one.

"It's no good," she growls. "I can't get above it. It's all around us."

"Does anyone else smell that?" Tara asks, wiping the cups we just used.

Zeph glances around. "What? All I can detect is the dank water."

"Something else, more like hops or yeast," Tara answers.

"I can't smell anything," I admit.

Rosa glares at me. "*You* shut up. This is all your fault."

I can't even defend myself. We wouldn't have had to flee from Summer if I hadn't incapacitated Tempest. I wonder how they're doing; I hope I didn't hurt them too badly. They didn't seem sick, but sometimes it's not obvious from looking. Guilt rebounds, even after the ritual, and I crouch, burying my face in my hands. Tara comes up behind me and puts a hand on my shoulder.

Then she raps on my noggin with her knuckles. "That's enough. We have no time for self-blame past this point. It won't change anything."

That is partly why I adore Tara. She never lets me wallow. Somehow she manages to be both charming and pragmatic. I'm sure Toad in the Hole benefits from her presence on a daily basis. She pulls me to my feet, and I offer a hug again.

This time, she accepts it, and it means everything that she's not afraid to touch me, after what I did to Tempest. I don't know how I'd cope if Tara treated me like a monster.

She tries to keep our spirits up, and she's telling an amusing anecdote about Nerys when it hits me. "Nerys," I say, as she's getting to the good part.

"What about her?" Tara gives me a confused look.

"Water is everywhere. I don't know if the water here ever passes back to the wildlands, but if it does—"

"We can get word to Nerys!" Tara finishes, her citrine eyes sparkling.

I nod. "It might not help immediately, but it can't hurt." Crouching down, I stir the water carefully with two fingers. "Nerys? I don't know if you'll ever hear this, or how long it'll be. But this is Thea. Tara and I are trapped in the In-Between. Can you please tell my dad...?" Here, I hesitate. "Tell him I love him."

"That's all?" Rosa asks.

"It's everything."

Tara goes next. "Nerys. This is Tara. I have my own message for my parents. I love them bunches, and I'll see them again. Don't know if it'll be soon."

Zeph joins us and takes a knee, earning a scoff from Rosa. "Nerys. You don't know me, but my name is Zeph. Please tell Lady Mirralee not to worry."

I blink at them. "Isn't Lady Mirralee the queen of the Autumn Court?"

"Is she?" This blasted fae never answers a direct question.

With a muttered curse, Rosa shoots an arrow into the water. "Nerys. This is Rosa. Ignore all these sentimental saps. Send help!"

We wait for a while. But the brackish water doesn't stir with anything like a reply, and Kerboros doesn't come back.

"Has he left us?" Rosa asks aloud. "Found a way out on his own, and off he went—to report back to that asshole cousin of his."

"He wouldn't," I say.

"Are you sure?" Zeph counters.

At first I want to say that I am. I've kissed him. I wanted to do more. And over the time that we've been traveling together, I've come to know him. He doesn't seem like the type who abandons his responsibilities. But he might view a trip to the In-Between as a chance to slip the leash. If the hunter goes missing, who can the Lord of Winter send to track him down? They do say this is where people who don't want to be found go to get lost. So if Kerboros intended to run—to stop being Winter's hound—this would be the perfect place to disappear forever.

"Even if he did run off," Tara points out, "where would he go?"

Zeph sports a smug expression, a half smile on their lips. "Good question."

I refuse to jump to conclusions, but it *does* feel like it's been a while. There's no way to track time in this place. It's so featureless. Rocks and water and mist.

And that reminds me that we're running out of time. Endless setbacks and delays will end in failure—my dad in a dungeon and me dying in the mortal realm. They will cut off Kerboros's head. While I'm known for causing trouble, I also know when to stop. And things have spiraled so far out of control that I'm scared to death.

"Maybe Kerboros got turned around," Tara says. "No landmarks."

"You're suggesting our scout got lost?" Rosa asks.

Zeph's semi-smirk blossoms into a grin. "Is that better than him abandoning us? I'm not certain we have use for a tracker who can't perform."

"I'll take incompetence over betrayal any day." Tara frowns in their general direction, but there's no heat behind her gaze.

I can't stop myself from defending him. "Not necessarily incompetence. I doubt he's been here before. Magic must react differently. It's more—"

"Any earthen lump knows that you don't set out alone here," Rosa counters.

Is she calling Kerboros an earthen lump? Oh no, she didn't. I'm ready to fight.

Before the argument can escalate, Kerboros strides into the clearing. "The answer is neither abandonment nor incompetence. I could not find an obvious path out of here, but I did find...him. Convincing him to accompany me required some doing."

A gnome steps into view behind him. "I can't believe this. After all this time, people!"

Judging by her expression, Rosa is even more irritated. "Another mouth to feed, one who couldn't even save himself, it seems."

"Govannon," the gnome says, bowing slightly, and it's a courtly gesture, made more so when he sweeps off his hat.

The name tickles the back of my brain. I snap my fingers. "Ragh mentioned you!"

Suddenly, there's a gnome beside me, though I didn't even see him move. "Do you know him? Is he well?"

"He misses you," I tell him.

Hollowed eyes well up with tears, and he presses a hand to his tattered vest. "I have no idea how long I've been here. It feels like forever, so I figured he had forgotten me. I can't believe he's still thinking of me."

"He gave us the impression that you're the love of his life," Kerboros says.

"Is he truly still waiting? For me?" The tears spill over and run into his beard.

I hesitate, then pat his shoulder lightly. "He thinks you're the one who's moved on. He has no idea that you're trapped here."

"Speaking of moving on," Rosa prompts, "we can't wait around forever."

"We could try to orient ourselves through magic," Zeph suggests. "Kerboros seemed able to navigate despite the mist, and I presume he relied upon tracking magic to do so."

I'm pretty sure Rosa would approve any plan Zeph suggests. "Let's try."

"What's the worst that could happen?" Zeph says.

30

Uncovered

This piece adorns the bookshelf beside the bed, and it's hidden inside a sliding door. If you slide back the panel, you'll find a pastoral scene carved as a frieze at the back of the cupboard. There are two figures seated in a field, surrounded by lambs gamboling around them. Use of different pigments highlights the scenery, a color-washing technique the artist has experimented with before. Other wildlife is present within the picture, and it registers to the eye as a puzzle with hidden figures rather than a single scene. Some animals are dangerous and could be taken as predatory, a threat to those enjoying the ostensible tranquility, and the obscured borders with irregular lines lend the impression that something more ominous yet may lie in wait for these two, a threat that has yet to be unveiled. The piece offers an interesting dichotomy, presenting a complete juxtaposition betwixt first impressions and objective truth.

KERBOROS

"HERE WE GO AGAIN," THEA mutters.

"What's that supposed to mean?" Rosa asks with a scowl.

"It means that you're tempting fate," I answer.

I smile at Thea, hoping she's pleased that I remember our exchange. Her lips curve just a little, not quite a smile, but her eyes linger on mine, and it feels warmer than a touch. I'm so glad we're together in this. After what happened to my family, I haven't trusted anyone in so long. But Thea has become so important to me; I can't change the way I feel, even if there's no chance of a happy ending.

Other matters demand my attention anyway. I stare at Zeph, who is still glowing with the intensity of my fading spell. On my return, I overheard Rosa blaming Thea for our predicament. That is incorrect. The responsibility resides with the party who tampered with my portal spell. I wonder if Zeph will admit it if I come directly at them. If they insist, I can cast the spell again and set the parameters so *everyone* can see proof of guilt.

"Tempting fate?" Rosa repeats.

"Challenging the universe," Govannon clarifies. "Speaking for myself, I'd rather not worsen our situation."

"How have you been surviving here?" Thea asks.

"I can't starve, can I?" Govannon says with a weary half shrug.

"You must be parched." Taragon immediately starts making a drink with pinches of this and that from her supplies, and then she passes the mug to him.

He accepts with a grateful smile, sipping with so much appreciation that I feel vague regret that it didn't occur to me to inquire about his physical comfort. Thea is the only person I've ever been inclined to look after.

"Magical pathfinding," Rosa prompts, flitting about my head.

I repress the urge to swat her away like an irritating insect. While she might be foulmouthed, I don't want to antagonize her before I reveal the truth about Zeph. I notice their eyes on me in turn, and they fold their arms, seeming curious but not concerned.

"I haven't had any particular success in that area," I say. "Perhaps someone else should take a turn."

"Are you suggesting I do it?" Zeph asks.

Thea answers before I can: "It's certainly not within my sphere of expertise."

"I could try..." Taragon doesn't sound confident.

Govannon is still cradling the warm beverage in two grimy hands. There is a peculiar pathos in the contrast between how well he's dressed and how disheveled he's become during his exile. "If I could cast a spell and depart this terrible place, I'd have done it ages ago. I wish I knew how long I've been gone."

"From the way Ragh spoke of you," Thea says gently, "I do believe it's been a very long time indeed."

"I would concur." I back her up on reflex.

She continues, "We gave him a flower, etched in rose quartz. He said it reminded him of a present you gave him when you were courting. He seemed so happy, remembering those times."

"They were the happiest of my life," Govannon admits.

"Why did you leave?" Thea asks.

Rosa practically snarls with impatience. "Uh, I don't care. Does anyone else think this is a colossal waste of time?"

Taragon takes a gentle tone. "Not at all. We need to know how he ended up stranded and what things he's seen while he's been here. Information is valuable. We'll be better prepared. And moreover, he's a new member of our group. Just as you contribute as an irreplaceable team member, so will Govannon, once we work out his strengths."

Now I see why Thea wanted Taragon along.

As Taragon speaks, the pixie's bristling anger subsides. "Irreplaceable? Me?"

Thea jumps in then. "Certainly. You've scouted for us so many times and offered invaluable intel. We never would have made it out of that flower field without you."

"That's true," Rosa says. "But...it's nice to be acknowledged."

"And that's what we're doing for Govannon," Taragon concludes.

"Then I suppose hearing his story can't do any harm," the pixie allows.

"For what it's worth, I agree," Zeph adds.

They have been listening intently, eyes dancing between the speakers while volunteering nothing. I've noticed they behave this way a lot, favoring neutrality and observation, but my instincts tell me that they're collecting data, storing it away and possibly making judgments that concern everyone. Everyone but Rosa, perhaps. I think she knows more than she's letting on.

"It's not a long tale," Govannon says, after a long sip of tea. "I tinker. I invent things. Magic and metal, that's my purview. Some light smithing, betimes. The climate in Summer wasn't hospitable to some of my wilder notions, and I wanted to try my luck in Autumn. I used the mushroom circle that I've always favored for such travels, and it should have deposited me a reasonable distance from the village outside the palace."

"It didn't, obviously," Thea says.

"Indeed not. I suppose I'd call it a freak happenstance, a rogue mana-storm, and suddenly, I'm here. Alone. Where I've been until that one"—he points at me—"found me."

"I'm not sure how much we'll need smithing or inventions," Taragon muses.

Thea seems like she doesn't want him to feel bad. "You never know."

Nobody is looking at me at this moment. They're not watching Zeph either. But I am. And I witness how their expression changes, the harmless facade shifting to reveal a sly calculation. I can't hold my tongue any longer.

"I have critical information," I say.

"About what?" Rosa asks.

"I've determined that my last portal spell didn't fail on its own. Someone interfered with my magic and sabotaged my efforts to transport us safely."

Thea's eyes widen while Taragon merely looks puzzled. Neither of them reacts otherwise, and they don't speak.

"Sabotage?" Govannon repeats.

Rosa remains silent as well. *You knew, pixie. While you were shouting at Thea, you knew the truth.*

"How can you be sure?" Thea finally asks.

"Because I followed the tracking spell back to the culprit." I detonate those words among the group, and they all start talking at once.

Zeph finally responds: "You're implying that the saboteur is among us. Are you expecting that party to admit their guilt?"

I accuse them directly at last. "If you choose not to, it changes nothing. The trail led me directly to *you*."

Instead of appearing remorseful or even mildly alarmed, they grin, showing a few too many teeth. "Congratulations, hound! You finally figured it out. I'm surprised it wasn't sooner. Didn't things go wrong as soon as I showed up?" Zeph laughs, an edge to their voice.

"That's true," Thea says tightly.

Zeph continues, a trilling taunt in their tone. "Didn't it seem like a coincidence? That I wanted to help you out of the goodness of my heart? I'm agog you allowed me to tag along, hound. Not surprised about Thea. She's known to be a gullible soul."

"Asshole," Thea mutters.

She prowls toward them, and Taragon grabs her wrist as she winds up to slap Zeph. The hobgoblin wears a thunderous scowl, matching Thea's expression. "Let's talk first. If we don't like what they have to say, we can rough them up later."

Zeph staggers back, pretending to be hurt. "How brutish. And here I thought not all hobgoblins are thugs."

"They're being offensive about you *and* my dad. I need to hit them," Thea grits out through clenched teeth. "Just a little."

"I wouldn't stop you," Rosa says, surprising all of us.

Especially Zeph, if their expression is any hint how they're feeling. "You too, Rosa? But you knew—"

"Not that we'd get stuck in a place like this!" she screeches.

I couldn't agree more. "Explain yourself."

"You owe us that much," Taragon adds in a thick voice. "And tell the truth. Remember that the beating is still on the table."

Thea has one hand curled into a fist, and she eyes their jaw. "Zeph wouldn't know the truth if it slugged them."

Govannon sighs. "I have no idea what's going on. I'd forgotten other people can be so exhausting and complicated."

"How can you be so relentlessly awful? I only asked for some honesty!" Taragon is clearly hurt, not just by the lies but the prejudiced remark as well.

She's wrapped her arms around her body, bracing herself against the injury inflicted by those careless words. Immediately Thea's anger fades when she realizes how Taragon is feeling, and Thea wraps both arms around her friend, wrath abandoned for consolation. They lean together, until Taragon pulls back.

Then Thea whirls on Zeph. "Apologize to her! Right now. For what you said and what you did. She's worried sick about Tempest, and she can't even find out how they are."

She cares enough about Taragon to feel her pain, and that is reason enough for me to slice Zeph to ribbons, burn their bits to ash, and then bury the char at a crossroads. I'm holding the leash on my temper only with great restraint. They had best watch their behavior—and their tone from this point on.

"I'm sorry," Zeph finally says.

I can't tell if they mean it.

Thea glares at them, one arm still around Taragon. "Who the hell are you anyway? What do you get from screwing us over?"

"Time," Zeph replies.

Thea and Taragon swap a look while Govannon drinks the last of his tea, allowing our complications to slide right off him. Then Taragon says, "Can you clarify?"

"Macha's tits, big folk are slow," Rosa complains.

Zeph chides, "Don't be cruel, my friend. The answer is obvious if you think about it. I've been wasting your time, not allowing you to complete your quest. But now I'm caught, and you *have* completed your quest." They bow in a ridiculously courtly gesture, full of sweeping arm movements that make them look curiously boneless. "Devan J. Fenelon, at your service. The *J* is for *Jozeph* but—"

"You go by *Zeph*," Thea finishes.

The truth sinks in. It explains the odd atmosphere and the antipathy

I sensed now and then. We've been traveling with Thea's contracted spouse for a while now, and they've witnessed everything. Everything about us. Everything *between* us.

I strangle the urge to curse like a pixie.

31

A Spell for Discord and Dishonesty

While I do strive to calm troubled waters, conflict isn't always bad, my jewel. When stress and tension build, sometimes there's nothing for it but to vent it. All the harsh words and recriminations need to be spoken and acknowledged before healing can begin. When you pass the point of no return, there's no remedy better than a proper row, a dustup to end all dusting. Air those grievances. Don't let them fester.

This also works if you have dear ones being stubborn, keeping feelings repressed. This magic solicits the truth, regardless of how willing the speaker is to share their thoughts. There's an element of coercion to this charm, so don't use it lightly. Best be sure you're ready to hear those home truths before you unleash them on the world.

Cast this spell at the hour of your greatest need, and leave no doubts in your spell work. You'll require:

- *Iolite*
- *Ginger, skullcap, and hops*

- *A copper pot*
- *Dank, smelly water*

This spell will infuriate those you cast it on, so be ready for that. Put the herbs in your pot, and burn them to bits with your magic. Once you have the char, simply add the foulest water you can find. The worse it smells, the angrier they will be, mind. And that's not only the magic. What a working! The fastest way to start a fight indeed. Now, then, you've got your terrible mixture, so take the iolite in your off hand and hold it close to your heart. Now you can wield the pot in the other hand, for yes, 'tis a weapon of great power.

Now sling the concoction on those you want to quarrel with! If you can bear to do it, it's even more effective if you dash it in their faces. And let the shouting start! You might want to run now, my gem. Because furious fae tend to chase. Sometimes they also attack amid the screaming as well, but once the anger's purged, it'll be possible to come to accord once more. You'll know if you need to do this, judging each situation on its own terms. This is an extreme measure, and people seldom forget that you used this charm, even if they forgive you.

THEA

I DON'T KNOW WHERE TO start with any of this.

To say I'm stunned would be an understatement. Alternating waves of fury and humiliation wash over me, until I can't speak while I adapt to my new reality. I've been traveling with my so-called spouse for a while, and based on their behavior, they're most definitely an asshole. I understand why they deceived Kerboros—he's directly related to the Winter Court—but it was pretty clear *I* had been pressured into making this deal. Yet Zeph chose to continue deceiving me as well.

I find that difficult to understand. Everyone seems unwilling to speak in light of this new development, and I know exactly what to do. I've wanted to use this spell for ages, and if ever a group needed to get their crap out in the open, it's this one. Silently, I dig into my bag for the hocus pocus handbook Da wrote for me and race through the steps. I take pure, unfiltered delight in gathering the disgusting gray water all around us. The others watch me, each of them seeming puzzled.

You'll find out very soon.

Once I have the warm, stinky brew, I dash around splashing it in everyone's faces, laughing like a backward banshee. The way they jerk and hiss, I can tell the magic's taking hold. Since pixies have a loose hold on their tempers at the best of times, which this isn't, Rosa is the first to boil over. But instead of screeching at me, to my utter astonishment, she whirls and takes aim at Zeph.

"You are"—she fires an arrow—"such"—fires arrow—"an irredeemable asshole! In the endless time I've known you, have you ever asked how you can help *me*? Made anything up to me like you're constantly saying you will? No! It's all empty smiles and pretty words with you, Devan J. Fenelon, and I'm sick to death of defending you to people who rightfully think you're a selfish stinkweed!"

Zeph dodges and bristles. "You follow me like a pet, Rosa! Am I not supposed to treat you like one? Maybe if you respected yourself more, I would too!"

"I hate you," the pixie shrieks. "Hate you for a million years plus ten!"

"And I have more important things to worry about," Zeph snaps back.

Tara wades in, going at Zeph verbally without missing a beat. "People are important. But you don't care about them, do you? Only Important Matters. If this is how you treat a loyal friend like Rosa, I'm glad we're enemies."

"I just met all of you, and I already wish I were back in my tree," Govannon exclaims.

Everyone quiets at the sound of Kerboros unsheathing his weapon. "You must answer for this treachery," he growls.

Oh crap. I didn't mean for things to escalate this much.

Zeph lets out a mocking laugh. "Don't pretend you're challenging me to a duel. You can't fight unless your cousin orders you to do so. Everyone knows—that's the worst-kept secret in Winter."

Kerboros smiles grimly in response. "The best-kept secret in Winter is that I broke that tether long ago. I maintain my own secrets, traitor. Defend yourself."

"Yet you continued to serve? Spineless." A dagger appears in Zeph's hand.

They circle, eyeing each other's stances. If I had to guess, I'd say they're searching for a weakness. Kerboros has reach on Zeph, but Zeph...I don't know what they're capable of. Right now, I feel like I don't know them at all.

"Stop this!" Tara has a knife at Zeph's back. That's my best friend, and nobody saw her coming. She seems harmless, until she isn't.

Rosa has her bow trained on Kerboros. "Stand down. If anyone's killing them, it'll be me. Get in line."

"Your poison won't end me," Kerboros says.

"Maybe not. But it'll make you wish you were dead."

Kerboros and Zeph lock eyes. Then, coming to some silent consensus, they lower their weapons at the same moment. In response, Rosa slackens her hand on her bow, and Tara lets Zeph back up a step. I observe, unable to believe how well that spell worked. The air feels lighter now. My dad was right. Sometimes truths need to be spoken.

"Apologize," Kerboros demands.

Zeph affects a bored aspect. "For what? I already apologized to Tara for hurting her feelings. Isn't that enough?"

"For tricking us. For lying to Thea, *especially*. And for stranding us here."

"I can't say I disagree with any of that," Tara says. "An apology is the least of what you owe us, if you're the reason we're stuck in this awful place."

Govannon shudders, visibly horrified. "Did you *really* do this on purpose?"

Zeph doesn't answer.

Rosa says, "For the record, I'm with Tara. I'm done pretending I don't find this shit troubling. I knew about Zeph's plans to delay the group, but they didn't mention *anything* about the In-Between."

All at once, their bravado drains away, leaving a different Zeph. Their face is wan and worried, past the uncaring glamour they've maintained. "I don't know if I've done the best thing. At the time, it felt like the *only* thing. If you had all the details about my background and the situation, if you understood my—"

"We need to talk," I cut in. "Now."

Narrowing my eyes, I glare to stress how much I don't care about their problems.

Zeph replies, "It's not that I disagree, but we're short on privacy, and I don't have the hound's facility for tracking. If we wander off, we might not see the others again."

"Then we step to the other side of the rock and whisper." I stomp over to where I've pointed, though standing water turns my angry footfalls into splashes instead of the thunderous pronouncement I'd prefer.

Somewhat to my surprise, Zeph follows. "Go ahead. I suspect you'd like to call me a few choice names before we get to the real issue."

They're right, dammit. And by saying that, they've made it impossible for me to do it without seeming predictable. "Which is?"

"How we're avoiding this marital alliance."

I stare at them silently, not giving any sign of my thoughts. Zeph deserves to sweat over what they've done. And now, put in context, I recall how they said it would be convenient to seduce me. *Is that why...?* It's not that I'm *interested* in them, but it stings how quickly they dismissed me.

For the first time, their eyes widen as they evince surprise at my reaction. "Don't tell me you're in *favor* of this charade? We don't have an ounce of chemistry."

Unlike Zeph, however, I can't lie even to make them uncomfortable. The truth spills out. "You're more like an annoying sibling than someone I can imagine myself marrying."

"We have that much in common," Zeph exclaims, beaming.

I scowl at them. "*I'm* not the liar, though. Or the saboteur."

"Right, I should have clarified, you're not annoying in the slightest. But you're not the sort of person who could move me to romantic interest either."

It's hard not to feel vaguely offended. "Agreed, we have all the spark of wet kindling." Sighing, I add, "I feel like such a soft touch. You must've realized that I'd agree to *any* plan to get me out of our contract marriage. Why didn't you tell me a long time ago?"

"At first, I wanted to take your measure. And then I became wary of your bond with Kerboros. I did think *you* would cooperate, but I also suspected you'd share anything I told you with Winter's hound. And I believed he was still compelled to report everything he learned to his cousin. No one has any notion that he's managed to break his geas."

I grimace. Unfortunately, that makes sense, not that I think logical explanations justify our current predicament. "So secrets got us here. Yours. His. Well, no more of that. It's time to reveal your genius scheme."

32

Fearful Symmetry

This is the only painting the artist has ever completed. It's clearly an experiment, and the brushwork is primitive and unskilled. There is only the vague suggestion of what might be a feline creature, a cat-sith, surrounded by dark shapes, looming in green and brown. Familiarity with the artist's work might allow one to guess that those are trees. A forest, perhaps. The rest of the hand-stretched canvas is washed in darkness, eclipsing other details. A jagged slash violates the upper portion of the painting, an expression of utmost rage. That, too, speaks as much as the depicted images. Some truths can only be carved with knives.

KERBOROS

"ARE YOU SERIOUS?" THEA SHOUTS. "How can you *not* have an exit strategy?"

I step closer, ready to take her side. But before I reach Thea and Zeph, the mist thickens, and as it becomes more opaque, it also darkens, shifting hues from bone to charcoal. Now it's an inky swirl, obscuring my vision entirely. The fog coils around me, soft susurration whispering around me, soulless hunger born from the void.

Self-preservation forces me to stop. Without my intending to use it, my magic flicks out, an eternity of training that makes it my instinctive reaction. Except it's not to save myself; I'm looking for Thea. And the trail simply…ends. As far as the tracking magic can determine, I'm alone in this place. The living shadow envelops me, crawling over my skin like a swarm of insects, all skittering feet and obsidian eyes.

"Thea!" I call to her, but the fog does more than swallow me whole. It also steals my voice and carries it away in dying echoes.

"Taragon? Rosa? Govannon?" Finally, I'm desperate enough to shout, "Zeph!" even if I did nearly stab that bastard.

No replies. The silence holds a smothering weight, and fear chews at the corners of my mind with pointy rat teeth. Perhaps the In-Between is more than a liminal space; this feels akin to the torments of the afterlife that mortals write about, sometimes in terms of deeds that will result in eternal damnation. I cannot imagine a more powerful punishment than being trapped with myself for time unbounded.

Something flashes in the distance, and then I'm somewhere else. Still alone, but this—the scene that resolves before me—isn't possible. First, because there are no green meadows anywhere in this dreadful realm, and second, because my brother died long ago. And yet he's here with me. Even knowing that this is some wicked snare and that I'll likely be devoured by whatever evil creature has donned his skin, I still stride toward Geraint, who clutches me close and pounds my back. Then he steps away to look at me, a ready smile on his face. Tall and thin, dappled with cinnamon freckles, and hair as red as—who? Who had the red hair?

The question tickles at the back of my head, making my mind feel itchy. Conviction grows that I've forgotten something incredibly important, but Geraint allows me no time to process that flickering awareness. He slings an arm around my shoulders and beams, all light and joy. He's just as he was, while I'm no longer a child. It's unusual for a fae couple to produce more than one scion, but my father was obsessed with the family line. With legacy and proving our rightness to rule.

"Just look at you! It's been an age, hasn't it? Are you ready?" he asks.

For a moment, I can't speak.

"For what?" I finally manage to reply.

"I promised to train you! I've been putting it off because I didn't like the thought of teaching you such skills when it's so obvious that your talents lie elsewhere."

Now I remember; it's been so long. Geraint was the one who first showed me how to handle a blade—reluctantly, I must concede. This specter isn't lying. Our sire insisted that I be made useful to his planned rebellion. He had no use for art, either before or after his determined return to contention for the lord's laurels.

There is still mist, but it's gentle, dew clinging to the greenery beneath my feet. I remember that it was early when this happened the first time. Though I don't register Geraint drawing his weapon, suddenly he brandishes a dull practice sword, carved from fallen wood. He stands with his shoulders straight, toes angling outward. I mirror his stance, but unlike the first occasion, I notice that his feet aren't properly set. My years as Winter's hound have taught me more about matching blades than my brother ever knew.

"Loosen your shoulders," Geraint tells me. "You're too stiff."

I'm stiff with shock. Disbelief. He demonstrates a smooth swoop with artful flair. And I smile as I realize my beloved elder brother wasn't particularly skilled with a sword. Those fancy flourishes won't serve when one is locked in vicious combat. My smile fades. Perhaps that's why he died. He believed in a better world, but he lacked the ability to carry his vision to fruition. A dreamer, our Geraint, not a doer.

Geraint launches a controlled attack, and I parry. My blade is everywhere as he searches for a gap in my defenses. But there isn't one, at least not that such a shadow can discern. I go on the offensive, a flash of feints, and Geraint stumbles, breathing hard. He can't block my blade work, and I clip his shoulder, hard enough to sting.

"I don't think you have anything to teach me," I say then.

My "brother" sneers. "You *would* think that, hound."

The mist surges, and my brother's form morphs into Lord Liskaal, the person I loathe most. The practice sword has become a deadly weapon, a real sword with a razor's edge. I need no invitation to attack, even though this will mean my death if this is truly his avatar, if he's run me to ground in this wretched place. Hate boils up in a red-hot wave, spilling over into the violence I imbue in each slice into his defenses. He has sparred with me before, but I've always been careful to conceal my true skill and to let him win for the sake of his overweening pride.

Not this time. Even if it's just an echo, I'll kill him if I can.

Shadow Liskaal gets his blade up in time, resulting in a jolt up my arm that feels fearsomely real. Our swords scrape and shing, sharp metallic sounds as I adjust my stance. His next strike comes fast as fate, inches from my throat. I dodge. And fury floods me—cold, precise, and unrelenting. He cannot predict my movements because he's never viewed me as a worthy foe, whereas I have observed his fighting style at length.

That lends me a crucial edge. I press the attack, varying high attacks and low feints to the point that he can't anticipate where my sword will be. The world narrows to blade and breath, advancing toward the moment when I annihilate him. Emulating my style, he bluffs left, then lunges right, nicking my side.

"First blood," he taunts. "If you surrender, I may be merciful."

Surrender? No. Never again.

While I may have set aside my plan to disappear, I will never return to his service. Ignoring the pain, I angle my sword and slam the pommel into his jaw. As his head snaps back, I whirl alongside him, slashing his hamstring, and his leg buckles. Shadow Liskaal dips to one knee, forced to acknowledge my victory, but his eyes seethe with hate.

"I have bested you."

"You lack the courage to finish me, spineless cur made in your father's image."

Without the slightest hesitation, I run him through. My blade pierces his chest, and it's only after I've done it that fear takes hold. What if I've been fighting one of my own group? What if I've just murdered Zeph or—my sword drops from my numb fingers—Thea? There's no corpse, however, and relief nearly takes me out at the knees, just like Shadow Liskaal.

Thea's safe. She's whole. She has to be.

I don't think I can live in a world where she doesn't exist.

Instead of a body, the changeable enemy shifts for the third time, this change spinning in a swirl of formless energy, shimmering gold and then orange and then red, all wild magic and unharnessed chaos. Not an enemy at all? Just...magic, born from my own brain? That creates questions about the monsters we fought earlier, but I can't linger on them with the smoky tendrils creeping over me again.

When the murky mist subsides, I find myself in the desolate clearing as if I never left. The others stand frozen in awkward positions. Rosa hovers with her mouth open, as if she was about to speak, but her wings aren't moving. Taragon is half bent over, while Govannon is caught mid-stride, like he intended to leave our company entirely. Zeph and Thea remain on the other side of the rock; her arms are akimbo, her face tight with displeasure, and as for Zeph, they are in the process of turning their back on her.

I'm the only one who can move, I think. I walk among them, tapping, touching gently, shaking, and in some cases, slapping. Not too hard. Zeph had it coming in my opinion. Nothing rouses them.

Perhaps they must defeat their own internal enemies to regain external agency? There must be *something* I can do, some way I can help. The heaviness of truth settles on me like a drunken gruagach.

I never imagined myself as a hero, but I might be the only one who can save them.

33

A Spell for Mettle and Moxie

Everyone is frightened sometimes. This charm will help you to marshal your boldness and take heart. No matter how dire a situation seems, you can face it, though a magical boost may help. Heroes do not emerge fully fashioned with a sword in hand. Instead, they battle fear and worry at every turn, and yet, despite knowing all the terrible things that could happen if they do this difficult thing, they still choose to take that path. That is courage.

You have spent your whole life fearing to take up space, afraid you'd be sent away from the only home you've ever known. I've done my best to assuage those fears, but I'm aware that you still carry deep wounds. For you, my dearest daughter, I hold fast to the hope that you'll one day believe what I've always understood: You're a treasure.

This one is best cast at midday, and be firm in your convictions. You'll need:

- *Agate, carnelian, and jade*
- *Basil and lemon balm*
- *A silver censer*

Burn the herbs in the censer with the spark of your magic. Clutch the agate, carnelian, and jade in your left hand. And speak aloud what you fear. Breathe in the smoke and out again. Push it forward, until it dissipates. Once it clears, your fears will be dispelled as well, and you'll feel stronger, ready to confront any situation. This applies to emotional strength, primarily, but if you cast the working fiercely enough, there may be some physical impact.

You may not realize how potent you've become, but then you're so careful that I can't imagine you harming anyone with careless wrath.

In fact, as a wee one, you took great pains to help all the little creatures. You and Tara hatched a clutch of abandoned lizard eggs in the stable loft and didn't tell me. The two of you took such good care of them that nobody knew. Until they grew up, had babies of their own, and the palace was eventually overrun with lizards.

I smile when I think of swarms of lizards. And you.

THEA

IN THIS DREAM, I'M VERY small.

This is the first house I lived in, a large and luxurious manor that felt too big, too empty. The pattern of the stone mosaic on the floor is symmetrical, slate gray—or is it blue?—smoothed to a preternatural shine, while the walls are washed a cool white. I walk through various rooms: a bedroom that nobody sleeps in with midnight velvet hangings, a library crammed with books, and a parlor overlooking an exquisite garden full of night-blooming flowers so rare that if they exist anywhere else, I've never seen them.

When I lived here before, I wandered around alone for what felt like a long time, crying, until the cook took pity on me and let me sit in the corner of the kitchen. Like always, I was looking for Rain and Fen and not finding them. They should have engaged someone to look after me, but I have never factored into their considerations. I exist and they feed me. That is the extent of our interactions.

Their indifference is breathtakingly cruel.

Today, they're in residence. The staff is buzzing about it, and it's like we've been visited by the gods when they're present.

I creep up to the library door. These are my "parents," though I've only seen them a few times. They're gone a lot, and they seldom speak to me—or even glance at me—but I'm always looking at them. Their wondrous beauty makes me ache; I can never compete with the child they lost, the one they never stopped trying to find. The one I can't replace.

I hear them talking, but I can't hear everything, and they don't even notice when I slip into the room and curl up in a corner. I wrap my arms around my knees, trying to make myself smaller, always smaller. If only I could disappear and stop being the wrong child, the wrong person. Unwanted.

"What are we supposed to do with her?" Rain asks.

Fen shrugs. "I don't know. I feel sorry for her, pitiful little thing."

Rain says, "Can't we leave her with Mudge? He seems to like her."

"Shouldn't we formalize the arrangement?" Fen asks.

I love Mudge. He takes me out into the wildlands, and I don't feel sad there. There's no one to tell me that I don't belong. I would prefer to stay with him if I was offered the choice. Not that I will be. Rain and Fen don't seem to think of me as a person, not even a small one. That means my wishes are irrelevant.

I fight the urge to cry. Loneliness is a weight on my chest, tightening, tightening, *tightening*, until I can't breathe. Light flashes, white-hot intensity.

Rain and Fen are gone. Shadows deepen, slithering toward me like shades of dead things that want to swallow me whole. Into that silence comes a little *scratch-scratch-scratch* at the back of my mind, and at first I try to resist, imagining it's some awful intrusion. But then it starts to feel familiar.

I know this person, don't I?

"Let them in." That feels like an instruction from someone else, but I sense no malice in the directive.

So I lower my guard. When the shadows recede, I'm no longer alone. No longer small. My mind matches my body, and the rapidly shifting circumstances make this feel like a dream, but he's here. How is he here?

I breathe his name, overwhelmed with joy warring with astonishment: "Kerboros. You came for me."

"There is no distance I would not cross to find you." His tone contains no levity, only devotion, and of such a singular nature, I marvel that I seem to possess it.

He takes my hands. There is a chill to his touch, but it's echoed in mine, and the points of contact on our skin warm swiftly until heat blooms between us. That warmth suffuses me, sweeping through my body until my nerves are singing. I want him so much that my body aches, and my toes curl.

"I'm so glad you're here," I say then.

"This is all a dream. You have to wake up. And return to me."

My eyes snap open. Kerboros hovers nearby, but we are not touching. He reached me in the depths of my despair, trapped in the past, in the pain. And he *dispelled* it. Now I can recall the scene where Rain and

Fen discussed what to do with me, as if I was a stray kitten they'd found, without pain threatening to double me over.

I throw myself into his arms, a creature of impulse to my core, and he catches me close, caressing up and down my back. I have never felt like a treasure, though my dad often calls me one. But the way Kerboros touches me, the gentleness of his hands, makes me *feel* like a wonder.

"How can we help them?" I ask, stepping back. I could have lingered in his embrace, but not with the others counting on us.

"You're close to Taragon. Perhaps you can reach her."

I nod. "Tell me how you did it, then."

"I focused on you, the essence of you, and magic did the rest."

"Magic." I speak the word like a curse.

Will it always be my downfall? But I *must* try. I'll never forgive myself if anything happens to Tara. I talked her into joining this mad endeavor; I can't allow her father's suspicion of me to become an accurate estimation of my character, of the danger I pose to those around me, those who trust me.

"Keep watch?" I ask.

Kerboros assents immediately, and I close my eyes. First, I simply remember Tara, what she means to me. When we first met, I hadn't been long in Mudge's custody. He would never admit it, but I suspect Da came to some arrangement with the Toadpearl family so I would have some company. He must've been worried about me, friendless waif that I was.

I remember the essence of her, everything we did together, and then, with all the fervor I can muster, even though I'm exhausted by what we've already endured, I spark up my magic. At first, there's nothing. Silence and void. Then, a faint pull on what feels like a thread tying me to her; I follow it—such a nebulous strand—and a narrowing sensation fills my mind, as if I'm passing through an impossible tunnel.

I'm with her. Standing in the tavern kitchen, though not as clean as it was when we visited recently. Everything is dingy, dishes piled high, and Tara is little too. What we witness as we grow leaves a lasting mark, it seems. Raised voices go back and forth, an argument gaining in sound and fury. I don't see Tara's parents, but they must be in the common room.

"We don't even have enough to pay the grocer!" Tara's mother shouts.

"I'm doing my best! We just need to get past this rough patch and—"

"You always say that! We need a miracle, not more of your nonsense. I've made a deal with a hobgoblin in Winter. He'll pay good coin if Tara helps him for a few seasons."

"You sold our daughter?!"

"Not sold. Rented. She'll be treated well and fed delicious food while learning about another culture. What could be better?"

"Woman, I swear—"

"Tara!" I touch her lightly on the shoulder. I put aside the pinprick of pain about being right; Da *did* buy me a friend.

Well. He rented me one. But that means what we have now is real. She could have turned her back on me, especially after I hurt Tempest. The fact that she didn't means everything to me. It doesn't matter why we're friends now, only that we are.

"Thea?" She blinks at me like one awakening from a long slumber.

"Focus on my voice. None of this is real. I need you to resist. And to follow me out. Take my hand if you trust me."

For a moment I'm afraid—I'm so afraid—that she won't. But just as she trusted me in the real world, she takes one step, then another, and soon her fingers wrap around mine. She doesn't doubt me.

"I don't understand," she says in a small voice. "This isn't the Toad in the Hole. At least, it hasn't been like this for a long time. And you're so tall."

"You can be too. It's a dream, and you control what happens."

Frowning, she seems to concentrate, and her form slowly shifts. "Oh, I see."

Still holding on to her, I stretch my magic to its limit. I didn't think about getting back, but when I picture Kerboros pacing, waiting for me, I feel the tug on the other end. He's the thread that allows me to pull her out. His strength, his resolve. I don't dare to put other labels on it, not when I'm promised to someone else. Outrage sweeps through me, fresh and piping hot. *Damn Zeph anyway.*

My eyes snap open. Tara gasps, stumbling forward, but I catch her and give her a huge hug. "Steady. We made it."

Tara touches her forehead to mine. *Because of you. Because you love me.*

Tears fill my eyes. We haven't mind-sung to each other since we were children. It's confirmation of an old and intimate bond. Doing this without surety of your welcome in someone else's head is not only unwise, it's also the height of discourteous imposition. I wouldn't have done this without an invitation.

But she's right. I do love her.

I do, I reply.

I love you too, Tara says silently.

The others are fearfully still, but just then, Rosa swears, turning the air blue with her affront. "When I get my hands on the stinkweed that dared to ensnare me, I will cram their nose up their butt!"

Tara laughs, easing out of my hold. We break the mental connection because it's rude to do that when others are present, especially wild fae like Rosa who can tell they're being excluded from the conversation. Kerboros might not have realized what was happening between me and Tara since he's high fae, but I don't want him to feel shut out either. He's more observant than people realize.

"Welcome back," I offer.

Tara smiles at Rosa. "You're the only one who got out on their own."

The pixie preens visibly. "I have a stubborn streak."

"We still need to rouse Zeph and Govannon," Kerboros says.

I summarize how Kerboros roused me and the way I did the same for Tara. Then Rosa says, "Understood. I'll get Zeph."

She's incredibly efficient. No more than a handful of heartbeats—and I've no idea what the pixie says to Zeph in the dream realm—but they awaken in a foul mood. They pace, ignoring the rest of us, seeming unsettled by whatever they experienced. If the trial remained consistent, it was a traumatic event from when they were young.

I don't welcome them back or try to comfort them. I would like a proper apology, fewer of these *I did the wrong thing for the right reasons* excuses. Whatever their motives, they fooled me, sabotaged our travel multiple times, and treated me like an accessory to a plan they haven't troubled themself to share. In fact, just before this magical entrapment, they claimed they didn't *have* a plan to exit the In-Between per se.

"How can we save Govannon?" Tara asks. "None of us have strong ties to him."

Kerboros answers, "I'll try. I'm the one who brought him back to the group, for whatever that's worth."

"I believe in you," I tell him in a bracing tone.

"I'm glad to hear it, Thea." People don't use my name a lot, so it gives me a start, hearing it in such a velvety tone. The unusual softness makes it seem like an endearment.

"Wait," I surprise myself by saying.

Kerboros offers me an inquiring look, and I don't look at the others as I cross to him. There's no point in pretending he isn't precious to me, and I don't want to regret letting this moment pass. Rising on tiptoes, I kiss his cheek. "For luck."

His smile is so beautiful that it breaks my heart for all the moments I *haven't* seen it.

He gathers himself, and then he's ensorcelled again with the fate of our party resting squarely on his shoulders.

34

Endless Spiral

This piece is aptly named, as a spiral has been carved into the wall, though the unsteady cuts indicate that it must have been an early effort. There has been no attempt to smooth the roughness of those lines, so it lends a rustic rather than mythical look to the curls turning ever inward. Lighter wood grain peeks out from the grooves that have been winnowed out with time and patience, so the pattern has a certain illusive quality that makes one think that it might, in fact, be a portal or a doorway—that if one touches a specific point, an aperture might open to allow us access to the inner sanctum, where greater treasures or artistic endeavors might be stored, secured against prying and judgmental eyes. But finding the pressure plate, that might be a riddle that only someone who loves the artist could solve.

KERBOROS

I CAN'T BELIEVE I'M HERE again, after volunteering to save a stranger.

This isn't the person I've been, but it feels more natural than the role I've been forced to play. I center myself, mentally collecting the few facts that I know about Govannon like overripe apples plucked from the ground. He loves a brownie named Ragh, he invents things and uses magic on those innovations, and he's been stranded alone. I imagine what his inner landscape will look like, and I envision that terrible tree growing on the rocky outcropping surrounded by stagnant water. My mind carries me there, and I *do* discover him perched on that branch, just as he was when I found him the first time.

I waste no time in saying, "We must go. This is an illusion."

Govannon snaps, "If it was so simple, don't you think I would've done that already?"

"It's not simple at all, for you have to trust me."

"Trust you? I barely know you."

I clench my jaw. "You'd rather remain immobile and defenseless, easy prey for whatever might be hunting you through mental warfare?"

"Perhaps I don't care anymore. If I get eaten, I'll be done with fear and loneliness."

The impatience I've been battling eases. I cannot fathom his torment. Others suffering such a lonely exile might have already broken beneath the weight.

With some effort, I gentle my tone. "If you give up, you will never see Ragh again. Against all odds, against all common sense, he's still waiting for you, though he'd never admit it. The pain he feels at not knowing why you left will never cease. What's it worth to you? The chance to hold him, explain what happened, and cry happy tears together?"

I can't believe those words emerged from my mouth; Thea has changed me, an alchemical shift transmuting lead to gold. And that's truer than anyone will ever know. Before getting close to her, my heart felt heavy as a stone, and now it glitters at the mere thought of her.

"Everything," Govannon whispers.

"Then leap! I'll catch you. And you will awaken." I speak with enough confidence that he launches off the branch immediately.

I keep my word, and together, we chase the distant warmth that binds me to Thea, soul to soul. My head feels fuzzy and strange, as if I have spent too much time apart from my physical form. Thea steadies my elbow when my knees wobble, and I encircle her shoulders with my arm, pretending I need the support more than I do.

Govannon rouses, stretching his arms over his head. "Another trial passed. I appreciate the fact that you searched for me," he adds.

"You're one of us now," I respond.

Rosa groans. "Macha's tits. Get me out of here before something worse happens."

"We can't linger," Tara agrees. "Exploration is out. Resting is unwise. This place is a threat on all levels. I'm surprised Govannon managed to keep his wits."

"Debatable," the gnome mumbles. "I do talk to myself rather a lot."

Thea speaks in a hesitant manner. "I have a suggestion. My dad wrote a spell…" She produces a little book that she reads often, opening it to a particular page. "This one. It deepens connections, and I thought maybe we could use it to pool our magic. One person might not be powerful enough to produce a portal and hold it long enough for us all to escape, but if we cooperate, it might work?"

"Fascinating idea," Zeph comments. They have been eerily silent since emerging from their private hell.

"I'll try anything," Govannon adds, desperation etched on his weary features.

"I'm with the gnome," Rosa says. "I'm in too."

While I'm not thrilled with the notion of being bonded to everyone, even temporarily, I'll attempt this since Thea suggested it. I hope that *only* our magic will be shared, not my private ambitions and the threads I've been weaving. I've given up on faking my death, but those who helped me slip my bonds could be harmed if others betray our connections. Erdene exists at the epicenter of a silent resistance that has been undermining Liskaal for ages. I hesitate, then make the decision. Though it's potentially perilous and I could be responsible for so much harm if there's too much overlap, I nod. This is a necessary risk.

"Can I read this spell before we begin?" Zeph asks, more tentative with Thea than they've been.

Thea stares at them, eyes narrowed, before deciding to allow the request. She hands over the book, and once Zeph scans the page, everyone takes a turn doing so. The ritual is simple enough, and she has the components in her bag. I admire her graceful hands as she arranges everything just so.

"So this is how you do fae magic?" The pixie doesn't sound mocking or hostile. It's just a question.

"My dad thought it would help me focus. It doesn't come easily to me, you see."

Rosa flutters over to Thea and pats her cheek. "Nobody's good at everything. My handwriting is rubbish, nearly illegible, and I can't even draw a straight line."

Thea smiles. "Really? Your honesty is so comforting."

"Is it? I'm just telling the truth. Pixies are straight talkers, you know. Never get any bullshit from our people, take us or leave us."

"I prefer your approach," Thea tells Rosa. "They drive me wild in the courts, never saying what they mean, taking forever to get to the point."

"Tell me about it!" Rosa exclaims.

When Thea smiles, the atmosphere warms between them. Rosa settles on Thea's shoulder as she leads us in performing the steps together. Next, we join hands, and at first, it seems like it's not working. We're just awkward people holding hands. But soon, my magic trickles out, joining Thea's in a teasing tangle. Her threads entwine readily with Taragon's, and Zeph has woven their startling strength through Rosa's tapestry of power. Govannon's shy magic surges last, until all our energies connect in a chaotic tangle. All around us, wild mana crackles in reaction, slashes and arcs of color in hues that match our personalities. This primordial energy is wild and uncontrollable.

"We'll either open the strongest possible portal," Tara gasps, "or blow ourselves up. Not sure which, but at least we're together."

Govannon manages a tight laugh. "I'll take *any* change at this point."

"Ready?" Thea asks.

Everyone nods.

Zeph turns to me with an unreadable expression. "You have the greatest skill with portal magic. I swear upon my life that I will not interfere this time. To give us the greatest chance at success, you should control the aperture."

I don't respond, but I take control of our joined energy, using my will to shape it. The veil thins, and I reach for a familiar mushroom circle near the Autumn village, my intended destination before. As the vortex forms in shimmering gold, Govannon cries out nearby. A hideous, oozing thing rises from the water, red as blood, pocked with sticks and stones and moss and bones. The monster seethes with mindless hunger. The gnome shrieks and dives through the portal before I'm entirely sure it's stable. I don't even know if I had the destination properly set. If he ends up lost again—

I struggle to hold the portal open as the creature undulates through the mire toward me, and I speak through clenched teeth: "Go! Get yourselves safe. Get out *now*."

I can't picture the mushroom circle at all, and oddly, there's such a familiar pull, like Thea is on the other side of the portal. But that's impossible. *Perhaps it's the last place we were? Please, not the Summer market—that would be no help at all.*

Zeph is the first to comply, beckoning to Rosa. "Hurry, let's move."

The pixie follows him with a troubled glance in my direction. Taragon rushes through right after, leaving Thea to cast me a desperate, frightened look. The vortex hurts, screaming in my head as the magic tests the limits of my will. As she dives, I move, trying to seal the portal as I tumble through, but the arcane force blows me off-balance, and the vortex oscillates wildly.

I need to close it, but it resists my tether. Something is pushing, pushing, relentless need, and then I hear a thunderous pop—the monster follows us out, flopping with a slime-ridden squelch. It keens and snuffles, and then come the slurping, hungry sounds. The creature slithers toward a mortal woman, frozen nearby, mouth open in astonishment.

I'd ask who she is and what she's doing here alone, but the portal is melting my brain, and that monster intends to eat us.

35

A Spell for Crossroads and Connections

There comes a point in every journey, my gem, when you realize you're not where you've intended to be. For me, in my various travels, that has often been a literal truth. If you're lost and you could use some aid getting on the right track, this working will work like a charm. Hopefully my wordplay put a smile on your face, even as you wrangle with veering off course. If you're not near a proper path, even a worn pooka track will do, best if there's signs of passage in all four directions, as a crossroads emboldens magic.

Now, then, this spell has two stages. The first will present a suggestion as to what direction you should set out, so you'll need ingredients suitable for orienteering, and the second part aims you toward someone within the vicinity who will prove helpful to your situation. I have said this before, but it bears reiterating. You might be borrowing help today so it won't be available the next time you need it. Magic can be a boon or a curse, and I never want to see you on the wrong side of a pixie's hex. You'll know when you need to cast this.

This one is best cast right before departure. You'll require:

- *Azurite and hematite*
- *Cinnamon and peppermint*
- *A copper teapot*
- *Clean, clear water*

Heat the water, and make a lovely pot of peppermint cinnamon tea. Savor each sip, and feel your head becoming clearer and lighter. Drink it all down to the last drop, then take the crystals in hand and press them to your heart. Allow your magic to rise, and you should feel a pull. Let yourself walk in that direction. Whichever way you're facing, that's the right path for this moment.

Once, you went off with Ferghus, but I didn't know where you'd gone. I scoured the palace and went to Miremorel, thinking you might've gone home without me. Everywhere I looked, no Thea. I was frightened half to death when you showed up on that pooka's back, all smiles and wild hair and dirty face. When I said I was worried because you'd gone missing, I'll never forget what you said with a roll of your eyes.

"I wasn't lost, Da. I was adventuring."

THEA

THE MONSTER HAS RAGH'S FACE.

That thought occurs to me as everything happens at once. As the monster rushes, a human woman shouts something, but I can't make out the words. The portal is a trembling golden vortex, expanding, twisting, writhing, and I don't know how long Kerboros can keep it open. I remember my dad telling me to trust myself, and the idea pops into my head, fully fleshed out.

But exigence forces me to be brief. "Push that beast back," I call.

Our magic is still linked, or the portal wouldn't be open. I give an experimental tug, and the energy surges toward me. Instead of trying to fight the monster, I envision the magic as a giant wall and exert force. The creature rebounds against the shimmering field and tumbles toward the wavering portal.

Zeph locks their will onto mine. "I see what you're trying to do. All hands, push!"

"Everyone, together!" Rosa grunts with effort, and her will is *astonishingly* strong.

Tara settles into the bond, adding her determination, and then Kerboros and Govannon lean in. Their colors swirl around me. While we're joined, I can see their auras, shaded by their moods and personalities, but I don't let the magical rainbow distract me. Another heave, and the immense creature careens toward the vortex as it snaps closed, severing our magical connection and bisecting the beast. The back end plops to the ground, jerking in death spasms; it doesn't dissipate. Rather, the unwholesome flesh unbinds, oozing into a more liquid state, so the objects that were lending mass squirt out into a crimson puddle.

The smell is indescribable.

"We should burn it, just to be sure," Kerboros says.

Zeph spearheads the magical initiative. They set the first sparks, and I add my will to the flame. One by one, the others commit to this course, until there's a conflagration before us, a pyre immolating our foe.

A human woman has been observing our struggle with wide eyes and finally speaks. "Who the heck *are* you people?"

I finally turn to look at her fully as the flames die to ash, cooling from orange to gray with magical precision. And then I blink. Rub my eyes and look again. Because she looks like *me*. She's softer and rounder;

she has deep dimples and incredibly kind eyes, but there is no mistaking the resemblance.

I've never met *anyone* who looks like me. Good chills pepper my skin as I take a step toward her, confused but drawn by her mere presence.

Kerboros gazes at her, head tilted, and it makes his ridiculously beautiful hair shimmer. "I would be inclined to ask that you answer the same question," he says.

"Why?" I ask.

He explains without looking at me: "Amid all the chaos during the attack, I lost the mushroom circle. But I felt a pull. A presence that felt like an echo of you, Thea."

"Thea?" the woman repeats.

It's not really a question, more like an expression of joy. Her eyes are wet with it. Then she rushes forward without hesitation and wraps her arms around me.

"Feels like I've been searching for ages. When I heard you were missing, I had to come. I'm Olive. And we're sisters."

Tentatively, I raise my arms, hugging her back. "Really? Are you sure?"

"I'm sure. You're the only one here who's…not fae." Suddenly, she pulls back, careful with what she says.

Maybe in case they don't know that I'm different? I suspect Olive doesn't want to alienate my friends, and I adore her for that moment of caution, her instinct to protect me. I step back after giving her a gentle pat on the shoulder. I have no idea how I should feel.

I have a sister? I have resisted the urge to try to learn more about my mortal family because I feared it would hurt Da. That he'd think I didn't love or appreciate him enough. Though some fae are all about the bloodline, Da doesn't care about that. Neither do I. What matters to me is how people treat me, if they love me for who I am without trying to change me.

But the sad little girl inside can't stop smiling. Because someone I've never even met cared enough to come looking.

"Wait," Tara cuts in. "You're Thea's actual sister?"

"Biologically," says Olive. "Yes. We are sisters. Though I won't force a relationship if Thea is uncomfortable. I just had to make sure she was safe."

Rosa waves her arms. "Uh, can we go back to the part where Thea is missing? And you've been searching?"

"Technically, I haven't seen her since she was born. But that's not exactly what I meant. You see, the fae notified Rain and Fen that Thea disappeared while on some official dispatch for the Winter Court. Rain and Fen told Iris, who told me about it."

"Who's Iris?" I ask.

Here, Olive hesitates. "Rain and Fen's natural daughter. Raised as my sister, but she never fit in with our family. They're…they can be difficult. Right now, she's only talking to me and, occasionally, our dad."

Oh. So Iris is the daughter they abandoned me for, and she grew up with *my* family.

I can't believe I'm asking this: "What's she like?"

Olive takes a moment to consider. "Kind. Creative. She's never met a stranger. And she can be impulsive. It frustrated our mother, who cares more about achievement than joy."

"She sounds a lot like you," Tara says.

If that's the case, maybe I wouldn't have been a good match in that family either. "What do you mean, 'achievement'?"

"I'm a doctor," Olive answers. "Our sisters—"

I blink. "How many are there?"

"Four, if you count Iris. We're all named for flowers. Sort of. Iris, Lily, Rose, and me, Olive. I'm more of a vegetable. My dad named me, and he said olive trees do flower, so it doesn't disrupt the theme."

"Sorry, I think I interrupted the answer to my own question," I admit.

Olive smiles. "No problem. It's a lot to take in. You asked about the achievement thing. It means our mom cares more about success. She loves bragging about how well we're doing in our careers. Rose is an attorney, and Lily is a therapist."

"Are those good jobs?" I flush because it's embarrassing how little I know about the mortal world.

"Mother thinks so."

Belatedly, I realize we've kept the group standing while I questioned this woman—my sister, though I still can't wrap my head around that—relentlessly. "Sorry to be so inquisitive. This probably isn't the time or place, but I hope I'll have a chance to ask more later."

"Not at all. I'm just happy I found you."

"I'm stunned that you came looking," I admit.

Olive says, "I was concerned from the beginning, but time wore on, and there were no updates from the Winter Court. Rain and Fen did make a few inquiries, but nothing came of that. And I…well, let's say I also needed a break. For personal reasons."

"It's not easy for a mortal to visit," Zeph says. "How did you manage it?"

Olive smirks. "It's better to leave you wondering, isn't it?"

Zeph narrows their eyes, but they're absolutely sparkling. "Tease. How did you know that I prefer delayed gratification?"

I frown at the two of them. I can't believe Zeph is flirting with the sister I just met. "Seriously? Now? Of all times."

Pink rushes up Olive's throat and blooms to her cheeks. I watch Zeph track the heated flush with an indecent level of interest. They smile and lick their lips.

Kerboros clears his throat. "I agree with Thea. This isn't the time."

"Yeah," Rosa says. "Keep it in your pants, you two."

"Oh my God. Sorry!" Olive whispers, pressing her hands to her cheeks. "I don't know what came over me. Normally, I'm not like this, I swear."

"It's the Devan effect," Tara says, not unkindly. "They're legendary for smooth talk, seductive lies, and irresistible charm." She glances at Zeph with a single-shoulder shrug. "Sorry. But working in a tavern, I hear things. Or rather, I heard about *Devan*. I didn't know you prefer to be called *Zeph*."

Truth. People drinking deep from their mugs love to gossip. And I do recall Tara warning me about Devan over drinks at the Toad in the Hole. Seeing Zeph try their luck with the sister I just met aggravates me; it feels disrespectful since we're technically married. Maybe that's hypocritical of me since I've been kissing Kerboros, but at least he's not Zeph's brother.

Olive nods, a certain shift in her aspect that indicates she's taken what Tara said seriously. "I won't fall for it again."

Zeph makes a wordless sound of protest at being summarized and dismissed.

I ignore them. "Back to the original topic."

Deadlines. Mishaps. I mean, we *did* go off course, and thanks to Zeph, things haven't gone as planned. And I admit that I've lost track of time, but—

"How long have we been gone?" Kerboros asks.

Zeph gets out their magical timekeeping device, and we all stare at it, stunned when it displays the date and time. *Four months.* We lost four months in the In-Between.

Time passes differently in the fae realm. It can be faster or slower depending on the magic and the ruling entity of a territory, and a lot of complicated factors, but either way, we're certainly past the allotted span that Lord Liskaal set forth.

That's it. I've failed.

It's a death sentence. My dad must be so worried. I feel physically ill. I exhale unsteadily, trying to control my emotions. Really, all I want is to fall over and burst into tears. But I don't want my sister to think I'm pathetic. She came all this way. For me. The least I can do is hold it together a little longer.

"Did your parents send you to look for me?" I ask.

Should I have said *our*? No. I can't. Mudge is my dad. I don't know the people who raised Olive. A hot flush washes up her neck and onto her cheeks as her silence tells me what I need to know.

"I came on my own," she replies. "And I'm not entirely sure how long I've been here." She waves a hand. "I don't know anyone, and I've just been...wandering." Her voice goes shaky, and I realize she must've been frightened. By the journey, by the enforced solitude, and then by our arrival since we came bearing monstrous gifts.

"What a dreadful welcome," Zeph murmurs in a silky tone. "I can do better for such a legendary beauty." They eye Olive as if they'd like to eat her up from head to toe.

She bursts out laughing, deepening the dimple in her soft cheek. "I see what Tara means. You really *are* a liar. That was so thick and greasy, I could butter bread with it."

"She's not wrong," Rosa says, smirking at Zeph.

Their skin flushes. Actually flushes. "I had impeccable reasons for those deceptions! Everything will work out. You'll see. There are simply a few more hurdles—"

"A lie is a lie," Olive says simply.

This is the most agitated I've ever seen Zeph. I might not be their type, but clearly Olive gets under their skin. They start to defend themself but Kerboros cuts it off with a slash of the deadwood he's been using to churn the char, making sure the creature can't rise from the ashes like a phoenix. I don't think phoenixes ooze, though. Hopefully not.

"Nobody wants to hear it," Kerboros snaps.

Zeph quiets, visibly chastened.

Govannon tips his face back, staring up at the sky, so different from the endless gray veil of the In-Between. "I'm finally free."

"Nobody knows you were with us," Tara tells him. "Our situation is complicated. But yours doesn't need to be."

I nod. "Make your way back to the Summer Court on your own if you prefer."

"No! I've certainly had enough of traveling on my own. And I didn't do so well the first time, did I?"

"I probably wouldn't take off either," Rosa admits.

The gnome continues, "Ragh has no idea what befell me. I would much prefer an escort back to civilization since I have no idea where we are. If I set out willy-nilly, it could delay our reunion even more."

"Then stay with us," Kerboros invites.

"Indeed I shall. I'll try to make myself useful," Govannon answers.

"Then we've increased our numbers by two," Zeph says.

They seem to take it for granted that Olive will accompany us, once we figure out where we're going. My stomach roils, fear battling with disappointment. I wanted so badly to fix this—to succeed instead of making a mess.

Kerboros whirls from the embers, his face cast in shadows, faintly sinister in the waxing light, likely because he's wrestling with what I've already realized. "My cousin gave us less than two weeks. It has been significantly longer. And he does not take failure lightly."

Tara curses, and I swear she's been learning from Rosa. "At this point, I suspect we're considered fugitives."

"There will be a bounty," Kerboros confirms. "Hunters too, albeit not of my caliber."

That's not hubris; there's a reason Lord Liskaal kept Kerboros so tightly leashed and forced him to track Winter's enemies. Kerboros is the best. So perhaps his knowledge and expertise will buy us some time.

"We have options," I say, trying for a smile. Judging by the look of the people staring back at me with varying degrees of concern, I've failed spectacularly. "My dad has a spell for this occasion too. It can help us figure out where to go next."

I keep the true worry secret because it's too bleak to speak into existence: whether the hunters have orders to arrest us or slay on sight.

36

> ***The Maze***
>
> *The carving is etched onto the ceiling above the artist's bed. From a distance, the maze scans like a geometric tapestry; up close, the craftsmanship reveals subtle variations in depth and edge crispness. Those who have studied the artist's work might find it fascinating that the creator wished to gaze at this work each night before falling asleep. Is it a symbol, a threshold to be crossed, or an indication of the artist's emotional state? It might, instead, be an expression of hope, that there is always an available path. The complexity of the pattern can be soothing to busy minds, allowing them to focus on tracing the lines to find their own center.*

KERBOROS

NOW THAT THE INITIAL DANGER has passed, I take stock of our surroundings.

We've landed in a meadow, bordered in all directions by distant trees. One side has a mushroom circle, the other a row of standing stones. To the right, the approach has a rocky path that's been laid on purpose, leading to a deep and dreary wood. On the left, there's a profusion of wildflowers in purple hues—violet, lavender, lilac, and periwinkle. Some are tall and ferny, while others grow close to the ground. I don't sense danger from any of these areas, but I'm not in top form right now.

"My head," Rosa groans.

"It's unbearable," Taragon adds.

Govannon sighs. "We overextended ourselves, I fear."

"It was the only way out of the In-Between," Zeph says.

My head pounds as well. Light hurts my eyes, and my skull feels heavy. Until now, I didn't realize it was possible to have a magical hangover. It's so painful that I can't think properly, and it takes me longer than it should to realize this.

"Even if the new trackers lack my skill, we must stay ahead of them."

"My dad wrote a couple of spells that might prove useful," Thea says, producing the battered grimoire that saved us before.

I worry that she may not be strong enough to tap magic again, as she struggles with it at the best of times. It might have been better to do this as a group, but when the portal closed, it also ended our link. She won't appreciate me questioning her, however, so I will support her, whatever she chooses to do. And if she stumbles, I will catch her.

Thea appears to rush the first charm, and I cannot discern whether the initial working had any effect. Next, she completes the second spell, and she takes a step toward the flower path. She bites her lip, glancing over one shoulder to see whether we'll follow. I do. And the others fall in behind me, silent, most likely in exhaustion.

We have already suffered so much. And now we must run, just like those I once hunted. The appropriate nature of this trial does not escape me.

"You're sure we should head this way?" Taragon asks Thea.

"I think so," she answers.

"I would have gone with the mushroom circle," Govannon says.

Zeph shakes their head. "The obvious transport hubs will be guarded. We can't travel openly through known portals. For my plan to succeed, we must stay ahead of pursuit and reach the Autumn Court within the next ten days."

"What plan?" Thea gripes. "As far as I can tell, you don't have one."

"Thea has a point. Do you ever intend to *share* your incredible plan?" Taragon asks with audible skepticism. "Because I agree, it's starting to feel as though you're winging it."

"How dare you," Zeph says, entirely without heat.

At the back of the group, Govannon is talking quietly with Rosa. Their voices are too low for me to discern the topic of conversation, which is fairly unusual. The pixie isn't known for her discretion, so I wonder what that's about. Taragon, walking quietly beside me, casts more than one look back, as if she might be thinking the same thing.

The mortal woman, Olive, speeds up to fall in step with Thea. "I came from the stone circle over there. It's farther than it looks."

"How did you get here, anyway?" Thea asks.

As I'm directly behind them, it's impossible not to overhear. I won't join the conversation unless Thea addresses me directly. People may one day call me her hound instead, for the way I feel, I would follow her to the end of the world for a gentle word and a soft caress.

"I drove to a grouping of stones in Massachusetts. Local legends claimed that when all conditions aligned, it was possible to pass through to the fae realm from there. So I did the research, and there was a blood moon happening, so—"

"You just dropped everything and took a chance?" Thea sounds so surprised.

When she turns her head, I can see that she's smiling. And her eyes are very bright. I'm so glad that someone proved to her she hasn't been forgotten by the mortal realm. Once Olive gets to know Thea, she'll treasure her even more, as Mudge and I do.

"Of course! You're my sister, and I was *so* scared I'd never even get to meet you. I started a sabbatical as soon as I heard you were missing. I didn't have a plan past getting here, but I had to try. And here we are."

"This means a lot to me," Thea says softly.

"The sky is so different," Olive muses, gazing upward.

I have never visited the mortal realm, so I quicken my pace slightly, ensuring that I stay close enough to hear what she has to say. Taragon appears curious as well, and I can tell by Thea's quick head tilt that she's interested. Her hair is tangled, darkened with the filthy water from the In-Between, and yet to *me*, she's still so beautiful that I find myself smiling at her back.

"How so?" Thea asks.

"There's no sun here. I'd imagine there are no stars at night either. Just…colors. It's like living beneath the aurora borealis all the time."

"What's that?" Taragon asks.

Though I'm loath to admit it, I'm curious too, drawn by the information Olive must possess. As we enter the forest, the path narrows, so we can't walk together, even if Olive seemed inclined to. She doesn't budge from Thea's side, though she smiles at Taragon to acknowledge that she heard the question.

"It's also known as the northern lights, visible only at certain times and in certain parts of the world. Something to do with charged particles or solar wind, interacting with the planet's magnetic field. I think it also relates to oxygen and nitrogen somehow, but this isn't my area of expertise. I'm a physician, not a physicist."

"I don't understand anything you just said." Taragon frowns, as if she doesn't enjoy feeling left behind.

I cannot say I comprehend the terms either. While I have read some fiction from the human realm, the stories I perused seem to have been written long ago. I rather enjoyed some detective stories by a Mr. Doyle, though I found his protagonist rather lacking in social graces. Rather like me, come to that.

"Sounds complicated," Thea says. "If the northern lights look like the sky here, then maybe it's glimpses of the fae realm slipping through where the veil is thin."

"I like that explanation," Taragon declares.

"A physician is a medical doctor?" I am fairly sure I read that in some mortal tome that made its way here.

"Yep! I specialize in virology. And...I'd rather not talk about work." Olive smiles at Thea, seeming alight with happiness. "Have you learned to manage your abilities?"

"You mean my endless craving to leech from people until they collapse? I wouldn't call that an ability. More of a curse." Thea's bitterness is tangible.

I wish I could comfort her, but I stay quiet. Olive is likely better suited to the role.

"It shouldn't be like that. What do you know about our physiology?" Olive asks.

"Nothing. My dad tried to figure out what I need, but there are no resources. The fae aren't terribly interested in others, at least not beyond seeking some territorial advantage."

"They sound like cats," Olive says.

"That is accurate," Rosa pipes up. "Pet us, give us treats, offer what we want when we want it, and we are the dearest creatures. But should anyone prevent us from having what we desire?" The pixie's smile chills even me.

"I'll teach you as we travel," Olive says, touching Thea's arm in a comforting gesture.

We've reached the tree line, and Zeph whistles, high and clear. A bird swoops down, a glossy black-winged beauty, circling above our heads with raucous calls. They converse in chirps and trills; it's fascinating to hear such sounds come from Zeph. They don't realize that I'm conversant in crow, not fluent but knowledgeable enough to get the gist.

How do you fare, madame crow?

Well enough, though you've caused me no end of grief.

Is my mother well?

She worries. As she should, considering your predicament.

Update?

The conversation becomes more intricate, and this crow seems to realize that I'm listening. She peppers her talk with nonsensical sounds that make it more difficult for me to parse the meaning. At the end of the exchange, Zeph tosses a treat to the bird, who snaps it up with a greedy beak.

Zeph explains, "I have a network of informants. Crows mainly. I've just received an update."

"What did Crow tell you?" Rosa demands.

Govannon blinks. "The crow's name is Crow?"

"No, but crows don't share their names with anyone who isn't crow," Zeph says with a touch of impatience. "Can I tell you what I learned?"

"Please do," Thea invites.

"It would be a welcome change," I mutter.

"There is, indeed, a substantial price on our heads and the Houses of Summer and Winter hover on the brink of war."

37

A Spell for Finding and Foraging

You might have noticed that most of the spells I've written are designed to see you through tough times. I don't know if you'll ever wind up lost and far from home, but if you do, I want to help as much as I can. Hunger is an unpleasant condition, and I am unsure how it would affect you long term. Most fae don't need to eat, though we enjoy it socially and take pleasure in flavors and textures. It'll come as no shock to you, after witnessing courtly revels, that we all contain some measure of hedonism.

This working will find dew pear and winter berries, honeyheart, wild phlox, fenelon, beetsnips, and savory caveroot. With a few of these ingredients and some water, you can make stew. The spell might also locate pigweed. With a little magic, you can turn that into flour, which would make a beautiful porridge with some honeyheart or winter berries. Or you could whip up some flatbread to go with the stew. If I can't cook for you, my gem, then I must provide the tools to allow you to fend for yourself.

This one is best cast right after you awaken. You'll need:

- *Green agate, moonstone, jet*
- *Meadowsweet, sweet marjoram, and thyme*
- *A copper pot*

Put the crystals in your pocket and the herbs in the pot. Use your magic to burn the herbs until there's a savory smoke. Now follow it the way the wind blows. This may seem random, but imbued with your magic, the smoke will guide you to natural resources. It'll be up to you to identify them, and I hope the wildcraft I've taught you will stand you in good stead. You know the difference between honeyheart and bitter palm. The latter shouldn't be eaten, though it can be boiled down and added to other ingredients to make a salve that soothes irritated skin. I used it on your bottom when you were small.

You should have good results if you fix your mind on the type of ingredients you're looking for. If you need a hearty breakfast, you'll want pigweed and winter berries. For a variety of flavors, I'd look for wild phlox, fenelon, beetsnips, and savory caveroot. I've made that stew for your supper many nights, and you always cleaned your bowl and asked for more.

THEA

"THE ALLIANCE HAS FAILED," KERBOROS says.

He understands the intricacies of court politics better than anyone, except possibly Zeph, who holds their secrets too close for me to be sure what they know.

"There may be soldiers on the move, not just hunters," Rosa says.

Govannon rubs a hand across his already-disheveled hair. "Just when I thought it couldn't get worse. Perhaps I ought to have gone off on my own?"

"Too late," Tara tells him cheerfully.

Olive turns to me, lowering her voice. "If your world is anything like mine, a war will be terrible and devastating."

"The stories are," I admit. "But there's only been peace in my lifetime. I'm so young compared to everyone else here."

Her eyes widen. "So am I, actually. We're surrounded by immortals."

"There's nothing we can do about it," Rosa says then.

Zeph nods. "I have Crow keeping an eye on the situation, and she will report back. For now, we should seek shelter."

"Or make camp," Kerboros suggests.

I suspect it'll be the latter. We don't know what became of Tempest, so I might be a wanted criminal for reasons other than failing at the task set forth by Lord Liskaal. Everyone needs rest, and I suffer a painful wave of longing, recalling how the court ladies coddled me in the bath. I haven't been clean since we ran away from the Summer market.

Nobody has much to say, and we push onward in silence; it feels like my whole life has been reduced to walking. Olive leavens the journey with explanations about our shared nature, answering questions I didn't even know I needed to ask. I've been starving myself when I should be focused on a light, continual pull. No deep drains, just skimming from everyone, always.

"That doesn't hurt people?" I ask, incredulous.

Olive shakes her head. "I suppose if you lived alone in the woods with only one person, it might become an issue. But for psychic vampires—"

"Is that what we are?" I cut in.

I've been called a leech, a siphon, even a demon or parasite. But this is the first time I've heard the correct term for my heritage. There might even be books for me to read in the mortal realm. Maybe I'll read them when I'm sent away. After Kerboros is executed.

My heart clenches. Are we truly doomed, either to run forever or be punished in perpetuity for one failure? Well. Nobody ever accused the Lord and Lady of Winter of being fair.

My sister gazes at me, wide-eyed. "Did no one tell you?"

"I don't think my dad knows. Rain and Fen…" I hesitate, unsure of her relationship with them. "Never devoted much time to my education."

That seems like the best way to describe their emotional neglect.

"That's unforgivable," Olive snaps. "They have all the time in the world for Iris. And I love Iris, she's my sister too, but it's wrong that they just…"

Didn't care? Regifted me like an unwrapped parcel? I don't fill in those blanks, and she hugs me instead of speaking, and then we hurry to catch up with the others before they get too far ahead. It's all woods, all the time.

And I love the woods. I do. But I'm so tired. And hungry. And now there are two of us who need to drain energy. I realize that's something else I need to worry about.

"Do you feed on anger too?" I ask.

Olive shakes her head. "For me, it's pain. That's part of why I became a doctor."

At least we're not competing for the same *type* of energy, but feeding from the same small population doesn't seem like the best idea. "Do we need to worry about having two of us dependent on the others for sustenance?"

For the first time, she looks troubled. "Over time, it might become a problem. Normally, psychic vampires surround themselves with people to avoid situations like this. But in our circumstances, that's impossible."

Fantastic. As I suspected. I don't ask any further questions because the answers might weigh me down past what I can bear. From that point, we move in silence. None of the others break it, and my feet ache from the endless march. We've been trudging for what feels like forever, until we're deep in the woods, when Kerboros calls a halt.

The lights Olive mentioned have dimmed to a purple glow, but they're not visible through the dense canopy. Unlike the woods that border Macha's territory, these trees are lush and vibrant, fully covered in leaves that run the gamut from emerald to citrine. Zeph picks up a rock and charges it with magic so it offers a faint glow.

With that scant illumination, I process how much the ordeal has impacted our little band. We're all filthy, covered in cuts and bruises, from various clashes with beasts and behemoths. Though we purchased supplies, I wonder what's left. Our packs tumbled around the In-Between, just as we did. And that means the contents probably got soaked.

I don't intend to eat anything that could be contaminated by that foul water. Nobody suggests a fire. In our situation, that would be unwise. Zeph drops their pack with a thud, digging into it to check the staples they were carrying.

Their lip curls. "Spoiled."

"We should strive to leave no traces here," Taragon says. "If we discard our things, it will only prove that we were here."

"And give them a greater signature to track," Kerboros adds.

"Then we carry everything, whether we can use it or not." Zeph seems enervated by that necessity, or maybe it's the situation. They sink to the ground without doing anything that could be construed as setting up camp.

"Do we have tents?" Olive asks.

Rosa chuckles. "Even if we did, I wouldn't sleep in one. I'll be nestled in the branches overhead, if anyone needs me."

"I never thought I'd say this, but...me too." Govannon appears to despise the idea, but he's resigned to seeking refuge in the boughs above.

"It's kept you alive so far," Kerboros says.

Olive frowns, glancing at Zeph as if they've personally disappointed her. "No food. No fire. No tents. We just sit and hope we're not discovered?"

"I'll set magical wards around the perimeter," Kerboros says.

He slips away to do that before anyone can question him. Since I think it's a good idea, I wouldn't protest anyway. While I'm watching the direction he disappeared in, Rosa and Govannon also vanish, small enough to tuck themselves out of sight. Every rustle of leaf and creak of branch makes me jump; I'm nervy as heck, listening for the crunch of boots, the cold whistle of Winter magic cutting through the dark.

No, I trust Kerboros. He'll make sure we have time to run. His traps will sound the alarm and delay our pursuers, but his absence leaves me with Olive and Zeph, who watches my sister like she's the most wondrous being they ever beheld.

Is that how Kerboros looks at *me*?

My face feels hot, and I press my hands to my cheeks to cool them.

Olive turns to me, ignoring their fascination as she whispers, "I've extrapolated somewhat by context and active listening, but I was wondering if you'd mind sharing everyone's pronouns?"

"Rosa and Tara use *she*," I whisper back. "So do I. Govannon and Kerboros use *he*. And Zeph—"

"I can speak for myself," they say silkily. "If you were interested in me, beautiful, you had only to come closer and ask."

Olive dismisses them with a flick of her fingers. "I can hear you fine from here."

"Well, then. Sometimes I feel he-ish and sometimes I feel she-ish.

And sometimes I feel they-ish. It varies from day to day, but I generally use *they* for simplicity. Have you met anyone like me in the mortal realm?" Zeph asks, shifting closer. They move until they're next to Olive, drawn to her like she's pulling them with magical traction.

She regards them with serious eyes. "As it happens, I have. But what does my opinion matter? In this situation, only your feelings do."

Zeph smirks. "My feelings? What if I feel that I'd rather do you?"

If they're trying to disconcert her, it doesn't work in the slightest. "Then I'd say you need to try harder."

Peals of laughter ring out as the branches above us shake. "Shot down. I never thought I'd see the day." Rosa cackles. "Serves you right!"

I get a glimpse of a bearded face peeping through the tangled foliage. "Indeed, most entertaining, a bird's-eye view of romantic failure. I do hope I have better luck with Ragh."

Kerboros returns, settling beside me as the others quiet. I lean against him, and he wraps his arms about me in a natural gesture.

Keeping my voice soft, I say, "I couldn't survive any of this without you."

I can't be *without you now.* But I can't say that part out loud.

"I can't do *anything* without you," he whispers back, creating pleasurable chills with his mouth next to my ear.

This fae warrior has changed so much. Or maybe this is who he was all along; he just couldn't be himself while following Lord Liskaal's orders. I raise my face and kiss his cheek, then bury my head in his chest. He doesn't let go.

After we sleep a little, I use the foraging spell to source fresh water and make porridge. Then the alarms sound, a high-pitched wail that warns us of mortal peril.

38

Hunter's Blind

This is a rare freestanding sculpture, one of the final works produced before the artist's disappearance. Exquisitely carved from the bones of a massive creature native to the mortal realm, the statuette depicts a hunter lying in wait, though the prey remains hidden. The hunter is a prone figure with cross-hatch carvings to detail the leather armor he wears while his features remain smooth, lending him an eerie, faceless aspect. He is simultaneously every hunter and no one at all. That erasure of identity hints at deep, repressed pain, possibly the anguish of following wrongful orders. Note: Scrimshaw is not widely practiced here, as it carries unsavory associations in relation to humans.

KERBOROS

THEA DROPS THE COOK POT, and her gaze snaps to me, as if seeking guidance.

I lift a single finger to my mouth as I silence the shrieking alarm. Wordless, I gesture for the others to take cover. Govannon and Rosa hide in the boughs above as Zeph pulls Thea and Olive into a glamour. They are truly skilled, as I know they're there, and I still can't distinguish where they end and the foliage begins.

It's good that they didn't catch us in our bedrolls. In the distance, I hear movement. One set of footfalls, and they're not skilled with wildcraft. A stick snaps beneath feet more accustomed to palace tiles than stalking in an Autumn grove. The hunter emerges from between the trees, and I glide in the opposite direction, circling behind him.

Indeed, he wears Winter's colors, not even trying to blend in with his surroundings. And he's vain, sporting a cloak the color of moonless snow, edged with frost that does not melt. Such extravagance doesn't match the setting and provides no protection whatsoever. In fact, the light shade makes it easier to track him against the scarlet and gold of the turning leaves.

A weapon hangs at his hip. Another mistake. It should already be in his hand, a curved blade forged for aesthetic appeal, not for balance. I feel insulted that Liskaal thought this incompetent buffoon could face me. Yet he has found us. So perhaps he hunts better than he prepares for battle.

But then, there won't be a fight. Only an execution.

Whisper quiet, I ease up behind him. He bends to touch the cook pot and murmurs, "Still warm," to himself.

When he straightens, I strike, slicing my dagger sideways across his throat. Hot blood jets from the wound, and he presses both hands to his neck, gurgling as he fights for life. If there are others nearby, he might survive.

Unlikely.

"Let's move," I call.

Thea skirts the fallen hunter and retrieves her pot, shoulders hunched. I wish there was time to comfort her. But we cannot tarry. The others give me a wide berth, and I cannot say I'm surprised.

It's one thing to know someone is deft at meting out brutality, quite another to witness that firsthand. I hope this doesn't change how Thea feels about me. In unwilling service to my cousin, I have done so many dreadful things.

Olive passes me as Rosa leads the way from our campsite. Thea's sister lingers long enough to say, "You did what you had to. To keep us safe."

It helps. Possibly because Olive doesn't know me well, and she's under no obligation to comfort me. I scan the site one last time to ensure we've left no traces other than the body, and then I follow the group.

At our first break, Thea draws some water from a brook and washes the cooking pot. I pause beside her, not knowing what to say. She feels distant, and I can't tell if it's the stress of our situation or—

"I'm sorry," she whispers.

"For what?" Of all things, I never expected an apology. Not from her. She's done nothing wrong. I'm biased, but I hardly think she's capable of wrongdoing that would warrant such a profound expression of remorse.

Her eyes are wide and tearful. "You're in this situation because of me. But I'm also sorry you've had to live this way. Doing bad things for that bastard."

"Not to argue with you, but I'm in this situation because of my father. And I didn't mind playing my role. I'm *good* at it."

"You hate it," she snaps.

She's right. I *loathe* putting weapons to flesh. It's part of why I'm obsessed with using blades to create beauty instead.

"It's better killing people I don't know," I say softly.

Thea sucks in a sharp breath. "He…he made you…"

I only nod, because if I start talking, I might never stop. And I don't see how she could feel the same if she knew. If she knew everything.

Suddenly, her arms are around me, tight about my waist. "As the wild spirits are my witness, I will see him brought low for what he's done to you."

Sweet and tender Thea vowing vengeance in my name—what does it say about me that this feels like a declaration of devotion? Moved beyond any ability to speak, I press a quick kiss to her forehead.

"This spot is too open," Rosa says. "We have to keep moving."

I glance around, stepping away from Thea. "True. We march on. And look for a safe place to rest for a while."

If there is such a place.

The next seven nights are nightmarish.

Once, we left an entire group of hunters for dead, courtesy of the poison-mist potion we apparently bought from Tempest. Twice, we fled in the middle of a meal. Three times, we scattered and regrouped after my wards sounded the alarm as we tried to sleep.

We cannot continue this way.

There has been no peace. Liskaal grows ever more desperate, throwing all his resources at capturing us. Everyone is worn to the bone, weary beyond bearing, and we barely escaped the last time. They're getting better at predicting our movements, and the others are losing hope. Only my tricks at obfuscation have kept us safe thus far, and I have little faith that I can prevail against my cousin's relentless soldiers.

Visits from Zeph's coterie of crows have kept us supplied with information, at least, and we know that we're in the wildlands halfway between Summer and Autumn. Not that the knowledge helps.

Morale is low.

Thea pretends to be in good spirits, encouraging the others, but nobody likes our chances. Privately, I have caught Rosa whispering first to Govannon and today to Taragon. If nothing changes, she will likely split the group. I suspect she's saying that the size of our party makes us easier to track.

Unfortunately, she's correct.

We can't move as swiftly as a single hunter, nor can we disappear. As Zeph predicted, the stone and mushroom circles are guarded, impossible for us to pass. And the usual routes are being watched as well. I'm running low on alternatives and hope.

The forest offers plenty of forage at least, though people are tired of endless variations of pigweed porridge and vegetable stew. Thea and Olive *need* to eat, along with their regular infusions of energy, and since they're limited to how much they can draw from our small population, both Thea and her sister are looking peaked. From what I have gleaned from their conversations, Thea should feed constantly, a delicate skim of negative energy that makes others feel better. According to Olive, their existence is symbiotic with humanity, reducing violent urges and preventing wider harm.

To me, it seems as if Thea grew up hating the hunger that drives her, and in the past, she often refused to feed until the need grew ungovernable. Which explains what happened with Tempest. I can tell that she's worried about so many things: how Tempest is faring, getting caught by Liskaal, being banished, Mudge, and now her newfound sister. But I don't press her to confide in me.

I have just called for a brief rest when Crow circles twice, then dives for Zeph. They communicate too swiftly for me to follow, and then Zeph faces the group. "This is the message I've been waiting for."

"Spill it," Rosa orders.

Their dynamic has changed since we left the In-Between.

Zeph complies. "We've received an offer of asylum. I knew Lady Mirralee would welcome *me*, but I've been negotiating for the rest of you. Today, Crow carries good tidings. Autumn is willing to host us on neutral territory as they facilitate cessation of hostilities between Summer and Winter."

"Can we manage that?" Thea asks.

"They have a plan," Olive predicts in a wry tone.

The flirtatious fae flashes her a wicked smile. "You know me so well already."

Taragon frowns, hands on her hips. "Why didn't you tell us before? It's fine for us to risk our lives, not fine to be in the loop? Enough of that nonsense."

For the first time, regret flashes in their facile features. "It's not that I don't trust you after everything we've endured together. But if I speak of these matters, it's possible I could be overheard. That is why I communicate indirectly, via the crows. There aren't many who can speak their tongue, and translation can be…tricky."

"Just like you," I mutter.

Zeph eyes me with a narrow look. "I'm well aware that you neither like nor trust me, hound. But you can believe this: You'll be amply rewarded for your cooperation."

Raising a brow, I rejoin, "I doubt you have any notion of what I would consider suitable recompense."

"You might be surprised," they say. "But be that as it may, we need to double our pace to rendezvous with the Autumn envoy on schedule."

That galvanizes everyone, and we push hard, practically running, to make it in time for the meeting. Though I have doubts, an elegant fae awaits at the forest's edge, clad unmistakably in Autumn's livery, shades of brown and gold with red accents. For some reason, she bows deeply to Zeph.

Then she says, "It is a pleasure to meet you—"

"We have no time for niceties," they cut in.

I have the sense that they're preventing her from revealing…something, but I am not certain what they're hiding. What other secrets might Zeph be keeping? I watch them carefully, failing to discern anything other than nervous energy.

"Understood. But it would be impolite if I didn't introduce myself to the group. I am Leifan, first adviser to Lady Mirralee."

Lady Mirralee governs the Autumn Court alone and has never agreed to any formal partnership. She has two offspring, one of whom will rule when the lady tires of courtly intrigue. The other is shrouded in mystery, a scion born from some fleeting passion.

Zeph offers an impatient nod. "Crow said that you can guide us to a hidden portal."

"Indeed I can. Follow me."

Wards I laid at our prior rest point twang in my head. "The hunters are closing in."

"Hurry," Thea calls.

Leifan responds by breaking into a run, and now it's a race. I pour my magic into the terrain all around us, and the branches snap to life, as do the leaves and vines. The trees themselves will defend our passing. Thea shoots me an awed look as she dashes headlong, putting her whole heart into this final sprint for freedom.

Olive falls behind. Her body is built for comfort rather than speed, and Govannon is flagging as well, poor fellow. He spent so much time sitting in a tree in the In-Between that it's unfair to expect his stamina to withstand this level of exertion. I extend a hand and pull him off his feet. Thankfully, he's both small and light, and I settle him on my back without breaking stride.

"Hold on," I say, increasing my pace.

Thea slows to make sure Olive doesn't get left behind. The sisters have already bonded, and when they join hands, I can see the brightness of the energy flowing between them. Though they're at the edge of my earshot, I hear the tail end of Thea's encouragement.

"...stronger together. You can do this."

Leifan leads us into a rocky outcropping that wends ever downward, and sounds indicate a huge hunting party pelting through the tunnels behind us. Zeph curses in a manner worthy of Rosa as we careen around a corner. The passage widens, ending in a silvery pool.

"Dive," Leifan calls. "Don't hesitate. Take a deep breath and swim straight through."

"Won't they follow?" Olive asks.

Leifan snaps, "I bear the portal stone, and they'll have to pry it from my cold, dead hands. Which could happen if you don't hurry!"

Zeph leaps first, then Rosa. Taragon plunges headlong, and I nudge Govannon forward. "I'll be the last."

Leifan shakes her head. "That is my role. I promised to escort you all safely back to Autumn, and my lady will be gravely disappointed if I abandon that oath."

"Then I will wait until the others pass. Is that acceptable?"

She nods as Thea and Olive leap into the water, only a breath apart. Now it's my turn. The subterranean pool is icy, nearly stealing the breath I saved, and I cannot see. It's all dark rock, so easy to become disoriented, and yet it cannot be far, or Leifan would have warned us. I press forward.

Just as my chest begins to burn, I break the surface in a different space. I splash my way out of a fountain in a private courtyard in the Autumn Palace. We stare at the water until Leifan breaks the surface, and Taragon whoops with triumph. My gaze finds Thea, so precious, so inexpressibly dear.

We did it. Everyone's safe.

Against all odds.

A gentle voice speaks, light as dry leaves rustling in the breeze: "Welcome to my domain. I am Lady Mirralee. We have much to discuss, but I can see that the journey has been difficult. Please avail yourselves of every comfort before our conversation continues."

"That sounds heavenly," Rosa declares.

"Zeph." There is a certain tension in the lady's voice. "If you would be so kind as to accompany me, briefly, before your sojourn to the baths?"

"Of course," they say.

More secrets.

But I'm incapable of greater curiosity with the promise of a bath and fresh attire at hand. I will never take such luxuries for granted again. The group parts ways, each seeking the services that sound most enticing, whether it's a massage or a skin treatment or a deep scrubbing from the castle staff. It's only after I reach the bathhouse that sudden wariness shouts at the back of my brain.

Divide and conquer? This overture came from Zeph, who has never once confided their intentions or their endgame; can Lady Mirralee be trusted?

And if she's yet another enemy, one who wages war with guile and not force, do we have any options or allies left?

39

A Spell for Lessening and Letting Go

There may come a time when people leave your life forever. Much as I wish that I could protect you from all hardship and suffering, I cannot. And you may need help letting go. Time does lessen the pain of partings, but some losses linger like an ache in your bones once they've been broken. Even after the wound heals, you might feel hollow. On the longest, loneliest nights, you might envision the face you've been missing your whole life.

This charm might help. They do say that if you love something, or someone, that you should let them go. I did fight against that common wisdom in my time—fought and fought and fought again. Then I came to accept that some of the old sayings are true. And that some treasures are too dear for keeping.

I believe that since I accepted the necessity of letting go, I received the blessing of you. At the height of my despair, you entered my life like a sunrise. You gave me a reason to wake up. First, it was your wide eyes and hungry mouth and your grabby hands. In the end, I regret nothing and cherish each moment I have been granted with you, my dear daughter.

This one is best cast after a painful parting. You'll need:

- *Pink rose petals*
- *Rose quartz*
- *A silver censer*
- *A large red maple leaf*

Etch the first initial of your loved one's name on the leaf with the rose quartz. Wrap up the rose petals, and tie the bundle with any type of string. Your own hair will do in a pinch, though that may give the spell too much power, and it will smell horrendous when you burn the packet, which is the next step. Before that, speak your thoughts to the wind. It can be as simple as, "I love you, and I am letting you go." Or it can be more philosophical: "This ended so something else can begin." Others might take a more formal approach: "I honor what was and welcome what will be." Whatever words you choose will be right for the occasion, my gem.

Next, place your leaf bundle in the censer and burn it down to ashes. Scatter the ashes around you in a circle; then step out of it without disturbing the line you've created. This symbolizes letting go and moving on. There is no fate but our own choices, my jewel.

I trust you to make the right ones for you.

THEA

THE AUTUMN PALACE IS THE most beautiful place I've ever seen.

While the Summer market was charming, this is exquisite, and I'm no stranger to luxurious surroundings. Where Winter is austere and ostentatious, Autumn exudes comfort and warmth. Even the walls glimmer with veins of gold, marbled through with luminous color. Splashes of red with brass accents adorn the bath chamber, where an attendant has just finished scrubbing me from head to toe.

Though I tried to wash on my own, she offered with such gentle insistence that I didn't have the heart to keep fighting. Not when it feels this nice to let someone else take care of me for a while. Afterward, she offers a selection of fresh clothing, and it reminds me of the way Erdene tricked me into getting dressed for my own wedding.

But things are different in Autumn, right?

It would be a mistake to trust Lady Mirralee completely, but I doubt she wants the realm involved in open war. Skirmishes between Summer and Winter have the palace staff gossiping. I heard bits and pieces on the way here.

I'm here to make up for my failure. To keep the peace and save my dad. But first I have to get dressed. Naked people seldom stop wars.

The outfits are all beautiful. They range from formal gowns to split skirts with smart jackets to flowing trousers with a matching top that laces up the back. I like the last ensemble best; there's something piquant and piratical about it. And I love the color, a pale gold that should go nicely with my hair and sun-kissed skin.

But I hesitate, wondering about the dress code, and point at the third outfit. "Will that be suitable for public appearances in the palace?"

"Everything I've laid out will suffice for any occasion," the attendant replies.

That's all I needed to hear.

After I dress, she guides me to the suite I've been assigned, and we pause outside the rounded door, gilt tracings on all the trim. "I requested a light repast for you. It should be set up already. Can I assist you further?"

"I'm fine for now. I appreciate your effort and expertise."

"My pleasure. Ring the kitchens and ask for Sarene if you need anything else."

"Get some rest," I tell her because I know how hard palace staff works to keep important guests happy.

Then I slip inside. The room takes my breath away. I gaze up at the vaulted ceiling adorned with burnished copper tiles that match the sconces bathing the room in an amber glow. There are gold velvet chairs arranged around a table crafted from red jasper, laid with delicacies, just as Sarene promised: a silky red soup, creamy white cheese, crisp flatbreads, mushroom tartlets, and a platter of fresh sliced fruit.

Once I finish exploring, I'll feast. In the opposite corner, I find a built-in bookshelf surrounded by silken pillows and overstuffed cushions all in the warmest of jewel tones. I can imagine how it would feel to lounge there with a book, sipping some cool honey wine or a cup of hot spiced tea.

I'm sure there's a bed in here somewhere, maybe past the fringed curtains. It feels strange having all this space. I've hardly been apart from Kerboros since we left the stables together. I'm not sure how to measure the time we were trapped in the In-Between, as it didn't *seem* like that long to us, but it was for the rest of the realm.

As I head for the unknown portion of the suite, the curtain parts, and Kerboros steps past, fresh from the bath. He smells of honeyed soap and jasmine lotion, and I can't stop smiling. He moves toward me with intentional patience, and I glimpse the response in his eyes, a brightness he can no longer conceal. Not from me.

"I hope you don't mind. I told them I'd rather stay with you," he says.

My pulse flutters. "I'm glad you did. I was just thinking that it's odd."

"What is?"

"Being without you."

His voice deepens to a rough and sensual purr. "I suspect you're the only one who feels that way."

It's time for me to stop pretending. "Do you *need* anyone else?"

"No," he says at once. "Only you."

"Then what are we waiting for?"

I've ached with wanting him, and I'm done with the aching *and* the waiting. I need him like air, and while I haven't had a ton of lovers, I enjoy driving someone else beyond control, taking them until they're spent and boneless and gazing with shining, wonder-filled eyes.

"What about dinner?" Kerboros gestures at the table.

I give him what must be the wickedest smile. "We'll need the energy more after."

"I see your point." Without another word, he follows me into the sleeping chamber, where he'd been lounging when I arrived.

Another gorgeous space, this one is dominated by a four-poster bed draped in red silk curtains. The linens are a gentle gold, while the coverlet is a copper brocade. More matching sconces add a warm glaze to the jasper tables on either side of the bed. There's no wardrobe, but one of the walls has drawers and shelves, all gilded to the point that it's an excess of opulence. And the drawers each have hand-painted frescoes, different pastoral scenes that might interest me if I wasn't already slipping out of my top.

Kerboros watches me with twin fires blazing in his intent gaze. "You're so beautiful. Are you certain about this?"

"I don't know what will happen after tonight," I admit. "And I'm not sure there's a path where we're allowed to be together. But if I can be with you like this, even once, just for tonight—"

"It's worth it," he finishes. "And I agree. I will relive this moment for the rest of my life, however short it proves to be."

The ache in my body intensifies in my heart.

We both know the truth. Our failure to meet Lord Liskaal's terms means that Kerboros is marked for death and me for banishment. This might be our last chance. I won't waste this moment, as it may never come again. When we meet at the end of the imposing bed and he pulls me to him, the shock of pleasure is edged with a bittersweet bite. In that moment, I resolve to focus only on the sweetness, the delight of melting my beloved, who has known only endless winter.

But here in the heart of Autumn, he burns for me.

"I need you so." His voice is rough and deep with desire, his tone reverent.

"Yet you're still wearing too many clothes."

He disrobes swiftly, leaving me to admire his body. But when I wrap my arms around him, I feel ridged tissue instead of smooth skin. Scars? Punishment, perhaps. I don't ask because those questions will ruin the mood. But after? I'll hear everything.

He reaches out, grazing my cheek with a tender touch before trailing down my throat, tracing the line of my collarbone. I raise up on tiptoe, and his lips claim mine. The stern line is all heat now. A nibble, a taste, and then his tongue tangles with mine. I moan, pressing even closer. He shudders at the sound and lifts me so easily that it feels like flying.

With a little growl, he drops me on the bed, hard enough that I bounce. Now I'm the one shivering in anticipation. He kisses a worshipful path down my body, and I arch, barely able to breathe for the gorgeous sight of his hair spilling across my bare belly.

I melt for him utterly, giving him everything. He drinks everything up, insatiable as I've only dared to imagine. And then I take him as mine, leaving him trembling in my arms. Finally, we collapse together, sweaty and smiling.

Stroking his damp hair, I smile. "No regrets?"

"Never," he vows, curling into my arms. "It was… That was…"

"What?"

"Beautiful." But he's frowning.

I don't believe that's what he intended to say at all. "Tell me the truth, Ori." The name is a test. I'm not sure if I should call him that, if it'll remind him of the fact that he can't remember his mother.

But his eyes sparkle. "Only in private, please. That nickname is for us."

I grin because his expression is both charming and infectious. "A pillow secret? I love that. But seriously, what were you about to say?"

"That was my first time," he whispers, hiding his face in my shoulder.

I open my mouth, then close it, unsure what to say. "How?" I finally ask.

He lifts one shoulder, trying to make light of his prior isolation. "Liskaal allowed me no friends, and he made me murder those who regarded me with affection. When would I have had the opportunity?"

"I want to strangle him with my bare hands," I snarl.

Ridiculously, that makes him smile. "Me too."

"Did he give you those scars?"

Kerboros nods without showing his face, and I take that as a sign that he'd rather not discuss these matters.

"He'll get what's coming to him," I promise. "Somehow."

"Now that I have you, I find that I don't care about retribution. Happiness is so much more powerful than I knew," Kerboros admits.

His sweetness and candor take my breath away. "You have a point."

"Are you hungry?" he asks.

That's right. They left us a veritable feast, and I'm sleepy but also famished. No question that I'll rest better with a full stomach.

"Starving," I say. "Do we have to get dressed to eat?"

"Why would we?" In a playful swoop, he cradles me against his powerful chest and carries me to the lounge, where an elegant repast awaits.

I end up perched naked on his lap while we feed each other the choicest morsels until only crumbs remain. It's sheer bliss. There are worries waiting in the wings, but I can forestall them for one magical night. I focus on him. On us.

We make love again, this time with more tenderness. If he asked, I'd have let him know that Shereth charmed me to prevent conception and only she can dispel it. Afterward, a yawn catches me off guard, and he shifts, settling me in his arms.

A kiss to my temple. "We should get some sleep. Tomorrow will be..."

I bestow a sleepy good-night kiss in return somewhere in the vicinity of his mouth. "Yes. Tomorrow will be."

Drowsy with delicious languor, I close my eyes, letting the sound of his heartbeat sing me to sleep.

40

Star-Crossed

This piece is whimsical, adorning a curio cabinet in the artist's quarters. Stars of all shapes and sizes have been carved into the cabinet doors, creating a dizzying complexity. Some stars contain others, a nesting pattern that required a steady hand and infinite patience. Some of the stars overlap, creating triangles within the arms of an intruding star. The line carvings are delicate on some stars, while others are deeply grooved, irregular. Impassioned, perhaps. Viewers have wondered whether the artist meant for this to be a tribute to the mortal realm or a quiet monument to marvels unavailable to fae eyes. Stars are an unusual choice, not normally represented in this culture. A few critics have called this piece maudlin and said that it speaks too directly to the symbol of lost love. The artist has not addressed any of the questions to date but has stated that this work represents someone in particular.

KERBOROS

WHILE THEA DREAMS, I HOLD happiness in my arms.

I have never experienced the afterglow that follows sharing myself, body and soul, with my other half. She rendered me mad with ecstasy more than once, and I would live for her, if I could choose my course. My entire being thrums with the joy of being chosen by someone who spreads brightness wherever she goes.

Once she awakens, this moment will pass. We will be forced to respond to the needs of others and play the roles we've been assigned. When my cousin arrives for the quorum, he may demand my execution, as my survival depends on following his commands and succeeding at the tasks assigned to me. For the first time, my efforts have resulted in abject failure—and yet I have never known such contentment.

I regret nothing, no matter what follows this magical night.

Ever so lightly, I stroke her hair, enjoying the wildness of her curls. Her skin is soft and warm, and I want to kiss every inch of it again. Left to my own devices, I'd let the courts burn and spend the rest of my allotted time between her legs, licking her until she screams.

My breath hitches with the images that conjures, and with effort, I control myself. She's tired and needs the rest. Adding a glimmer of magic, I trace a pattern on her bare back, etching symbols that I hope she'll feel when she rouses later.

Despite my best efforts, sleep eventually claims me. When I awaken, Thea is gone. This solitary stirring strikes me like a blow, yet I didn't expect her to whisper words of love or even teasing enticements as she did the evening before. As I wash and dress, I tell myself this is enough.

The memory will sustain me.

As I step out into the hallway, I surprise Olive with her hand raised to knock. "I thought this was Thea's room."

"It is," I say. I don't elaborate on our relationship or why I'm staying with her. Whatever Thea chooses to share with Olive, it should be up to her.

"Do you think I could come in?"

I raise my brow. "To wait for her? I do not know when she'll return."

"No. If I didn't find her, I was planning to look for you next anyway. I'd like to ask you a few questions, if you don't mind."

In answer, I retrace my steps into the suite, inviting her in with a gesture. "Please make yourself comfortable. There are no refreshments, I'm afraid."

We licked the dishes clean last night before curling up together in bed. The enterprising staff removed the trays before I emerged today.

Olive gazes around the suite with a half smile. "I see they take their early Ottoman Empire seriously in the Autumn Court."

"I suspect that's some human reference?"

"It is. But I won't bore you with a history lesson. And this is a gorgeous place, don't get me wrong. It's just…intense. Anyway." She sits at the table, propping her chin on her hand. "I hope I'm not overstepping, but it's obvious that you're close to Thea. So I was wondering if you'd tell me about her childhood. From what I've gathered, Thea has a strained relationship with my other sister's biological parents."

"Rain and Fen," I supply. "That's true. They detected the deception swiftly, but they didn't know where Thea came from, so they couldn't…" I hesitate.

"Return her?" Olive guesses.

"Precisely. They focused on finding their real offspring. I don't believe they gave Thea much thought at all."

"She must have been so hurt and confused," she whispers.

"Yes." I could add that she carries deep wounds, but some things, she ought to confide herself. I will confirm facts but not speculate about her emotional state.

"And she was raised by a hobgoblin named Mudge? Her foster father."

"Don't refer to him that way in front of her. He's her dad," I correct.

"You're right. I'm sorry, that was clumsy. 'Real family' are those who love you, no matter what," Olive says.

"Their relationship is precious."

"I'm glad to hear it. If you've known her for a long time, can you share any stories?"

"What kind?"

"Anything about what she was like growing up. I missed so much." Olive sounds wistful, genuinely regretful that she'll never get that time back.

And that's what prompts me to share. Though I wasn't close to Thea for her whole life, I've been observing her and smiling at her antics for some time. I talk about pranks she played in the castle, swarms of lizards, the kindness she's always shown, and her most recent stunt, freeing the pookas from unwilling participation in royal pageantry.

"I'm glad she wasn't lonely," Olive says, when I pause for breath.

"I didn't say *that*, necessarily. But she's the sort of person who seeks happiness and scatters it like flower petals for others to find."

That puts a brilliant smile on Olive's face, and the resemblance to Thea is stunning, though Olive is the more muted of the two. "I'm glad she has you."

"It is the other way around." I stumble a little over the words.

She rises then. "I won't keep you. I'm off to pester Taragon for some childhood stories too. I have so much to learn. But I was wondering..."

"Yes?"

"I'm almost out of protein bars. I rationed them in the woods, and I did have some of the porridge and stew that Thea made. What will happen to me if I eat too much fae food? I'm not precisely human, but I *am* mortal. Legends suggest that taking even one bite is too much, but I'm not ready to leave. I just met Thea."

"It's a spectrum. One bite won't trap you forever." I pause, trying to think of an example that will make sense to a mortal with a scientific bent. "In some human texts I've read, there is a thing called radiation. People who have been exposed to it experience symptoms and then, eventually, physiological changes. Is that correct?"

"More or less. Is there radiation here?"

"In the sense that there's a higher concentration of magic. Magic is possible in the mortal realm, but the spells are weaker, and the effects are less lasting. Here, magic suffuses everything, including our food. In Thea's case, she's lived here her entire life, and her body has adapted to this environment. The mortal realm doesn't have enough mana to sustain her."

"I think I understand. So I can eat fae food for now, but if I linger for a long time, there might come a tipping point where I'd have absorbed so much fae magic that I wouldn't be able return either."

"Precisely. But for your purposes, that would require decades of meals in mortal timekeeping."

"An excellent explanation. I've jumped into the deep end without my usual planning, and I want to be useful or, at the very least, not to cause complications."

"A worthy aspiration," I say, smiling.

I *like* Thea's sister. As Thea does, Olive cares with her whole heart. In rare sympathy for another soul, at least one who isn't Thea, I see Olive out. She waves as she heads down the hallway, presumably to find

Taragon. I haven't seen any of the others since we separated, and I'm surprised to find that I feel concerned, particularly about Govannon. I coaxed him out of that blasted tree twice over, so I search for him to ensure that he's well.

After asking four castle staff members, I find the gnome ensconced in a small reading room. The copper-and-gold theme is understated here, mainly repeated in the delicately patterned rug. Govannon glances up as I enter; he has metallic pieces arrayed on the table in front of him. I'm pleased to find him clean, hair and beard tidily trimmed, and wearing a dapper new suit.

"You look well," I observe.

"I'm trying to decide if I should try to reach the Summer market on my own. With the patrols and the conflict..." He doesn't look eager for another adventure.

I don't blame him; he must be wild with missing Ragh, however, and I imagine he's frightened of getting lost again. Perhaps those are problems I can solve.

"I could send a message, advising Ragh that he's needed urgently as a character witness in the quorum proceedings. If I said Thea needs him to speak on her behalf, I think he'd come."

Govannon nods at once. "That's brilliant. While he might seem gruff, he has the kindest heart. Once he decides you're one of his, he never wavers."

In the desk against the far wall, I locate stationery and writing implements. I settle in, crafting a message that should draw a certain brownie out of the courtyard he's guarded all this time, waiting for his true love to return. The prospect of reuniting two star-crossed lovers fills me with delight, and I hope with all my heart that I live long enough to see this plan come to fruition.

"There, that should do it. I'll dispatch the message with one of Zeph's crows right away. You'll see Ragh presently, my friend."

Though my heart may soon be broken, I'll take *this* happy ending in trade.

41

A Spell for Reunions and Revelry

Just as people leave your life, there will also be joyful returns. If there's someone you can't wait to see, this spell nudges things along so you're reunited sooner rather than later. I've written before about balance, but this working doesn't borrow from future happiness. Someone who loves you will always want to see you, so it doesn't contribute to energies becoming unbalanced. This only greases the wheels and makes your desired outcome more probable. A word of warning—if you put too much force behind this working, it could become a portal spell, and you might startle someone nearly to death if you drop a vortex on them.

This charm has two parts, one to encourage the reunion, and provided the first half works, you finish with your loved one, a joint charm to celebrate seeing each other again. It's important to mark those moments and count your blessings.

This one is best cast when you first awaken, and go gentle with your concentration. For the wishing-for-reunion part, you'll need:

- *Chalcedony, hematite, jasper*

Hold the gems in your hand, and touch them to your heart. Focus on the person you're longing to see, and speak aloud whatever truth you'd share with them if the universe delivered them to you. (Try not to literally open a portal.) If the spell roots correctly, they'll feel the call and make their way to you as soon as possible. Hint: If you want them to hear your voice, speak near any body of water, as sprites love to gossip.

Once the reunion occurs, invite your loved one to cast the count-your-blessings part with you. For this, you'll require:

- *Chicory and cinnamon*
- *Clean water*
- *The joint spark of your magic*
- *A copper teapot and clay cups*

Together, brew the herbs into a tea, and drink the entire pot while catching up on all the moments that you've missed. It may seem like small magic, but when you're done, the pot will be empty, and your hearts will be full.

Nerys and Shereth send their love.

THEA

LEAVING THE SUITE THIS MORNING was agonizing.

I should have woken Kerboros or addressed the night of passion we shared. Now it feels more like a dream than something that actually happened. But I had a note waiting from Zeph, and they specified I should come alone. That worries me on some level, but I still emerge into a private courtyard, where the meeting is supposed to take place.

A fountain carved from sunstone occupies the center of the plaza.

Glittering crystals adorn the sides, and the water cascades from the top, forming miniature waterfalls as it spills down the obelisk into the shallow basin at the bottom. Red and copper tiles create an abstract pattern beneath the shining surface. Smooth brown flagstones create a path suitable for pacing around the rim.

Greenery grows wild up the walls, muffling any sounds from the palace proper, and the vines are dotted with blooms. The landscaping is perfect, all the flowers chosen in complementary hues—starting with yellow, blushing to orange, deepening to red—and each plant occupies the right amount of space, neither too wide, nor too tall.

Perfection makes me nervous. As I gaze into the water, it ripples, and then a liquid, bubbling voice reaches me. "Thea! I finally found you."

"Nerys." I kneel on the stones, delighted beyond measure to hear her voice.

"I did eventually hear the whispers you sent, and I passed a message to your dad. I couldn't dispatch help, but I did send word as the others asked. How are you, my girl?"

"Worried, but bearing up. What news can you share? Is my dad safe?"

"He's traveling to you as we speak. Or might be there already, as it's been a while since the river reported the last sighting."

Relief sparkles through me. "You're the best."

"I can't linger. This is an intrusion, and I don't want to add to your troubles. Be safe."

The fountain stills and returns to its original state. Nerys has gone.

And Zeph is late. On my fifth circuit of the fountain, I remember a spell my dad wrote for me; it's been too long since I've seen him. If Nerys is right, and she usually is, he's traveling right now. He might need a helping hand to get here safely. I get out the right crystals and hold them to my heart, whispering to the water.

"I miss you so much, Da. With all the unrest, I need you to be safe. And frankly, I need you here with *me*, the sooner, the better."

A musical tone sounds, and I turn to see Zeph slipping past a wind chime hung on the eaves near the door. "I'm sorry for the delay. There were a few complications to resolve."

"What's going on?" I demand.

"Before I answer, there's someone who desperately wants to greet you." They step aside, revealing…

My dad. He looks exhausted and more than a bit frazzled. Though Nerys gave me the news, I stare, unable to believe that my luck has finally turned. No more traps, no more sabotage. Hunters didn't cut him down on the road; Liskaal didn't lock him up in the dungeon. Da trusted me to keep myself safe. He remained at Miremorel as promised, and then he came at the hour of my greatest need. My dad *never* lets me down. Once I process the fact that he's really here, I rush right at him. He hugs me so tight that my ribs cave a bit, but I hug him back just as hard.

"I doubt my spell had anything to do with this, as I just cast it, but I'm so happy to see you."

"Now, hearing that's made me the happiest person alive, indeed it has, my gem." With gentle hands, he brushes my hair back and pats my cheek.

Zeph smiles. "What's important is that you're together…and out of Winter's grasp. And that's what I need to talk to you two about."

I perch on the edge of the fountain, still cuddled up to my dad. "I'm listening."

"First, let me secure the site," they say.

Their unwillingness to speak freely or divulge information makes me think they might actually have a plan, but I can't fathom what it is. The only thing I'm certain about is that they're desperate to escape marital ties to me. Not that I mind because Zeph gets on my nerves without even trying. I watch as they cast a spell that creates a blue shimmer, encasing us in a soundproof barrier.

"Satisfied now, are you?" Da wants to know.

"What if I said I could depose Lord Liskaal without a single soldier raising a weapon?" they ask.

I make scoffing sound. "It sounds too good to be true."

"Then answer this first: Do you enjoy formal status in the House of Winter? Either of you?" Zeph seems to be holding their breath, as if everything hinges on our reply.

I glance at my dad because while I've always been a nonentity, tolerated but not embraced, I can't be sure of his situation.

"Why do you need to know?" Da asks.

"This isn't the time to be cagey," Zeph says in an impatient tone. "The quorum starts soon, and if I fail, there are *no* second chances. Not for any of us."

Something in their manner makes my dad think twice about pushing for more insight. "No. I'm wild fae. I work in the palace, but I've neither an official title nor any protections from reprisal. Lord Liskaal treats us all according to his whim."

Zeph closes their eyes and lets their head fall back, shoulders easing. "Bless all good and generous spirits."

"What's this about?" I ask.

But they lose themself dancing around the fountain with more spontaneity than I imagined they possess. "No stopping us now. Lord Liskaal will *never* see this coming. His type seeks martial action and military readiness. He's brutal, not clever."

"It might be too soon to celebrate," my dad points out with gentle wisdom.

"You're quite right. I shouldn't rejoice prematurely." Zeph circles back to the front of the fountain and delves into their jacket. "I have papers here for you both. Review them quickly, for they must be filed and legally binding before the quorum begins."

I take my set of papers while Mudge accepts his, and we skim the pages in silence. Da finishes a little before I do, and he wears a baffled expression. "If I understand aright, you're authorized to adopt me into the House of Summer, conferring upon me a titled rank. You're also prepared to recognize Thea as my daughter officially, which grants her that same status."

Zeph displays a toothy grin. "Precisely."

"I don't see how that defeats Lord Liskaal," I say.

"You wouldn't. Not yet. But I swear on my life that no harm will come to either of you if you sign these agreements. Indeed, you might even find that doors will open beyond anything you could have imagined." Desperation laces their tone, reflected twice over in the anxious flutter of their hands.

I suspect they'd promise anything for our compliance. Maybe that's reason enough to refuse?

"Yeah, I'm right back to 'if it seems too good to be true'..." I mutter.

"Time is running out," Zeph says softly. "And I am aware that you don't trust me. But will you fare better if you take no action and remain vulnerable to Lord Liskaal's judgment?"

When they put it that way, I swap a look with my dad. "What do you think?"

"I've no interest in social climbing, but I will never let Liskaal harm you. According to Erdene, he was ranting about banishment as his hounds tried to hunt you down." He hesitates. "And if it means you'll be my daughter on paper and all...well, I want that more than anything. I'd love for official records to reflect what we know in our hearts to be true."

Tears fill my eyes. "I want that too."

Everything else is secondary; it doesn't matter what Zeph is scheming. They'll use us however they see fit, I have no doubt, but they're also offering us both a safe haven and formal recognition. It's enough to make up my mind.

Quickly, I hug Da, then turn to Zeph. "Find a pen. I'm ready to sign."

42

Resilience Rising

This is a tree, rising from a rocky outcropping, carved into a piece of fallen wood. The tree seems desolate at first, withered beyond all recovery. The trunk is desiccated, and only two branches remain, spreading in opposite directions. There are no leaves on this skeletal framework, and it is impossible to discern what kind of tree it was based on the lines presented. Unlike many works by this artist, this piece has been carefully polished so that the warmly layered colors of the wood grain contrast with the seemingly lifeless subject. In another departure, the work is contained within a box frame, protected behind a layer of translucent crystal. And when one views the piece from the proper angle, a secret reveals itself to the committed or the deeply curious. Though it seems all hope is lost, at the tip of the leftmost branch, there exists the suggestion of a single bud, the promise that renewal hovers at the edge of possibility.

KERBOROS

FOR GOVANNON AND RAGH, I risk communicating with one of Zeph's crows.

There is a chance someone will realize that I've hidden this ability, and I loathe sharing my secrets for free. I'm already itching to set my spiderlings loose to see what I can learn about the quorum, and I have contained myself only because I fear offending Lady Mirralee. Our status is precarious to say the least.

Zeph was correct when they said few speak the language. Crows are endlessly clever, and they're everywhere, nearly as good as having access to a garrulous water spirit. But any water spirits here would be bound to work toward Autumn's interests. I doubt Mirralee would be concerned about Ragh and Govannon's reunion.

Once Lady Crow hears the story, she agrees to carry the note to Ragh in the courtyard near the Toad in the Hole. *I will not carry a reply back to you*, she caws. *This is a favor offered because of all the tasty treats. The one you name, Ragh, has fed my children. I do hope he comes to find his lost love.*

"Me too," I say, making my way back inside the palace through a side entrance.

Suddenly, I feel a bone-deep chill and duck into the nearest doorway. My cousin passes with a ridiculously large entourage while I focus on keeping every hint of my existence scraped to silence. If he spies me, he will immediately call for my execution. And while I did once plan to slip out of this life by pretending to die, I have long since abandoned that aim. Now I have too much to lose, a beloved soul who completes me, though I've yet to speak those words to her.

Come to that, I wonder where Thea is. I understand that she and

Zeph have some complicated marital matters to unravel, so she may be tending to those issues before the quorum. Delegates have been arriving constantly; Autumn is in an uproar, and they're running out of room for visiting dignitaries. I slink around the palace, poking into dark corners and listening to gossip. Even now, two brownies who work in the kitchens walk ahead of me, speaking in low tones.

"I heard it from Dainis, who's in charge of accommodations. Apparently, the Lord and Lady of Winter refused to stay in the quarters they were assigned. They said they were 'unfit for habitation.'" The brownie mimics Lady Valnevi's shrill, entitled tones with uncanny accuracy.

The other one shakes his head. "Can you imagine? Leifan has been run ragged all day, carrying messages between factions."

"I'm surprised they trust her."

"Winter doesn't. But Lady Mirralee is well respected in Springtide and beloved of Summer. Do you think anyone in the Winter Court knows Zeph's true identity?"

True identity? What does that mean?

"They're so impressive," the first brownie says with a dreamy sigh.

They turn toward the kitchens, and I can't follow without attracting attention. If only I could send my spiderlings—but no, better not.

I consider what I've learned. Lady Mirralee must possess critical intelligence about Zeph, and since *she* knows, her staff has ferreted out the secret. This is likely why Zeph has been so reluctant to disclose the entirety of their plans. As long as they don't reveal all the moving parts, it's impossible to derail.

Much as I hate to admit it, they were correct to be cautious, as they could have been overheard. As long as we were traveling in the open, unable to set up an infallible, soundproof shield, it was best to assume that others might be eavesdropping. Somehow. I lived with constant surveillance, resorting to all manner of trickery for a moment to lay my own snares. Not that I'll use any of those preparations now.

Regardless, whatever Zeph's scheme, I hope it deals Liskaal a debilitating blow.

As I explore, I search for Thea, but she's nowhere to be found. No news from the rest of the group either. Though I saw Taragon earlier and I made a point of locating the gnome, I haven't encountered Rosa at all. Zeph has made themself scarce as well. In the course of my wanderings, instead of running into the woman of my dreams, I find her father outside the reading room where I met with Govannon.

Mudge greets me with a pat on the back. "You have my gratitude and goodwill for keeping my girl safe."

"I was lucky to be with her. In our travels, she saved me more than once."

"I'm not surprised," he says with a beaming smile. "Thea is a treasure. A treasure! It's pure madness around here, isn't it?" he adds, glancing around at the palace staff rushing past in all directions.

"They're preparing for the quorum tomorrow night."

With representatives from all four houses present, the pressure is high in Autumn to host an advantageous event and succeed where Winter failed. That would be a feather in Lady Mirralee's cap. And Liskaal will be furious, humiliated beyond all bearing.

I cannot wait.

"Do you know what Zeph is planning?" Mudge asks.

"I wish I did. They're irritatingly secretive, even when it would make sense to gather allies or accept assistance."

"They might have good reasons." Like Thea, Mudge is prone to thinking the best of people and giving them the benefit of the doubt.

With an example like his, no wonder she grew into such an incredible person.

"Possibly."

"Well, I could stand to get away from the hustle and bustle. Could I interest you in getting a drink? We could sneak out!"

"Do you have a destination in mind?" I ask.

"Right as rain, I do. A kitchen brownie told me about a place in the village, and I can't wait to taste their honey ale."

I surprise myself by nodding immediately. "That sounds good. Let's go."

Mudge has already learned Autumn's hidden ways, so I follow him. If I employed magic, I could siphon secrets too, but Lady Mirralee might view that as treachery and deliver me to my cousin's judgment. I won't make it easy for Liskaal. Never again.

It doesn't take long for us to slip out of the palace, and soon, we're in the village beyond the reach of foxy nobles and wily royals. Unlike Winter, the area surrounding the palace is well-kept, clean streets and thoughtful greenswards. Mixed buildings—some wood, some stone, and some formed of mounded earth with flowers growing on top—make up the artisan district.

We pass through a night market, where hanging lamps cast a golden glow over handmade wares and necessary sundries, but only a few stalls are open at this hour. It reminds me of the time I spent shopping with Thea as we searched for Taragon. Back then, we thought we'd need her silver tongue for persuasion. In hindsight, I can't *believe* I didn't guess that Zeph was responsible for the way our luck soured. Though I was suspicious, I imagined that sprang from my chary nature, not their irrevocable guilt.

"Something on your mind?" Mudge asks.

"Just battling some regret for being foolish."

"Looking back, it's often easy to see where you went wrong. But when you're in the thick of things, sometimes it's not obvious at all."

Perhaps he doesn't intend to comfort me, but I take heart in his words. Mudge doesn't speak again as he navigates to a narrow wooden building on the far side of the market, mustard-yellow paint peeling to reveal a layer of faded turquoise beneath. This ramshackle structure lists to one side, nearly touching the building beside it. The wood is weathered and warped, and moss clings to the exposed right half. Round windows peep from the top story, matching the round door, wide enough for a gruagach to pass through. A small hand-painted sign reads, THE ICKY PUDDING.

Mudge glances at me with a grin. "We won't get the pudding, hey?"

Before I can reply, he enters without hesitation. *Just like Thea.* Inside, the tavern is full of wild fae, and the place is furnished in a rustic style, fallen wood and found stone. A wooden beam crosses the entire bar, hung with dried herbs, garlic, and onions, and for reasons known only to the proprietor, a massive white tooth. Mudge claims the last free table, leaving me to fetch the drinks.

"Two honey ales," I say to the one-eyed hobgoblin behind the bar.

"Coming right up." He fills two mugs with a foamy-topped golden liquid.

I trade some coin for the drinks, not my usual choice, but I want Thea's father to like me. I suspect he might chuckle if I brought back a glass of white-blossom wine. As I turn, I wonder if he would disapprove of what's passed between me and his daughter. Mugs in hand, I dodge drunken brownies and hobgoblins as I cross the floor to settle on a rough-cut stool across from Mudge.

I slide his drink across the table and say, "Bottoms up."

"Ah, that's the stuff." He smacks his lips after taking a long pull from his tankard. "Now, then. I do believe we have something important to discuss."

"What's that?" I ask.

"Your intentions toward Thea, of course."

I nearly choke on my honey ale and gape at him before managing to say, "My…intentions?"

"Did you think I wouldn't know? People talk." Though Mudge is smiling, his eyes are intent. He tends to be a kind, playful person, but not when it concerns Thea's happiness.

This might anger him, but… "I shouldn't speak of my feelings to anyone else before I share them with her. But I'll say this much: To me, she's the most important person in this realm or any other. I'm not in a position to make promises, but—"

"You would if you could," he finishes with a broad smile.

"Yes." There's no reason to hide how completely I belong to her, how she's marched into my heart and brightened even the darkest corners.

"Then that's all I needed to know." He raises his mug and clacks it against mine. "To futures that might be, the present that is, and the past that can't harm us anymore."

"I'll drink to that."

43

A Spell for Masking and Misdirection

While honesty is the best policy, occasionally there's a call for craft. If you're cornered and you need to create some breathing room, you require a working that causes people to focus elsewhere. It's best to choose a diversion that's naturally dramatic so it doesn't strike your audience as strange that they're invested in the outcome. Meanwhile, that intrigue allows you the space to complete whatever you're trying to achieve. Mind, this isn't a permanent solution. The charm doesn't mean they'll look away forever or never think about you again.

They say you don't regret the risks you take in life; rather you regret the ones you didn't. As for me, I'd always rather know what would've happened if I had taken a chance. While I do want you to be safe, my gem, I also want you to be happy.

And you've a bold, bright spirit, and I am awed by the person you've become, even as I wait to see what more you'll accomplish. Our life together has been so much more than I ever imagined for myself, back when I was a young hobgoblin. Oh, I'm still green, just no longer young, but I fancy I've some wisdom yet to impart. Bless you for coming to me, my darling daughter. I wouldn't be me without you.

- *Smoky quartz and tourmaline*
- *Valerian and foxglove*
- *A smidge of magic*

This working is deceptively simple, and that's the power of it. The components serve as a focal point for your magic. Place the gems in one pocket and the herbs in another. Now close your eyes, and imagine your magic cloaking you from notice, not invisibility, not even like the skulking spell I taught you early on. No, you're perfectly visible. You're just not worthy of attention. Their eyes will slide right over you and fixate on something—or someone—else. The amount of power you pour into this spell might impact its duration. I once cast it too strongly, and people thought I'd gone missing. Used that to my advantage, I did, and kipped off from work for a week.

We had a splendid holiday in the wildlands, didn't we, my gem? You swam with Nerys in icy brooks and Shereth painted you blue because that's the color you wanted to be that week. I made pigweed flatbread and mushroom stew until we were weary of it.

*That's the next point I need to make. This spell will never work on people who truly love you. Don't even *try* to trick us. We're coming to the end of this guide, only one spell more in my repertoire. And I saved the best for last.*

THEA

BEFORE THE QUORUM'S FIRST SESSION, I cast the masking-and-misdirection spell.

Now Lord Liskaal shouldn't be able to punish me before Zeph executes their plan. It's a peculiarly lonely day, the final one before all our fates are sealed. I speak with Tara and my dad, but not Rosa or Zeph. On the way to the great hall, those two pass without pausing. Likewise, Govannon doesn't see me either. I'm braced for the worst when I turn the corner and spot Kerboros striding down the hall toward me.

I wait for him to pass. To not see me. And my dad's words, written in the magical handbook, echo in my head: *This spell will never work on people who truly love you.*

But…Kerboros stops, a quiet smile lighting his usually somber features. "I missed you yesterday. I thought you'd be in our suite at night, at least, but—"

"I was with my dad most of the day," I tell him. "And overnight. We had a lot to discuss. I didn't have a chance to let you know."

He tips his head, seeming curious. "Did you mention me? Is that why he took me for a drink?"

Oh no.

In fact, I *did* mention my feelings for Kerboros yesterday afternoon, and I didn't think I needed to ask Da to be discreet, but apparently, I was wrong. "I wondered where he went." Before he can respond, the announcements begin, a resonant-voiced staff member calling out titles of those entering the quorum. "We should go separately. It'll be safer."

"I'll go first," he offers at once.

And I understand the reasoning without him articulating why—he's offering himself as a sacrifice. Lord Liskaal will be livid when Kerboros appears, after having failed his last task. Based on what I know of his past, there was dark magic, a compulsion binding his actions, and as far as Liskaal knows, Kerboros shouldn't be free to refuse whatever Liskaal demands. The Lord of Winter could order Kerboros to fall on his sword, and he is willing to die for *me*, even though he could flee.

"Stay safe," I whisper, watching him go.

He passed the test I didn't intend to set for him. The spell doesn't work on people who truly love you. And Kerboros sees me, always.

I haven't run into Olive, but that might be for the best. We're sisters, and it would hurt if she doesn't love me, but it might be unreasonable to expect love so fast. For now, it's enough that I like her and that she cared enough to search for me.

After counting as high as my patience allows, I slip into the great hall to take a position at the edge of the room. Liskaal is screaming invectives at his cousin, being held back by two burly boggarts in Autumn colors. "I will not—"

"Silence!" Lady Mirralee raps three times on the table where the other representatives are seated. I don't recognize the rulers, but I can tell Summer from Springtide based on their colors. "Lord Liskaal, you will have an opportunity to address the quorum, but you have not been recognized."

"Sit down, Liskaal." The lazy order comes from a handsome fae in Summer's hues. That must be Lord Sorren.

"You requested the first speech," Lady Mirralee says to Zeph. "I am prepared to indulge you."

"Of course," the Springtide ruler says with a snicker.

I can see why people say they're eccentric. "Call Me Pell" is wearing what looks like a dressing gown over a long skirt paired with sturdy mud-encrusted boots. If they've combed their hair in the last week, I can't tell. They carry dishevelment to the next level, cultivating it the way some fae do perfect beauty.

Their levity earns a mordant look from Lady Mirralee, but Zeph glides to the center of the room, untroubled by the rising tension. "I'm here to address Winter's inadequacies. They were entrusted with the task of renewing the peace accords between Summer and Winter. As of tonight, they have failed most ingloriously."

"I will see you dead for that insult," Lord Liskaal spits.

Lady Mirralee levels a killing stare at the Lord of Winter. "Have a care who you threaten in my demesne, or you will be the one to lose your life."

Zeph continues as if the interruption didn't occur. "This is the contract I prepared and signed. Please note the fine print."

Lady Valnevi sucks in a sharp breath. "What—"

"Hope they can read my writing," Rosa says with a muffled laugh.

A memory pops up—Rosa mentioning her terrible handwriting. I don't entirely understand what's happening, but Zeph presents the contract to Lord Springtide, along with a magnifying lens. "Please read this codicil aloud, milord."

"Please! Call me *Pell*."

Zeph smiles. "Please read it, Pell."

"As you wish!" For some reason, the Springtide ruler decides to do so in an uncanny imitation of Lady Valnevi's shrillest tone. "'If the marriage between Thea de Winter and Devan J. Fenelon is not consummated within forty-five respites, the marriage shall be annulled, and the House of Summer can choose a different representative for the peace treaty. If Winter fails in this compact, they agree to select new leadership by rationale of incompetence, per past precedent for a vote of no confidence. The quorum of the four courts is bestowed with full jurisdiction in this matter.'"

Pell's vocal stylings are so distracting—and amusing—that titters come from the crowd. Until people realize what's actually been said.

Then the room explodes with reaction as Liskaal thunders, "What trickery is this?"

"No trickery, just pixie penmanship," Zeph says.

It seems like they hid an entire clause in the ornate swirl of an *o*. This is… I don't even have a word for the joy sparkling through me with all the fizz of sparkling honey wine.

"Unacceptable," Lady Valnevi shrieks. "We will fight to the death before honoring—"

"No." The simple word from Lady Mirralee quiets everyone in the room. "This is not dishonest. The words were written so you could have seen them, had you been more observant or if you had a trusted pixie in your employ. I opine that this contract is valid, the required time has elapsed for failure, and the quorum now has jurisdiction over Winter's affairs. What say you, Pell? Lord Sorren?"

"Valid," the Lord of Summer says.

"It's valid," Pell agrees. "Delicious! Ridiculously apropos. To think I considered missing this entirely. I'm *so* glad I put on my good boots."

Those are the good boots? I sneak another peek at them. Still muddy. Fascinating.

Lady Mirralee makes a gesture, taking the contract from Pell. "Your complaints are noted and dismissed. The next order of business is—"

Lord Liskaal draws a hidden dagger and rushes at Mirralee, but one rather handsome gruagach in Autumn livery restrains Liskaal casually, forcing him to his knees. "Our people will rise up in revolution! They will never accept this travesty!"

Lord Sorren bursts out laughing. "You're delusional. You must have no notion how much they hate you."

"He's right," Pell adds. "So very right! They'll likely throw a party. Oh, I do love parties. I hope there's cake."

"We can do that once all business is complete," Mirralee says. "Zeph, I believe you have a nomination for the Summer marital alliance with Winter?"

"I offer Thea Summer, formerly affiliated with Winter, but she held no official titles. Here are the documents formalizing her relationship with our house."

"Everyone knows that Devan Fenelon has ties to Summer and Autumn," Lady Valnevi screeches. "This is all bias and corruption!"

Ties to Summer and *Autumn?* I glance at Lord Sorren, who merely smiles at the accusation. Does that mean Zeph is the mysterious scion, born to Lady Mirralee and, maybe, the Lord of Summer? This is a game changer.

"And who is next in line for leadership in the House of Winter?" Pell asks. "Lineage is such a nuisance. Let's do a lottery instead! Everyone who belongs to Winter, put your names in a bowl! Any boggins could do a better job at ruling than those two." They indicate the pair screaming and twisting in the guards' custody.

Pell has a point.

Zeph ignores that suggestion, as it likely doesn't fit their vision. Random boggins rule assuredly doesn't suit this complicated scheme. "That would be Kerboros."

"Does anyone object?" Lady Mirralee asks.

They ignore the futile shouting from Lord Liskaal, now being forced onto his face, cheek smashed against the glossy tiles. Lady Valnevi receives similar treatment as the voting takes place. Within moments, it's over, a unanimous decision resulting in a bloodless coup.

Kerboros seems stunned, too shocked to speak, by his sudden rise to power. He's escorted to the high table and offered the seat that belongs to the Lord of Winter. His gaze meets mine across the room, and I smile.

He's saved. I can breathe again. So this was Zeph's gambit? Hide a fail-safe in the marriage contract and then misdirect and delay, delay, delay? Well. It worked. It likely helps that they were getting constant reports from Summer and Autumn, at least until we wound up in the In-Between. I do believe that wasn't part of the original plan.

Pell indicates the two prostrated before the assembly, spitting hate. "Whatever shall we do with them? They'll cause trouble, left to their own devices. Oh! We could cover them in metal and turn them into statues!" They seem so very delighted with the idea that they don't realize how everyone is staring in wide-eyed horror.

I hope things are all right for the wild fae in Springtide. I don't think this ancient fae has many tethers left to reality.

Lord Sorren clears his throat because there's no way to respond to any of that, turning to Kerboros. "Lord Winter? What is your decree?"

Everyone glances at Kerboros, who displays a menacing aspect. "Strip them of their magic and banish them to the mortal realm."

"That's a death sentence," Liskaal snarls.

"Not immediately. You'll suffer. And that's the judgment you imposed on Thea. It's fitting for you to experience it for yourselves."

"I like you," Lady Mirralee says in an approving tone. "House Winter is certain to improve under your leadership."

Only afterward do I realize what this means. They intend for me to marry Kerboros to seal the peace accords between Summer and Winter. Without Liskaal and Valnevi agitating for war, it's largely a symbolic gesture, and I suspect it's also an apology from Zeph. For not sharing their intentions sooner.

When the new Lord of Winter glides through the crowd to join me, I feel like I could burst with joy.

44

The Way Home

This piece is so realistic that it looks like something that the artist carved from memory, not imagination. Shaped from fallen wood, this is a freestanding mushroom cottage. Honey hues imbues the creation with warmth, and the roof overhangs the walls with vertical slits beneath that mimic the gills of a mushroom, standing in for roof tiles. In a real structure, they might also offer ventilation.

The roof rises to a domed cap, and the doors actually open to reveal the incredible detail within. This seems to have been crafted in two pieces, lending it a three-dimensional coziness. There is a tiny hearth made of stone and the minuscule furnishings are meticulously sized to scale. Curved shelves line the walls with tiny artifacts set atop them as proof of a full and happy life. One might believe that tiny folk truly make their home in this magical, whimsical place. There is a small sign above the front door that simply reads, MIREMOREL. *Below that, two words:* WELCOME HOME.

KERBOROS

I PULL THEA FROM THE edge of the gathering to the center, where she belongs.

As long as I live, I will not permit people to ostracize her or make her feel that she doesn't belong because she was born somewhere else. Newcomers bring new ideas, though in truth, she's essentially a native. She remembers nothing of the mortal realm, as she was stolen only a few hours after her birth.

Though I'm unaccustomed to attention and I never shared my father's desire to hold the reins of power, I pitch my voice to carry. "First, I must say I didn't seek this role."

"People who don't want power are the only ones who should have it," someone calls. It sounds like Thea's dad, but since Mudge isn't tall and the crowd is huge, I can't be certain.

"Agreed," Zeph says.

I acknowledge them with a nod, then turn my attention to Thea. Since I'm already holding one of her hands, I take the other and raise it to my lips. This isn't an arranged marriage. It's not a marriage of convenience either, an agreement we'll reluctantly sign to prevent worse consequences. No, I intend to make it clear to this assemblage that I chose her long ago and that I can imagine myself with no one else until the end of time.

"You have been ordered about your entire life," I begin.

"So have you," she says quietly. I might be the only one who hears it.

"And so, before this assembly, I must ascertain one thing beyond any shadow of a doubt. Do you want this? Do you wish to marry me? Forget the peace accords, Winter and Summer be damned. Do you want *me*?"

She smiles with her entire soul, a luminous glow behind her beautiful eyes. "Always. My answer is yes. I'm glad we can prevent further conflict, but you're everything I ever wanted in a partner, and I've been searching for you my whole life. I'm sorry I didn't recognize you sooner."

"Recognize me?" My voice lilts on the question.

"Yes. Soulmates should quicken to each other on sight." Her smile says she's teasing me, but the word *soulmate* fills me with joy.

Lady Mirralee interrupts the moment to decree, "Remove the exiles. Carry out the sentence immediately, before they seize an opportunity to escape and foment unrest."

The former Lord and Lady of Winter are bound, both with magic and with cold iron, and the palace staff drag them from the great hall. Liskaal and Valnevi are still screaming in protest. I don't watch them go. In fact, I only have eyes for Thea.

"It seems to me," Pell drawls, "that we are dressed and gathered in a manner that's entirely suitable for a wedding. Weddings always have cake! They should get married right now." They glance around looking for support of the suggestion.

I tilt my head. "What do you think?"

"It's a little sudden," Thea says. "But I have no doubts about you. Or us."

"A wedding!" Mudge shouts it first.

Others take up the cry. I hear Rosa and Taragon, louder than the rest. Lady Mirralee restores order by rapping on the table again. "This could have been a wretched ordeal, but thanks largely to Zeph's machinations, it shall be a joyous one instead. Let us witness as Winter and Summer plight their troth. Then there shall be revels unlike any experienced in recent times."

"After tonight, we'll live as legends." Lord Sorren speaks his agreement with what seems like a warm look at Lady Mirralee.

Yes, there's definitely something between them. Though I have no proof, I believe Zeph has blood ties to both royal houses, Summer and Autumn, though they were raised by Lord Sorren. Perhaps Zeph has no desire to hold a title in either court. It occurs to me that they might have orchestrated *all* this to win their freedom by offering up me and Thea in their stead. It's diabolical: a coup, a bait and switch, and a fox slipping a snare all at once.

Clever, clever Zeph.

Since I'm so pleased with the outcome, I don't mind that they used both of us for their own ends. Lady Mirralee whispers to Leifan, who hurries to another staff member, and soon an entire regiment of workers is rearranging the look of the great hall, carrying tables to go with the seats, and someone has conjured lights, while a brownie hangs bright banners, and yet someone else hurries about with vases of fresh flowers.

In less time than I could have imagined, the sonorous speaker who announced all the arriving guests calls us to the center of the hall. "Lord Kerboros. Lady Thea. Please take your places and speak your vows before this assembled company."

I haven't thought about this; I never imagined I would be so fortunate. But I shall not let this moment pass or permit this blessing to slip from my grasp. Still hand in hand, I walk with Thea, feeling the weight of the collective eyes fixed on us.

"You first," she whispers.

We are surrounded by people. But my focus narrows to Thea's smile, her sparkling eyes. I can only speak the truth and hope it's enough.

"I will always see you. I will always listen to you. I will always believe you. I promise that I will disagree with you when you're wrong but with gentleness, never in anger. I will protect you with my last breath, and I will heed your counsel because you are a kind and brilliant person. I love you with my entire soul, and I promise to be there when you need me. Will you take me as yours?"

"I will," Thea breathes.

I kiss both her hands in a courtly gesture, hoping she can tell how happy I am. "Your turn," I murmur, beneath the thunderous applause.

When the room quiets, she inhales deeply. "Some people picture how this moment will go, and I never did, likely because I was too busy causing trouble." She pauses for the ripple of surprised laughter. "But even if I'd imagined my wedding, it could never compare to the reality of surviving the darkest days with the perfect partner by my side. Over time, you earned my trust and never once let me down.

"In turn, I promise to wreak havoc on your enemies—in the silliest ways imaginable—and I promise to make you laugh when you're in the doldrums. I promise to pull you into bed at the least provocation and make you wonder a thousand times a day what in the world I'm thinking. I promise to keep the mystery alive and never explain anything until the last moment. And most importantly, I promise to love you until I die. Still want to be mine?"

She startles a laugh out of me, and I answer with the chuckle caught in my throat. "Yes. More than anything. It could only ever be you."

Lady Mirralee applauds, rising to motion at everyone else. "Citizens of Autumn and assembled guests, please join me in welcoming the Lord and Lady of Winter."

All around us, fae surge to their feet, applauding with joyous abandon. Someone starts calling for a speech or a toast. The demand becomes overwhelming, but for once, I have something to say.

A nearby waiter places a glass in my hand, and I raise it, indicating that I'm about to cooperate. The hall hushes, eager to learn what sort of ruler has taken power in Winter. I smile slightly, considering how outraged my father would be over what I'm about to do.

But my brother? Geraint wouldn't be able to stop smiling.

"Earlier, I said I don't want this responsibility. Before, all I wanted was to disappear—to be left alone to focus on my art." It's the first time I've acknowledged that particular passion in public. "Now that I have the freedom to do as I wish? I refute the strangling levels of control my cousin embraced. I intend to convene a ruling council in Winter. I'll discuss issues with them, and we'll determine the best course via consensus. I plan to appoint representatives from all classes of wild fae.

"Our system is stagnant. This is the wild fae's home too, and they deserve a voice. I shall see that there is a fair distribution of power. Not only is it more equitable, but it also grants me the chance to be with the people I love. So don't be startled if I spend more time creating beautiful things than imposing my will. Nobody asked how I intend to handle this responsibility, and so I believe I am free to do as I see fit within my territory."

"Macha's tits," Rosa says loudly into the silence. "It'll be absolute chaos. I love everything about this."

Thea rises up to kiss me in front of the whole of fae society, both high and wild. When she pulls back, she grins at me. "Chaos, hmm? This is indisputable proof that you've married the right person. That's basically my middle name."

The other rulers confer quietly, and then Lord Sorren rises with honey wine in hand. "We shall observe this democratic experiment with great interest."

Pell is grinning with a glee that seems borderline deranged. "Oh! I've never been so entertained. I want a council too! I know, I can do the lottery idea." Immediately, they signal to staff and ask for paper, pen, and ink.

I feel mildly concerned for the people of Springtide, but it won't be worse. I hope.

Lady Mirralee rises as well. "Now that all official matters are attended to, let the festival begin!"

45

A Spell for Festivity and Fireworks

We have come to the end of the handbook, my gem, and since this is the grand finale, I offer you a spell to celebrate the happiest of times. When the greatest of good things happens to you, there should be a way to mark the occasion. Well, I say if it's worth doing, it's worth doing big and loud and proud, which is what I've always taught you. Take up space. Speak your truth. Put dancing pookas made of fire in the sky. (Yes, you can do that with this spell, and why not?) Go wild. You only live once, and I want you to eat everything you desire at the table of life, leave nothing untasted, no wine unsavored.

With this spell, your will is paramount. But we've been working on your focus and your belief that you have a full right to use fae magic. Even if you weren't born here, you're everything beautiful and glorious about this realm. You can create flowers of fire or pookas made of light or images that move and glow and speak and melt into something else entirely. The limit is only your confidence and your imagination. I believe—even if you don't—that you can do magic without these rituals. Because the truth is, the magic comes from you, my jewel. The metals and gems and herbs may aid focus or channeling, but if you'll pardon my trickery, they can do nothing without you.

That's the last lesson left for me to impart. You are enough. You're perfect as you are, even in your imperfections, and you are loved. Use this working well, my precious daughter.

This one is best cast at the moment of your greatest joy. You'll require:

- *A reason to celebrate*

I hope that I'm present when you cast this for the first time. I'd love to perform the spell with you and see what wondrous, mythic scenes we create. To cast this spell, simply imagine what you want to appear, and be as specific as possible. Envision the colors, the effects, whether there's sparkle or glow, streaks of light or popping embers. And then release your vision into the world.

The best illusions begin in your mind's eye, and then you share them—on the ceiling, on a wall, or in the sky, wherever you're celebrating. I can't wait to see what beauty is born from someone as wonderful as you, my jewel. My work is complete, but yours is just beginning. Whether you have adventures or settle down, all that is yet to be written. I will be proud of you, whatever path you choose.

Love always,

Da

THEA

I'VE HAD MORE TO DRINK than I normally would, and I can't stop smiling.

So many people know my name and insist on speaking with me or shaking my hand. I've hardly had a moment to myself, and Zeph dragged

Kerboros away, all amped up to discuss the idea of choosing delegates among the wild fae. I hugged Tara earlier, and right now, I'm having a surprisingly pleasant chat with Rosa. She even apologized for her part in deceiving us.

"I owed Zeph, you see. And while I didn't support what they were doing, I understood the need for secrecy. Liskaal had eyes everywhere."

"I get it," I say, gracious because I lose nothing by being generous.

And isn't that *usually* the case?

"That's lovely to hear. I know that I can be rather"—she pauses, as if seeking the right word—"candid. Not everyone's cup of tea. And I don't have many friends. So…"

"You have one in me," I tell her.

A delighted smile splits her somber face. "I knew it! I'll visit once you're settled in Winter. If I'm welcome?"

"Anytime you like."

"Well, I can see people lining up behind me, so I won't keep you."

"Thea."

My knees buckle a bit, and I catch myself on the table nearby. I whirl, recognizing Tempest's distinctive voice. "You're awake! I'm so sorry. I didn't mean—"

"It's all right. Not your fault. I do faint from time to time anyway."

"Tara said you seemed sick." It's not a question, but they seem to take it as one.

Tempest sighs. "In fact, I am. I wasn't trying to keep it a secret, but…"

Since they pause, I fill the silence with a question I must ask, even if the answer hurts. "Have you recovered from what I did to you? And can you ever forgive me?"

Since Olive explained what I needed to be doing, I've finally lost the sense that I'm slowly starving to death, the infinite, underlying hunger that plagued me since childhood. In a gathering like this, I skim like a bird across the water, and the mood lightens. There's no anger anywhere, only joy, and I'm full to bursting.

"Already forgiven and forgotten," Tempest says. "And you forced me to rest. I feel better than I have in a while, but my outlook isn't good."

I suspect that's what they didn't say before. "Is there anything I can do? We have good healers in Winter. My dad might know someone too. Mudge knows everyone." I use his name in case Tempest doesn't know who my dad is.

"I've seen dozens of healers, and no one has any clue what's the matter with me. Since I come from rather a rare lineage, that doesn't aid matters."

"I'm sorry to hear that."

Olive eases up to my right side. "I wasn't trying to eavesdrop. I just wanted to congratulate you, Thea. But I did hear something about a mysterious illness, and well…"

"That's your area," I guess.

"Yes," she says baldly. "I know this is a party, but I'd love to pick your brain." She's locked on to Tempest, eager to help.

This is why she became a doctor.

"And if you're experiencing any physical pain at all, I can ease it without you suffering ill effects. It's a perk of the energy-transfer process." She makes it sound…beneficial, as if she doesn't see it as receiving undue rewards.

Maybe I've been looking at this the wrong way my entire life. Kerboros even said that he felt *happier* when I ate up his anger.

"I don't mind. But perhaps we can speak elsewhere? It's rather loud in here, and I'm trying to avoid Taragon. Her gaze goes right through me."

"I know just the place," Olive says.

Before they take more than one step, Zeph appears next to my sister. "Where are you going, goddess? I've had no chance to spend time with you in days. Don't abandon me in my hour of greatest need!"

Olive rolls her eyes. "You seem to be misunderstanding something. I don't exist to entertain you, and I'm only interested in Tempest right now."

She swans off with Tempest in tow, leaving Zeph more flustered than I've ever seen.

"That was tough to watch," I say, smirking.

"She is utterly magnificent." They're not remotely put off by that rejection, it seems. Their mercurial gaze returns to me with obvious reluctance. "Do I need to apologize? Rosa said I do, but I tend to think the ends justify the means."

"I still think you're an asshole, but it worked out for me." Right now, I can't muster any rancor, though I was plenty furious when their treachery was first revealed.

"Our people respect chicanery," they say loftily, "and a truly convoluted scheme, successfully executed. And they adore a dramatic reveal. It all landed perfectly."

"Don't be insufferable," I say.

Kerboros threads through the crowd, hunting for me with a singular intensity. I love being the focus of his devotion. He eyes Zeph, then says, "Go away."

To my amusement, the commensurate schemer complies, but before we can escape, my dad darts toward us, drinks in hand. "I need to give my blessing...and I'd love for us to provide some entertainment, if you're game, my gem."

Entertainment... I recall the final spell in the handbook. *Time for a big leap.* I can manage this. Da believes in me, and more importantly, I now believe in myself.

"Let's do it."

Appearing baffled, Kerboros stands back as I hold my dad's hand and close my eyes. This began with pookas, so it's fitting it'll end with them too. I picture Ferghus and the rest, and I imagine them stampeding through the walls, hooves sparking fire, purple smoke trailing from their tails. And then I unleash the magic.

People scream.

It's my wedding, of *course* they do, and I let the images fade. The guests break out into nervous laughter when they realize there's no substance to the smoke.

Dad takes his turn next, and tears fill my eyes when he opens his. On the blank wall opposite, he creates a slowly shifting panorama of my life: Thea as a round-cheeked infant. Thea, barely able to walk and already pulling pooka tails. Thea missing her front teeth and running like the wind with Taragon. Thea with a newly shaped figure and a wild mane of hair that didn't see a comb for longer than I care to recall. Thea as I am now, weeping happy tears as I hug my dad, the person who has always, always loved me and been there for me.

Nobody in this room is as lucky. I am rich in family and friends and now in my chosen partner too.

Spontaneous applause shivers through the crowd as my dad turns to Kerboros. "Here's what I have to say to you, son. I'll be your biggest supporter, so long as you're good to her. If you hurt her, I have a shovel."

"I never will," Kerboros promises.

But I knew that already. He has such a tender heart, though he's been forced to growl like a wolf and hunt like a hound for most of his days.

"To the happy couple!" Da calls out.

And we toast along with everyone in the room. At some point, Kerboros tugs on my hand, guiding me toward a side door. We slip outside, and I know he wants a moment alone with me, because that's precisely what I'm craving too: a little privacy, a stolen kiss.

But someone else—*two* someones—have gotten here before us. Ragh and Govannon break apart, breathless and red-cheeked from the intensity of their kiss. I'm so happy, I could scream.

"You're here!" I exclaim, delighted. "Together!"

"Thanks to Kerboros," Govannon says. "I was so afraid Ragh couldn't forgive me."

Ragh kisses Govannon tenderly. "My love. There's nothing to forgive." He turns to us with wide, shining eyes. "Bless you. Bless you for giving my love and my life back to me. All this time, I didn't even know he was missing. I didn't know I should be looking!"

"Because you always doubted you were worth staying for," Govannon whispers.

They're lost in each other again, making up for time apart, and we tiptoe past, leaving them to their epic and boundless joy. I'm so glad we took the time to talk with Ragh and learn his story. I'm proud of the role we played in putting happiness back into the world.

Kerboros reaches for my hand, and it reminds me of the moment in the Summer market when he bought me cake and I hugged him with sheer happiness. We receive nods and greetings from various wild fae, and some of them want to talk. By tacit consent, we respond to everyone with the same courtesy we'd show a ruling power.

Because I meant it when I told Ragh that everyone matters.

At last, we reach that secret courtyard with the fountain at its heart, and I curl into my true love's arms, flushed with radiance. I lift my face, and he kisses me as if he needs my lips to live. I kiss him like he's air and light combined.

"I love you," I whisper when we break apart, and I realize we're saying it in unison.

I've never felt like anyone's other half before, but I'm sure of him—of us—and of the incredible future that awaits us. At one point, the odds were stacked against us, but Olive has shared some mortal sayings, and I love this one especially: Never tell me the odds.

I'll beat them every time. I used to be no one except my dad's daughter, and now I realize what I should've known all along: That was enough; I was never nobody.

To love someone else truly, madly, deeply, you have to love yourself first. And I *do*—as much as I love Kerboros.

As much as I love my family and friends.

And together? We're unstoppable, and we'll change the world.

DISCOVER MORE FROM ANN AGUIRE
IN HER CHARMING COZY
PARANORMAL BOOK

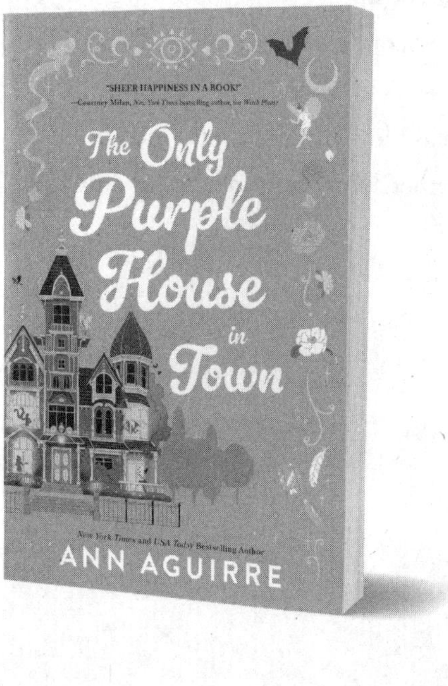

CHAPTER ONE

WHOEVER SAID IT WAS ALWAYS darkest before the dawn clearly had never lived like Iris Collins.

Sometimes she felt like a cave creature that never saw sunlight; it was dark at sunrise, sunset, and all the hours in between. She stared at her account balance on her phone with anxiety chewing away at her insides, a behavior she mirrored by gnawing on her cuticle until it bled. Her roommates would be home soon, and she didn't look forward to that conversation. They'd covered her for the last two months, but she doubted they would be willing to triple down.

I can't even leave until I pay them back, and I can't find a new place either.

She had no clue how to earn her back rent or come up with what she needed for this month. Her sisters had money, but Rose would lecture if she bailed Iris out; Lily would refuse to help while talking about how Iris should live within her means; and Olive didn't have reliable internet since she was currently doctoring without borders. Her three sisters were a how-to guide for success, while Iris was the cautionary tale. Her mother had made life hell the last time she lent financial assistance, so that was out of the question.

Should I sell my car?

In the movies, vampires were essentially immortal and had been accruing wealth for centuries. Unfortunately for Iris, she came from a different line entirely. Her type didn't feed on blood but human emotions, and Iris had come up shy in that department as well. Unlike the rest of her family, she had no special abilities that sprang from her vampiric nature. At least, nothing had ever *manifested.* Olive could feed on her patients' pain and improve their lives as she did so. Lily feasted on grief, and Rose thrived on anger, whereas Iris was basically *human.* Or so her mother had said more than once; her tone made it clear that wasn't a compliment. But then, even among the paranormal community, psychic vampires weren't well liked. They were known as "takers" for obvious reasons. Five years ago—when the witches made their big announcement—others had followed suit.

Now, Iris didn't have to hide who she was, and there were dating apps devoted to various types of supernatural folk. Iris had been on Shifted for a while, but she kept meeting lone wolf types who just wanted to hit and quit. In this case, they happened to be able to turn into actual wolves. Then she tried Bindr, but witches could be touchy about lineage, apparently. The skeptics and conspiracy theorists amused her the most. There were forums devoted to debunking magic, calling it "the greatest hoax since the moon landing," and sometimes Iris did a deep dive through the most ridiculous suggestions to distract herself from the reality of how screwed she was.

In fact, she was doing that now. She scrolled on her phone, snickering. "Sure, lizard people have replaced all our nation's leaders—that's real. And there are mole people living underneath Capitol Hill."

Enough of that.

From there, she clicked through to a site offering various magical charms. *I could really use one for prosperity, but they're so expensive. And what if it doesn't work?* Shaking her head, she resisted the urge to max out her card with an impulse purchase. But damn, it was tough. She *really* wanted to find out if the magical lipstick was permanently kiss-proof. In the news, Congress was trying to pass a new law requiring all paranormal individuals to self-identify and register in some kind of national database. *Yeah, that won't end well.* And some douchebag senator in Iowa wanted even sterner sanctions, special housing projects, and tracking devices. Someone else had proposed a *tax* on supernaturals. *How does that even make sense? And good luck enforcing it.* She shook her head and went back to window-shopping. So many cool magic items she'd love to get her hands on…

For Iris, life hadn't changed that much. The paranormal communities were still close-knit, and most didn't reveal themselves readily, even if a few people had identified themselves for clout and were giving interviews about what it was like growing up "other" among humans. Some were pursuing a fortune or building social media empires, capitalizing on the interest focused their way.

I can't even do that. Too bad—it would help the shop.

Sighing, she trudged to her room, currently crammed with supplies for her jewelry-making business, but nobody was buying the finished products. She'd invested in the idea, but she hadn't earned more than twenty bucks on her pieces. She supposed she could register as a driver, but she was scared of letting strangers get in her car. Iris lowered her head. It was ridiculous that she was afraid of…so many things. Pacing back to the dining room, she feverishly tried to think of a solution.

Do I have anything *left to sell besides my car?*

"You owe me six hundred bucks," Frederic said.

Iris let out a cry, juggled her phone, and then dropped it. Screen down, because of course. That was how her luck ran. When she picked it up, there was a tiny nick on the corner, exactly what she didn't need today. *I didn't even hear him come in.*

Stifling a squeak, she spun to face Frederic.

She'd been dodging the others—Regina, Frederic, and Candace—for the last week, even though she had nowhere to go. The diner staff was sick of her ordering a cup of coffee and staying for hours, while the dollar cinema didn't seem to care if she stayed all day. But now, it was too late.

Frederic tapped her shoulder briskly. "Did you hear me? Where's my money?"

He owned the house and had rented three of the four bedrooms. It was a decent place, decorated in bachelor style, and everyone was nice enough. But like everywhere else Iris had lived, she didn't quite fit. Frederic hadn't even wanted to rent to her in the first place since she didn't have a day job, but Iris had gone to high school with Regina, and she vouched for Iris. Now Regina was mad because Iris was making her look bad, and Candace was tired of the tension.

Everyone quietly wanted Iris gone, but she had to *pay* them first. She raised her gaze from the polished-oak dining table, trying to figure out what to say. *Sorry, I'm broke* was only three words, but she couldn't make herself say them, mainly because she'd said them so often, and she'd burned through any good will the others felt for her.

But before Regina and Candace arrived to exacerbate the situation, the doorbell rang. "I'll get it," she said swiftly.

Iris raced past Frederic to the front door where a postman in a blue uniform asked her to sign for a certified letter. *That's never good news. I hope it's not another bill that I let slide until it went to collections.* The way her luck ran, it probably was, and the return address stamp on the envelope only reinforced that impression. Digby, Davis, and Moore sounded like a law firm.

I hope I'm not being sued.

She didn't want to read it, but the alternative was facing Frederic, so she closed the door with a quiet snick, blocking the early-autumn breeze. Through the window, she watched the leaves skitter on the sidewalk, caught by that same wind. She tore open the packet and found a wealth of legal documents.

IN THE ESTATE OF GERTRUDE VAN DOREN, DECEASED…

Poor Aunt Gertie. I wish I'd gone to her funeral.

Iris skimmed the pages with growing disbelief. Her great-aunt Gertrude had left the bulk of her estate to Iris: a small amount of cash, her collection of ceramic angels, and a house in St. Claire, Illinois, including all contents within. Iris had no clue why Great-Aunt Gertie had done this, but the bequest burned like a spark of hope. Her great-aunt—her paternal grandfather's sister—had been reckoned rather odd, something of a misanthrope just because she never married.

Maybe she thought I'm the weirdest, the most like her. Or the one who needs the most help? Either way, true enough.

Iris hadn't seen Great-Aunt Gertie since the summer after graduation, when her parents had dragged her to St. Claire for a courtesy visit. Iris had sent yearly Christmas cards, however, mostly because she enjoyed the ritual of writing them out and mailing them, and occasionally, her great-aunt sent snail mail in return. *Maybe that haphazard correspondence meant something to her?* Whatever the reason, this inheritance couldn't come at a better time.

Quickly she read the letter telling her how to proceed, and when she folded up the packet of papers, she had a response for Frederic at least, who was standing behind her with his arms folded. "Well?" he prompted.

Iris handed him the will. "It'll take a little while, but I'll pay you soon. You can start looking for someone to take over my room."

Acknowledgments

Since I'm not fae, I can thank people freely. First, I need to thank my wonderful editor, Christa Désir, who must have started to suspect that this book was a figment of my imagination. Thank you for your patience and your insight and your expertise while I tinkered and rewrote and did my absolute best to bring this story out of my brain and into the world. Next, thanks to the amazing team at Sourcebooks, who always collaborate fully to create the most beautiful books. I love my cover art; I adore working with everyone on the team, particularly Siena, Pam, Angela, Lindsay, and Courtney.

Next, I thank my agent, Emily Sylvan-Kim, for her extraordinary patience. I appreciate her thoughtful feedback and the lack of pressure as I adapt. I'm getting my groove back.

This book has been a long time coming, and I'm so proud of it. The story is timely and touching, and the ending made me cry like a baby. I've been playfully referring to it as *The Book That Bookstores Built.* See, as I was writing it, I was also on tour during the summer of 2025 for *I Think I'm in Love with an Alien.* I visited so many amazing indie stores, and I wrote in many of their spaces. It was a magical experience, and I want y'all to have the chance to visit those amazing stores as well. The ones I visited are:

- Village Books in Bellingham, WA
- Third Place Books in Lake Forest Park, WA (near Seattle)
- Grand Gesture in Portland, OR
- Ruby's Bookstore in Folsom, CA
- L'il Book Bug on the Blvd in Lancaster, CA
- Mysterious Galaxy in San Diego, CA
- Changing Hands in Tempe, AZ
- King's English in Salt Lake City, UT
- Spicy Librarian in Denver, CO
- Watermark Books in Wichita, KS
- Under the Cover in Kansas City, MO
- Love's Sweet Arrow in Tinley Park, IL

Definitely stop in. The staff is amazing and knowledgeable, and they'll recommend amazing things for you to read.

As I traveled, I had the chance to reconnect with old friends, people who've inspired and supported me for many years. Those people include (but are not limited to): Dina James, Lilith Saintcrow, Victoria Helen Stone, Courtney Milan, Sharon Shinn, Shawntelle Madison, Jeannie Lin, Suleikha Snyder, Skyla Dawn Cameron, Charlotte Stein, Kate Elliott, and Silvia Moreno-Garcia. Thanks to local friends, Jocelyn and Sarah, and to the whole team at DVSAS. I'm forgetting others, I'm sure, but that's because I'm fallible, not because they're forgettable.

Thanks to my family—for everything.

And finally, last but *never* least, thanks to my readers. After all these years, you're still with me, and I will never take that trust lightly. I adore you all.

About the Author

New York Times and *USA Today* bestselling author Ann Aguirre has been a clown, a clerk, a savior of stray kittens, and a voice actress, not necessarily in that order. She loves video games, Korean dramas, music, dogs and cats, and staring at the sea. Though she writes all kinds of genre fiction, she has a major soft spot for a happily ever after.

Discover more from Ann Aguirre...